Trail Of The Wolf

A Novel

by

W. Richard Trimble

Clear Stream Communications

Shiloh

Copyright © 2002 by W. Richard Trimble

Manufactured in the United States of America

Library of Congress Cataloging-in-Publication Data is available

ISBN 0-9659564-0-7

1 2 3 4 5 6 7 8 9 10

I. Title

Trail Of The Wolf

Author's Note

When writing or reading of times past, one must of course take into consideration that some conditions have changed over the years. For example, in the 1870's, a lot of men and women married earlier than is socially acceptable today. Marriage at sixteen was not uncommon. Some youngsters matured when they were fourteen, others not until they were seventeen, and others not until they were twenty-five. That situation has not changed; it is the same today; but public opinion about it has changed, and some laws have been passed making eighteen the magic age. In the 1870's, some men and women of eighteen were already married and had children of their own.

Now, while most of the language is the same, a few words have fallen out of use. *Line shack*, for example. A line shack was a bare bones shack built out on the range by some ranchers where cowboys could sleep and cook when they were tending cattle more than a convenient ride from the ranch house. Depending on the size of his range, a rancher might have one or several line shacks. When there were no line shacks, there were "cow camps" where the cowboys pitched tents or slept in the open.

Somehow, the Spanish word *hacienda* has gotten misunderstood in American English. In the United States in recent years it has been used to mean "house." However, *casa* is the Spanish word for house. An hacienda in Mexico was and is a huge ranch, extending for miles and miles. A rancho in Mexico was a small ranch. (This is in contrast with early California where the term rancho included a huge ranch.) It is important to know these distinctions because the words are used in the following story.

In Training is a phrase that has fallen out of use today. Roughly equivalent to today's phrases, "in shape," or "in condition," it was more specific. Applied to both animals and humans, it meant that the muscles needed for a specific task, running, for instance, were built up and ready for use. If you wanted a horse able to run twenty miles, you put him in training. After that, so long as he could still do it, even if not being formally trained, he was considered "in training." But, if the muscles had deteriorated from lack of use, he was "out of training."

Today, we go to the stable once a week—if we go at all—and take our horse out for a three hour ride. When we come back, he is tired. In the 1870's, many people who made their living on horseback were in the saddle from dawn to dark with a few breaks for a meal and such. The horses they used were in training and could carry them all day if necessary. And, in that regard, good horses could travel four hundred miles in eight days. Excellent horses could do better. Moreover, if you were willing to ruin them or kill them, you could do even better. Butch Cassidy and his men, who often rode thoroughbreds, driving spare horses ahead of them, sometimes traveled one hundred miles in twenty-four hours during getaways.

To a degree, movies have been guilty of corrupting our view of history. In western movies, for example, every man seems to own and carry a revolver in a sturdy leather holster. The fact is that only a minority of men owned pistols in the 1870's. While everyone was free to own any gun he wanted, rifles were the generally preferred weapon for protection and hunting. Moreover, most of the guns owned in the 1870's were muzzle loading rifles and muskets. Breech loaders, employing paper or brass cartridges, were newfangled and costly. Only "out west" were these in the majority. In addition, most revolver owners carried their weapons in their belts or pockets or on their saddles. A few had leather holsters of varying quality.

A final point: the primitive-looking maps contained herein reflect the state of common map making in the 1800's.

WRT

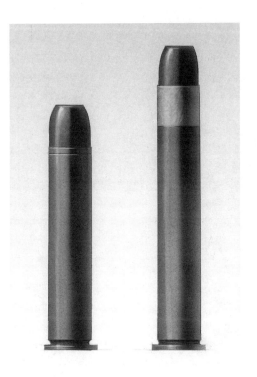

ACTUAL SIZE
Left: .45-70   Right: .45-110

Cartridges used in two Sharps
rifles in the 1870's

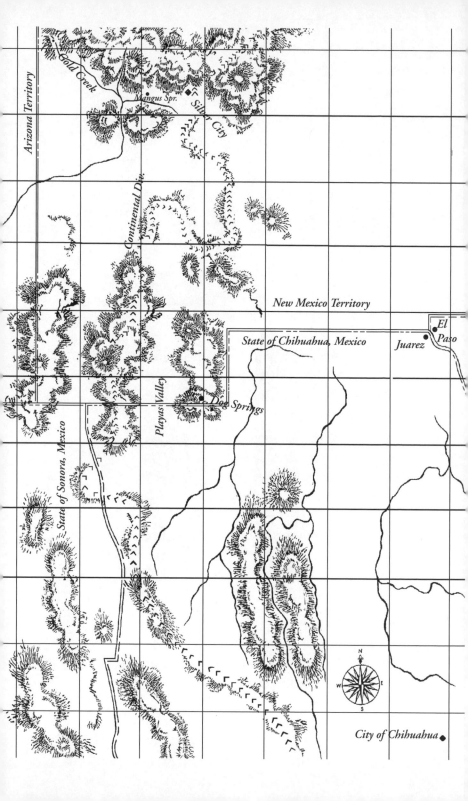

One

H e came up here all right," the big man said quietly to the rider in front of him. He could see the tracks on the trail they were riding. The big man was about forty and was slim with broad, sloping shoulders. Pinned to his vest was a silver star engraved with *Marshal of Gold Creek*.

The front rider, who rode a black horse, did not say anything.

It was mid-August of 1878, and the two riders were angling up a ridge on the western slope of the Mogollon Mountains in southwestern New Mexico Territory. The Marshal led a pack horse, and both riders had their rifles out of their scabbards and laid across their laps. They were looking about them, searching the chaparral. The Marshal of Gold Creek squinted noticeably when he looked farther than about fifty yards. His distance sight had been bad for eight years now.

The Marshal's name was Morgan Blaylock, but most people simply called him Morgan. He preferred it that way. Consequently, most had forgotten or never did know his last name.

Morgan watched as the front rider crested the ridge. The front rider, whose reins were tied together at their ends, suddenly dropped them onto his horse's neck, steering the animal now with his knees. In the same moment, his rifle, an octagon barreled .45-70 Sharps, came up in one fluid motion, sweeping slightly, following a moving target, and fired. The gun recoiled, blowing a puff of bluish smoke. The smoke came from the seventy grains of black powder that propelled a massive forty-five caliber bullet.

Morgan asked, "You get him?"

The front rider turned in his saddle to the Marshal. He was seventeen years old and cleanly handsome with lively blue eyes and, under his hat, blond streaks in his brown hair. He grinned good naturedly at the Marshal.

1

"You ever know me to miss?"

Morgan gave a slow smile. "No, as a matter of fact, I've never known you to miss."

Morgan slid his own rifle into its saddle scabbard. A lever action .44-40 Winchester, it shot the same cartridges his new Colt revolver did.

The boy looked back to what he had shot. About a hundred yards out lay a dead deer with a red spot just behind its shoulder. A neat heart shot.

They rode down to the deer and dismounted. The boy moved the deer so that its head was downhill and then, with his "sticker," the sharper and straighter of his two knives, he slit its throat to drain the blood from the carcass. After it stopped bleeding, and while Morgan held its legs, the boy quickly and expertly gutted the animal. He discarded most of the innards, including the shattered heart, but put the liver and kidneys into oilcloth sacks.

Together, they loaded the deer onto the pack horse. The boy, whose name was Blackie Sheffield, was just under six feet tall, was slim, and was very hard. He could have loaded the animal by himself; but, because they were partners on this hunt, he let the bigger man help. Blackie Sheffield was the market hunter for the town of Gold Creek, and had been so for the last three years, since he was fourteen. Before that he had apprenticed at it under his father. Long ago, he had developed all the necessary muscles and technique to lift deer carcasses onto pack horses by himself. A gutted mule deer can weigh from one to two hundred pounds. Unlike a live animal, it will be floppy and hard to manage; it takes a powerful grip, and powerful arms, back, and legs to snatch and swing one onto a pack horse without help.

So now they mounted their horses and rode down the mountain single file, the pack horse in the rear.

A couple miles down the mountain, following a trail beside a very shallow creek, the hunters came upon a placer gold mine and were presented with a grisly sight: what remained of a man dangled upside down by rope from a tree limb. The rope was knotted crudely around the feet. The legs, although withered and turned black in decay, were pretty much intact; but the man's head and trunk had been torn down, apparently by coyotes and vultures, and so bones and clothing were scattered around an area of several yards. There was the stench of rotting flesh.

Morgan dismounted and went over and with his boot carefully moved the bones and debris from beneath the hanging legs. He found what he had thought he might: the dirt there was dark with charcoal. A small fire had burned beneath the head, and the man had died in agony, jerking and screaming, while his head had cooked.

Looking around, Morgan spotted the skull where it lay about twenty feet away; the crown was scorched black.

"Most likely this is Apache work," he said.

The boy nodded. He had heard that Apaches sometimes did this, but he had never seen it before.

"There might be another body around here," the boy said. "There were two men working this claim."

"When were you last by here?"

"A couple months ago."

"Do you know their names?"

"No."

"Would you look for the other man? I'll look for a claim marker; that should give us their names."

Morgan soon found one of the claim markers—a tobacco can was lodged in a pyramid pile of rocks; and inside the can was a paper that described the claim and named the two owners. Morgan then turned to helping Blackie look for the other man. When a half hour had passed and they still had not found him, he hailed Blackie. They met back at the pack horse where Blackie shooed flies from the deer carcass.

"Let's get your deer delivered," Morgan said. "I'll come back here tomorrow afternoon with a couple of idlers from town. This man's been dead for two or more weeks by the looks of things. Wouldn't you say? One more day won't make much difference. If his partner was taken prisoner, he's already dead somewhere."

They rode on down the creek about two miles, coming upon a four tent camp where nine miners, dirty and shaggy, were sluicing for gold. As the hunters approached, a couple of the miners waved. The hunters waved and rode up and dismounted.

Morgan asked, "Do you boys know a miner was killed up the creek two or three weeks ago?"

Everyone stopped working.

One man asked, "Who was that?"

Morgan pulled the claim marker from his vest pocket and glanced at the names again. "Either Roy Clampet or Ike Miller. One of them had his brains cooked and the other one is missing."

"Apaches?"

"I'd guess that."

One of the miners said to the others, "That must be why they never returned the mercury." He explained to Morgan and Blackie, "They borrowed some mercury three-four weeks ago."

A miner from Georgia joked, "They got a lotta nerve, gettin' themselves killed before they paid back that mercury."

Another miner scowled. "Oh, Ned, hush up!"

Ned grinned. He had been in two terrible battles in the Civil War and had seen thousands of dead, so he was not about to be impressed by two more.

Morgan said, "There wasn't enough left of the dead man to know what he looked like. Could you boys describe the two of them?"

Morgan listened with care while the men gave a description. Then he looked at Blackie who nodded confirmation.

Taking their leave, the hunters rode on down the creek to where it put into Gold Creek. They then headed south down Gold Creek Canyon, and after about three miles, they rode past the tailings of some large mines, the largest of which was the last, the Yellow Lode Mine. Just past those tailings, on

Yellow Lode Mine land, was Morgan's office which was also his home. Nearly three hundred yards further south they entered the town of Gold Creek, a community of around seven hundred people.

The town was about a half mile long and was built along Gold Creek and had three parallel dirt streets. The creek ran on the east side of the canyon, near a shear rock wall; and right now, in mid-August, it was about six feet wide but only inches deep; however, during rain storms it often spread out in its bed to about fifty yards wide. There was a lot of high brush in that fifty yard wide creek bed, some of it taller than a horse. There had once been trees there too, but they had been cut down by townspeople years ago and used for firewood.

On the west bank of the creek bed was Carver Street, named after the man who had discovered gold here. Main Street was on higher ground west of that; and School Street, on which the first school had been built, was west of Main on yet higher ground. There were no more streets west of School Street because the ground rose sharply up the mountainside. Nevertheless, about sixty people had lived on that steep mountainside in shanties and dugouts until three weeks ago when a fire had swept through there and burned everyone out. For the past three weeks, those same people had been living in tents and machinery crates down in town.

Morgan and Blackie rode on down Main Street, passing a hodgepodge of businesses and homes, passing the butcher shop where Blackie often sold his kills. They rode about two-thirds of the way through town to the two-storied Gold Creek Saloon where they dismounted and tied their horses to the hitching rail. The proprietor of the saloon, Jasper Odin, a portly man of about forty, had spotted them through a front window and now came out onto the boardwalk.

He could see very well what the hunters had brought, but he asked good naturedly, "What'd you bring me, Blackie?"

"Venison."

"How about skinning it for me this time?"

"It'll cost you a dollar extra."

Jasper Odin considered briefly. The extra dollar would make the deer cost him six. "Well, all right."

Blackie untied the oilcloth sacks and handed them to Odin. He un-lashed the deer and slid it off the pack horse, and he and Morgan carried it by its legs in through the front door of the building and into the kitchen where they hooked the deer's hind legs onto meat hooks attached to the rafters. Then the two older men went into the bar and sat down at a table with a newspaper while Blackie skinned the deer with such skillful rapidity that he made it look easy; and for him it was.

Morgan told Odin about the dead miner. Odin just shook his head. There were a hundred miners, give or take a few, working claims in the mountains surrounding Gold Creek. They all knew—or should have known—that it was dangerous out there. A band of Warm Springs Apaches under Chief Victorio had been on the rampage since the snow had melted. The remains Morgan and Blackie had discovered today would make a total of four miners that those Apaches had killed in the area this summer. The missing man would make it five. There might be more victims out in the hills that nobody knew about. And this spring, twenty miles from here, down on the San Francisco River, Apaches after horses had hit a small ranch, burned it to the ground, and, excepting the horses, had killed every living thing.

You didn't lose a lot of sleep over such things, though. If you did, you couldn't stay on in this part of the country.

When Blackie was through skinning the deer, he wiped his skinning knife with a damp cloth and put it into its sheath on his belt. He poured water into a wash pan and washed his hands and forearms with soap. Finished, he threw the water out the back door onto the ground. He walked into the bar rolling his sleeves down.

Jasper Odin looked up from the newspaper and smiled. "Through already?" He liked the boy.

Blackie smiled at Odin. "When you've skinned as many deer as I have, it doesn't take long." His eyes went to Morgan. "Morgan, have you got time to give me another punching lesson today?"

"Sure have."

Odin said, "Oh, say! Morgan, I hear you used to be a prize fighter. That true?"

"Yes, a long time ago."

Morgan did not often talk about that part of his background. Prize fighters, men who fought with bare fists for money, were, as a rule, such awful ruffians that the profession was looked down upon by a lot of people.

"Morgan, you do nothing if you don't amaze me. First, I learn you went to college—'course, I shoulda known that by the way you speak. Now I learn you were a prize fighter." Odin shook his head. "A strange mix."

Morgan conceded, "It is at that."

"Where did you do your fighting, by the way?"

"Boston, Savannah, New Orleans. Towns like that. Anywhere you could get people to bet against you."

Odin turned to Blackie. "I hope you aren't thinking of becoming a prize fighter."

"Nope. I just want to be tougher. Isaac Underwood's been spoiling for a fight with me for a couple of months. We'll come to blows sooner or later. I'm sure I can whip him; but, if I whip him, I know I'll have to fight his brother Zeke. Zeke's a lot bigger than I am."

"And older. They're both bigger and older than you."

Blackie protested, "I'm seventeen!"

"I know you are; but Isaac must be twenty. And Zeke's twenty-two or three."

Morgan cut in, "Odin, you don't have to be a big man to whip a big man. You just have to know what you're doing. Most big men don't know how to fight. They win fights because the other man doesn't know how to fight either."

"I'd hate to see Blackie get hurt by biting off more than he can chew."

"Take my word for it, Odin, men—big, medium, or small—who know how to fight are rare. Most of them end up on the ground, thrashing around. They hurt the other man only because he gives them plenty of chances." Morgan stood. "If anyone comes looking for me, I'll be out at Blackie's barn."

"I'll tell 'em."

To Blackie, Morgan said, "Let's go change the note on my door so people will know where to find me." Walking out of the saloon, he added, "We'll spend the rest of the day working on your left. We already know you've got a knockout punch in your right."

He was referring to a recent fight Blackie'd had at the livery stable with a man who had tried to intimidate him. Blackie had talked back sharply, and the man had come at him thinking to slap the youngster around a little. The man had walked into Blackie's right fist and had been knocked unconscious for more than a minute.

It was Morgan who, only a couple of weeks ago, had shown Blackie how to get such power into his right hand.

* * *

The Sheffield place was a small ranch about a quarter mile south of town, downstream on the creek. It had a good size house that had been built almost two feet off the ground to avoid flooding during thunder storms. A roofed porch ran the length of the house. Inside, there was one big room that served as living room, dining room, and kitchen; and there were two bedrooms. Behind the house, there were a dark red barn and several other outbuildings including three large chicken coops and a shed for ducks.

Morgan and Blackie unsaddled their horses and put them in the corral behind the barn. Inside the barn, they hung a burlap sack of oats from a rafter. Blackie removed his shirt and hung it on a peg. His torso was slim and hard with cleanly defined muscles. Each of them wrapped his left hand with strips of cloth that Blackie had gotten on an earlier occasion from his mother's rag bag in the house. The purpose of the wrapping was to protect the skin of their fists from the rough burlap.

Their fists wrapped, Morgan started the lesson:

"Your left fist is your most effective weapon," he said affably. "Why? Even though you're right-handed and can hit harder with your right, when you stand correctly," Morgan demonstrated the proper placement of his feet, the left foot forward of the right and turned inward at a slight angle, "and your body is turned just right," he had his left shoulder forward and his right shoulder back, "your left fist is closest to your opponent. Consequently, your opponent has less time to see your left coming and react to it. And when you have a knockout punch in your left, you might seldom have to use your right."

Morgan then demonstrated in slow motion how to throw a left hook. Then he threw one for real. His fist struck the bag powerfully, making it swing away.

Morgan now drilled Blackie in slow motion on the left hook. Everything, from the position of the feet, and including the spring from his toes, and the bend of the knees, through the swing of the shoulders, and even to where he held his other fist was attended to. Morgan coached him until Blackie got the form perfect. Finally, when Morgan was satisfied, he instructed Blackie to put speed into it. Whenever he noticed Blackie's form weaken and not correct itself within a couple of repetitions, he would stop him and correct him and start him at slow motion again; then he would have Blackie speed it up. Finally, he had Blackie put power into the punch. "Follow through," he said, "like you're going to drive your fist right through the other man." He would correct any lingering errors of form and re-start Blackie in slow motion, coming forward to power very quickly. This took them a couple of hours of drilling, and by then they had lit two lanterns because it was getting dark inside the barn. Blackie, now landing powerful lefts over and over again, had the bag of oats swinging high away from him.

The lesson came to an end when the barn door swung open and an extremely pretty woman of thirty-five stepped into the barn. She had rich brown hair and deep blue eyes, and there was something very, very female about her.

"Blackie?"

"Oh, hi, Mom."

Morgan's pulse had quickened upon hearing Sarah Sheffield's voice. A wave of pleasure rushed over him. "Evening, Sarah."

She replied warmly, "Good evening, Morgan." Her cheeks flushed slightly.

Blackie had long ago become used to the effect that his mother had upon men. He was proud of her.

Sarah Sheffield spoke to her son: "Blackie, it's getting late, and you haven't milked the cows. And supper's almost ready."

"Oh, okay. Oh, Mom, can Morgan eat with us?"

"Of course. Morgan is welcome at our table any time."

She spoke to Morgan: "How's your pupil doing?"

"Very well. He's got a knockout punch in either hand."

*　　*　　*

Later that evening, on his way home, riding the quarter mile to town, Morgan gave thought to Sarah Sheffield. She had been a widow for three years now. Morgan wondered if she thought of taking another husband—especially now since they had found Butch's body last year, erasing any doubt that might have lingered about his actually being dead.

Not even considering companionship, there was good reason for her to marry again. She had a small ranch that required plenty of work to keep up. She had several milk cows, some steers, and a whole lot of chickens and ducks with which she supplied the town with milk, butter, eggs and meat. And her sixteen year old daughter, Dusty, had gotten married two months ago and had moved to an outlying ranch. That left Blackie, of course; but he might marry soon. Who knows? Granted, he would be unlikely to leave his mother without help. You could see that Blackie adored his mother.

Allowing himself a flight of fancy, Morgan imagined himself married to Sarah Sheffield; he experienced a warm, whole, satisfied feeling, a feeling of completeness. He knew then that he could live out the remainder of his years and feel that he had made something of his life.

He wondered how the two kids would take it if he married their mother. He did not know the daughter as well as he did Blackie; but she was easy to like. She had a joy of life about her that infected you when you were around her. On the other hand, over the last few months Morgan had grown to know Blackie well. He liked the hell out of the young man, and Blackie gave every indication of genuinely liking Morgan.

Morgan had first ridden into Gold Creek nearly two years ago. He had noticed the Sheffields in the first few days—you couldn't miss them, of course, they were so damned good looking. People said that Butch, the kids' father, had been awfully good looking too. Blond and handsome and fun loving, people said. Probably they had been a pretty sight, the entire family together.

There had been another Marshal when Morgan had first come to town; but he had gotten himself murdered in an argument with a miner. Nobody else seemed eager to take on the job after that; besides, it didn't pay much. Morgan volunteered to take the job because he needed it, and because he wasn't afraid. Well, here it was almost two years later, and he had sort of slipped into the easy routine of it. Partly because of his size, he seldom had trouble. But, probably his attitude had more to do with his not having trouble; he preferred not to arrest anyone; he would rather escort a rowdy drunk home than put him in jail. Anyway, things seemed better now than when he had taken over.

Morgan inhaled the mountain air as he rode into town. The cold night air, moving down the mountain into the canyons, was laden with the odors of chaparral.

For some months now, Morgan and Blackie had been occasionally going hunting together. Until these hunting trips had begun, all Morgan had personally known of the boy was that he had an infectious smile—a remarkably attractive smile—and, with most people, a polite manner. (The boy did have a quick temper sometimes.) As a result of the hunting trips, they had gotten to know each other pretty well. And when Blackie had told his mother that Morgan was an educated man, she had invited Morgan to "readings." When someone in town would receive a book, it would be lent around town among some of the families. Sometimes, a family might host another family or two and someone who had a good voice would read to the others. At the Sheffield's, though, the adults and older children were encouraged to take turns reading aloud from the books. Even when the books weren't all that good, Morgan had enjoyed the company. It had been a pleasure to sit with the Sheffield's on such evenings, taking one's turn reading aloud. There was Blackie, at other times and places rambunctious, a professional hunter since he was fourteen, sitting, well mannered, hair combed, listening to or reading the world's literature.

Well, that was Sarah's influence. She had no intention of her children coming of age illiterate like some of the miners hereabouts. Morgan remembered his surprise and pleasure when he had discovered how widely read Sarah herself was.

So now this evening Morgan rode up Main Street to Buzby's Livery where he boarded his horse. Putting his horse away at Buzby's corral, still thinking of Sarah, he realized that his stomach had butterflies. *My god,* he thought, *just like a youngster again!* He walked toward the upstream end of town, toward his office which was also his home. He reckoned that Sarah could still have children—if she wanted more. A pleasant thought.

Morgan walked the nearly three hundred yards beyond the end of town to his home and office, a place which had started out as a one room cabin, constructed and lived in by the original owner of the Yellow Lode Mine. That was before the man had sold out to the current owner who lived two days ride southeast of here in Silver City. The current owner now donated the cabin rent free to the Marshal in the interests of law and order. A jail cell had been added onto the cabin about three years ago.

As Morgan opened his door he glanced at the empty store building across the road. Mainly as a convenience to employees of the Yellow Lode, it had once supplied food and general merchandise to miners hereabouts; but when other merchants had come to town it had been closed.

Tonight, looking at the darkened building, Morgan had no inkling that it would play a role in the hellish disaster that would soon strike this town.

Two

E d, how about another shot?" It was evening and Blackie stood leaning on the bar at the Gold Creek Saloon. He pushed his empty glass toward the bartender, a friendly twenty-two year old bachelor named Ed Ringsley.

The barroom was softly lit by coal oil lanterns and was filled with dusty miners eating and drinking at tables or drinking at the bar. There was a general hubbub of conversations, and there were brass spittoons located strategically about the saloon. Most of the miners had come directly from work, and the hard rock miners, those who worked underground, had their lantern hats with them.

Supper tonight at the Gold Creek Saloon was antelope which Blackie had killed earlier in the day nine miles to the west, down in the San Francisco Valley below the Mogollon Mountains. This was the first game he had sold to Jasper Odin since he and Morgan had brought in the deer eight days ago.

Ed Ringsley uncorked a whiskey bottle and poured Blackie his second shot. He took a nickel from Blackie and threw it into a can behind the bar.

Ed asked, "You hunt every day, Blackie?"

"Not every day. I could if I wanted to, though. With all the people in these parts wanting fresh meat, I could make a lot of money."

As it was he made more money than any of the local mine workers did; and that was more than he needed. The mine workers hereabouts made a good wage: eighteen dollars a week for six ten hour days. Blackie, however, made at least five dollars every time he went out, and sometimes he made two big game kills in one day.

"Maybe I ought to take up market hunting," Ed remarked.

"Sure. Are you a pretty good shot?"

Ed grinned. "Naw. I ain't much of a shot. I guess I'll stick to bartending." A pause. "That reminds me. I saw you split your take with Morgan a couple weeks ago. Are you and Morgan partners?"

"No. We just go hunting together once in a while—whenever he gets broke and needs some money. You know, he only gets thirty dollars a month for being Marshal."

"I guess that ain't much. Is Morgan a pretty good shot?"

"Not for deer. His eyesight's bad. He sees all right up close, say fifty or sixty yards, and he's a sure shot up to that range with either rifle or six shooter; but, much farther than that, he doesn't see well."

Ed snorted. "So, Ol' Morgan's the Marshal and he ain't much of a shot. That's a hell of a thing."

"Hold up, now. I didn't say he wasn't a good shot. I said he doesn't see well at long range. So, he can't shoot well at long range. But he's real quick with a six shooter....and, up close," Blackie spoke slowly and with meaning, "he hits what he shoots at."

"Oh. Okay. So, anyway, you do the killin'. So why do you split with him then?"

Blackie shrugged. "It's only now and then. And he's good company. He's a hell of a story teller. He sure has done a lot and seen a lot. He was born in the East, you know, and he went to college. His dad was a lawyer, and his people wanted him to be one. But he quit school and came West."

With a youngster's pride in a tough friend, Blackie added, "Morgan's killed five men."

Ed was jolted. He'd had a talking acquaintance with the man who had murdered the previous marshal and who had then hightailed it out of town; and he had once known another man who claimed to have killed someone. But it shocked him to find out that someone he saw every day had killed five men. It also gave him a new and careful regard for Morgan.

Behind Blackie, a poker game had been in progress at one of the tables. There was a pile of money in the center of the table, indicating that the hand being played had been heavily bet. Starting with the man to the left of the dealer, the players were now spreading their hands. The fourth man spread a full house—three queens and two jacks. From the stack of money in front of him, you could see he had been having a lucky night.

The sixth player, who had bet his last money, spoke up bitterly: "Nobody could win like that and not cheat!"

The fourth player registered amazement that anyone would accuse him of such a thing. Then he turned angry.

"Aw, you're just a sore loser!"

The sixth player retorted, "I oughta knock your head off!"

There was a scraping of chairs as the two men quickly stood.

The fifth poker player, a man bigger than either of them, spoke up: "Hold on, boys!" He got to his feet. "There ain't no sense in fightin' over a little ol' poker game."

The sixth poker player was suddenly ashamed of what he had said, but he was not man enough to admit it. Instead, he glared hatefully at the other players, and then turned and stalked out of the saloon. The others sat back down, and the fourth poker player raked in his winnings with shaking hands.

Blackie and Ed turned their attention back to each other.

"Hey," said Ed, "I been meanin' to ask you: Is Blackie your given name?"

Blackie smiled. "No. My dad nicknamed me that, oh, about seven years ago, and it stuck. My real name is James."

"Why'd he pick 'Blackie?'"

Blackie shrugged and grinned, "Oh, I went through a time when I liked the color black. I kept after him until he bought me a black colt I wanted—it's the same stud you see me ride now—and I bought a black hat and had my mom make me some black duds. So he started calling me Blackie and it caught on."

Ed grinned and nodded. A man asked for another shot of whiskey. Ed poured it and then returned to Blackie and said, "They say your pa died in a snow storm."

"Yeah, he did. He used to do most of the market hunting for this town, and one day three years ago, he went into the mountains, and a blizzard came up of a sudden." Blackie paused and gave a little sigh. "We never saw him again.... It wasn't until last year that somebody, a prospector, found his bones."

"I guess it's hard, losin' your pa at that age. What were you? fourteen?"

"Yeah." Blackie smiled. "He sure was a lot of fun. We spent a lot of time together. He taught me to shoot when I was four."

"They say your pa was a dead shot."

Blackie spoke with pride. "He was. You know, there are people in this town from everywhere; and I heard a lot of people say they never saw anyone who could shoot like my dad. I think that says a lot."

"I guess it does at that."

"He used to make me shoot competition against him. The loser would do the winner's chores that day. Now, when I was small, he'd give me an edge. I'd shoot from, say, twenty-five yards while he shot from a hundred. He always made it fair; but not easy. I could never get careless or lazy, 'cause I'd be doing his chores.

"Anyway, when I started winning too much, he moved me back to fifty yards. Then to seventy-five. When I was thirteen, we were shooting even up—both at the same distance, or at the same things. But, after I turned fourteen, I got to be just a tiny bit better than him."

Ed raised his eyebrows. "How'd you do that?"

"I think my timing was just a hair better."

"Timing?"

"You can never hold a gun perfectly still, you know. It weaves and bobs ever so slightly. So you have to let your shot off just when your sights pass the spot you want to hit. Your finger and your eye and your breath and your mind have to be right together on it. It was on the long distance shooting at moving targets that I could best him."

Ed mulled that over. He smiled. "Well, I guess that says a lot about you."

Blackie grinned with pride.

While Blackie and Ed had been talking, a sour looking bully of about twenty had moved up to the bar and stood listening to their conversation without appearing to do so. Covered with dust from the mine, he was about Blackie's height, but stockier. His name was Isaac Underwood, and he had drunk just enough liquor to make him bold. He was, as Blackie had told Jasper Odin eight days ago, "spoiling for a fight" with Blackie.

Isaac Underwood spoke loudly so that plenty of people could hear:

"All right, you bragged about how good a shot you are. But, what I'd like to know is how good you are with your dukes. I'll bet you ain't worth spit."

Startled for only an instant, Blackie turned suddenly dangerous.

"You can find out by coming outside with me."

Blackie removed his arm from the bar top. Ed tried to grab it. Blackie glanced at Ed who shook his head in warning. Blackie's eyes went back to Isaac where they stayed while he spoke with barely controlled anger.

"Ed, Isaac's been saying things to me for a couple of months now. This time, he's gone too far."

Ed warned, "Isaac never fights alone. He and Zeke always gang up on somebody. Zeke's right over there."

He nodded in the direction of Isaac's brother, Zeke Underwood, who sat at a table with some other miners. Zeke had turned in his chair and was watching the confrontation. He was about three inches taller than his brother, and much better looking with curly black hair. He too was covered with dirt from the mine.

Blackie's temper had gotten the better of him. He ignored Ed's advice, and blurted recklessly, "I'll fight 'em both, then!"

Isaac announced to everyone, "Bring some lanterns! There's goin't'be a fight outside!"

Blackie walked rapidly for the front door. Most of the miners jumped to their feet. Several grabbed lanterns from tables. Blackie, Isaac, and Zeke walked quickly outside, and a lot of miners piled out after them.

Ed Ringsley came out and complained, "Two against one ain't fair."

But he had no inclination to join Blackie in a fight with two men he knew to be tough and brutal. Nor did anyone else.

In the dirt street, the spectators, tensely excited, formed a wide, loose circle around the three fighters. Most of the spectators were miners, so most favored the two brothers; but Blackie had his backers too.

The fighters circled for position. Blackie kept his distance at first. For a moment, the thought crossed his mind that he had taken on more than he could handle; but he pushed that thought away and threw his whole attention onto how he could win. His alertness was a thousand times his normal. He could see no advantage to charging into two men who were bigger than he; so he backed away in circles and made the brothers come to him while he waited for something to happen, while he waited for one of them to make a mistake. Each brother tried to flank him a couple of times, but Blackie was too quick. When one tried to flank him on the left, for example, Blackie darted backwards to the right, leaving the flanker out of punching range. So they had to approach him from his front, and they got in each other's way, making one have to get within punching distance first. This last fact was not lost on Blackie who immediately made it part of his tactic. He determined to make one or the other of them arrive alone within punching distance.

After a few seconds of this, the brothers were a little confused. No fight they had ever been in had gone this way; usually, several blows had been struck by now. Finally, Isaac grew impatient. He concluded that Blackie was afraid and therefore not really dangerous. He dropped his head and charged, his right fist drawn back. Blackie nimbly moved out of his way and pushed him stumbling past. While Blackie was thus engaged, Zeke stepped in and socked him hard to his eye. Blackie rocked back. Zeke moved in on Blackie only to run into a hard left to the chin that staggered him. Surprised by the power of Blackie's punch, and hurt, Zeke stepped back.

Isaac rushed in now and hit Blackie solidly on the nose.

Blackie sprang away backwards, his nose immediately running blood. While the brothers stalked him, he backed away for three or four seconds, recovering from the blow.

Isaac rushed again. This time, Blackie smashed a right to Isaac's face and Isaac's legs gave out and he crashed to the ground, face down.

While striking Isaac, Blackie had momentarily become a stationary target, and Zeke leaped forward and landed his hardest punch to the side of Blackie's head. Blackie was stunned and he staggered sideways, and then dodged and weaved for four or five seconds to avoid Zeke's wild follow-up punches. Blackie recovered and drove his left fist into Zeke's jaw. Zeke stumbled backwards.

Isaac had gotten to his feet and now; and from behind he leaped and grabbed Blackie in a bear hug, pinning his arms to his sides. Blackie looked down, spied Isaac's instep and, with all of his weight, stomped *hard* with his heel. Isaac howled and released Blackie and fell to the ground groaning and holding his foot. But Blackie had been momentarily stationary, and Zeke hit him solidly with a powerful right to the face. Blackie went down on hands and knees but quickly righted himself, standing upright on his knees. His ears filled with the noisy shouts of spectators, some of them shouting for Zeke to finish him, others shouting for him to get up.

Zeke drew his right foot back and kicked at Blackie's side. Blackie saw it coming and shielded his body with his arm. He felt the kick land; but, in his frame of mind, felt no pain. He grabbed Zeke's leg and held it to his body. He got to his feet quickly, lifting the leg with him, throwing Zeke off balance and spilling him to the ground. Zeke rolled over and started to get up. Blackie allowed him to get partway up and then, during the instant that Zeke was in that defenseless position, Blackie stepped in and smashed a long right to his face. Zeke went down and out cold.

Isaac had gotten to his feet and now limped uncertainly. With his brother out of the fight, he was without courage. Blackie moved to him and landed a tooth shattering left to his mouth and Isaac went down. Isaac was out for a moment; and when he came to, he saw Blackie starting to crouch beside him.

"I've had enough!" Isaac slurred through his bloody mouth.

Cheers rose loudly from the spectators. Even those who had been for the brothers now cheered Blackie.

Blackie was breathing heavily through his mouth. The flesh around his right eye was swollen and somewhat red, and blood was running from his nose down over his chin onto his clothes. Some blood had gotten into his mouth and had colored his teeth.

All during the fight, standing on the boardwalk, almost breathless with excitement, had been Cathy Haggarty, a pretty twenty year old. Now she ran down through the other spectators and up to Blackie.

"Oh, Blackie, you're a mess! Come on inside and let me clean you up."

The spectators started whooping. One of them shouted, "To the victor go the spoils!" There followed whistles and shouts. Blackie, with battered face, grinned at the spectators. He allowed Cathy Haggarty to lead him inside the saloon and into a back room.

"Pull off your shirt," Cathy told him.

While he removed his shirt, she got out two wash pans and poured water into them from a bucket. Turning from the wash pans, she gave Blackie's shirtless torso an appreciative once over; the muscles were hard and knotted and cleanly defined under smooth skin. She took his shirt from him and submerged it in cold water.

She remembered her foster father's instructions for a bloody nose when Cathy had been a tomboy kid. She told Blackie, "Sit down and press your finger against your gums just below your nose. That'll help stop the bleeding."

Blackie did as he was told. Cathy came over with a cool damp cloth and began wiping the blood from his face and chest. As she worked, she rinsed the cloth in the pan of cold water. After cleaning the blood away, she continued wiping his face soothingly. She felt wonderfully useful.

She said, "Well, I hope those bullies learned their lesson."

"So do I, Cathy."

"Oh, Blackie, you fought so good!"

Blackie's swollen face grinned proudly.

Turning now to the wash basin that contained Blackie's shirt, Cathy ran her hand over his bare shoulder. She sloshed his shirt in the water.

"We'll have to leave your shirt in cold water all night to soak the blood out."

She dried her hands and then, standing behind Blackie's chair, ran her hands over his shoulders, down his chest to his hard belly.

She said softly, "Spend the night with me, Blackie."

"I don't have enough money."

"Now, Blackie, don't tell tales. I know you sold Mr. Odin an antelope today."

"Yeah, but I gave most of the money to my mother."

"You must have kept a half dollar for yourself."

"Yeah."

"That's all I'll charge you."

"Four bits is a lot of money."

Cathy took her hands off of him. "Blackie Sheffield! I charge everyone else two dollars, and that's just for a few minutes!"

She came in front of him. With a playful grin and a sparkle in her eyes, she grabbed his hands and tugged.

"Come on, you miser, let's go upstairs and have some fun."

Blackie laughed, got up, and let Cathy draw him through the doorway.

Three

The sound of a pair of boots running up the stairs awakened Blackie just before sunrise. He rose up on one elbow. Early morning light came in through the window of Cathy Haggarty's little upstairs bedroom at the Gold Creek Saloon. The flesh around Blackie's eye and cheek bone had turned black in the night. Next to him, against the wall, Cathy still slept. The running boots reached the top of the stairs, and a young man named Charles Cistrom burst into the room.

"Blackie!"

"What is it?"

"Your sister just rode through town in a nightshirt. Looked like she was heading out to your place. Wasn't anybody with her—and she had a black eye. About as big as yours."

Blackie was nonplused.

The young man continued, "What do you reckon happened?"

Blackie grabbed his pants from a nail on the bunk post. "How would I know? All I know is she must've come in from the Renner place."

Cathy threw an arm over Blackie's chest, seeking the sensation of hard muscles beneath smooth skin. She asked sleepily, "How old is Dusty now?"

"Sixteen."

"She's got spunk," said Cathy. "You won't catch me riding half the night out there alone, what with the Apaches so active now."

It was rare for Cathy to compliment another woman, but this morning she had a feeling of completeness that made her momentarily generous.

Charles Cistrom said, "By the way, she was toting a shotgun."

Blackie dressed quickly and hurried down the stairs and out into the street that was just beginning to show early morning activity. He walked briskly along without his shirt in the cool air. He was conscious that he should have been home and in the barn milking the cows right now. A quarter mile outside of town he came to the creek and crossed it, stepping from rock to rock. The Sheffield house faced the creek, was fifty yards back from it, and was surrounded by big shade trees. As Blackie walked up the steps of the front porch, his sister Dusty opened the front door. She was a blonde, taking after their father, and except for the black eye she was beautiful. The cheek that was not bruised was delicately pink. The pupils of her eyes were blue, surrounded by lighter blue irises that seemed transparent and to have depth. She wore only a short nightshirt, showing a lot of leg.

"Blackie!"

She stared at his bruised face, and then burst out laughing. She darted forward and kissed him and hugged him affectionately; then she leaned back, still holding him, and looked at his face.

"Aren't we a pair!" she laughed.

Blackie looked at her black eye with concern. "What happened to you?"

Dusty's face got a hard look. "My no-good husband hit me. Knocked me clean off my feet."

"Why?"

"We were quarreling. We've been doing a lot of that lately. In fact, not long after we got married, he started picking at me. I couldn't do anything right, if you believed him. And he'd make fun of me in front of his people.

"Living in that house with all his people wasn't any fun either. His mother didn't like me, and his brothers were all trying to get me into bed.

"About three weeks ago, I took some hot food out to one of the line shacks where he was staying. I just wanted to do something nice for him. He wasn't there. He was out moving the herd. But a half-breed girl was there. I left the food off and rode back. You should have heard the lies he tried to make me believe.

"Anyway, last night, after he beat me up, when he went to sleep, I got up pretending I was going to the outhouse. I couldn't very well dress and pack a bag with all his people there; so I just grabbed my shotgun and went out like this and saddled my horse and rode straight here.

"I expect John will be along here after me in three or four hours."

"What do you want to do?"

"I'm staying here. He can rot in Hell."

*　　*　　*

About midday, Dusty's husband John Renner rode across the creek and up under the big shade trees. He was a muscular, good looking young man twenty years of age. A single shot .45 caliber Springfield rifle was in the scabbard attached to his saddle. Dusty was standing in her night shirt behind the porch railing to John's right. Blackie, at the center of the porch, leaned against a post at the top of the steps.

Dusty spoke: "You can just turn your horse around, John Renner, and ride right on back where you came from, because I'm not going with you."

"Aw, Dusty, I'm sorry about last night...."

"It doesn't matter, because I'm not going back with you."

John Renner dismounted. "Dusty, you have my word that it will never happen again."

"You're word! You sleeping with a half-breed and I don't know who else!"

John Renner walked toward the steps.

"Don't come up here! Just get on out of here!"

"Aw, Dusty, calm down."

John neared the bottom step.

Blackie spoke: "You heard her, John. Don't come up here."

John Renner was suddenly furious. "Blackie, I've come for my wife! Now get out of my way or I'll black your other eye!"

Blackie moved to the center of the top step. John saw it as a challenge. He charged up the steps only to run into a powerful right smashed to the point of his chin. He tumbled backward to sprawl in the dust, unconscious.

Blackie jumped down beside John, saw that he was unconscious, and then looked up at Dusty. She stood gripping the porch railing. Pale, she looked steadily into Blackie's eyes.

John was still unconscious when Blackie led John's horse over. Instinctively, Blackie squatted and raised John's limp hands to his ashen face. This seemed to revive John, and his face turned suddenly red. His eyes were still closed, and he squinted in pain. Then, in low agony, holding his chin and jaw, John rocked his head from side to side, groaning. Finally, he opened his eyes and weakly sat up. He was dazed, and all of the fight was out of him.

Blackie spoke calmly: "Go home, John."

John got dazedly to his feet. He glanced at Dusty and then looked away. He missed the stirrup with his left foot on first try. He got it the second time; but he could not get up. He tried again, and Blackie gave his other foot a boost. John swung into the saddle, glanced at Dusty, and rode out of the yard toward town.

Blackie turned and looked at Dusty again; she returned his gaze steadily. He climbed the steps, and together they went inside the house.

Sarah Sheffield stood looking through a window at John riding away. She let the curtain fall and turned to the youngsters. "Is it over, Dusty?"

"Yes, it's over." After a moment's reflection, Dusty added, "I'd have to be crazy to go back to that house."

"All right." A pause. "It wouldn't be wise now to send Blackie after your belongings. We can wait a few days for things to settle down, and then ask a friend to do it.

"In the meantime, Blackie, give it about an hour and then go in town and buy Dusty some clothes. I'll make out a list and give you some money."

It was just about an hour later when Blackie walked into town carrying the shopping list in his shirt pocket. He walked up Main Street and was in front of the hardware store when something caught his eye about seventy yards up the street. Someone had jumped up from a bench on the boardwalk in front of the Hard Rock Saloon. Blackie saw the man's rifle going to his shoulder, and in the same instant he recognized the man as John Renner. Blackie weaved to his right, toward the hardware store. He heard the blast of the rifle.

Blackie's intention had been to run into the hardware store. But several horses were tied to the rail there and they were stamping and jerking and colliding nervously at the sound of the gunshot. Blackie turned and ran for the other side of the street. From the edge of his vision, he could see John stuffing another cartridge into his rifle's breech.

Blackie ran at full speed for the Victorian house across the street. He was at the edge of the front yard when a little boy there began scrambling to his feet from where he had been playing on the ground.

Up the street, John wrenched the rifle to his shoulder and took excited aim. He knew he should kill Blackie before Blackie could arm himself. He jerked the trigger, causing the barrel to dip a fraction of an inch, spoiling his aim. The gun roared and recoiled, belching bluish-white smoke.

The little boy had gotten fully to his feet just as Blackie ran by. The bullet hit the child in the upper chest. He was dead before he hit the ground. Blackie did not see this, as he was inches past the child and running all out.

Blackie ran up the steps of the Victorian house, turned the door knob and burst into the living room. Inside the kitchen, a thirty-three year old woman named Mabel O'Connor turned and stared through the kitchen doorway at Blackie. She was startled and confused by his entrance.

Blackie demanded, "Where's a rifle?!"

"I....I....I don't know!"

There was no time to waste on a confused woman. Blackie ran down the hallway and threw the back door open and ran out. He leaped from the porch to the ground and ran across the back yard, ran across the next street, and burst into another house.

John Renner had reloaded and had run down Main Street to the Victorian house. In a mortal fear to kill Blackie, he gave the dead child no thought. He ran up the steps and through the open front door of the house. His rifle was at the ready.

Standing at the kitchen doorway, the woman, Mabel O'Connor, was terrified now.

John shouted at her, "Where'd he go?!"

Mabel O'Connor was momentarily paralyzed with fear. Finally, she looked toward the hall. John saw the back door standing open at the end of the hall. He ran the length of the hall, down the back steps, and across the back yard. As he entered the street, he paused, looking this way and that.

The door of the house directly across the street stood open. Several feet inside the house, armed with a rifle now, Blackie moved so that he could aim through the open doorway. He fired from inside the house. The rifle blasted, recoiled, and puffed smoke.

John Renner fell over backwards in the street. The shirt over his heart began to turn red. He was dead.

Blackie walked calmly out of the house toward John's body. Suddenly he heard, one after another, three very loud and long screams. The screams came from Main Street. Blackie started cautiously for Main Street.

On Main Street, crazed with shock and grief, Mabel O'Connor now sat on the ground in her front yard, holding her dead little boy in her arms. Neighbors and others were gathering around.

Mabel O'Connor wailed, "They've killed our baby! They've killed our baby! They've killed our baby!" She did not sound quite human.

Morgan was just getting there. He pushed his way to the heart of the crowd. The dead child with its bloody chest was a total surprise to him. "Mrs. O'Connor! What happened?"

Mabel O'Connor did not answer, did not even look up.

A man in the crowd stated the obvious: "Somebody shot the boy."

Meanwhile, Blackie had run cautiously between buildings, and had stopped upon seeing the crowd. Now he came over and pushed his way to the crowd's center. He was thunderstruck at sight of the dead child.

A pretty, light-brown haired girl Blackie's age ran toward the crowd holding her skirts to her knees. She called out with dread, "What's happened?! What's happened?!"

She had to push and bump her way to the center of the crowd. She saw Mabel O'Connor holding the bloody little boy. "Mama!" the girl screamed.

Mabel O'Connor cried, "Oh, Stella, they've killed Billy!"

The girl, Stella O'Connor, fell to her knees, screaming and crying.

Mabel O'Connor gazed around at the onlookers now. Her eyes had a crazed look. At the sight of Blackie, she jolted. She pointed at him.

"There! There he is!"

The crowd stared at Blackie. Those nearby pulled back from him. Morgan was incredulous. He looked at Blackie questioningly.

Blackie shook his head at Morgan, denying the charge. "John Renner must have hit him when he shot at me. He shot twice. Once when I ran through this yard."

Morgan said, "I heard three shots."

"The third shot was mine."

Morgan looked a long moment at Blackie. "Where is he?"

"On the next street."

"Let's go have a look, and you can tell me what happened."

They walked around the house toward the other street. Part of the crowd detached itself and followed them. Blackie told Morgan about Dusty coming home, about John coming after her, and about the fight in the front yard. He described being shot at in the street and described running through the

O'Connor yard and through the house. He told of borrowing a rifle from a housewife in the second house he had barged into.

When they arrived at John's body, the crowd got silent and spooky. No one but Morgan stood next to Blackie or said anything. They were afraid of him for no rational reason.

The housewife who had lent Blackie the rifle watched the bunch of them from her front window. When Morgan and Blackie walked over to her house, she came out onto the front porch. She was a freckled and plain woman in a faded blue gingham dress.

Blackie handed her the rifle. "Thank you, Mrs. Peters. I'll come back later and clean it."

Mrs. Peters answered gently, "Now, Blackie, you just don't pay it no mind. I'm sure you'll have enough bother today. Mr. Peters'll clean it when he gets home."

Morgan said, "Mrs. Peters, Blackie says he was unarmed when he ran into your house."

"That's so."

"Would you please write down all you were a witness of? I'll return later to pick it up. Don't sign it until I bring someone to witness your signature."

"Marshal, I ain't too good with words."

"That's all right. I want it in your own words."

"I'll do the best I can."

"Thank you."

Morgan and Blackie walked back over to John's body. Other onlookers had shown up. One was Charley Bateman, the part-time undertaker for Gold Creek.

Morgan spoke to Bateman: "Charley, would you cart the body up to your place and hold it for the Renner people?"

"Sure enough, Marshal."

Bateman was properly grave; but Morgan thought he detected something else there. Something like being glad to have the work.

* * *

Morgan had no reason to doubt that Blackie was telling the truth. Nevertheless, for Blackie's protection, he went through what he felt to be good procedure. Because of the men Morgan himself had killed elsewhere, he had had to attend more than one coroner's inquest; so he knew more or less how an investigation should be handled.

He and Blackie went together to the Gold Creek Saloon where Morgan borrowed several sheets of paper, a bottle of ink, and a pen. He gave Blackie two sheets of paper and had him write out his statement. While Blackie did this, Morgan asked Jasper Odin to ride out and let Sarah and Dusty know what had happened. Blackie finished his statement and signed it, and bartender Ed Ringsley and a bar patron signed as witnesses to Blackie's signature.

During all of this, Cathy Haggarty stared intently at Blackie from where she sat on the third step of the stairs.

Blackie and Morgan then walked up the street to the Hard Rock Saloon and Blackie showed Morgan where John Renner had started his shooting. There they found two spent .45-70 shell casings in the dirt beside the boardwalk. Morgan put them in his shirt pocket. The bartender and six saloon patrons came out to watch. Two of them, Jake McCracken and Billy Cape, along with the bartender, acknowledged having been there when John had started shooting. Furthermore, they were able to name five others who had been there but were now gone.

There was a bench on the boardwalk beside the saloon door. Morgan indicated it.

"Blackie, would you mind waiting outside here while I ask these fellows some questions?"

Blackie was surprised, but he said, "No. Not at all."

He took a seat on the bench while Morgan herded the three witnesses inside. Morgan stopped on his way in and laid his hand on Blackie's shoulder.

"It's just for appearances," Morgan said. "I don't want anyone to say that because you were standing by, a witness couldn't say what he wanted to."

Inside, Morgan indicated a table and he and the three witnesses sat around it. He said casually, "Okay, let's start at the beginning."

The bartender said, "Well, now, John walked in here and asked for a shot of whiskey." The bartender was about thirty and already appeared to be over the hill.

"When?"

"Oh, about an hour ago, I reckon."

Jake McCracken broke in, "I'd say more like an hour and a half ago." Jake McCracken was a big man, slim with broad shoulders. He had a couple days growth of beard.

The bartender agreed. "Yeah, I guess he's right. More than an hour ago. Anyway, he ordered a shot of whiskey."

Morgan asked, "He say why he was in town?"

The bartender was surprised by the question. "Well, no. I just figured he'd driven some cattle up here to slaughter. Why? Why did he come to town?"

Morgan did not answer. Instead, he asked, "How'd he seem?"

The bartender answered, "Well, now as you mention it, he seemed kind of queer."

"How so?"

"Well, he looked kind of sickly...."

"Peaked," said Billy Cape. "And quiet."

Billy Cape, twenty-two, a gambler, was pleasant looking even though a bit puffy from drinking too much and not getting enough exercise.

The bartender went on, "That's right. John's usually a talker. But he didn't have nothin' to say when he first came in."

Billy Cape said, "I asked him why he was so quiet, and he just looked up at me and then looked away. I swear he looked like he was in pain."

"That's right," the bartender said. "Anyway, after he got that shot down, he sort of loosened up."

Billy Cape added, "He said Blackie was at tryin' to break up his marriage. Now, I know for a fact that there's aplenty men around hereabouts would give their left arm for a chance at that girl; and they'd like to see that marriage broke up; but it seemed like ever'body jumped onto John's side when he said Blackie was at tryin' to do it. Seemed like ever'body claimed that a brother-'n-law ain't got no right meddlin' in a man's marriage."

Morgan looked questioningly at Jake McCracken.

Jake McCracken said, "That's about how it went."

Morgan asked, "What happened then?"

The bartender answered, "Somebody bought John another shot."

Billy Cape said, "And ever'body was at givin' him advice on what to do about Blackie. They got pretty carried away. Some of 'em said John oughta give Blackie a good whippin'. But then, one of the fellas said he was at the Gold Creek Saloon last night and saw Blackie whip the two Underwood boys at the same time. So, he kinda threw cold water on that idea." Billy Cape smiled slightly.

Jake McCracken said, "Things got kinda outa hand, though; 'cause John started talkin' tough and said he had a score to settle."

There was silence, and Morgan asked, "What happened then?"

The bartender said, "Well, now, somebody tried to buy John another drink and he wouldn't take it. Said he didn't wanta get drunk or somethin' like that. Said he had to do some thinkin'. He went on outside and I thought he was gone until about a quarter hour later he starts shootin' out there. I s'pose he was out there all along."

Morgan looked at the other two for confirmation. They nodded.

Morgan asked, "Did any of you see what he was shooting at?"

"I didn't," said Billy Cape. "And I was one of the first to the door. I saw him take his second shot. I kinda thought he must be shootin' at Blackie. But I didn't know for sure. He reloaded and then took off runnin' down the street. I went outside then and saw him run up to the O'Connor house and run inside. I didn't see the kid layin' there till I got down there myself."

"How many shots were there? I mean, before he ran into the house?"

"I only heard two," said Billy Cape.

Morgan looked at the other two witnesses. They nodded.

McCracken said, "There was only two shots. The other one came afterwards from the next street."

Morgan then handed paper to all three. He set the pen and ink on the table.

"Would you three mind writing down what you just told me?"

Billy Cape looked embarrassed.

He said quietly and apologetically, "Morgan, I don't know how to write."

Jake McCracken said matter of factly, "Me neither."

"That's all right," Morgan said. "I'll do it for you."

The bartender proudly took up the pen, inked it, and laboriously began writing his own statement.

When the bartender finished writing his statement, he signed it and then Morgan and a customer witnessed the signature. Morgan wrote down the other men's statements. Another customer then read those statements back to Cape and McCracken; after which each of them signed with a trembling "X." The customer and the bartender then signed as witnesses to their signatures.

Morgan walked out of the Hard Rock Saloon carrying the statements.

He spoke to Blackie, "I reckon you can go on home now if you want to."

"I've got to buy Dusty some clothes at Belvedere's."

"All right. I'm going to try to get all the witnesses down on paper this afternoon. I'll be out to talk with Dusty too. Then I'll be going out to the Renner place to tell them what happened. I think it'd be best if you don't come in town tonight. Or tomorrow either. They'll be coming for John's remains tomorrow." After a pause, he added, "And keep a rifle with you when you're outside. The Renners might get hot headed. I don't know."

The boardwalk ended at the Hard Rock Saloon, and there was a vacant lot between it and the next building up the street. That vacant lot was occupied by six tents which housed Spanish speaking families, people who had just four weeks ago lived up on the hillside to the west of town and had been burned out by the fire. Blackie and Morgan stepped off the boardwalk and then separated. Blackie walked on up the street, and for a few seconds he could hear Morgan questioning in Spanish some of the women who lived in the tents.

Blackie walked up the dirt street until he came to a cluster of eight buildings built close together with a covered board-walk along their fronts. He stepped up onto the boardwalk and then walked into Belvedere's Dry Goods Store. The door, opening, struck a little bell that tinkled. There was shelving to Blackie's left holding bolts of cloth, boxes of shoes, ready made pants and shirts, and other dry goods. To his right, the counter stretched twenty feet down toward the back of the store. To protect them from soiling by grimy fingers, the more expensive bolts of cloth resided on shelving behind the counter, as did easily pilfered things like buttons and threads and fancy items. The exit to the counter was at the far end, near the back of the store. Directly in front of Blackie, at the far end of the store was a curtained doorway that led to the living quarters occupied by the Belvedere family. The family included John Belvedere, his wife Margaret, and their sixteen year old daughter Trudy. At the tinkling of the bell, John Belvedere came through the curtained doorway. Brown haired and blue eyed, he had once been a good looking man; but now at thirty-five he was forty pounds overweight, soft of muscle, and puffy in the face. He registered surprise at seeing Blackie.

Blackie spoke calmly, but in a slightly subdued manner. "Hi, Mr. Belvedere."

Belvedere had heard of the shooting, and he simply did not expect to see Blackie here in his store so soon afterward. Surely Blackie would have had the decency to go home after such a somber event. After killing two people.

"Hello, Blackie. What can I do for you?"

"Dusty's home; and she didn't bring her clothes and things." He reached for the list in his shirt pocket. "My mom made out a list. Could you fill it for me?"

John Belvedere figured that the order would include some underwear, and he never filled such orders because some ladies felt embarrassed when he did. So, from habit, he turned and called to his wife.

"Maggie!"

Margaret Belvedere came through the curtain. A dishwater blonde in her early thirties, she still had some prettiness left over from her youth. She too was surprised at Blackie's presence.

"Blackie's got an order for Dusty," John Belvedere explained.

Blackie handed the list to Margaret Belvedere who could not help staring at his black eye.

Blackie said, "Mrs. Belvedere, could you tell Trudy that Morgan doesn't want me to come in town tonight; so...."

"I'm here, Blackie," a girl's voice called from the living quarters.

Trudy Belvedere pushed the curtain aside. She was sixteen with a slim, fully developed figure and a serenely pretty face. She was one of Dusty's friends, and this summer, after Dusty had moved away, she and Blackie had occasionally taken twilight walks together. She had had a crush on him ever since she could remember, but tonight was to have been their first real date. They were to have gone, in the company of Blackie's mother, to the Jethro Stevens' for supper. She had looked forward to tonight, going as Blackie's date to the house where her friend Jettie Stevens lived. She suspected that Jettie had recently taken an interest in Blackie that was not just friendship.

Right now, Trudy stared at his bruised face.

"Look, I'm awfully sorry," Blackie said, "but, Morgan doesn't want me to come into town for a couple of days. And besides, I don't think anybody'd be in the mood for a supper party tonight anyway."

"All right. I understand."

John Belvedere was relieved.

Trudy asked, "What happened to your face?"

Blackie gave a slight smile. "One of the Underwood boys hit me last night."

"Why?"

"Oh, Isaac was shooting his mouth off, so I took him and his brother both on at the same time."

"Oh, Blackie you shouldn't have done that. You should've gotten help. Wouldn't anyone help you?"

"Don't worry about it. I whipped them both." Blackie gave a little smile, showing his pride. He knew it was unseemly now so soon after the shooting, but he could not help it.

Trudy could not help it either. She tried to repress her pride in him. "Really?"

Blackie nodded, smiling. "There were plenty of witnesses."

John Belvedere could not make up his mind how he should feel about it. He did not like the Underwood brothers; they had an insolence that was infuriating. Yet, he could not congratulate Blackie who, after all, had just killed little Billy O'Connor.

Trudy asked Blackie, "What was the shooting about? We've heard these crazy stories."

"What did you hear?"

"That you shot John Renner and Billy O'Connor."

"I did *not* shoot Billy. Mrs. O'Connor was just confused and she got everything mixed up. When I ran past Billy he was alive, and right about then John shot again. So, he must've hit Billy then. Mrs. O'Connor was in the kitchen when I ran in, so she couldn't have seen it anyway.... I did shoot John; but what would you expect me to do? Let him kill me? He'd already shot at me twice."

When Blackie got home with the package of clothes for Dusty, who was clad now in one of Sarah's robes, he was relieved to see no disapproval of him in her eyes.

"Thank God," said Dusty, "you're safe."

Four

It was dusk when first one dog started barking, pointing eastward, and then three others joined in. They were barking at someone riding toward them where they stood near the ranch house. Cattle were intermittently bellowing too, as usually happens about dusk, especially if someone or something is moving about.

The ranch house sat alongside the San Francisco River, maybe eight miles west of the Mogollon Mountains. Surrounded by outbuildings and corrals, the house was a rambling affair that had been built in stages as the family had grown and needed more space. Central to the house was a large room that served as living room, dining room, and kitchen.

The family was at the supper table when the dogs commenced their barking. There was a forty-five year old man and his forty year old wife, four sons ranging in age from fifteen to twenty-four, and a daughter ten years of age. Two coal oil lanterns on the table lighted the room.

The eighteen year old boy, listening to the dogs barking, said, "I reckon that'll be John."

The woman, Cordelia Renner, John's mother, said crabbily, "I wonder if he's got that fool girl with him."

The ten year old girl, Cecelia, Dusty's only friend here, looked down at her plate and smiled privately at the thought of Dusty coming back. She got up from the table and went to a window.

The girl said, "It's just one rider, and it ain't John."

The twenty-two year old son got up and joined his sister at the window. "It's Marshal Morgan from Gold Creek."

Morgan had pressed his horses hard to get to the Renner Ranch before sundown. He had wanted to get there first with the story before someone else could arrive with an altered version that might inflame the Renners.

40

Morgan rode on into the clear area in front of the house. He had one of the Sheffield pack horses with him for carrying Dusty's possessions back to Gold Creek. The dogs stood back but continued to bark. Morgan dismounted and tied his horses to a post.

The little girl, Cecelia, ran out to meet him. Overcoming her shyness, she asked, "Do you know if Dusty got home all right?"

Morgan gave her a tender but sad smile. "Yes she did."

"Oh, I'm glad! Sometimes the Apaches come down here at night and sneak around and steal our horses and butcher our cattle. I was worried for her."

"I'll tell her you were."

Cecelia was pleased.

The girl's father walked out of the house followed by his boys. He was tense.

"Well, Morgan, I reckon you wouldn't ride all the way out here unless there's something wrong. Is John in trouble or something?"

"Mr. Renner, I've got bad news....John was killed today in a gunfight."

Death was no stranger here. Like many families in these times, the Renners had lost other children. A three month old boy had died of "natural causes," that is, from some unidentified illness. A six year old girl had died within hours of being bitten by a rattler. And a ten year old boy had died three days after being kicked in the chest by a horse. Nevertheless, that did not make it any easier for them. When Morgan said that John was dead, Mr. Renner's legs went weak and his vision dimmed. Cecelia squealed, and broke out crying, staring half-disbelieving at Morgan; finally, she turned away, crying uncontrollably. The boys turned pale and silent, and stood around helplessly. Mrs. Renner came to the door and stared hatefully at Morgan.

Morgan told the events as briefly as possible while at the same time giving enough of the story so that the Renners could have no doubt that it was John who had initiated the violence. When Morgan finished, Mr. Renner merely nodded. His wife harshly told Cecelia to stop her bawling. The girl ran around the side of the house, and they could hear her crying out back. The Renners did not invite Morgan in, and after about a minute of silence, he knew there was nothing else to be done but to ask for Dusty's things. He felt very awkward doing it so quickly after announcing John's death.

Finally he said, "I think it would be easier on everyone if I carry Dusty's belongings back with me."

*　　*　　*

Morgan slept late the next day. He had ridden half the night to get home. He had hoped the Renners would invite him to stay the night, but they had not done so. On account of Apaches, everyone knew that riding a well worn trail at night down there could be dangerous. The safest route at night was cross country; because, in the vast open country, the chance of being in the same place at the same time with a party of Apaches was very remote. But Morgan's eyesight kept him from taking his bearings from landmarks at night with the telescope he always carried. So he had had to stay on the trail.

Five

W hoa!" The driver pulled back on the reins, and the six horse team brought the stagecoach to a creaking halt in front of Buzby's Livery. The driver set the hand brake.

It was afternoon, the day after the shooting.

The driver was a rugged looking man of medium build who wore his hair long. He had a bulge of tobacco in his cheek. Beside him, the guard, big and hostile-looking, wore a waxed mustache and had a .45-70 Sharps rifle across his lap.

The horses, the coach, the luggage, the driver, the guard, and the four passengers were all covered with dust raised by the horses' hooves and the coach wheels.

Having heard them arrive, old man Buzby, who owned the livery, came out to meet them. He called out, "How was your trip?"

The driver answered, "The same as always."

"Didn't see no Apaches?"

"No, thank God."

The driver and guard climbed down to help Buzby unhitch the team. While they were doing this, the passengers—three men and an attractive woman—stepped stiffly down to the ground for a welcome change from the shaking, jolting, and lurching that had been their lot for many hours. Two of the men wore long duster coats which they now removed along with their hats. They proceeded to beat the dust from their dusters and hats. The woman and the other man slapped at their clothes. Dust flew.

When Buzby led the team away, the driver turned to the passengers. "Well, folks, if you haven't already guessed, this is Gold Creek. We'll be stayin' overnight. Now, we'll be staying at the Mother Lode Rooming House which is pretty good. And for two bits extra you can get a bath—if you're feeling any need for it—and they'll haul the water and heat it for you."

The stage company had contracts with inns and road houses along the way, and beds and food were provided as part of the price of passage.

The driver now climbed atop the coach and handed down very dusty carpet bags to the passengers who immediately began swatting the dust from them.

One of the passengers, who now had his duster draped over his arm, had a gold star pinned to his waistcoat's left breast pocket. A Federal Marshal destined for El Paso, Texas, he was in his mid-thirties and had a rugged, leathery face with a full mustache. His name was Timothy Wiggins, and he was smartly dressed in the latest fashion.

As soon as the passengers all had their hand luggage, the driver climbed down and led the way down Main Street toward the center of town. As they neared The Sawdust Bar, the driver said, "By God, I want a stiff shot of good whiskey. Anybody join me?"

Marshal Tim Wiggins answered, "Don't mind if I do."

The woman, of course, said nothing. And the other three men protested that they wanted to get settled and cleaned up for supper.

The driver and the Marshal broke off from the group and walked into the saloon and across the sawdust covered floor to the bar. There were no spittoons, and so the driver spat his tobacco into the sawdust on the floor—that was what the sawdust was for. They both ordered whiskey from the young bartender, both took a swallow, and both exhaled heartily.

The driver turned to Tim Wiggins and said, "Well, Marshal, I want to tell you how much it eases my mind to have a lawman aboard. Someone who's used to handlin' a gun when the chips are down, and won't get buck fever when shootin' at a man. When we leave here in the mornin', we'll be carryin' a shipment of gold all the way to El Paso. There's only one bank vault between here and there, and that's in Silver City. So, the gold's at risk almost the whole way."

Marshal Tim Wiggins was pleased to have some importance in the eyes of the driver. Hiding his pleasure, Wiggins replied calmly, "I'm always glad to help out."

The driver raised his shot glass to Wiggins. "To your health."

"And to yours."

They both drank and exhaled a sort of, "Ahhhhhhhhhhhh," to relieve the burning sensation in their throats and vocal chords induced by the straight whiskey.

The driver turned to the young bartender. "We passed the graveyard comin' into town. I'd say there was forty-fifty people out there."

"They're buryin' a little boy belongs to Bill and Mabel O'Connor. He got shot by a stray bullet from a gunfight yesterday."

Marshal Wiggins said, "That's terrible!"

"Sure is," said the bartender. "Bill O'Connor's the manager of the Yellow Lode Mine, the biggest mine hereabouts. I guess it's out of respect for him that so many people turned out."

While the stage driver and the Federal Marshal downed the rest of their whiskey, a man with dull brown hair and a gray tinge to his skin walked into the saloon and up to the bar. He had soft hands and a paunch.

The bartender turned to the newcomer. "Howdy, Doc. Whiskey?"

"Yup."

Doc Zale was the only medical doctor in Gold Creek. He was opinionated and self-important—a big frog in a little puddle.

The bartender poured Doc Zale a shot and said, "Been some excitement around here the last couple of days."

"Sure enough. That Blackie Sheffield's been a busy boy. Yesterday morning, Zeke Underwood fetched me over to Tillie's to tend to his brother. Now, Zeke didn't look none too good himself. His face was all swelled up like it was snake bit.

Said Blackie took a wagon spoke to him and Isaac. Isaac had two teeth knocked out and a broken foot."

Marshal Wiggins and the driver were taking this all in.

The bartender protested, "I heard that Blackie took 'em both on with bare fists!"

"Naw. Couldn't've been. Those two brothers are tough; and Blackie's still a kid. He's only seventeen, you know."

"Yeah, I s'pose you're right. When I heard it, I kinda wondered. You've got to be careful what you believe nowadays. I heard a couple of different stories on yesterday's shootin'. What'd you hear?"

"Well, there's no doubt that Blackie killed his brother-in-law. Now, little Billy O'Connor was killed in the crossfire. Blackie says it was his brother-in-law that shot the kid, but Mrs. O'Connor says it was Blackie. Now, I don't see no reason for her to say Blackie did it when it ain't so. Do you?"

"Guess not. What's Marshal Morgan gonna do about it?"

"Aw, he ain't gonna do nothin'. He and Blackie are thicker'n thieves. Besides, Morgan's sweet on Blackie's mother."

The bartender grinned. "Can't say as I blame him about Blackie's mother."

"Me neither. There ain't a handsomer woman in these parts."

Marshal Wiggins turned to the doctor. "What'd this fellow kill his brother-in-law for?"

Doc Zale's eyes took in Wiggins and his gold star. When he spoke, he chose his words more carefully. "I don't rightly know. I heard it was because the brother-in-law hit his wife, Blackie's sister."

Marshal Wiggins was indignant. "My god! A fellow can't go around killing men just because they hit their wives!"

"I know...."

"Does this sort of thing go on here all the time?"

"All the time," said Doc.

The bartender disagreed. "Oh, I wouldn't say it goes on all the time. Once in a long while, maybe, but not...."

Doc deliberately cut the bartender off. "All the time. And robberies too. Why, just three weeks ago, Belvedere's Dry Goods was held up. Fellow got away with eighty dollars!"

"Sounds to me as if you need a new marshal," said Wiggins.

"Or maybe," said Doc, "we need a *U.S.* Marshal to spend some time here and tame things down."

* * *

Later that evening, Doc visited Bill and Mabel O'Connor and their two surviving children, seventeen year old Stella and twelve year old Hank. The O'Connor family, subdued in speech and behavior, sat in the parlor with only one coal oil lamp burning. Each of the family wore something black to tell of his or her grief at the death of Billy. Mabel still was a bit crazed.

Doc had wasted no time in telling them of having met a United States Marshal; and he was just now adding, "Furthermore, Marshal Wiggins said if the town wanted him to, he'd stay on here for a couple of months. Of course, he said we'd have to fire Morgan Blaylock. But, as I see it, that ain't no loss."

Bill O'Connor, a slim, good looking man of medium build, asked, "What would this Wiggins do that Morgan can't?"

"He'd make it impossible to pull armed robberies, for starters."

"Armed robberies? There've only been a couple of armed robberies in this town since I've lived here."

"Any robbery is more than enough."

"I suppose so."

"And he'd make it impossible for anyone to get shot in town."

Mabel O'Connor was suddenly keen.

Bill O'Connor asked, "How?"

"He said he'd do it the same way Bill Hickock did in Abilene or Dodge City or someplace. Hickock didn't allow guns inside the town limits. Everybody had to keep their guns at the Marshal's office."

"I don't know as the miners here in town would allow that."

"Marshal Wiggins said that all we have to do is call a Town Meeting and fire Morgan and vote in the law about the guns. He said he'd see to it that the law is obeyed."

"Still, I don't think the miners would vote for such a law."

"Now, I said the same thing. But the Marshal said to have the meeting on a work night, and late. After ten hours in the mine, the miners'll be tuckered out and most won't want to attend a late meeting. And if we prepare our friends before the meeting we can catch everyone else by surprise, and pass the law without much opposition." Doc smiled at the cleverness of the plan.

Bill O'Connor frowned. The deceit of it bothered him. "I don't know whether I'd be for that."

Mabel O'Connor burst out, "Oh, do it, Bill!" She added more quietly, "For Billy's sake."

Bill O'Connor looked away for a long moment. Finally, he said, "All right, I'll do what I can."

Doc could not conceal his elation. He knew he needed Bill O'Connor's prestige and influence to achieve his end. His end was to bring change, to create an effect; it gave him a feeling of power.

Doc said, "Now, you bein' the manager of the Yellow Lode Mine probably makes you the most important man in town. If you'll just visit a few families with me, I think we can make it so. And we should take Mrs. O'Connor with us. The ladies will all be sympathetic to her loss; and we all know the power of the ladies over us menfolk."

Six

Six days after the shooting of Billy O'Connor and John Renner, Morgan saw a handwritten announcement spiked to the outside front wall of the Gold Creek Saloon. The announcement said, "Town Meeting tonight. Ten o'clock at the Gold Creek School." Morgan knitted his brow and then went on into the saloon. Inside, Jasper Odin sat at a table looking through a mail order catalog from Chicago that had come in on the stage five days ago. The catalog was printed in black ink on white paper. It had pen and ink style drawings of the items for sale; and it offered everything from farm implements to dresses and boots, to lanterns and knives and forks. Odin looked up at Morgan pleasantly.

Morgan asked, "You see that announcement out there?"

"What announcement?"

"The Town Meeting tonight at ten o'clock."

"Ten tonight? Why, most everybody'll be in bed."

"That's right. Now, who would have a Town Meeting at ten at night?"

"Well, I dunno. Are you sure you read it right?"

Morgan turned and went out and pulled the paper from its nail and carried it into the bar and laid it in front of Odin. Odin read it and looked up.

"Why, there must be some mistake. Whoever wrote this must've made a mistake."

"That's Gene Turner's writing."

The handwriting was beautifully elegant and absolutely legible. Eugene Turner was the Secretary for the Town Meeting and had been elected to the job because of his penmanship.

"Well," said Odin, "I suppose somebody oughta talk to Gene."

"I'll drop by and see him."

Morgan took the meeting notice and walked a few yards down the street to the hardware store. Inside, there were no customers, so the owner, Eugene Turner, sat relaxing in one of the chairs near the un-lit stove.

Turner looked up and said, "Howdy, Morgan."

"Morning, Gene." Morgan handed him the handbill. "Is this ten o'clock a mistake?"

"No, sir, it isn't."

"Why ten o'clock?"

"Well, I don't know. Doc told me to write it. You know, he's the President of the Town Meeting nowadays."

Morgan nodded. "Why such a short notice?"

"I don't know. I'm just the secretary. I just do what I'm told." He added abruptly and rudely, "If you want to know all those things, go ask Doc."

Morgan frowned at him, surprised and puzzled by his behavior. Under Morgan's gaze, Turner averted his eyes. Morgan turned and walked out. He walked up the street toward the house that Doc used for home and office. On the way, he saw a few more meeting notices spiked here and there along the boardwalk. At Doc's house he knocked a couple of times but no one answered. Then he saw a note on a nail beside Doc's door. It said that Doc was away for the day. Morgan shrugged and went on about his business.

*   *   *

Morgan and Odin arrived for the Town Meeting at around ten minutes to ten. There were already about fifteen men there. Odin and Morgan sought out Doc who was nervously going from one person to another. Doc glanced at Morgan and moved away and commenced talking with someone. Odin and Morgan followed. They waited nearby. Doc moved away again. They caught up with him.

Doc whirled and looked intently into Morgan's eyes, trying to determine if Morgan knew what was about to happen. He decided that Morgan probably did not know. His eyes now danced this way and that, never staying on Morgan's more than an instant.

He smiled brightly. "What can I do for you, Morgan?"

"We just wondered why we're meeting at ten o'clock."

"Oh, uh, well, uh....you see, Bill O'Connor wanted to have the meeting, and he can't make it till ten. Got to work late at the mine or somethin'."

"Why couldn't we have it tomorrow night, then?"

"Well, he wanted to have it tonight."

Morgan was sincerely puzzled. "What's so important that we couldn't wait a day and have more people here? And why such short notice?"

"You'll have to ask Bill. I'm just doin' what I'm told. You know Bill. He's used to tellin' people what to do. And I'm used to doin' what I'm told."

Morgan knew Bill O'Connor. He had never seen Bill push his weight around outside of the mine. He was quiet and unassuming on a social level. Morgan knew Doc too. Doc almost always tried to have his own way in a secretive manner. Looking at Doc now, Morgan saw that Doc's usually gray face had turned slightly red. Doc still smiled brightly; his eyes danced around the room.

Jasper Odin asked, "So you don't know what this is all about either?"

Doc turned his head and looked away. "You boys'll have to excuse me. I've got to go get things ready."

He walked away toward where Eugene Turner was sitting, unwrapping his writing materials. Odin and Morgan looked at each other, raising their eyebrows. They took seats nearby.

In the next few minutes, about a dozen more men came in and sat down. At ten sharp, Bill O'Connor came in. Doc quickly called the meeting to order and turned the floor over to O'Connor.

O'Connor spoke: "Men, I guess you know that my family was recently the victim of a shooting. It's an awful feeling to know that someone you've known and loved for the last five years is gone forever. Someone you've nursed through sickness, and hugged when he took his first step, and laughed with. I'll never see him again.

"I sympathize with the Renner family too. Maybe their loss is greater—I don't know. They had their boy for a lot more years. In those years, there was more sickness to nurse, more tears to wipe away, and maybe more joy to share. And now he's gone too.

"Well, I'll leave off from that. This isn't a funeral. What I want to talk about is the future. I think it's time for a change. Morgan Blaylock has been the Marshal for almost two years now. He's not done too bad of a job, in my opinion, but I do think someone could do it better."

Needless to say, Morgan was surprised. He and Jasper Odin glanced at each other and then looked back to O'Connor as he continued.

"There's a United States Marshal in town right now who has agreed to stay on in Gold Creek for a couple of months to tame things down around here. During those two months, we can take our time and look for a replacement for Morgan. If we have to we can bring someone in from out of town. Now, of course, we can't have two Marshals in town at the same time. It's like having two foremen on the same job. They get in each other's way. So, the U.S. Marshal will only stay if we let Morgan go. Therefore, I move that we terminate Morgan as of now."

Bill O'Connor sat down with his back to Morgan. Doc stood up and asked, "Anybody else have anything to say?"

Another man stood up. Doc nodded at him. The man said, "I second the motion."

Morgan stood up.

Doc said, "Morgan has the floor."

"Now maybe I have been too long on the job. I could probably do better for myself in some other kind of work. The Marshal's pay is barely enough to live on in a boom town. I don't mind losing the job, but what I do mind is someone saying that I'm not doing a good job. And despite the way Bill said it, that is what he meant. Now, I think this town is safer than when I took over. What I'd like to know is how any marshal would have prevented what happened to Billy and John. You know, marshals are not gods. They don't know what goes on inside the heads of other men. They can't always predict what someone is going to do. Now, what I'd like to know is what you think this Federal Marshal can do to make it any safer in town. Would someone tell me that?"

Morgan sat down. No one stood up to answer him.

Doc said, "Well, Morgan's had his say, and the motion has been made and seconded. All in favor of, uh....terminating Morgan say aye."

Nearly everyone said "Aye."

Doc then said, "All against, say nay."

Only four men, including Odin, said "Nay." Morgan did not even vote after he heard the ayes.

Doc said, "The ayes have it. Morgan is fired. Now for the next couple of months, United States Marshal Timothy Wiggins will be our local lawman." Doc's eyes glanced at Morgan and immediately flicked away. "Morgan, if you could move out of the Marshal's office by noon tomorrow, it sure would be appreciated."

Doc glanced around the room and cleared his throat. "Now, men, Marshal Wiggins suggested a law that'll make his job easier and make our town a lot safer. His suggestion is that nobody be allowed to keep a gun with him inside the town limits. Everybody would keep their guns at the Marshal's office—actually in the empty store across the road from his office. A gun owner could fetch his gun any time he wanted it, just so long as he was headin' out of town."

Doc looked around the room. "Now, I think it's a sensible law. I think everybody has to agree that if there ain't no guns in town there's nobody gonna get shot in town. I don't see how anybody could argue with that.

"The law is for the protection of everybody. But I'd like you to think especially about our children. We got a lot of children in town. We have to think of them. We got to protect our children; so any inconvenience that this law brings is made up for in the safety of our children."

Morgan noted Doc's words, "our children." Doc had no children of his own, and was not even married. He spoke as if the children belonged to the town instead of to the families. The peculiar thing was that whenever Morgan had seen him dealing with children, Doc had treated them as if they were nuisances.

Doc went on, "So, I'm proposin' a law." He pulled a slip of paper from his shirt pocket and read from it aloud:

"No guns shall be allowed in town. All persons coming into town must leave their guns in the Marshal's care until they leave town. All persons living in town must leave their guns in the Marshal's care while they are in town." Doc looked up. "Now I'll open up the floor for discussion."

Morgan stood up. Doc made a face calculated to ridicule Morgan. In a tired tone, he said, "The Chair recognizes Morgan."

Morgan said, "I think Doc's proposed law is dangerous. A citizen may never have to use his gun in self-defense; but, if he should ever need it, it's his right to have it at hand. Now, the Marshal can't be everywhere at once. Let's say he's at the south end of town when some gunslinger comes into the north end of town and doesn't give up his gun. The gunslinger could pull a robbery or kill someone with no opposition."

Doc butted in. "Aw, Morgan's just trying to save his job."

"I don't have a job. I've already been fired. But, that doesn't mean that I can't speak up for all the law abiding citizens of this town." Morgan paused. "You know, Chief Victorio's Apaches are raiding and killing wherever they think the pickings are easy. There's no way you could keep Doc's law a secret from them."

Jed Simmons, a big man with a black beard, stood up and cleared his throat. Morgan looked his way.

Jed Simmons said, "The Apaches are at war only because they fear the white man. If we show 'em that they don't have anything to fear, I believe they'll come down out of the mountains and live in peace. I think Doc's law is a step in the right direction. When they come down here and find we don't want bloodshed either, you'll see 'em laying down their arms too."

Morgan responded, "Now, Jed, I don't question your sincerity. But, I can't agree with you. Most Indian culture is built around theft and bloodshed. They don't see another way to live. Before the white man, the Indians of the different tribes stole from each other and murdered each other for centuries."

Jed Simmons said irritably, "My wife is one of the gentlest people I know." His wife was Apache.

"I don't mean to say anything against your wife. I'm sure she's a fine woman. But she's living in a white man's culture. As imperfect as it is, it's more peaceful than the Apaches'."

Doc broke in. "Let's not argue over Jed's wife. Mr. Belvedere wants to speak."

John Belvedere was momentarily surprised. He had gotten so interested in the argument between Morgan and Jed that he had forgotten his part in the meeting. He now got to his feet.

"As many of you know, my dry goods store was held up recently. The scoundrel came in just before closing and pulled a six shooter on us. Nearly scared my wife and daughter out of their wits. Now, with Doc's law, that couldn't happen. If the robber hadn't had a gun, the three of us could surely have overpowered him. I say let's stop arguing about Doc's proposal, and take a vote."

Eugene Turner stood up. "I second the motion."

Doc raised his voice. "All in favor say aye."

Odin, Morgan, and three other men were the only ones who did not give their ayes.

"All against, say nay."

The five gave their nays.

Morgan was bewildered by the lopsided vote. What he did not comprehend was that almost all of those men voting yes had been committed to vote so before they had entered the room; consequently, his arguments had come too late and, for the most part, had fallen on deaf ears. Moreover, to the majority, the notion that the Apaches might attack such a large town seemed a remote daydream from Morgan's over-active imagination.

*   *   *

At sun up the next morning, Morgan rode away from his home of almost two years. Behind his saddle horse walked a pack horse loaded with his clothes and a few other posses-sions. He rode south to the Sheffield Ranch. When he crossed the creek, one of the two Sheffield dogs trotted out to greet him. At the house, Morgan dismounted and tied his horses to the hitching rail. He climbed the steps and knocked at the door.

Sarah Sheffield opened the door. She was pleased at the sight of him. "Good morning, Morgan. Come in."

Inside, Morgan could smell meat cooking on the stove. The table was set for three people.

Sarah asked, "May I set you a plate?"

"Thank you no; I've eaten. I'll take coffee with you, though." He paused. "Where are the youngsters?"

"They're milking the cows. They should be coming in any time now."

Sarah went to the cupboard and took down a cup for Mor-gan. There was a sudden scratching at the back door. It was the "milk dog," the one that always went with the milkers and watched until they were done, and then raced to beat them back to the house.

Sarah went to the back door and opened it for the dog. Morgan followed and stood beside her. Her closeness made him feel light headed. They stood like that, neither wanting to move and break the spell.

"Here they come," said Sarah.

They could see Blackie and Dusty coming around the side of the barn. Both carried two large pails of milk. Each had a somewhat discolored eye, although the swelling had gone away. They were talking and smiling.

"Look at them," Sarah said with pleasure. "They get along just like two peas in a pod. I can't remember when they last had a real quarrel."

"I sure quarreled with my sisters," Morgan remarked.

Sarah nodded. "I didn't get along all that well with my brother either. He was four years older and seemed to think I was his servant."

They watched the youngsters come across the back yard.

Sarah remarked, "They're very different in some ways. Blackie has a quick temper sometimes...."

"I've noticed."

"I'm not sure where he gets it. But anyway he's hardly ever cross with Dusty. And when he is she just gentles him right down."

Dusty and Blackie came in and exchanged greetings with Morgan. They poured their milk into a zinc plated milk can and placed a lid on it. Sarah now broke eggs into a frying pan while Blackie and Morgan carried another milk can, containing last night's milk, cooled now, out to a buckboard sitting under some trees. Sarah would drive the buckboard into town in a few minutes and sell the milk along with fresh eggs.

The four of them sat down to the table. There was venison steak, eggs, biscuits, and gravy. Sarah talked Morgan into taking a buttered biscuit with his coffee, and Dusty convinced him to try some wild berry jam that she had made last fall.

Morgan said to Blackie, "Looks like you got yourself a haircut."

Blackie smiled and glanced at Dusty. "My barber's back." He was obviously delighted about his sister being home.

Morgan marveled at how everything seemed to pivot around this girl wherever she was. He had seen it here as well as at other households when he had gone with the Sheffields to those households to listen to books read aloud. The funny thing was that she did not seem to seek attention; on the contrary, she seemed more interested in other people's affairs—listening attentively to what others had to say, asking pertinent questions. She spoke freely about her thoughts and feelings, but she spent more time finding out what others thought and felt. She seemed such a happy person, and it rubbed off on the people around her. People seemed to brighten up whenever she was around. Morgan knew that he surely did.

Morgan waited through the breakfast small talk until everyone had finished eating and then said, "There was a Town Meeting last night."

"Oh?" said Sarah. "What was it about?"

"I got fired as Marshal."

The Sheffields were stunned.

Morgan went on: "There's a Federal Marshal been hanging around town the last few days. It seems that he, Doc Zale, and Bill and Mabel O'Connor were behind this. The meeting was a stacked deck. It was set up like a stage play; some of the men knew just what they were going to say and do beforehand. I cornered Gene Turner afterward, and he admitted the whole thing."

Sarah asked, "But, what's Doc got against you?"

Morgan snorted. "Doc." A pause. "He sure fooled me. Gave me to think he was my friend all this time. I should've known better. He was constantly complaining to me about other people behind their backs. To their faces, he smiled and pretended to be their friend. I don't know why I thought he felt differently about me. I don't think, in the bottom of his heart, he likes anybody."

Blackie asked, "What's this Marshal got to do with it?"

"Well, he's going to stay on and be the local Marshal for a couple of months. As far as I can see, he's just a busybody. The day after he came to town, I looked him up, and he got slippery about what he was doing here. He avoided me from then on. According to Gene, he met Doc on his first night in town, and, together, they hatched this whole thing."

Dusty asked, "What are you going to do now?"

"I'm heading out to Collier's ranch. They're always in need of a hand. They lose about one man a year to Apaches or rustlers. I'll work out there for a few months until I've got some money saved. Then I'll come back this way and maybe do some prospecting."

Dusty asked, "Couldn't you get a job in one of the mines?"

"Well, yes, I guess so. But I think I'm better suited for ranching."

"But the mines pay a lot better. You could make your grub stake a lot faster."

Morgan thought that it seemed very important to Dusty that he stay. He was surprised.

"Well, I guess you're right. But I'm more of a cowboy."

Dusty seemed hurt. "I don't want you to *go*."

Morgan felt suddenly physically weak. He knew that he should not be going. He had a sudden glimpse of the real reason he was going, and he experienced a terrifying confusion. He said lamely, "Well, I'm already on my way."

Blackie said, "I'll ride out part way with you, and shoot something on the way back."

Sarah spoke up: "Oh, no you won't, James Sheffield. You'll stay right here and do your grammar and composition." She turned to Morgan. "I let his tutoring lapse during all this upset over the shooting. And Dusty hasn't studied since she married. Its high time for both of them to get back to it."

As if explaining to someone who did not understand, Blackie said, "But, Mom, Morgan's going away."

"He's not going so far we'll never see him again. When he next has time off, he can come and stay with us."

"I can study tomorrow."

"You *promised* you would do it today. You promised you would help your sister catch up. No one respects a man who doesn't keep his word—least of all, the man himself."

Blackie smiled at Morgan and shrugged, turning his palms up as if to say, "I'm stuck."

Morgan grinned and drank his coffee. Finally, he put his cup down and got serious.

"The Town Meeting passed a new law last night. Nobody can keep his guns with him in town anymore. The Marshal will keep everybody's guns. When someone comes to town, he has to leave his gun with the Marshal. The Marshal will lock it up in that empty store across from his office. When a fellow leaves town, he has to look the marshal up to get his gun. I'm a little worried what might happen if the Apaches find out the town is disarmed.

"Now, you folks are outside of town, so the law doesn't cover you except when you go into town. But, it does effect you; if the Apaches were to raid the town, you might be included.

"So, what I suggest is that you all keep guns at hand. When you're out rounding up the milk cows, take a rifle with you. Never be more than a step from a gun of some sorts. And keep a knife in your belt."

There was silence while the Sheffields considered what Morgan had said.

Finally, Blackie asked, "By the way, what did you learn about that dead miner we found?"

"Nothing." Morgan turned to Dusty and asked, "I suppose you heard what we found up in a canyon a couple weeks ago?"

She nodded.

Morgan continued to Blackie, "I went back the next day with two men; but we never found a trace of the missing partner. I think it's safe to presume he's dead. I checked with the Post Office; there's no mail for either of them. Nor does Millie recall ever having any mail for them or ever seeing them. So, I wrote to the Sheriff in Socorro about it. That was about all that could be done as things stand."

Morgan paused and then said, "Well...." He got to his feet. "I'd better get going if I want to make Colliers' before dark."

Everyone stood.

Morgan said, "There was one amusing thing about that meeting last night: they were in such a hurry to shove their law through, they forgot to pass penalties for not obeying it. So, if you don't obey it, they can't legally do anything to you."

Everyone smiled. Sarah then turned to her youngsters and said, "You two clear the table and get busy on your studies. I'll see Morgan off."

Blackie was momentarily surprised, and then he understood. He and Dusty said good-by to Morgan as the big man went outside with their mother. Sarah closed the door behind her. Her two offspring grinned at each other.

They cleared the table and Blackie set the grammar book, paper and ink, and two pens on the table.

Dusty went to the front window and looked out. Morgan, tall and trim with big shoulders, stood beside his horse, looking down at her mother. Dusty liked his eye-pleasing ruggedness. Moreover, she liked his easy-going manner, and she liked it that he admired and respected her mother a lot—it was obvious in the way he behaved around her. Dusty wanted him to stay in Gold Creek and court her mother. And Dusty was pretty sure that he was leaving not because he was a "cowboy," but for some other reason—one that she did not understand.

Behind Dusty, Blackie scraped leavings from the breakfast dishes onto two old chipped plates while the two Sheffield dogs waited attentively. Something was on Blackie's mind again. He chose to discuss it now.

"You know, you haven't said one way or another....but you didn't seem upset by John's death."

Dusty turned. Hesitated. "I wasn't. It was a little shocking; but I wasn't upset." She paused. "The night I left him, I knew with all my heart that I'd washed my hands of him. I was on your side when you whipped him out front here, and I was on your side when I heard of the gunfight." She paused again. "I'm not glad he's dead, but I'm not bothered by it."

Blackie nodded.

"How about you?" Dusty asked. "How did you feel after you killed him?"

Blackie mulled it over. "Dangerous," he finally said. He put the dogs' plates on the floor where the animals promptly licked them clean. He straightened up and looked at Dusty. "I realized how dangerous I can be."

Dusty nodded, thinking. Then, genuinely curious, she asked, "Were you afraid when he started shooting at you?"

"You bet. I was scared right up to the time I got a loaded rifle in my hands. Then I wasn't scared anymore; I knew exactly what was going to happen."

Dusty studied him while he put the breakfast dishes into the dish pan that sat warming on the edge of the stove. She said in gentle agreement, "You *are* dangerous."

When Dusty was again looking out the window, she saw Morgan pull some papers from his saddle bag and hand them to Sarah. Seeing them up close a few minutes later, Dusty found them to be the written statements by witnesses to the shooting of Billy O'Connor and John Renner.

Seven

That same morning, a man, a Sonoran, sat on a horse in the Mexican State of Sonora, on a grassy knoll not quite a day's ride south of the Arizona border. The man was dressed simply and wore a simple hat with a medium brim. He had a lever action .44-40 Winchester in a saddle scabbard, and, tucked into his belt, a new Colt revolver that shot the same ammunition. Behind him, rolled up and tied to the saddle were his pancho, his blanket, and his petate, a mat to sleep on, made of woven palm leaves. A canteen and a bag of food were tied in front of his saddle horn. He scanned the hills around the southerly end of the semi-arid valley.

The man, whose name was Francisco Moran, finally saw what he had been looking for. Without haste, in a manner of someone of much experience, he pulled a large mirror from his saddle bag. He looked measuringly at the position of the sun, and then began flashing the mirror at what he had seen.

He continued flashing. There was no code to it. Only flashing to gain attention. Finally he stopped and waited.

Presently he saw, on a mountainside six miles away, the flashing of a mirror. It went on for a few seconds, and when it stopped, Francisco Moran flashed an acknowledgment. Then he put the mirror back into his saddle bag.

Six miles away on the mountainside, seventy mounted men trotted their horses down the slope into the valley. A man rode point about one hundred yards ahead. The rest rode in disciplined order, two by two. They wore civilian clothes, with all sorts of different hats. Further back in the column, some of the riders wore their bandannas over their noses because of the dust raised by the horses. They were Sonora State Militiamen—farmers, ranchers, businessmen—from Ures, the then capital of Sonora, and they had been on the trail for many days.

They were armed as well as could be expected of volunteers. A few had single shot breech loaders which shot brass cartridges. Others had paper cartridge breech loaders. Still others had shotguns. But most had muzzle loaders.

The column rode down into the valley and progressed across it to the grassy knoll where Francisco Moran had been sitting on the ground to give his horse a rest. He mounted now.

The leader of the column, Esteban Jerez, spoke to Moran, "Hola, Francisco."

"Hola, Esteban."

Esteban Jerez asked in Spanish, "What did you find?"

Francisco Moran pointed down between this knoll and another where there were an adobe house, three outbuildings, and a corral made of branches of dead brush. Behind the buildings, trees and brush indicated the existence of a spring. In back of the house there were ashes from several fires and remains of dead goats and a cow. In front of the house a man lay dead.

Francisco said in Spanish, "They camped there last night."

Esteban Jerez nodded grimly.

Francisco continued in Spanish, "Three bodies down there. A man, and a boy and a girl both under twelve. All have been scalped; and the children were stripped and raped."

"Bastards!" Esteban Jerez said in Spanish.

Francisco continued, "There are signs of a woman. Clothes and things. She's not there. They must have taken her with them."

While he spoke, the nearby militiamen sat in their saddles silently and grimly with tight jaws.

Francisco went on. "They got more horses here. They are driving more horses than they are riding."

Everyone within hearing knew what that meant: with fresher horses to switch to, those being pursued could leave the Militia in the dust.

Esteban said, "We'll take them by surprise, then."

Francisco shook his head. "They will cross the border into Arizona today."

"We can try."

Francisco shrugged, then nodded doubtfully only to be agreeable. He was sure their quarry was lost. Two years ago, in 1876, the Mexican dictator, President Diaz, had canceled the agreement of "hot pursuit" that had allowed forces from either side of the border to pursue renegade Indians or outlaws into the other's territory.

Esteban Jerez turned and spoke to the other men in a raised voice. "Water your horses!"

The men started their horses toward the spring.

Francisco said, "I go now."

He turned his horse and rode down the knoll, heading north.

Later in the day, in the early afternoon, Francisco Moran sat on a rock in a low mountain pass. His rifle lay across his lap, and his horse grazed nearby.

Esteban Jerez and his militiamen were riding their horses up the southern slope of the pass at a fast walk. As they came up to him, Francisco mounted his horse.

Francisco had to shout to be heard over the collective creaking of saddle leather, snorting of horses, and talking of the men. He pointed northward, down into the next valley, and shouted, "El Lobo!" The Wolf!

They could see, about five miles distant, down in the semi-arid valley, many dots—over one hundred—and much dust.

With Francisco riding point, the militiamen trotted their horses down the north slope of the pass. With their quarry in sight, the men had a new tenseness. Their fatigue was forgotten.

Five miles down in the valley, forty-nine desperados walked their horses briskly along an ancient trail. Ahead of them, they drove more than sixty riderless horses. The horses and riders were, all of them, dusty and dirty from many days of riding. A handful of men rode in front of the spare horses. On each side of the spares rode a man with a long, coiled whip. The front riders had their bandannas down around their necks; but, rearward, most of the men wore their bandannas over their noses because of the dust. All had rifles or shotguns and many had pistols in their saddlebags or in their pockets or tucked into their belts. Only a handful of men had holsters for their pistols. Each man dressed in his own way. All were Mexicans except one, a sandy haired American.

Some of the desperados glanced behind them from time to time, looking for the pursuers whom they knew were somewhere south of them.

A woman rode with them, the one they had taken from the little ranch. She was barefoot and her dress was torn. She was a study in misery.

The third rider from the front was dark and big—very big—with cold black eyes and a sharp, hooked nose. He was about fifty years old, and had gray flecks in his black hair. He was the leader here, the man called "El Lobo." He was a killer many times over. In the last thirty-some years, he alone had killed more than a hundred men, women, and children; and he felt no more remorse than a hunter would who had killed a hundred rabbits.

To the rear of this gang of thieves and murderers, a man was looking backward, squinting. He spotted something.

He cried out, "Jinetes!" Riders!

The desperados looked back at the dots coming down the pass which they themselves had ridden down just an hour before. In an undisciplined surge, they moved to a gallop. Whips cracked at the spare horses.

When the Militiamen perceived that they had been spotted, they too accelerated to a gallop.

The desperados raced across the valley heading for the pass at its north end. The Militiamen raced after them. They ran their horses at full gallop for more than one and a half hours.

Eventually, the desperados climbed the grade to the top of the pass. At the summit of the pass, El Lobo pulled up, raising his arm.

He cried out, "Alto!"

The desperados, their horses wet with sweat, came to a milling stop.

The sandy haired American looked at their situation. The pass was wide, and there was no cover. Nevertheless, they would have the advantage of high ground. Furthermore, they were sure to be better armed than the Militia. They stood a good chance of holding their own, and of even turning the Militia back. Of course, it could always go the other way. These things were never certain.

The American made his way over to El Lobo. He spoke in Spanish, shouting to be heard. "Lobo! Lobo! Will we stand and fight?"

El Lobo had made his decision days ago. Had he been riding with the men he had ridden with thirty years ago, he would already have doubled back and tried to ambush the Militia. The men he had ridden with thirty years ago had been seasoned killers of unmatched ferocity who had had no concern for danger. Forty-nine men like that would have cut these Militiamen to shreds. But that was thirty years ago. Today he rode with too many men whose attributes he doubted. They were bloodthirsty, but that alone was not enough. He estimated that in a pitched battle against superior odds, he could perhaps rely on less than ten of his men to be sufficiently ferocious and reckless. The American was one of those he trusted.

Sweeping his arm to indicate his men, El Lobo answered the American's question in heavily accented English. "Not with these cabrones." It was English that El Lobo had learned thirty years ago, when he had been a follower, when the leader had been an American.

El Lobo continued in English, "Why take chances? The border is not far! We change horses here, and split up."

In Spanish, El Lobo addressed the rest of his men. "Change horses! Split into groups of five and fan out! Meet at Cabeza Gordo Springs in seven days! No trouble in the United States! You hear?! Lie low! Pass the word!"

The men jumped to the ground and began moving their saddles to the fresher horses. When they were done, they mounted and broke up into groups of five and fanned out, driving their spare horses ahead of them.

When Francisco Moran reached the summit of the pass, what he had known would happen sooner or later had happened an hour before. The tracks were unmistakable. The desperados had changed horses and broken into smaller groups. He halted his horse, and took out his brass field glasses and scanned the countryside. Here and there were horses which had gotten loose because the various groups had been unable to control them. Francisco counted six horses.

The Militiamen, with Esteban in their lead, galloped up to Francisco and came to a dust roiling, milling stop.

Francisco said to Esteban, "As you can see, they've changed horses. We won't catch them today. Tomorrow, they will be in Arizona."

Esteban nodded and then said to those near him, "We'll camp on the border for a few days to make sure they don't come back across in our jurisdiction. Meanwhile, I want two volunteers to ride to Camp Huachuca to warn the Americans of El Lobo and his men."

Eight

That same afternoon, Dusty walked into town carrying two cheese cloth sacks, each containing two dressed chickens for the Gold Creek Saloon. She wore a belted, blue skirt that was cut to half-way between her knees and ankles. Above the skirt she wore a white, starched cotton blouse. Her shiny yellow hair spilled down over her shoulders. On her belt was a blue handled knife. She walked up the saloon's back steps and knocked at the kitchen door, and when no one answered the door, she opened it and went inside, pulling it closed behind her. There was no one else in the kitchen, so she peeked through the open doorway into the bar.

Leaning over the bar and sporting three days growth of beard, a bar patron saw her from the corner of his eye; he looked up and grinned. "Well, what have we here?"

Inasmuch as it was afternoon, there were only three other customers, and they all looked up and savored Dusty. Ed Ringsley stood behind the bar trying to look only a little interested in her. Cathy Haggarty sat in a wooden armchair beside the foot of the staircase. It was her favorite perch, since it allowed her to retreat upstairs when she wanted, or to take a customer up there unobtrusively. Right now, she did not like the way Dusty took the bar's attention.

Dusty called across the room, "Mister Ringsley, could you tell the Odins that I'm here with the chickens?"

Ed Ringsley was pleased at having her attention. He started for the stairs. "All right, Dusty."

Dusty withdrew into the kitchen. Cathy Haggarty got to her feet and walked for the kitchen. Her only contact with Dusty was during these occasional deliveries; so she hardly knew her; nevertheless, sometimes she liked her, and sometimes she disliked her. Dusty was altogether too wholesome looking to suit Cathy, and usually she felt an urge to degrade the girl.

Anyway, she had been hoping for an opportunity to talk with Dusty alone since last April. When the girl had married in June, Cathy had given up the idea. However, now that Dusty was back and husbandless.... Nervous, Cathy gave thought to what she would say to start a conversation.

She went on into the kitchen, and when she spoke, it was the best thing she could think of. "You know, your brother's awful tough with his fists."

"I know," Dusty agreed.

"I watched him thrash the Underwood boys last week, the night before you came back. As a matter of fact, I was with him upstairs the morning you came back. Charley Cistrom ran up and told us you rode through town in a night shirt. I'll bet dressed like that, you set some of them early risers' pants on fire."

So that was who Blackie had been with.

Finally getting to what she wanted to talk about, Cathy went on, "You know, in my kind of work, someone like you could make a fortune."

Dusty was taken aback by this statement.

Cathy continued, "I mean it. You could be rich like a princess. I talked you over with the girls up at Delilah's. And they all say so." Delilah's was the whorehouse at the north end of town.

Dusty's eyes went wide in surprise. "*Me?!* You talked *me* over?"

"Yeah."

Dusty was nonplused.

Cathy went on, "A couple of the girls up there used to work in New Orleans when they were younger and they know a lot about the business. They said someone like you should go to Nevada, to Virginia City, where they got the richest silver mines in the world. They got sixty thousand people there, and most of them are men. And they got rich men all over the place. You'd be set up in a suite, and you wouldn't take no one for less than a hundred dollars a night, maybe a lot more."

Dusty was blushing; but she was amused.

"In seven nights at a hundred a night, you could make what a well paid man makes in a year. You could make maybe thirty thousand dollars in a year. Maybe a lot more. That's what I mean about living like a princess."

Dusty still blushed. She said politely, "Thank you for saying so; but I just want to stay here in Gold Creek with my people."

Cathy leaned back against a table and looked at Dusty, not understanding her at all. "Me, I don't have no people."

"Don't you?"

"Well, none that I know about. I'm a foundling." Grief flashed for just an instant in Cathy's face.

"Oh."

"Yeah. The people who found me on their doorstep didn't want me either; so they gave me to an old couple who were barren. They took me and raised me. He was a preacher."

Dusty nodded.

"The old man, he was all right, I guess. But, the old lady.... She wanted me to call her Mother, but she never let me forget I was a foundling and that they'd sacrificed so much for me. She never let me forget that she wasn't my mother. There were times when I thought the old man really liked me and was proud of me—you know, when I'd get good grades in school, or something like that—but, then the old lady would tell him things that I did and make them sound so bad, and I sometimes overheard her tell him things when she thought I couldn't hear. And I suppose she told him lots of other things I never heard. Anyway, I know she didn't want him to like me, and she'd tell him things and he'd get cold to me. She never whipped me; she always made him do that. And when he was away, she'd wait till he got home and then tell him how bad I'd been, and then he'd whip me with a switch. I hated her and I got so I hated him for believing her."

They could hear Jasper Odin's heavy footsteps coming down the stairs.

As if summing up, Cathy added, "Anyway, I ran away when I was sixteen." She pushed away from the table and waved her clenched hand like someone cleaning a blackboard. "I don't know why I'm telling you all this stuff."

"Where was your home?"

"St. Louis."

Dusty wondered, but did not ask, how Cathy had gotten out here from St. Louis. As a matter of fact, Cathy had hitched a ride with a wagon train hauling equipment for Gold Creek. No virgin at the outset, she had serviced the bull whackers—the ox drivers—as payment for her passage. That is, she had serviced all but one of the bull whackers. That man had been one of the married men, and he had refused to have anything to do with her except when her feet had blistered in her shoes from walking—as everyone did—alongside the wagons most of the time and the blisters had broken and had gotten infected, and it had been he who had doctored her feet and wrapped them every morning so that they would be more comfortable in her shoes. Cathy had not liked him, but she had respected him. And whenever she thought of that trip, she did not think well of the other men, but she thought of him with respect.

Cathy was walking toward the doorway to the bar. She turned before going through the doorway and said to Dusty, "Anyway, if you change your mind about Virginia City, let me know. I'll go with you."

"I'm sure I won't."

Jasper Odin and his wife came into the kitchen. Mrs. Odin, a small, skinny woman with red hair that was just starting to turn gray, would have exploded if she had known that Cathy had been trying to talk Dusty into prostitution. It would have been the straw that broke the camel's back. She would have had her husband throw Cathy out of the saloon forever.

When the Odins had bought the saloon three years ago, Cathy, then seventeen, had already been working there for three months as the sole prostitute. And when the Odins, as new owners, had told her that she must leave, she had broken down crying, and had said that she would have to go live at Delilah's, a common whorehouse. Befuddled and sympathetic, and not wanting to contribute to Cathy's further degradation, the Odins had agreed to let her stay. They were real softies. Their reputations had suffered some for having her there.

It had turned out much better for Cathy than she had expected. Whereas the former owner had exacted a fifty percent commission from Cathy's earnings, the Odins would never have thought of such a thing. They simply required her to pay room and board and to help fill in when someone around there got sick.

Now, standing just inside the bar, Cathy listened to the Odins and Dusty greet each other in the kitchen. She was fearful that Dusty would tell the Odins that she had solicited the girl for prostitution.

Inside the kitchen, Mrs. Odin, who knew how much fun catalogs could be to youngsters, said to Dusty, "You know, we just got a new catalog from Chicago last week. Would you like to borrow it?"

Dusty broke into a pleased smile. "Oh, yes! Very much."

Mrs. Odin said to her husband, "We can let her have it for a few days, can't we?"

"Oh, sure. I'll get it." Odin went out of the kitchen and headed for the stairs.

Mrs. Odin asked, "How've you been?"

Dusty smiled. "Fine. How about you two?"

"The same as always. We just get older, that's all. We haven't seen you for a while."

"Well, you know, I was married."

"Yes. But, now that you're back, we hope to see you now and again."

Dusty smiled and nodded. The Odins were always pleasant to her.

In the bar, Cathy went over to a table and sat down. Having opened her past like a wound to Dusty, she was melancholy now. She sat there and felt sorry for herself. She compared herself with Dusty for a few seconds, and, for some reason, it floated into her awareness that she did not like herself, and that she did not really like this life she led. It was not as if she had to be a prostitute. No, because, after all, there was a shortage of women in town; and she was a well built, pretty young woman, and she'd had proposals of marriage even from some of her customers. But, generally speaking, she despised her customers.

She stayed with prostitution because the money was good. It was a fact, however, that she never really felt that she earned the money she made, and she spent it carelessly; and she would probably end up working in a seedy whorehouse somewhere, tired and old, with nothing to show for her years of work.

Cathy could hear Dusty's voice in the kitchen as the girl talked with Mrs. Odin. It was a nice voice, pleasing to the ears—happy sounding. It got under Cathy's skin. The idea of Dusty being a whore pleased Cathy. She daydreamed briefly, as she had several times since last spring, of managing Dusty in Virginia City and getting part of the girl's income. Maybe Dusty did not realize how easy the work was. You just had to pretend to enjoy the men as much as they enjoyed you. As a matter of fact, Cathy had not enjoyed men for a long time. The exception to that was Blackie the other night. Watching him thrash the Underwood brothers—the brutality of it!—she had felt sexual attraction to someone for the first time in over a year. And, later, it had been strange and exciting to press herself to his hard body and to gently bite his hard muscles. She'd had him make a fist with his right hand and she had rubbed that fist, so capable of brutality, over her face and her breasts and her ribs and her belly. Puzzled, he had asked her what she was doing, and she had answered that it just felt good. Afterward, when they had both been gratified, she had gently felt his swollen face and imagined that they were her bruises on her face, and that he had made them with that fist of his. Furthermore, the next day, having learned that Blackie had killed John Renner, she had been overcome by desire for him. From the staircase, she had watched him sitting at a table, writing out his statement, and she had actually shivered with excitement several times. Later she had daydreamed that she lived in Virginia City with him where he sometimes killed men and where he was feared and she was known as his girl and she supported him by selling herself.

But, since the day of John Renner's death, Blackie had not been inside the saloon while Cathy had been there. Beside herself, she had asked Ed Ringsley if he might drop by Blackie's house and hint that she wanted to see him. Ed had refused.

Now, sitting in the bar, listening to Dusty's voice in the kitchen, Cathy decided that she would send a message by Dusty. Dusty had been kind to her just now, had not turned away from her as did most of the women in town when she walked down the street. Dusty had listened to her when she had talked. So maybe Dusty would be kind enough to carry Cathy's message. She got up and walked out the front of the saloon and around the side and into the back yard where she entered an outhouse. She stood there peeking out the half moon cut in the door. Five or six minutes passed before Dusty came down the back steps carrying the Odins' catalog. As Dusty was about to pass the outhouse, Cathy stepped out as if she had just finished.

"Oh, Dusty."

Dusty looked at her. Cathy seemed pale and nervous. Her hands alternately pulled at each another.

"Would you do me a favor?"

"What is it?"

"Would you tell your brother....tell him that I'd like him to stop by....to stop by for a moment."

"When?"

"Oh....any time. Uh, the sooner the better, really."

"All right."

Cathy's relief showed. "Oh, thank you. It'd be a big favor."

Dusty nodded and walked out of the yard and toward home. She realized that Cathy was stuck on Blackie. It surprised her that Cathy, who must be awfully casual about sex and men, would have the usual anxieties about being able to be with the man she thought special. But, of course, why not?

Right then, going through the front door of the saloon, Cathy was thinking what a perfect fool Dusty was. Dusty lived in a dream world if she thought she could be happy staying here in Gold Creek with her family. Cathy was sure that happiness was a child's illusion. When you grew up, you realized that it was not possible. It would do Dusty good if some man would abduct her and rape her. The idea pleased Cathy.

When Dusty got home, her mother was cutting up vegetables for a stew, and Blackie was lying on the couch with his boots off. She whispered Cathy's message to Blackie who looked startled and got to his feet.

He spoke in a lowered voice to avoid Sarah's hearing. "Why does she want to see me?"

"Are you her lover?" Dusty teased, keeping her voice low.

"Hardly."

"She says you were with her the night I came home."

"That's true. She cleaned me up after the fight, and then took me upstairs to bed."

"How much did you pay her?"

"Nothing. It was free."

Dusty laughed out loud. She forgot to be quiet. "You see! You're her lover!"

"I am not! It just happened once!"

"Well, that's why she wants to see you."

Sarah had overheard the last few words. She asked without emphasis, "Who are you making love to, Blackie?"

Blackie turned crimson. "God, Mom, I'm ashamed to tell you. And it only happened once. And I'm not her lover. Dusty's just having fun at my expense."

He shoved his sister. Dusty chuckled.

"Well," said Sarah, keeping her voice gentle and conversational, "I hope you're being careful. If you get someone with child and you're not in love with her, you could make a lot of unhappiness for yourself and other people."

"I know."

"And it would be much worse with someone you're ashamed of."

"You don't have to worry, Mom."

Sarah was glad the subject had come up. Seventeen-year-old Hattie Redfield had been spending a lot of time out here at the ranch this summer. A moderately pretty girl, she was a bit timid despite the fact that she had worked up enough courage to chase Blackie. Whenever Sarah tried to engage Hattie in conversation, the girl usually tried to find out what Sarah thought on the subject and then agree with her. Sarah was sure that Blackie was not strongly attracted to Hattie; nevertheless, she suspected hanky-panky.

She asked matter-of-factly, "Was it Hattie?"

Blackie turned quickly away because he knew that his face would betray him. Although Hattie Redfield had nothing to do with what he and Dusty had been talking about, he had indeed made love to the girl.

"We weren't talking about Hattie," he said.

But, of course, turning away like that, under the circumstances, was almost as good as an admission of fact. Dusty, guessing whom Sarah must mean, turned a mildly surprised face to her mother.

Blackie sat down on the couch and grabbed his boots, intending to put them on and bolt from the house. Sarah, however, was not going to leave things half said.

"You know, of course, that if you get her with child, her people will expect you to marry her."

Blackie was pulling his boots on. He wanted to say that he had been careful. But to say so would be to admit the whole thing.

Anticipating his attitude, Sarah said gently, "Accidents sometimes happen. Precautions don't always work.... Well, I don't mean to badger you. You know the consequences, so I'll leave it at that."

His mother's method of handling him—giving him her viewpoint and then backing off to let him make his own decision—had always been effective with him. By conceding that he was responsible for what happened to him, that it was up to him to decide, she made it possible for him to consider her opinions without his feeling them forced upon him.

Blackie looked up into his mother's eyes. He was suddenly glad that the whole thing was out in the open. He had known that there were risks; but until this conversation he had found it a little easier to ignore them. It was a fact that he did not care all that much about Hattie, and he certainly did not want to marry her. It was also a fact, though, that she had made herself conveniently available to him. She had caught him at a vulnerable time: Dusty, who, besides being his sister, was his best friend, had just moved away and he had missed her company intensely.

"All right," he agreed, "when I see her again, I'll end it." A pause. "I don't want to hurt her feelings, though."

"I'm sure you'll be a gentleman. If you're honest with her, she'll be best served. It will give her a chance to find someone else....someone who can be in love with her."

* * *

Later that afternoon, out at the shed where the chicken scratch was kept, Dusty was filling buckets with scratch for the late afternoon feeding. Some of the chickens and ducks had seen her open the shed, and they were hanging around, waiting for the feeding, getting under foot. The rest, unworried, were off on the hillside or at the creek; they knew they would be called before scratch was actually put into the troughs. The chickens and ducks were pretty safe from predators because the two Sheffield dogs patrolled regularly and kept an eye on the surrounding area. The dogs themselves would never have been caught dead with a live chicken in their mouths. They were so good with the chickens that the chickens often pestered them; sometimes, catching them lying down, the chickens would jump onto them and walk on them.

Dusty heard the back door slam. She jerked a look that way and saw Blackie leap from the steps and hit the ground running in her direction. Inasmuch as she had teased him earlier, and inasmuch as he had nothing else to do this afternoon, she was pretty sure what this meant. Dusty dropped her buckets into the barrel and took off running around the corral, heading for the creek. She was pretty fast, but she was no match for him, and he overtook her before she got to the creek. She took a quick turn to the left and he overshot her. She laughed. He wheeled and caught back up with her. She feinted another turn to the left, but made a sudden right turn, and he overshot again. She laughed again. But he was closer and in only a few bounds he was upon her and, despite her last instant weaving, he threw his right arm around her and, while she screeched appropriately, he picked her up and tucked her under his right arm like a sack of potatoes. He held her against the side of his chest, his arm around her midriff, her head and feet dangling.

Dusty kicked and jerked and said, "Put me down, you big ox!"

"Not until you say uncle."

For Blackie, getting even with his sister was just his excuse to horse around with her. He could have closed the back door of the house normally, and walked calmly out to Dusty and thrown an arm around her and picked her up by surprise. But that was not the game. The game was to make a big ruckus as if he was mad at her, as if her teasing had been terribly resented. If she had not taken off running, he would have been disappointed and would have lost interest immediately.

Blackie carried Dusty back toward the scratch shed.

Dusty complained, "You're going to make me vomit!"

"You can't see my face."

She laughed. "No, I mean by carrying me like this."

"You haven't eaten since noon."

"Oh."

"All you have to do is say uncle."

Of course she could have said uncle right away, but that would not have been proper play. She had to give some little resistance as if she did not want to say uncle, as if he had to force it from her by carrying her around like this for a bit.

He carried her toward the shed, and after a few seconds he began to worry that she was uncomfortable. "Are you going to say uncle?"

"Oh, all right! Uncle!"

Blackie put her feet down and let her straighten up. She pushed her hair back.

"Now you've made me late," said Dusty. "You've got to help me now."

He had not made her late to any degree. She just thought it was fun when they worked together.

"Oh, all right," he said as if giving in. He had, of course, come outside fully intending to help her. Working with Dusty was never a chore, it was always a game.

At the shed, they shooed away the chickens that had gotten into the scratch barrel. Blackie held the buckets while Dusty filled them from the barrel with a scoop. At one point, when the buckets were practically full, and she was sure his hands were occupied with the buckets, she swatted his rump with her scoop.

"Ouch!" he exaggerated.

She grinned and said, "Oh, sorry."

"I'll bet you are. You're trying to give me the ague."

"What?"

"The ague. It's some kind of disease I've heard people mention. I was trying to make a pun. You know how when somebody hits you really hard they raise a goose egg lump on you?"

"The ague you're talking about is spelled a-g-u-e. You didn't make a pun. A pun needs a word that's spelled the same."

"You see! You've made a fool of me again! I daren't open my mouth around you. Everybody knows it. I walk into town nowadays and people sit along the boardwalk and I hear them snicker and say, 'Heh, heh. Looky yonder. There comes Dusty's fool.'"

"Oh, stop your whining."

"I can't help it. Oh, woe is me. Poor little old me. Me, who never did nothing to nobody, has to suffer you for his sister."

"If you don't shut up I'm going to tell Mom the grammar you're using."

"God, don't do that. I won't say another word."

Dusty finished filling the buckets and then stood on her tiptoes and grabbed Blackie's head and bit his ear.

"Ouch! My God. How much of my ear is left? I can hear the boardwalk people now: 'Yonder comes Dusty's fool. Don't he look just like a raggedy-eared cat?'"

Dusty swatted his rump. She liked to catch him with his hands full. She could rough house with him without getting it in return. Of course, he could have emptied his hands, but he seldom did.

They each took two buckets of scratch out to the feed troughs and stood there calling, "Chick! Chick! Chick! Chick! Chick!" The chickens came running from all directions, and the ducks came flying in from the creek on clipped wings about two feet off the ground. The youngsters made more trips back to the scratch barrel for buckets of scratch because there were a lot of chickens and ducks.

* * *

That evening, after supper, after the dishes were done, Dusty sat at the table looking through the catalog the Odins had lent her.

Sitting there by lantern light, leafing through the catalog, with her mother sitting across from her, darning some of Blackie's socks, and with Blackie sitting on the couch across the room petting their two dogs, Dusty's eyes were arrested by a drawing of a dresser. She studied it. It was a very nice looking dresser. It had lots of drawers and had a mirror on the top. She herself did not own a dresser. In the room she shared with Blackie, there were only nails in the walls from which to hang clothes on hangers; and, on the floor, there were two wooden boxes in which to put folded clothes, one box for her and one for Blackie.

The price of the dresser in the catalog was seven dollars and fifty cents. Add a dollar and a half for the mirror. Add to that the cost of shipping out here to Gold Creek by riverboat and freight wagon, and you had a ridiculous price. Moreover, the dresser could get damaged on the way. For sure, the mirror was unlikely to get here in one piece.

Sarah spoke: "Blackie, I've been darning a lot of your stockings lately. Are your boots loose?"

"Yeah. I can't seem to get ready-mades that fit. Next time I'm in Silver, I'll get a pair made for me."

"Silver" was what everyone called Silver City.

Dusty went on thinking about a dresser. It was funny: before she had seen that picture, she had not given a serious thought to owning a dresser. Nails on the wall and boxes on the floor had been good enough. But, why shouldn't she have a dresser? If only she could get one without being extravagant.

She turned to Blackie where he sat with the two dogs scrunched up against him trying to get all of his attention. If there was one thing she had learned in her sixteen years it was that if you could get Blackie interested in your project, it got done. Once he got started on something, he kept after it until it was done.

"Blackie?"

"Hmm?" He looked up from the dogs.

"Come here." It was a request.

He moved to get up. The dogs threw their paws over his thighs to try to hold him down. He got up, extricating himself from the resisting dogs, and walked over to Dusty. She patted the chair next to her. He sat down. The dogs came over under the table and leaned against his and Dusty's legs.

"Do you think you could make a dresser like this?"

He studied the drawing of the dresser, and then looked at Dusty and shook his head. "No. I wouldn't know how to do it." He saw a flicker of disappointment.

Dusty thought for a moment. "Do you think we could take the drawers out of Mom's dresser and see how it's made, and copy it?"

"I suppose so. I could make one; but, honestly, it wouldn't be worth a darn. I can make simple things, and even doors; but dressers take someone with a lot of practice. And you need the right tools."

Dusty nodded. "Well, it doesn't have to be perfect. Anything would be better than what we have now."

Sarah had looked over at the catalog. She said, "Why not have Mr. Deering make it?"

Mr. Deering was a cabinet maker in Gold Creek.

"It would cost too much," Dusty answered.

"Well, we're not exactly poor, you know."

Dusty was aware that her mother had a sizable bank account. Nevertheless, Sarah usually resisted taking any money from the account. She was very frugal. So her mother's remark surprised Dusty.

But it was Dusty this time who resisted spending the money. "I bet it would cost twenty dollars here in Gold Creek. Maybe more."

Blackie said, "Maybe we could get it for a lot less."

He had Dusty's attention.

He went on, "Maybe I could trade game at the sawmill for the wood. And maybe I could do a little extra hunting and make some extra money to pay Mr. Deering."

"Would you do that?! Would you?!"

"Sure. If everybody'll agree."

Dusty was excited. "Let's go see Mr. Deering right now and see how much it would cost."

"Okay." He was getting into the mood of it, infected by her excitement.

* * *

"Jettie! Jinny!"

Only this moment back from Mr. Deering's, Dusty had walked up the steps onto the front porch of the Sheffield house ahead of Blackie, and through the open front door she could see the two girls sitting at the table with her mother. They were good friends whom she had not seen since moving out to the Renner ranch.

Dusty ran inside and kissed and hugged both girls. Blackie came inside and hung back, exchanging flirting glances with them. He was glad it was starting again—the girls coming to see Dusty. Before she had married and moved away, the house had always been packed with her many girl friends. In Blackie's opinion, these two here now, along with Trudy Belvedere, were the best looking girls in town. Jettie, seventeen, a sparklingly pretty brunette with big brown eyes that shone with fun, was the daughter of Jethro and Sunny Stevens, the owners of the Little Sunny Mine. In Jettie's company, blushing under Blackie's glances, was fifteen year old Jinny Rowe, much admired for her fine features, her cameo-white skin, her curly auburn hair, and her light blue eyes. And, as if that was not enough, she had a firm, sleekly curved body. Blackie found her exciting to look at; and he figured that she would look even better in two or three years when she had finished filling out. Her father was the principal of the Gold Creek School, and her mother was one of the teachers there.

"Look at what I'm getting," Dusty said, showing the girls the drawing of the dresser in the catalog. "Mr. Deering's going to make me one just like it." She gushed about how Blackie was getting it for her.

Jettie turned to Blackie. "Oh, how nice! Blackie, you're sweet."

Blackie grinned. Dusty was always making him sound like a big hero.

"Oh, I'm not doing it for her. I'm doing it so's I can have a mirror to admire myself in."

Jettie's eyes lit up. And, as if suddenly recognizing him, she exclaimed, "Narcissus!"

Everyone chuckled.

Sarah was pleased at Jettie's quickness, at her associating Blackie's words with the Greek myth about Narcissus, the youth who fell in love with his own image reflected in a pool of water. Sarah had never said anything to anyone about it, but Jettie was her choice for Blackie. Jettie was a thoroughly nice girl, smart, and fun loving to boot. Moreover, her parents were quite nice, and they liked Blackie. That was important, having good in-laws.

The girls chattered there for a few minutes, and then went off into the bedroom and closed the door where they talked "girl talk" for three quarters of an hour. When they came out, Blackie was churning butter and Sarah was looking through the catalog. It was late, so Jinny and Jettie reluctantly said good night.

Sarah said to Blackie, "I'll finish that. Would you take a rifle and walk the girls to the edge of town?"

The girls were surprised at this precaution, but neither said so. They were pleased to have Blackie escort them.

Blackie went to the gun rack on the wall where there were four shotguns and four rifles. He took down a loaded ten-gage double barreled shotgun with a full choke. Such a gun would be best for nighttime shooting. From a brass dish below the rack he scooped up six extra cartridges and stuffed them into his pockets. The big, brass cartridges made his pockets bulge.

Blackie walked the two girls into town, taking School Street and ignoring the gun law. He and Jettie dropped Jinny at her house next to the school, and then they walked on, shyly, toward the north end of town without saying much. They had known each other for many years; but since July, when she had first flirted with him, they had been a little shy together.

At the back porch of the Stevens' big, three story house, Jettie suddenly asked Blackie, "You know, I was thinking the other day that I don't remember you ever being down in our mine."

"I've been in the first drift, but never down a shaft."

"Would you like to see it? I'd like to show it to you sometime."

"Sure. That would be fun."

"How about next Sunday?"

"I promised Tillie a deer next Sunday, but I won't promise anybody anything for the following Sunday if you want to do it then."

"All right. Sunday after next for sure?"

"For sure."

"I'll be looking forward to it."

"I too."

She said softly, "Good night."

"Good night."

Jettie went inside and Blackie walked out of the yard and down the street toward home. Inside the house, Jettie's brothers and sisters, all younger than she, were in bed; but her parents were waiting up for her. Her mother sat embroidering by lamp light while her father, his wavy black hair starting now to get streaks of gray, sat smoking a pipe. Leaning against her father's arm chair was his cane that he used to lighten the load on his lower back when standing or walking. Three years ago, Jethro had injured his back in the mine and he had never fully recovered. And now, when he sometimes turned wrongly, he would collapse in agony and be in bed for anywhere from a few hours to a few days.

Jettie came up behind her father's chair and threw her arms around him. "I'm going to show Blackie the mine Sunday after next."

Jethro pulled his pipe from his mouth. "Good, good. We might get a son-in-law yet."

Jettie laughed. "Oh, pooh, Daddy. Aren't you rushing things? Besides, Dusty says he isn't ready to settle down yet."

"Well, neither was I when your mother snared me."

Sunny Stevens spoke: "And Sarah told me that she wasn't thinking of marriage when Butch caught her."

"Well, anyway, I don't think you should make too much of me showing him the mine."

Jethro said, "Well, it's a start and you know it."

"Yes." Jettie laughed pleasantly and hurried to the stairs.

Her mother asked her, "Do you want me to invite them for supper that evening?"

Jettie paused at the foot of the stairs. "Oh, Mamma, I'd be afraid he'd invite Trudy again."

"I'll invite Sarah in such a way that it's only for the three of them."

"All right, Mamma." Filled with energy, Jettie ran up the stairs. At the top of the stairs, she called, "Daddy, if you're worried about having a son-in-law, I could get married to someone tomorrow. Someone from your mine, maybe." She was teasing him.

Jethro called back, "No, thank you. Blackie suits me just fine."

There had been this conversation between Jettie and Jethro on their front porch a couple of days after Dusty's wedding in June. He had pointed out to Jettie that he would not always be here; at forty-four years of age, he had already outlived most of his contemporaries. He feared that someday he might get down with his back and never get out of bed. That would be the end of him. Had she thought of marriage? Not yet? Well, as the oldest, she might expect that her husband would be the one who would run the mine and would take care of her family if something happened to her father. If she waited until after he, Jethro, was gone, there would be no way the young man could be trained to manage the mine. Did she have a young man she was particularly fond of? No?

Jethro had pretended to think at length. "What about Blackie?"

Jettie had caught her breath. She had known Blackie since she could remember. And she liked him; but there had been her mother's disapproval when Sarah had allowed Blackie to quit school at fourteen to take up market hunting full time. The way her mother had talked to her father at the time, it was as if Blackie could never amount to anything worthwhile if he quit school. This had effected Jettie's view of Blackie—no matter that under Sarah's tutoring he now had better grammar than most of the kids in school; no matter that he read books that daunted most readers. Jettie's mother, not knowing that Jettie was still effected by her words of three years ago, had not bothered to correct her obviously wrong prediction of Blackie's early ruin.

And once when Jettie was fifteen, her mother had talked about perhaps sending her to her grandparents in New Jersey where she could go to a girls school, and where she could meet the right people—specifically, the right young men. Her mother, Sunny, had merely been thinking out loud. Sunny, who had been born poor, had finally gotten it through her head that they were quite rich, and that, therefore, they had the power to do such things. But Jettie had formed the impression from her mother's remarks that she did not think the local crop of boys was suitable for Jettie. So, as a sort of consequence of her mother's thinking out loud, when that same year, Blackie had flirted with Jettie a couple of times, she had not responded. He had not flirted with her since. But, occasionally, over the last couple of years, when she had been out at the Sheffields' and she had seen him with his shirt off, had seen the hard, rippling, cleanly defined muscles, she had experienced confusion when it had excited her. Besides, in the last year, she had begun to think for herself more, and to depend less upon her mother for opinions.

So, then, sitting on the front porch last June when her father had asked her if she had thought of Blackie for her husband, she had replied, "Oh, Daddy, he's too wild."

"Why do you say that?"

She had tempered her objection: "Oh, Daddy, you know he's a little wild."

Jethro had chuckled. "Well, he's nothing compared with what I was like."

Blackie was a young man after Jethro's own heart. At Dusty's wedding, Blackie had drunk a goodly amount; and he had come over and sat with Jethro for a while and they had drunk some more, and the whiskey had made Blackie funny and quick and he had turned the slightest things into jokes that had made Jethro roar with laughter.

Jethro continued to Jettie, "I was much wilder than he is and it lasted into my twenties."

"Oh, pooh, Daddy."

"Ask your mother. Tell her I said it's all right to tell you the truth."

"I can't believe it."

"You ask her.... Sunny!"

Sunny Stevens had come out onto the porch to see what he wanted.

"Wasn't I wild when you met me?"

"Well, it's certainly nothing to brag to Jettie about."

Jethro had turned to his daughter. "You see?"

Jettie had asked her mother, "Was he as wild as Blackie?"

"Blackie's a lamb compared to what your father was.... What are you two cooking up?"

Jethro had then said to Jettie, "I'm proof that a good woman can make a man want to settle down. There've been wild young men since the beginning of time. And there've been good women since then too. And when a good man gets some babies, he just wants to be there with his family. That's the way I was, and I'll bet that Blackie'll be the same way."

"How can you tell?"

"Well, look at the way children like him. They gather around him almost as much as children used to gather around his father. I'll bet he'll be just like his father when he has kids."

Jettie had *loved* Butch Sheffield. As a child, she had always made a bee-line for him when the two families had gotten together. She had dreaded having to leave his lap, too, because she couldn't get it back—one of her brothers or sisters always ended up in it.

Sunny had cautioned her daughter: "You've got to pick a good man to start with, though. He's got to be good beneath his wildness or you'll never settle him down. Your father's a good man."

Jethro had asked his wife, "Well, don't you think Blackie's a good man?"

Sunny had smiled. She had always liked the boy immensely. She knew he was sometimes rambunctious. But he always conducted himself around her with the best of manners. And she liked the way he behaved toward his mother, too.

"If he treats his wife with half the respect he does his mother, she'd never have reason to complain."

Anyway, that conversation with her parents had planted the seed, and Jettie had started thinking of Blackie in a new way. And in July, when Blackie and Sarah had returned from visiting Dusty down at the Renner Ranch, Jettie, in the company of Jinny Rowe, had gone out to hear about the visit, and Jettie had shyly flirted with Blackie and Blackie had responded. There had been more flirtation since.

But, upon hearing the conflicting stories of the gunfight last week, Jettie had decided that she did not want a boy friend who killed people. Jethro, however, who was nothing if not resourceful, had invited Morgan to the house for supper and had requested of Morgan that he tell the results of his investigation. During the telling, Jettie had brightened up remarkably.

Tonight, walking down School Street on his way home, and now knowing for sure that Jettie wanted his company, Blackie thought that he would drop by her house a couple of evenings from now and invite her for a walk. He knew he would have to get there right after supper, though, and whisk her off; otherwise, he would have to share her with other young men who often showed up at the Stevens house in the evenings competing for her attention.

Blackie had no idea that this was anything more than an exciting flirtation with one of the prettiest girls in town. Jettie, playing her cards close to her chest, had not yet given him any reason to think otherwise. Certainly, he would have allowed that it could possibly develop into something more; but to him such an eventuality was vague yet.

When Blackie got home, Dusty, clad in a night shirt, was sitting up in her bed, reading by lantern light. She smiled expectantly when he walked into the bedroom.

He sat on the edge of his bed. "Jettie's going to show me their mine Sunday after next. And I'll probably drop by after supper some night soon and take her for a walk." He was pleased with himself.

"She'll like that. I didn't know she was interested in you until tonight in here."

"What did she say?"

"Oh, she beat around the bush. But she's interested in you."

Blackie nodded. Said, "Hmmm."

Dusty did not add that Jettie had asked too casually whether Blackie had any inclination to get married soon. Dusty had told her frankly that she did not think he was ready yet. Dusty thought that Jettie, until tonight, had been the only one of her girl friends who had not shown romantic interest in Blackie. And Dusty now felt that there was deliberation to Jettie's movements relative to Blackie. Jettie was not flighty; nor was she a scatterbrain. She had brains and looks and goodness; she could make Blackie a good wife.

After a moment, Dusty asked, "Do you think you're likely to get married soon?"

"Oh, I don't know. Maybe a couple years. I'm in no rush."

"Jettie's liable to be taken by then."

"I'd be presuming a lot if I imagined her liking my company means she wants to marry me."

Dusty gazed at him, amused. He never seemed to fully realize how attractive he was to women.

Blackie studied her amused face. Then asked, "Do you know something I don't?"

"I know that Jettie's old enough to be giving thought to marriage. And I'll tell you what I think—Jettie will make someone an awfully good wife."

"Yes. I'm sure you're right. A fellow probably couldn't ask for better."

"But, I also knew before I asked you that you weren't ready to settle down yet."

Blackie nodded and smiled at his sister. He drew pleasure from the fact that she knew him so well and could predict his mind and behavior.

"Well," said Dusty, "maybe Jinny will still be available in two years. I don't know, though."

"She excites me. Something about her makes me want to take her in my arms and hold her."

"You and about a hundred other men hereabouts."

"Yeah, I guess you're right. There'd probably be a lot of competition."

"If there's anyone she wants to excite, though, it's you."

"You think so?"

"I know so."

"How do you know?"

"God, Blackie. It should be obvious to you. The way she looks at you. The way she blushes when you talk to her."

"I thought she was just shy."

"She's only shy around you. She's pretty sure of herself around other boys."

Blackie digested this. Then, "I wish she was a year or two older. Do you think her people would let her go riding with me?"

"If I know her, she'll talk them into it."

Blackie was intrigued. "I guess I should've paid more attention to her before this."

"I'll bet she thinks so too."

Blackie grinned, encouraged.

After a moment, he said, "Oh," and got to his feet. "I've got something to show you."

He walked into the front room and over to the bookcase with its glass doors where he struck a match, and with its light he extracted his mother's small, scuffed, leather-bound book of puns and limericks. Seven or eight years ago, he had read four or five pages from this book, but that had been the last time he had looked inside it until tonight. He now carried it back to the bedroom and, with light from the lamp, found the right page.

"While you girls were in here tonight, I asked Mom what makes a pun, and she showed me this." He handed the open book to Dusty. "To make a pun, the word doesn't have to be spelled the same, just as long as it sounds the same or almost the same."

Dusty read the definition of a pun and then, only slightly embarrassed, looked up at Blackie and held her hand over her mouth, acting properly contrite.

"So," said Blackie in mock triumph, "the boardwalk people won't have me to snicker about tomorrow after all."

"Now they'll snicker at me."

"Not if they know what's good for them."

Nine

Two days later, Francisco Moran and one other Sonora Militiaman stood in front of the Camp Commander's adobe office at Camp Huachuca in Arizona Territory. They were in the company of the Camp Commander, an American Captain by the name of Whitside, and his aide, Corporal Juan Valdez.

The Captain was smiling and shaking their hands and saying, "Thank you for coming to warn us. Valdez, here, will see that you are fed, and have beds for the night. The groom will look after your horses. Anything we can do for you, just ask Corporal Valdez."

Corporal Juan Valdez translated the Captain's words into Spanish. The two militiamen thanked the Captain in Spanish. Captain Whitside smiled and nodded. He had instantly liked this Francisco Moran. The fellow was unpretentious; but, on the other hand, he was quite sure of himself without even seeming conscious of it.

Captain Whitside turned to Corporal Valdez. "Look up Captain Troutman and send him over."

"Yes, Sir."

A half hour later, when Captain Troutman entered the Camp Commander's office, Captain Whitside was sitting in one of two wing chairs pouring himself some tea. Whitside looked up.

"Oh, Bill. Good. I just made some tea. Grab a cup from the buffet."

Captain Troutman took a cup and saucer from the mahogany buffet and sat in the wing chair opposite his commanding officer. He placed the cup and saucer on the table between them, and Whitside filled the cup with tea.

Captain Whitside was a capable military man and an able organizer. And, although he did not know everything, he was smart enough to surround himself with a knowledgeable

94

staff, men whom he could turn to when he needed help. When he had been sent down here to found a military camp with the express purpose of controlling the marauding Indians, he had not known all that much about Arizona, its people, or its history. Before departing Prescott, the territorial capital, he had read everything he could find on Arizona and New Mexico, which was not much. He had been lucky, however, to discover a captain in his command who had been in the area for a few years, and who took a strong interest in everything about the Southwest including its history. That Captain sat before him now.

Whitside set the teapot down and asked, "Bill, have you ever heard of a Mexican outlaw called El Lobo?"

Captain Troutman was surprised. "Yes, Sir. He's a man of the worst sort. Why do you ask?"

"He and his gang of about fifty desperados crossed over into our territory a couple of days ago. They were running from the Sonora Militia. Two Militiamen were in here a few minutes ago to warn us."

Captain Troutman treated the news gravely.

Captain Whitside went on. "They told me something that puzzles me. Do you have any idea why El Lobo and his gang would be taking scalps from Mexicans?"

"Probably, Sir, to sell them to the State Governments in Ures or Chihuahua."

"Eh?"

"Some Mexican scalps can be passed off as Apache scalps."

"Since when have the Sonora and Chihuahua governments been buying Apache scalps?"

"Since the 1830's, Sir. You see, when the Spaniards still reigned in Mexico, they kept troops posted wherever the Mexicans might be molested by marauding Indians. It posed at least a little restraint upon the Apaches. But the Spaniards were turned out by the Revolution of 1821; and, subsequently, Mexico City lacked the will and capacity to deal with the Indians on the frontiers. And between 1821 and 1835 the

Mexican authorities recorded no fewer than five thousand settlers killed by Apaches in northern Mexico. And as you know, Apaches often do not simply kill—some of those victims were tortured."

Whitside shook his head in wonder. It was a staggering toll.

Troutman went on. "Anyway, the State Governments of Chihuahua and Sonora finally took matters into their own hands. They offered a hundred silver pesos each for adult male Apache scalps, fifty for adult female, and twenty-five each for children's scalps."

"That's a lot of money," Whitside said.

"Yes, but it's dangerous work. Now, until about 1855, four particularly bloodthirsty bands of bounty hunters operated in northern Mexico. They were very effective. Much more so than the Mexican and American armies have been. One band was of Mandan Indians from Kansas. Each of the other three was run by an American. About thirty years ago, El Lobo was a member of one of those bands."

"I see," said Whitside. He paused. "Killers for a cause may not always be nice people; but, ones who don't have a cause, who kill strictly for money, are among the lowest kind of people."

"Right you are, sir. So, for such people, it was easy to cheat. What with Mexicans being part Indian, many Mexican scalps look pretty much the same as Apache scalps."

"Do these four bands still exist?"

"No. But, the bounty still stands; because, of course, the Apaches still rampage; and, therefore, some small scale bounty hunting still goes on."

"If the Mexicans know El Lobo takes Mexican scalps, why do they buy from him?"

"I'm sure he has someone else take the scalps into Ures. He certainly wouldn't take them in himself. There's a price on his head."

Whitside nodded. "Bill, I'd like you to look up these two Militiamen and find out all they know of El Lobo's likely whereabouts, his tactics, and whatever else you think useful. Then, I want you to field a company of men to search for him and his gang. What about Lieutenant Hodges to command it?"

Ten

The Gila River flowed generally west from the Mogollon Mountains to where it cut through some mountains which made up the border of New Mexico and Arizona. In those border mountains, a small stream put into the Gila from the north. If you traced that small stream to its beginnings, you ended up at a spring which in those days some people called Cabeza Gordo. It was not a well known spring, and the country around it was semi-arid except in the small canyon where the spring was.

El Lobo had camped at that spring when he was a young man, when the country still belonged to Mexico; so it was a place that he knew, and it was also a place that was not often visited by other people. Consequently, he had used it on rare occasions when it had been necessary for him to go into hiding, to hole up, because things had gotten too hot for him in Mexico.

The sandy haired American bandit—Abner Waters was his name—had hidden out with El Lobo at Cabeza Gordo Springs once before, four years ago. Their party had numbered only fourteen bandits that time; but within three days they had killed and scared off most of the nearby game. As a consequence, they had spent several days eating the meat of spare horses. To make matters worse, they had had no vegetables and no salt. Abner Waters had no intention of reliving that experience, so he and the four men in his charge, only one of whom had been at Cabeza Gordo that other time, crossed the Gila River west of the springs, struck the San Francisco River, and followed it northeast for about thirty miles where they made camp at San Francisco Hot Springs alongside the river. The next day, they cut directly eastward toward the Mogollons. At the foot of the Mogollons, they picked up an established trail, and headed southeast into the mountains. After four miles, following the trail up over a ridge, they came down into the north end of the town of Gold Creek. Abner Waters was surprised at how much the town had grown since he had last visited it eleven years ago.

When the bandits, leading three spare horses, passed the Marshal's office, Marshal Wiggins was relaxing inside with his feet up on his table and the door open. The Marshal spotted the five armed men through the open door and got quickly to his feet. He went to the door and hailed them.

"Hello, boys!"

The desperados looked at him without any friendliness and kept walking their horses down the street.

The Marshal shouted, "Halt!"

The desperados halted and all five rotated their horses so that they faced the Marshal as he walked up to them.

From a few feet away, Wiggins could smell them, and he guessed that they had worn the same clothes for weeks.

"Do one of you fellows speak English?"

"I do," said Abner Waters.

"Well, now, there are no guns allowed in town."

"Whadaya mean?" Waters asked crossly. He had never heard such foolishness.

"I mean you can't carry guns in this town."

"Whadaya expect us to do? Throw 'em down on the ground before we ride in?"

Marshal Wiggins replied patiently, "No, no. I take them from you and lock them up across the street there." He pointed to the empty store. "And when you're ready to leave town, I give them back to you."

The American bandit summarized the Marshal's words to his companions. The Mexicans were suddenly suspicious of such an odd request. They belligerently refused, and Wiggins did not need a translation to understand. For the first time, the Marshal realized that he might be in trouble. He was suddenly afraid.

And Wiggins was suddenly and unpleasantly aware that he had not unhooked the leather thong that held his revolver in its holster. Under everyday conditions, the thong, attached to the holster and looped around the gun's hammer, kept the gun from bouncing or sliding out while he sat or rode. But it took a couple of seconds to unhook it. That time could cost him his life. Wiggins had not been called upon to draw his revolver in the line of duty for several years now; so, he had gotten careless.

Abner Waters said in Spanish to his companions, "Listen, Lobo said no trouble on this side of the border. Let's go outside of town and talk this over."

Waters addressed the Marshal in English. "We're gonna go talk this over."

While the desperados walked their horses out of town, Wiggins unhooked the leather thong from his revolver's hammer. It had been thoughtless, his walking out to these strangers with the thong still over his hammer. He went quickly into his office and grabbed a shotgun, checked to make sure that it was loaded, and crammed some cartridges into his pockets. From his window, he could see the strangers stop about fifty yards from him where they sat talking. Finally, the American departed from the others and, with the three spare horses in tow, rode back toward Wiggins' office.

Wiggins laid the shotgun on his table where he could snatch it up quickly. He stood inside now and waited.

Abner Waters rode up to the Marshal's office, dismounted, and walked inside. He took in the scene. There were a couple chairs and a table, a rumpled bed, and a wood burning cast iron stove. By the door was a small table on which stood a bucket of water with a dipper handle sticking out. There was also a wooden door to a back room. The door had a small barred window in it, and was obviously the entrance to the jail cell.

The American bandit grinned disarmingly. "I guess I'll have to do the buyin' of the grub. You scared my friends."

"Scared them?"

"They're not used to Americans. South of the border, if you rode into a town and somebody took your guns, he'd just as likely murder you."

Marshal Wiggins relaxed. "Oh, I see." He smiled. "Well, we mean no one any harm here."

Wiggins started for the empty store across the street. "Come on over and we'll check your guns."

They walked across the street where the Marshal unlocked the door to the building and held it open. Waters walked inside and was impressed with what he saw. There were more than a hundred muskets, rifles, and shotguns lined up along the walls. Less than ten pistols lay on a table.

Waters said, "Well, I guess you weren't lyin' to us. That sure as hell ain't no private collection."

"No, I wasn't lying. Everyone in town's doing just like you." After a pause Wiggins added proudly, "This is the safest town in the territory."

"I'll bet it is," said Waters. But he was thinking otherwise.

Waters left his rifle and revolver with Wiggins and then rode on into the center of town. He decided to take his time now, and went to three saloons, asking questions, and finding out a lot about the town and its residents. He rode up and down the streets, and noted where various establishments were—including the bank. He went to the hardware store and bought three packs for the spare horses. Finally, he bought supplies and loaded them onto the packs. All the time, he was asking questions and listening and learning.

Abner Waters looked the Marshal up and recovered his guns, and then rode out and rejoined his companions, and together, they skirted the town, riding down the brush filled creek bed, coming to the Gold Creek Road south of town, opposite the Sheffield Ranch.

Waters said in Spanish, "Look, you men go on to Cabeza Gordo. Tell Lobo I'll be there in a couple of days. I'm gonna look over the country around here for getaway routes."

Waters spent the rest of the day riding around the surrounding hills, occasionally meeting and talking with miners. That evening, he camped along the creek just south of the Sheffield Ranch, and he noted the eight horses in the corral. The next day, he continued his reconnoitering until about noon when he turned and headed south toward the Gila River. At the Gila River, he turned west, and followed the river through the Gila Valley, passing two big farms which grew hay and vegetables for Silver City and Gold Creek.

Two days after leaving Gold Creek, Waters stood under the shade of a tree at Cabeza Gordo Springs, sketching the town of Gold Creek in the dirt with a long stick, and describing his plan to El Lobo in Spanish. At the end he said:

"About half the miners outside of town have horses, some have burros, and almost all have guns. We'll avoid 'em. Now, the best getaway route is south to the river, and then south up Mangus Valley and over the mountain, picking up the Old Janos Trail plenty south of Silver City, and following that down into Playas Valley and crossing the border at Dog Springs."

El Lobo's smile was without mirth. He said in Spanish, "Looks good. We'll do it."

Ripples of excitement ran through the gang.

For emphasis, Waters restated something he had said earlier: "We'll take or kill every horse we see in town. We want any followers on foot."

Eleven

On Sunday afternoon, Blackie walked out of Tillie's Boarding House on School Street followed by Tillie Roberts, a tall thin woman in her thirties who wore her brown hair done up in a bun. Long wisps of hair had escaped from the bun, giving her an overworked appearance.

Tillie was saying, "Bring me another deer Thursday, Blackie. No antelope for a few days; the boys are tired of it. And tell your mother I'll be needing ten chickens next Sunday about noon."

"Okay."

Blackie's saddle horse and pack horse were tied to the rail out front. His rifle was in its saddle scabbard where he had left it while carrying the deer inside. He had ignored the gun law.

He mounted his horse and rode over to Main Street and headed south toward home. As he approached the Gold Creek Saloon, Marshal Wiggins, who had been standing on the boardwalk talking to Jasper Odin, stepped down into the street to intercept Blackie. It was the first time either had seen the other.

"Son, there are no guns allowed in town."

"Huh?" Blackie saw the gold star and suddenly realized who the man was. He instantly disliked him for what he had done to Morgan. "Oh.... Well, I'm on my way out of town now anyway."

Wiggins did not like the boy's manner. It lacked the submissiveness which Wiggins was used to and liked. When people knew you were a Federal Marshal, they were automatically respectful. Or scared.

Wiggins asked angrily, "Don't you know it's a law you're supposed to turn your gun in to me when you come in town?!"

"Maybe I did."

"Then, why didn't you do it?!"

"Your office is clear over on the other end of town; and I didn't know where you were. It was just a lot of unnecessary bother."

"That's no excuse. It's the law!"

"All right. I'll do it next time."

"A smart aleck kid like you needs a lesson to remember. You give that rifle to me, and I'll just keep it until tomorrow about this time. Come look me up then."

Blackie replied coolly, "I need the rifle, Marshal."

"That's too damn bad." Wiggins reached for the rifle.

Blackie's temper snapped. He kicked Wiggins' arm away. Wiggins was amazed at the young man's reaction. Instantly, his amazement turned to indignation and rage. His right hand darted for his revolver in its floppy leather holster. In his excitement, he forgot that he had the leather thong looped over the hammer. He jerked the revolver only to have it stop partway out. With both hands he snatched the thong off. But, by now, he was looking up the barrel of Blackie's rifle. Wiggins was momentarily afraid. But then he began to doubt that the boy was serious. His hand was still on his revolver and he wanted to draw. He could kill the boy and be legally safe.

Jasper Odin, wide eyed, shouted from the boardwalk, "For God's sake, Blackie, don't do it! Marshal, don't even think about doing anything! Blackie, for god's sake go home and cool off. You too, Marshal. Both of you cool down!"

With Odin's mention of the name, "Blackie," Wiggins suddenly realized whom he was dealing with. The boy had killed before. Wiggins' hand involuntarily moved away from the revolver.

Blackie answered, "All right, Mr. Odin, I'm going." Then, pulling back on the reins with his left hand, he spoke to his horse. "Back! Back!"

The horse backed down the street. The pack horse followed. Blackie's rifle was still pointed at the Marshal.

Odin said soothingly and quietly to Wiggins, "He's a crack shot, Marshal. Don't make a move. So long as he thinks you won't do anything, he won't do anything."

Blackie backed the horse into an alley to the next street. Then he turned and galloped out of town.

Wiggins took a few seconds to recover from being scared. Then, humiliated and furious, he marched into the Gold Creek Saloon. There were a dozen or so men inside, including Zeke Underwood.

"I'm raising a posse to go arrest that Blackie kid. Any volunteers?"

There was silence. Wiggins looked around the room.

"Come on! He's just a kid. We'll be back here in an hour. I'll buy the drinks."

One of the men said, "Since he's just a kid, you oughta be able to handle him by yourself, Marshal."

Wiggins stared at the man with a "You'll get yours" type of look.

"Dead or alive, Marshal?" It was Zeke Underwood.

Wiggins snapped, "Dead or alive!"

Another man exclaimed, "Dead or alive?! What're you arrestin' him for?"

"For murdering his brother-in-law and Billy O'Connor, and for not obeying the gun law."

A thick chested man said, "Now, hold up, Marshal. I was right outside here when that gunfight started. Blackie wasn't even armed. It was plain self defense. And it was John Renner who shot...."

"You can tell that to the judge and jury," said Wiggins rudely.

Zeke Underwood said, "You get me a shotgun, Marshal, and I'll go with you. I don't want no bird shot. Get me some buck shot."

"You'll get it."

Jasper Odin had been listening to this exchange in horror. Now he had heard enough. He slipped out of the saloon's back door and ran to the little stable he had out back. He decided there was not time to saddle the horse, and he slipped a bridle on it and led it out and over to a fence where he climbed up and mounted bareback. He galloped the horse down the street and out of town southward, toward the Sheffield place. It had been years since he had galloped a horse bareback, and now he had trouble staying on at the pace he set. Somehow he got there without falling off, and he brought his horse up at the front porch amid the two barking Sheffield dogs. He jumped off, ran up the stairs and pounded on the door.

Inside, Sarah and Dusty were cutting up a duck and six frying chickens which families in town had ordered. Dusty put her knife aside, wiped her hands on a cloth, and opened the door.

Odin came in, visibly excited. "Where's Blackie?!"

Sarah was surprised. "Mr. Odin! I expect he's putting his horses away. Why? What's the matter?"

"Marshal Wiggins is trying to raise a posse to arrest him."

"What in heaven's name for?"

"For the killings a couple weeks ago." Odin glanced at Dusty. "But what he's really mad about is that Blackie didn't give him his rifle when he went into town while ago. He's gonna charge him with that too."

"No jury will convict him of the killings," Sarah said firmly.

Dusty said, "They can't do anything to him for not turning in his gun, either. Morgan told us the dummies didn't think to pass penalties for not obeying their law."

"I'm sure you're both right," Odin fretted. "But, arrest isn't the worst of it. The Marshal told Zeke Underwood, 'dead or alive.' Zeke's the kind of man who'd kill Blackie after he turned himself in peaceably. So, just to save his own life, Blackie might have to shoot it out with the posse."

"In heaven's name!" Sarah went into action. "Dusty, run out and tell Blackie to saddle up and ride to Carpenter Springs. Tell him to stay there until I come or send for him. In fact, you go with him, and insist he stays there. He listens to you. Take camp gear and bedrolls. Hurry!"

*   *   *

While Sarah was giving Dusty those instructions, Marshal Wiggins, accompanied by Zeke Underwood, was in Belvedere's Dry goods Store, asking John Belvedere to join the posse.

John Belvedere, standing behind the counter with his wife, answered Wiggins, "You're darned right, Marshal, I'll be part of your posse. We can't allow contempt for our laws. We'll make an example of this boy. When we say no guns in town, we mean it!"

*   *   *

A half hour later, Blackie and Dusty were already galloping south on the Gold Creek road. A pack horse, tied to Blackie's saddle, galloped between them. Dusty carried her shotgun across her lap. Blackie, as usual, had his hunting rifle in its saddle scabbard. But, this time, aboard his pack horse was a long barreled, 1874 Sharps Long Range Express Rifle which shot a forty-five caliber bullet propelled by one hundred and ten grains of black powder.

*   *   *

Marshal Wiggins had gotten six men to join his posse, and now they were in the empty store across from his office where he was handing out guns.

Wiggins said, "I still can't believe that Doc refused to come with us."

"I've known Doc a long time," said Belvedere. "He's good with words, but he's a coward."

"I guess I learnt that today."

Sarah Sheffield's voice interrupted them. "Is the Marshal here?" Sarah was standing in the doorway in bluejeans and shirt.

Wiggins turned and was transfixed by the sight of her. Finally, he said, "That's me."

"I'm Mrs. Sheffield, Blackie's mother."

There was a long pause. Then Wiggins said, "Yeah?"

"May I speak with you in private?"

Wiggins did not know whether he wanted to or not. He wanted nothing to interrupt his revenge. Finally, he said to his posse, "You boys wait here."

Wiggins walked Sarah to the other side of the road where they stood in front of his office and talked.

*   *   *

Blackie and Dusty had picked up Sawmill Road. They rode at a brisk walk now, giving their horses a breather. The Carpenter Springs trail would branch off southward about an hour up Sawmill Road. Because it was a full day's ride to Carpenter Springs, Dusty had been there only twice before on family campouts four and five years ago; but Blackie had been there seven or eight times; and after his father's disappearance, it had been agreed between him and his mother that if caught in a very bad storm south of the sawmill, he was to try to reach Carpenter Springs. At least then she would know where to look for him.

*   *   *

In the empty store where the guns were stored, the posse was looking through the windows at Wiggins and Sarah across the road.

Zeke said, "I wonder what they're talkin' about?"

"I don't know," said Belvedere. "They've sure been out there a long time."

Finally, they saw Wiggins and Sarah separate, both smiling. Sarah mounted her horse and headed it down the road. The Marshal walked across the road and entered the empty store, still smiling.

"I won't be needing you boys today."

*   *   *

Sarah came into the kitchen of the Gold Creek Saloon through the back door. Jasper Odin and his wife were starting a stew for tonight's customers.

Jasper glanced up. "Oh, Mrs. Sheffield." He looked at her anxiously. "What happened?"

There was relief in Sarah's voice. "I've gotten it all straightened out. He's disbanding the posse. He said that if Blackie comes and apologizes, he'll drop the whole thing."

"Oh, good! Good!"

"Mr. Odin, I don't know how to thank you for warning us."

"No thanks needed."

Odin's wife spoke up. "The way my husband frets over your boy, you'd think he was kin."

Odin blushed. "Well, he's a good boy, that's why. He's always polite and respectful, and he listens when you talk to him. Maybe a little quick tempered once in a while, but his good side more than makes up for it. I like him, and I guess I don't know all the reasons why."

Sarah smiled. "I don't believe the Marshal thinks he's polite and respectful."

"Well, the Marshal's behavior, since coming to town, isn't deserving of respect. Now, I'll admit Blackie was a little impolite there at first. And he shouldn't've been. But the Marshal, being the kind of man he is, made matters worse by trying to bully him. Why, if I'd been the Marshal, I'd have taken the time right there to talk things over with Blackie. Explain to him what I was doing and why. And I'd have found out a little about Blackie and what he thinks."

Sarah nodded. "Yes, that's the way to handle him. I learned very early that he reacts to threats by fighting you. If you invite him to think things out with you, you can win him over. And sometimes he's right and wins you over."

Odin turned to his wife. "You see? This old man knows a thing or two."

Mrs. Odin smiled.

Odin turned back to Sarah. "Now, about fetching your youngsters home. How far is Carpenter Springs?"

"Round trip, it's a two day ride. I'll see if I can't pay one of Blackie's friends to ride out there tomorrow."

Odin grinned. "Oh, Mrs. Sheffield, I don't think you'll have to pay anyone to ride out there." His grin broadened. "Just let it be known your daughter is there. You'll have young men fighting each other tryin' to be the one you send."

Mrs. Odin said, "Oh, Jass!"

"Well, it's true. Every time she or her mother either one comes by the front of the saloon, the men all sprain their necks trying to get a look at 'em."

Sarah blushed.

Odin went on. "But, I was thinking about my bartender Ed Ringsley. Him and Blackie get along pretty good; and I know we can trust him not to tell anybody where he's going. I judge that's best."

* * *

When Blackie and Dusty got to where the trail to Carpenter Springs branched from Sawmill Road they bypassed it and continued up Saw Mill Road. Blackie knew that Sawmill Creek cut through some granite about three miles up the road. So, they rode on up Saw Mill Road, holding to the middle of it where wagon teams would obscure their tracks in the morning. A quarter mile down from the granite, they entered the creek and walked their horses up it to the granite. They climbed their horses out onto the granite, leaving no tracks, and proceeded across its hard surface until it ended. They then struck out cross country for the Carpenter Springs trail, picking it up about five miles from where it entered Saw Mill Road. It was getting on toward sundown by now.

Later, when it was well after dark and they were riding by the light of the full moon, Dusty asked, "How long before we get there?"

"Another four hours. Tired?"

"No."

Twelve

About sun up, Blackie lay in his bedroll watching Dusty pour steaming coffee from an enameled pot into two tinned cups. She looked up and saw him watching and smiled. There was a great deal of frank affection between these two, and they were quite open about it.

Dusty stood and brought the cups over, sat cross-legged on her bedroll and handed Blackie his cup.

He sat up and smelled the coffee, savoring the odor. "Mmmmm."

He blew on the cup's hot rim, and then took a noisy sip, drawing air between his lips and the cup's rim to avoid burning his lips on the metal.

"Mmmmm," he repeated. "Now, why can't I ever make coffee this good?"

"You let yours boil too long. Besides, I put eggshells in this."

"You mean to say that in all that rush yesterday, you took the trouble to bring eggshells?"

"I know you like your coffee made this way."

Blackie studied her fondly.

After a bit, he told her, "I sure missed you when you moved out to the Renner place."

"Really?"

"Yeah. I like having you around." A pause. "Everything's a lot more fun when you're around."

Dusty was pleased.

Dusty had missed Blackie too, but not so much at first. Everything had been too new and different and exciting and had taken up most of her attention. She had been learning to be a wife, learning to live with a man who, after all, was a bit of a stranger. An exciting stranger, she had thought at first; but nevertheless a stranger. Furthermore, she had been living in a strange household, with a strange family. They had a different manner and had different habits from the family she had grown up with. She had tried to learn, tried to be a good wife, sister-in-law, and daughter-in-law.

Things had not gone as she had expected them to.

John's mother had been a real problem. The woman had simply disliked Dusty. Dusty had mistakenly thought that once the woman got to know her, they could be friends. With a shock, one day, she had realized that her mother-in-law did not want to like her.

Dusty had entered into the marriage thinking of it as a wonderful kind of partnership. Gradually, by the first month of marriage, she had come to realize that John somehow saw her as an opponent, as someone to be lied to, as someone whose self confidence required undermining.

So, then, she had mistakenly thought that if she made it very clear to John that she was on his side, that she loved him, he would change. It had not worked.

It was she who had changed, although she had not realized how much until her mother and Blackie came to visit at the end of the first month. Being with them, she had realized how serious she had gotten, and how less fun life had gotten to be. And John had been snide about the affection she and Blackie had shown one another.

After her mother and Blackie had gone home, she had missed them both. Terribly.

What had trapped Dusty was her good intentions. She had entered into the marriage "for better or worse," as the minister had said at the wedding. She had wanted to make a go of the marriage. And she had wanted to make John happy. But she had been caught up in a morass of intentions which were not compatible with hers.

A week after Blackie and her mother were there, she had discovered the half-breed girl. To Dusty, the marriage had been clearly over then. John had tried to lie to her about the affair; but she had refused to be taken in. Then he had changed his tack: without admitting guilt, he had implied that he would change. Against her better judgment, Dusty had agreed to try again. Deep down, she must have known that it was futile.

Dusty had come to realize that the chances for happiness in the Renner house were nil. Three times, she had broached the subject of their moving to her mother's house where John could work in one of the mines. John had refused to hear of it.

The contrasts between the two households were too stark to miss. Mr. Renner was henpecked, and his wife often found fault with him and complained. There was no one in the household who did not squabble with others frequently. Perhaps that was why Dusty's squabbles with John had seemed to cause no significant notice.

At "home," things had been very different. Dusty's father, Butch, an extremely good-natured man, had had the last word around there when it mattered. Both her father and her mother had been openly affectionate toward each other and toward her and Blackie.

In the Renner household, no one really exchanged ideas. Mrs. Renner seemed to be the only one whose opinions had importance there.

At home there had been a lot of airing of ideas. And with the onset of Dusty's puberty, and afterward, there had been a few nights when she and her mother had sat up and talked, as friends, for hours after Butch and Blackie had gone to bed.

Of course, when John was courting her—a courtship that had lasted only four weeks—he had seemed interested in what she had had to say; but after their marriage he had often taken an opposing point of view just to be contrary. It had been as if he did not want her to believe that she was right about anything.

At home, she and Blackie had often asked each other's advice on things. And Blackie had a manner of listening to another as if that person were the most important person in the world right then. Consequently, it was great fun to talk with him.

For Dusty, the only bright spot in the Renner household had been the ten year old girl, Cecelia. The girl had admired Dusty so much that she had frequently mimicked her. When Dusty had washed her hair, for example, Cecelia had washed her own. She had even tried to talk like Dusty. The poor girl was in a situation she could not get out of for at least another five years when she might hope to marry.

Who knows why Dusty had been so wrong about John? Of course, with him living out of town, she had laid eyes on him only a few times and had had nothing at all to do with him until he had started courting her. And then, during the courtship, he had been on his very best behavior. He had shown her a face that was not his own. He had shown her a John that was seemingly good-natured, gentle, and considerate. But beneath it had been the real John: bitter, frightened when he did not have the upper hand, and mean when he did. He had been a good talker; and part of her mistake had been that she had listened to what he had said rather than waiting to observe what he did.

Riding away the night that she had left him, knowing that it was all over now, she had felt relief that amounted to exhilaration. All the oppression of the Renner household had blown from her, and she was the old Dusty again. Even the danger of meeting Apaches on the trail had failed to dampen her spirits. She had lost two months of her life in a bad marriage, but two months was very little.

Well, all that was past now, and here she was in the mountains with her brother who liked having her around, who believed that she was important and special, and who said the things he really thought. You always knew where you stood with him.

Thirteen

Carpenter Springs is in a westward facing canyon. Blackie had selected a lookout at a rocky place about three hundred yards up from their camp, on a ridge on the south side of the canyon. Influencing his choice had been the fact that immediately east of the ridge was a steep ravine—a ravine in which you could climb up to or down from the lookout without being seen from the west.

From his lookout, he could look westward down the canyon, down onto the foothills below, and see uninterrupted for miles.

It was dull work, in the hot sun, watching for pursuers that you did not know existed. He was pretty sure he was wasting his time, but it was not prudent to ignore the possibility that they had been followed.

To occupy himself, he oiled his Sharps Long Range Express Rifle, and then wiped the workings and the bore as dry of the oil as he could get them.

Occasionally, he watched Dusty from up there. He had been up there an hour when he saw her, carrying her shotgun, walk up the creek where she was sometimes out of sight. She being out of sight made him a little nervous on account of Apaches. Now and then, when hunting, he had seen one or more Apache in the mountains. They had never bothered him, but he was always on the alert.

At last, he saw Dusty turn and come back down the creek to the camp. There, she took an ax to a willow and cut off a long, slender limb. He watched her trim the twigs and bark from it and finally test it for limberness. A fishing pole.

If there was anything he knew about Dusty it was that she loved to fish. Unfortunately, she did not get much chance to do so nowadays because Gold Creek was practically fished out.

When it looked to Blackie that she had the pole all fixed up with line and hook, he saw her take a short-handle shovel from their pack and dig for worms.

Blackie stayed up there for three hours, until he could stand no more of it. It was one thing to hunt all day alone; it was another to sit still doing nothing and be pretty sure you were wasting your time. When he came down the ravine, Dusty was fishing, thoroughly enjoying herself. She had looked up and seen that he was off the lookout, and she had looked for him coming down the ravine.

Blackie walked up to where she fished. "How's the fishing?"

She beamed and pointed to the string of trout in the water, tied to a bush on the bank. He went over and properly admired her catch.

She asked, "Do you want me to take the lookout?"

He shook his head. "Up there, you can see somebody coming for more than an hour out. So, I've got an hour before I have to get back."

He stood there and watched her fish. They were quiet so as not to scare the fish with the sound of voices.

Dusty jerked her pole, burying the hook, and pulled in another trout. It flopped and jerked on the line. She unhooked it and strung it with the rest of her catch.

Now she baited the hook again, and by way of making conversation, she said, "Yesterday, Trudy Belvedere said that a lot of the boys want to come out to see me again, but, they're afraid of you now."

Blackie snorted. "Well, I guess if they don't hit you or take a shot at me, they don't have anything to be afraid of."

Dusty smiled at him. "It's all right. I don't feel like being courted right now anyway. There's plenty of time for that."

Presently, Blackie grinned. "So long as your girl friends don't stay away, I'll be satisfied."

"Hah. If you were to move away, I'd lose three quarters of my girl friends. I'm just their excuse to be around you."

Blackie's grin broadened. "Tell them they don't need any excuse. I'm available."

"Yeah, but these girls have marriage on their minds. They're not just thinking of romping in the bushes with you."

Blackie laughed.

* * *

Blackie went back up on the lookout for another two hours. This time, he took along a book that Dusty had packed for them. Toward the end of those two hours, he watched Dusty build a small, almost smokeless fire, and watched her get out the cast iron skillet. She waved him down. He took one last look around, and then beat it on down to camp, his mouth watering for trout.

* * *

The hot, mid-afternoon sun gleamed from Dusty's glossy yellow hair as she swept her shotgun, following a moving target. She let go with one barrel. The gun roared and recoiled. She took out running, high stepping and jumping over sagebrush. There was a joyousness about her. She came to the rabbit she had just shot, picked it up, and held it by its hind legs high in the air, smiling up to where Blackie sat lookout.

Up on the mountainside, Blackie looked down at her holding the rabbit for him to see. He smiled and waved.

Dusty exchanged the cartridges in her shotgun for buckshot, pea sized shot that could kill a buck deer or a man at fifty yards. (Her shotgun was always loaded with it unless she was hunting small game.) She then carried the rabbit back to camp and skinned and dressed it in less than five minutes; she had done it countless times before, preparing Blackie's kills for buyers. She wrapped it in a cloth, and, with a wire, hung it from a tree limb where coyotes or bears could not get at it. Then she went along the creek, picking herbs with which to flavor the rabbit.

Near their camp, someone, years ago, had placed rocks such that the stream backed up and formed a pool about four feet deep. In the afternoon, after looking the mountainsides over carefully, Dusty peeled her clothes off and stepped into the pool. The water seemed impossibly cold at first, but her body got used to it right away, and she found it very pleasant to sit in it up to her chin and float around for twenty minutes.

After looking the mountainsides over again, she emerged from the water and then busied herself around camp, letting the sun and the mountain air dry her body. By all reckoning, it was a stunning body. She built a small fire and placed a small wooden tripod over the hot coals. She hung a little chain on the tripod and hooked a covered pail to it in which she started cracked oats cooking.

Finally, she dressed and then climbed the mountain and relieved Blackie. He came down to camp and snoozed in the shade for an hour, and when he awoke, he put some more wood on Dusty's fire, and then bathed in the same pool that she had.

Later, when Blackie had climbed back up to take the lookout, Dusty had come down to the camp and had taken the cooked oats off the fire. Now, as supper time approached, she stuffed the rabbit with the oats and the herbs she had picked, and started the rabbit cooking on a wooden spit.

She was enjoying herself. Beside her was a sack of cooking and eating equipment. Her shotgun leaned against a rock next to her.

The noise she heard was so very small that a less alert person might have missed it. She snatched her shotgun and cocked both hammers. The clicks of the hammers cocking were loud enough to be heard several feet away.

Blackie's voice said, "It's me!"

He came through the trees and into camp.

"There's a lone rider about two miles out, coming this way. It's probably somebody Mom sent, but I'd better get into position just in case. Could you take the lookout? Somebody might be following him."

"All right. I'll finish this later."

She set the rabbit aside, and carefully dowsed the fire with water from a pan beside her. She rummaged in the sack and pulled out a cloth and a wire. She wrapped the rabbit in the cloth, and with the wire, hung it from a tree branch.

Meanwhile, Blackie had exchanged his long barreled Sharps for the shorter one.

The place where Blackie had chosen to intercept intruders was downstream from camp, at the east end of a meadow that ran for about seventy yards between canyon walls. The meadow was cut down the center by the creek; the trail, which followed the creek, was utterly exposed for the length of the meadow. The trail then passed under the rocky ledge where Blackie hid.

Ed Ringsley came into view on horseback at the downstream end of the meadow. He walked his mount—one of the Sheffield horses—steadily toward Blackie. He was about twenty yards away when Blackie showed his head, rifle aiming.

"Hold it right there, Ed!"

Ed visibly jumped and quickly reined in his horse.

"Oh, Blackie!" Ed laughed nervously. "You scared me." Still a little shaken, he said, "Your ma sent me to tell you and Dusty to come home. Everything's okay." He pulled a paper from his shirt pocket. "Here's a note in her hand."

"I'll come down."

"Boy, I'll tell you—I know there ain't much chance in me meetin' up with no Apaches, but I worried about it all the way. Your ma lent me this rifle." He patted the rifle in its scabbard. "But, like I told you before, I ain't that good a shot."

"Why did you come alone, then?"

"Oh, I don't know...." Ed looked around. Trying to hide his eagerness, he asked, "Where's Dusty?"

Blackie smiled. "Oh, she's around here somewhere. Let me take a look at that note."

Fourteen

I think I'd almost rather be shot," Blackie grumped to his mother.

It was sundown, and he stood leaning against the wall near the kitchen stove watching his mother drop pieces of chicken into a hot frying pan. He and Dusty had just put their horses away after the all-day ride back from Carpenter Springs.

Sarah said gently, "Our lives will be in turmoil until you handle this. Can you think of a simpler way to do it? We'll do it your way if you can."

Blackie thought for a bit, finally admitted grumpily, "I guess not."

Dusty said, "Oh, Blackie, please go do it."

"Oh, all right." He was suddenly less grumpy. He turned and headed for the door.

Dusty said, "I'll wait to eat with you; so, hurry."

Still a tiny bit grumpy: "Okay, okay."

He went on out and Dusty looked at her mother and smiled. Sarah was relieved. She had not expected it to be this easy.

Dusty said, "He's such a honey bear."

"More like a bear with a sore head sometimes."

"Yeah, but he's *our* bear."

"Yes, I guess we're stuck with him." Sarah was talking like this, but she did not really mean it. It was the concern peeling from her.

"Oh, Mom, you know you wouldn't want any other son. I know I don't want any other brother. I've compared him with my friends' brothers all my life, and he's the best as far as I'm concerned."

"Well, you certainly have him wrapped around your finger."

"No I don't."

"Oh yes you do. 'Oh, Blackie, please go do it,' and he trots right out to do it."

"I never ask him to do anything he doesn't want to do, because I know he won't do it."

"Well...."

"He knew you were right, and he wanted to do it, but his pride was in his way. So, I just gave him a little shove, that's all. I helped him do what he already wanted to do."

Sarah looked sharply at Dusty. Surprise mingled with pleasure. "Well, aren't you the clever girl."

Dusty continued. "Sometimes, when he's cross, he takes a little patience, that's all.... Well, you know that; I've watched you handle him all my life. But, anyway, he's worth it."

"Yes. As Mr. Odin says, his good side far outweighs his bad. He's awfully good about a lot of things. I couldn't ask for a harder worker. When you moved away, he never complained about the extra work he had to do. He's never complained about work since he was small that I can remember. Do you remember last spring, when Billie was foaling? He stayed with her all night, and in the morning he did his chores and then came in and slept only an hour and was up to go hunting because he'd promised someone a deer. And when he came home that evening, he did his chores just like every other night."

"I remember."

"And when he sets his mind to do something, there's not much he can't do."

"And besides, Mom, he thinks the sun rises and sets on you."

"On me? It's you he thinks that about."

Dusty laughed. It was a silly thing to debate.

"And, it's no wonder," continued Sarah, "the way you spoil him."

"Oh, I don't spoil him." Dusty would admit to pampering her big brother now and then. But, why not? It was fun. And he made such a pleasant fuss over the little things she did for him. It wasn't all one sided, either. He was always ready to even things up between them.

Sarah looked into her daughter's happy, ingenuous face and she thought what a pleasure it was to have her living at home again.

*   *   *

When Blackie walked into the Marshal's office, Marshal Wiggins was playing solitaire. A cup of coffee was getting cold at his elbow. Wiggins looked up.

Blackie spoke self-consciously. "I've come to say I'm sorry for the way I....uh....behaved the other day. I....uh....it won't happen again. From now on, I'll leave my rifle off at home before coming into town."

Marshal Wiggins smiled meanly. "I'm glad you came in, kid." His hand dropped to his revolver. There was no leather thong looped on the hammer today. He pulled the revolver out and snapped the hammer back. "Because, I'm arresting you for murder and violation of the gun law."

Blackie was momentarily amazed. Then he realized that the Marshal had set a trap for him.

"So, you lied to my mother."

"Sometimes you have to do things you don't want to do."

Blackie's voice was full of disgust. "You don't fool me."

"Kid, you got a big mouth. Give me the least excuse, and I'll blow you to Kingdom Come. Now turn around."

Blackie complied. Wiggins pulled Blackie's two knives from their sheaths on his belt. He patted Blackie down to his boots, checking for weapons.

"Into the jail cell with you."

Blackie walked into the cell. Wiggins locked the door and hung the key from a nail on the wall. Wiggins was pleased with himself. Inside the cell, Blackie was smoldering.

An hour and a half later, in the Sheffield house, Sarah stood looking toward town through one of the front windows. She was worried. Dusty sat anxiously across the room.

Dusty finally got up. "I'm going into town and see what's happened to him."

She went out to the corral, grabbed her sorrel mare by the mane and led her from the corral. She had raised the mare from a filly and had broken and trained her personally. Gripping the horse's mane, she leaped up onto her back without a saddle or bridle. She kicked her to a gallop, and, controlling her by tugs on her mane, galloped into town.

Dusty rode straight to the Marshal's office. The door stood open, and a lantern burned inside. Wiggins, illuminated by the light from inside, sat outside in the cool evening air on a bench with his back to the wall.

"Are you the Marshal?"

"Sure am."

"Have you seen Blackie Sheffield?"

"Yep. He's in there." Wiggins indicated the office door.

Dusty misunderstood what Wiggins meant by "in there." She thought he meant the office. She was relieved. She leaped from her horse. Wiggins jumped to his feet and barred the doorway with his body.

"Just a minute, young lady; you can't go in there. It's not visiting hours."

"What?"

"He's in jail."

"What for?!"

"A few things, including murder."

"He didn't murder anyone!"

"There's a witness says he did."

Dusty spoke angrily. "A woman who's lost her mind from grief! You ought to be ashamed of yourself, using that poor woman for your petty spites."

Wiggins was stung by her words and tone.

Blackie's voice came from inside. "It's all right, Dusty. I'm all right."

Dusty raised her voice. "Are you sure?"

"Yes."

"Have you eaten?"

"No."

"I'll bring you supper."

The Marshal cut in. "Oh, no you won't. It's past supper time. Come tomorrow about noon."

"He hasn't eaten since this morning!" She burst into tears. "You can't do this!"

Blackie said, "I'll be all right, Dusty! Go on home and tell Mom. I'll see you tomorrow."

With tears streaming down her face, Dusty spoke to the Marshal. "You're just a petty little man with a soul the size of a pea."

She grabbed her sorrel's mane and leaped onto its bare back.

She added, "You won't be with us very long."

"Is that a threat?" He sought to intimidate her.

She answered slowly and penetratingly. "No. I'm telling the future. I can feel it in my being. I can smell the death on you."

Dusty turned her horse and kicked it and galloped off.

Marshal Wiggins was thrown by her words. He stood there, staring after her. His face twitched. Suddenly, he wheeled into the office and locked the door. He pulled a shotgun from the wall and checked to see that it was loaded. He stacked cartridges on the table beside his bed.

He spoke with a raised voice to Blackie. "Kid, if anybody comes to try to get you out, I'm going to stick this shotgun through those bars and let go both barrels."

There was no answer.

"You hear me, kid?"

No answer. Marshal Wiggins grabbed the lantern, and with its aid looked into the cell.

"What's the matter, kid? Cat got your tongue?" He laughed.

Blackie looked at Wiggins without visible emotion.

Wiggins turned away from Blackie. He was worried. He perspired. He leaned the shotgun against his bed, then sat on the bed and took his boots off. He squinted at the window on the side of the building; lantern light reflected from the window, preventing him from seeing outside. He blew the lantern out. Moonlight flooded in. He went to the window and looked through it this way and that. Now he went to the window on the other side and looked out. He went back and sat on his bed. In the darkness relieved only by moonlight, he undressed to his underwear, swung into bed, and pulled a sheet over himself.

* * *

A furious Dusty raced her horse up to the front of the house, leaped to the ground and ran inside to tell her mother what had happened. Sarah experienced four or five seconds of consternation over the Marshal's duplicity; and then, quickly, she made plans to visit the Justice Of The Peace first thing in the morning and get him to urge the Marshal to prefer charges right away, and then get the Justice to set bail. With all of the witnesses' statements that Morgan had left with her, she had not the slightest doubt that bail would be set and that it would be minimal. Sarah would then go to the bank and withdraw the funds, and Blackie would be out of jail before the end of the day. There would probably be a coroner's inquest in a few days at which no indictment would be made, and Blackie would be free. The Federal Marshal would have egg on his face and that would be bad because he was obviously a vindictive person. Maybe she should write the Sheriff in Socorro and ask him to come down to press the Marshal to go on his way and stop meddling in affairs which are not in his jurisdiction.

After hearing her mother's clear-headed plans, Dusty calmed down and then went out and put her horse away. Back in the house again, she nibbled a little bit of chicken, and then, confident in her mother's cool effectiveness, she went to bed. For some time after snuffing the lantern, she lay in her bed thinking. The malicious injustice of the Federal Marshal not allowing Blackie to eat upset her some, but then there was nothing she could do about it tonight. Unable to sleep, her mind skipped from one thing to another. Eventually, it drifted onto Cathy Haggarty's infatuation with Blackie. Dusty thought about the strange conversation she had had with Cathy. Lying there in the dark, she deliberately re-lived the conversation several times in her mind. Something kept nagging her and, at last, rather suddenly, she thought she understood something. It came to her in a rush, and then she lay there and considered various angles of the idea.

Finally satisfied, she wanted to talk to someone; so she got up and went into her mother's bedroom and sat on the edge of the bed. The motion of the bed woke Sarah.

"Mom?"

"Yes, honey."

"You know how a person can catch a disease like scarlet fever from someone else who has it? Just by being around them?"

"Yes."

"Do you think a person who is diseased in the mind can pass her disease to someone else?"

"I don't know. I suppose it's possible. What do you think?"

"I think maybe it happens."

"Why do you say that?"

"Well, you know how when kids start running around with a different crowd, and they start acting and thinking like their new friends? They sort of copy the people around them. Some behavior they copy on purpose, and some of it I think they don't always know they're copying. And, even when they start running around with someone else, they usually still act and think like their old friends at least a little—and sometimes a lot. You know, when I was down at the Renners', I started acting like them some. It just sort of happened without me knowing it. I didn't realize how much I was acting like them until you and Blackie came down there to visit. I saw it then and I tried to stop it. But it was hard. It wasn't until the night I left that I seemed to shrug it off—to shrug off their influence, I mean—and I started acting like my old self. Maybe some of their influence that I can't see is still hanging on me. I hope not."

Sarah reached and patted her daughter's leg. "So you think that maybe some people mimic other people's traits and attitudes without realizing they're doing it?"

"Yes."

"Well, you might be right. I guess it would explain a lot of things.... In fact, the more I think of it, the more I think you're right."

Dusty did not say anything, and so Sarah asked, "What brought this up?"

"Oh, I was thinking of Cathy Haggarty. I think there's something wrong with her mind."

"Did she talk to you the other day when you took the chickens in?"

"Yes."

"What did she say?"

"Well, she wanted me to give a message to Blackie."

"What was it?"

"Oh, she wanted him to come and see her."

"Is that who you were teasing him about? Is that who he'd slept with?"

Dusty did not answer immediately. She felt she would be telling Blackie's secret. Finally, "Yes."

"He's not 'involved' with her, is he?"

"I'm sure he's not. But she's crazy about him. You should have seen her. She was a nervous wreck asking me to give him the message."

"She must have said something else to you for you to decide she's crazy. What was it?"

Dusty was silent for a moment. Then she started giggling. "She wanted me to become a whore."

Sarah sat up in the bed. "Well, of all the nerve!"

"Don't worry, Mom," Dusty giggled, "I don't think I'm going to do it."

"Well, I should think you wouldn't!" Sarah caught herself and started giggling too.

They both laughed for a little bit, and then Dusty told her in detail what Cathy had said.

When Dusty finished recounting it, Sarah said, "I want to feel sorry for her over her childhood, but people have had worse childhoods and have made decent lives for themselves. She doesn't have to be a whore."

"Yeah, I know it. Anyway, I was thinking that I don't want Blackie to have very much to do with her. It occurred to me that just by being around crazy people you might catch some of it."

"By mimicking their behavior and attitudes without knowing you're doing it?"

"Yes."

"I suppose the thing to do is to stay alert, then."

"I guess. Or to stay away from them."

"Yes.... I suppose that's all part of picking the people you want to be around. Because it's practically impossible to be around someone very long and not be influenced by them—not pick up some of their attitudes to some degree."

Fifteen

At first light the next morning, about forty-five minutes before sun up, the dogs of the town of Gold Creek were barking far more than was usual. Most people, sleeping soundly, simply did not hear them. Among those who did, only a handful got up to look out the windows. Of those who got up, not one saw anything unusual. Most went back to bed.

Spaced about twenty-five yards apart, standing beside their horses amid the tall thick brush in the creek bed that ran beside the town, were thirty-nine desperados of El Lobo's gang. Five more desperados surrounded the empty store containing the guns.

Another five surrounded the Marshal's office on foot. One crept below each of the two windows, while another stood at the door. The two below the windows rose up and looked inside. They both lifted their rifles and took aim. There were consecutive blasts as they fired through the windows. Immediately, the man at the door shot the lock panel and then kicked the door open.

Inside, United States Marshal Timothy Wiggins lay dead in his bed.

Blackie, a light sleeper all of his life, had heard the dogs barking; however, there had been nothing he could do about it. But when the two rifles had roared close at hand, accompanied by the noise of shattering glass, he had sprung over against the inner wall where it was difficult to see him or shoot him just by looking through the barred window on the cell door. He did not know what was happening, but he had heard the lock panel shot and the door kicked open and he now heard the clomping of boots in the office. He heard the men speaking in Spanish.

Across the street, a desperado had shot the door lock on the vacant store where the guns were stored. Men went inside.

The gunfire at the Marshal's office was the signal for which the rest of the desperados waited; they rode into town quickly. The town's dogs commenced frenzied barking.

From nearby houses, individuals—some partially dressed, others in night clothes—came outside to see what the ruckus was. The desperados began firing at them like shooters at target practice. They killed and wounded several, including children, until the townspeople gained enough sense to stay inside.

Desperados rode through the town, taking some horses and shooting those they did not take, and shooting anyone who looked belligerent or who tried to run from town.

South of town, inside the Sheffield house, Sarah and Dusty were awakened by the distant gunfire. Sarah was up quickly, dressing in bluejeans and flannel shirt. As always during emergencies, she was in full possession of her faculties, not the slightest bit confused.

Dusty, in a nightshirt, ran from the other bedroom to a front window and looked toward town.

Sarah said, "That's way too much gunfire. I don't know what's happening, but it could be Apaches."

"Could it have anything to do with Blackie?"

"I don't see how. Not all *that* gunfire. Get dressed. Hurry!"

Dusty dressed in bluejeans, shirt, and boots. Sarah pulled down a rifle and two shotguns from the wall and checked to see that they were loaded. She opened a drawer and pulled out gray boxes of ammunition and stacked them on the table. She pulled out a gray box of shotgun cartridges and looked at its label. The label showed pen and ink style drawings of BB sized lead shot spilling from an opened cartridge. It also showed a duck taking flight. The label said, "Fowl Shot," and "BB." She set that box aside and pulled out another gray box with drawings of lead shot the size of her little fingernail. It had a sketch of an antlered deer and said, "Buck Shot" and "00."

Sarah opened the box and stuffed cartridges into her pockets.

She spoke rapidly: "Do you have your knife?"

"It's right here." Dusty pointed to the blue handled knife in its sheath on her belt.

"Where's your shotgun?"

"Under my bed."

"Check to see it's loaded, and stuff all the cartridges you can into your pockets. And put a jacket on."

Dusty pulled on a jacket. She breeched her shotgun, saw the shells, and snapped it closed. She stuffed buckshot cartridges into the pockets of her jacket.

Sarah said, "We're going to go out carefully to the barn, and you're going to let me cover you with hay. I'm going to pile it high on you. You stay there no matter what you think is happening to me. I don't care if you hear me screaming. Don't come out from under the hay because of sympathy for me. If things get that far gone, you alone could do me no good. It would just be two deaths instead of one. Do you understand?"

Dusty was wide eyed. "Yes."

It was a plan Sarah had devised years ago when the children were small.

"Don't come out from under the hay until I come for you, or until things have been quiet for several hours. Do you understand?"

"Yes."

"The most important thing is for *you* to live."

Sarah began going from window to window looking to see that the coast was clear. Dusty followed her example.

"Mom, what about Blackie? Do you think he's all right?"

"I don't know. We can't worry about it right now because we can't do anything about it. As soon as things quiet down in town and stay quiet for a couple of hours, I'll ride in and see to him."

Sounding as if she might cry, Dusty said, "Oh, God, I hope he's all right."

"Honey, don't think about it. Look outside."

The coast looked clear. Sarah and Dusty ran for the barn. They opened the barn doors and shooed the cows out. If there were Apaches, Sarah wanted them to have no reason to go into the barn if she could help it. Sarah and Dusty climbed up to the hayloft. Sarah instructed the girl to lie on her back with her shotgun at her side. She pitched a fork full of hay over Dusty's feet.

"Mom," Dusty's voice was touched with sadness, "I don't want to lose you."

"I'm a pretty good shot."

Sadly, "I know."

Sarah pitched hay. "I'll do everything I can to live. I want you to do the same. Will you promise me to do everything you can to live?"

"Of course, Mom."

Sarah was pitching hay as fast as she could. "Put your arms up over your face so that you make an air pocket. Fresh air will filter down to it as you breath."

Sarah pitched hay until she had covered the girl well. You could walk over her and not feel her beneath the hay.

"All right, honey, I'm going inside now. Remember your promise."

*　　*　　*

With three swings of an ax, a desperado had smashed in the front door of Belvedere's Dry Goods Store. From the living quarters attached to the back of the store, John Belvedere, clad in a night shirt, having been awakened by the smashing of the door, had rushed through the curtained doorway into the store and met three armed desperados coming inside single file. He had put up his hands and backed around behind the counter. In silk night gowns, his wife and sixteen year old daughter Trudy had pushed the curtain aside and looked.

Belvedere waved frantically at his family. "Get back! Get back!"

Seeing the desperados they backed hurriedly from sight. The first desperado followed them.

Belvedere raised his voice to the desperados. "Don't go in there!" He picked up a cash box and shook it. "Here, see?! Money! Money! Dinero!"

With a forced smile, he handed the cash box to the third desperado. The man leaned his rifle up against the counter to take the box.

Belvedere waved at the shelves of dry goods. "You can have anything you want! Just take it. But, please leave my family alone."

Sounds of a scuffle came from the living quarters. There were grunts from the first desperado, Mrs. Belvedere, and Trudy. There was the sound of a blow, and of someone falling to the floor. Then the sound of cloth ripping. Trudy shrieked. Belvedere jerked toward the end of the counter, but stopped when the second desperado pointed a rifle at his chest. The first desperado pulled Trudy from the living quarters. With one hand, she was trying to hold closed the front of her torn nightgown.

The first desperado said in Spanish to his companions, "Look! Look at this!"

He ripped the nightgown from her. The other two desperados ogled her sleek, young body. Mrs. Belvedere staggered to the doorway, holding her head. John Belvedere opened a drawer behind the counter. From it he snatched a large, forty-four caliber Army revolver. Cocking it as he whipped it up, he blew a hole in the first desperado's head. The roar of the big gun was deafening. Blue smoke clouded the scene. The second desperado was pulling his rifle up when Belvedere shot him in the chest. The man fell to the floor. The third desperado had dropped the cash box, and now ran for the front door. Belvedere fired and hit him in the kidney. The man continued running out into the street where he collapsed, groaning in pain.

Horrified, Mrs. Belvedere blurted, "Where did you get the....?

"Shut up, you fool!"

Her husband ran past her to the front door. He aimed at the wounded desperado and fired. From across the street, another desperado fired his rifle at Belvedere. Belvedere fell, sprawling from the doorway onto the boardwalk. He was dead.

Two more desperados charged into the store. There was a shot. Presently, the two desperados came out. One carried the money box; the other, carrying the dead men's guns, kicked Trudy stumbling ahead of them. She tried to cover her nakedness with her torn nightgown.

Down the street, the door of the Gold Creek Hardware Store stood bashed open. Three desperados were cleaning the shelves of ammunition, and stuffing their pockets with anything that took their fancies.

A short distance away, on the front porch of the expensive-looking O'Connor house, a desperado bashed the front door with an ax. His name was Benito Gonzales, and he had a long, distinctive scar on his left cheek. The door gave way; he threw the ax down, picked up his single barreled shotgun, and stepped into the house.

Inside, a scared Bill O'Connor stood barefoot in pants and shirt at the foot of the stairs. He was armed with a butcher knife.

Benito Gonzales raised his shotgun and blew O'Connor's face to a lump of pulverized flesh. Gonzales reloaded, and walked over and went through the dead man's pockets. He found nothing. He looked up the staircase.

He could hear the low, rapid droning of a voice up there. He carefully climbed the stairs. At the landing, in night clothes, Mabel O'Connor was on her knees, saying the Lord's Prayer. Her hands were folded together high in the air. Gonzales hit her full in the face with his fist. She sprawled, and he kicked her three times to the head, leaving her unconscious.

A bedroom door stood open. He went in and walked around looking for valuables. He found only a five dollar gold piece, three silver dollars, and a dime. He tried the other bedroom door. It was locked. He stood back, aimed and blew the lock out. He reloaded, and then kicked the door open.

Inside the bedroom, in night clothes, Stella O'Connor and her twelve year old brother, Hank, sat cringing on the edges of their beds. Their father, confused by a situation he had not understood, had told them to stay in bed and lock their door.

Gonzales appreciated a pretty girl when he saw one. He walked in, leering at Stella, and grabbed her by the wrist.

Twelve year old Hank leaped at Gonzales, taking him by surprise. Gonzales stumbled back against a wall. They struggled. The desperado, holding his shotgun, had only one free hand. Stella, terrified, made no move to help her brother. Finally, Gonzales shoved the boy away far enough to kick him. That stopped the boy long enough for Gonzales to jam his shotgun against the boy's belly. There was a roar, and a spattering of blood around the room.

Stella, sitting on her bed, went into hysterics. She bounced where she sat, pulling at her hair with her hands. Her face was distorted and red. She made a peculiar "Uh, uh, uh...." noise in time with her bounces. She did not look so pretty now.

*   *   *

The desperados were under orders to do their looting and kidnapping swiftly, and it was not very long before they had thirteen girls and young women held at gunpoint on Main Street. All of the girls were in night clothes and their feet were bare and they shivered from the chill of the morning air and from terror. All were pretty—why take plain girls when pretty ones could be had for the same effort?

Stella was not there yet. Trudy Belvedere was trying to tie her torn silk nightgown together in the front, but in her shock and fear she could not concentrate and could not control her trembling hands.

Beside Trudy, trembled a seventeen year old redhead, Connie Watkins. Shocked and terrified, she was having trouble breathing. She had only a few minutes ago seen her father, Red Watkins, murdered when, unarmed, he had tried to prevent her abduction. Standing there in the street, trying to breathe, Connie's vision and hearing kept dimming and coming back as she almost fainted several times.

Behind Trudy, Jettie Stevens spoke in a quavering voice: "Turn around, Trudy. I'll help you." The Stevens' grand house had, of course, been looted, and she had been grabbed. Her father, when he had first heard gunfire, had leapt hastily from bed and had twisted his back; in agony, he had fallen there beside the bed, unable to move himself. Eventually, the bandits had come and looted the house and abducted Jettie, and Jethro had been unable to do a thing about it.

There in the street, another captive, fourteen year old Prudence Babcock, a small, fair girl with dark brown hair, had sought out the oldest girl in the group, twenty year old Rebecca Shales. Rebecca, a curly headed brunette, slim with large breasts, had her arm around the younger girl. Comforting Prudie somehow lessened Rebecca's own fear. Prudence wept without halt. She could not understand what was happening. Her father, with a house full of kids, had realized that he could not prevent Prudie's abduction. He would simply have gotten himself killed. And then what would have become of the rest of his family?

Rebecca Shales' husband had been as terrified as she when the bandits had barged into their one room shack by the creek. Otis Shales had offered no resistance, and Rebecca had been too terrified to do anything but go where the rifle barrel in her back had directed her.

Two more young married women were there: Suzanna Brown, an eighteen year old brownette, and Mary Jean Hicks, a sixteen year old dishwater blonde. Next to Mary Jean stood a single girl, Dianna Ramsey, eighteen. Head strong and independent, Dianna herself had at first resisted her captors. As a result, she had been knocked down with a fist to her jaw and then kicked thrice in the ribs. On the second kick, she had felt a rib crack and had screamed. The man had kicked her again in the same place. She had groaned and had ended her resistance.

Trying to hide among the several girls was fifteen year old Jinny Rowe. When first taken, she had hoped that it would be all over quickly; they would probably rape her and then turn her loose. She was now beginning to suspect that it was not going to be over quickly.

Next to Jinny was Ella York, sixteen, willowy with shiny, very light brown hair and gorgeous blue eyes. Her father, realizing that the men could not understand English, had told her to go along calmly. Everything would be all right. He and a posse would catch them before nightfall. She wanted to believe him, but she was badly frightened anyway.

On her knees in the street was blonde Etta Johnson, sixteen. She had an overpowering notion that she would not see tomorrow. And the thought of being raped kept sending stomach acid up her throat again and again. She had wanted to scream, but when she had tried, stomach acid had gotten into her lungs and she had collapsed to her knees in a coughing fit.

Squatting beside Etta, trying to help her, was Minnie Stapleton, fifteen, the oldest child of a family that had only just arrived in town last week. They had been living in a tent on the creek bank, and her fourteen year old brother had been trampled and severely injured when a desperado had ridden his horse right over their little tent. Minnie had dashed away on foot only to be overtaken by the rider and knocked down with the broadside of a machete to the back of her head.

Finally, there was Clarissa Blackford. She prayed constantly while she stood there. Her captor had originally taken a plain girl, Lila Roos, but when he had seen the prettier Clarissa, he had abandoned the Roos girl and taken Clarissa. Clarissa kept asking God why He was doing this to her.

The American bandit, Abner Waters, came walking by. He casually looked the women over. One of the three men guarding them addressed him in Spanish:

"Where can we hold these prisoners?"

Waters answered in Spanish, "There's a jail in the Marshal's office."

* * *

El Lobo, with twenty men, contemplated the cast iron doors and sashes on the rock and cement building that housed the Gold Creek Bank. There was a combination lock on the face of one iron door.

A man in trousers and suspenders, his shirttail out, and his feet bare, was marched up by Abner Waters and another bandit.

El Lobo spoke in accented English: "You own bank?"

The man nodded without looking him in the eyes.

El Lobo said, "Open."

The banker was scared, but he shook his head. El Lobo put his revolver to the man's head.

"I keel you."

The banker stood there, waiting to be shot.

Abner Waters interceded, "Look, mister, we can blow it open with powder from one of the mines. We'll get in whether you open it for us or not. So, why not make it easier on everybody, and save your own life to boot?!"

The banker, whose name was Fred Tyson, almost gave in. Then he shook his head. He could not bring himself to pay for his life with other people's money, with his depositors' money.

Waters said urgently, "Hold up, Lobo!"

Waters turned calmly to the banker. "You got a wife and kids, right? Sure, you do. I seen 'em. Three boys and two girls. Now, you open the bank for us, and I'll see to it myself that nothin' happens to 'em."

Fred Tyson looked at the ground.

Waters continued in a you-and-me tone. "Y'know, we got some pretty bad men here." He indicated the desperados.

"They get out on a long ride, and some of 'em start actin' like animals. They'll take kids like yours—the boys as well as the girls—and use 'em in ways you wouldn't ever wanta think about. Some of the things they do to kids just turns my stomach! It's a mercy that the kids don't live long. Now, Lobo, here, he's the boss. So, if you open up for us, he won't let them scum have your kids."

Waters turned. "That right, Lobo?"

El Lobo nodded as Fred Tyson looked into his cruel, black eyes.

Fred Tyson said sadly, "All right, I'll open it."

Abner Waters, pleased with himself, turned away. He spotted Blackie standing there with two of the three bandits who had been guarding the captive females.

He spoke to one of the guards in Spanish. "What's he doin' here?"

"We found him in the jail."

Waters was immediately taken with the young man's clean good looks. He asked Blackie, "What were you in jail for, boy?"

Blackie hesitated. "Killing a man."

Waters grinned. "Well, I can't hold that againya; I've done a bit of that myself."

Waters turned to watch the banker working the combination lock. He turned again to Blackie.

"Over money?"

"No."

Waters half smiled. "Never kill anybody unless it's for money. It ain't worth it."

Fred Tyson completed the last turn on the combination lock. He turned the door lever. There was a noisy clunk as the door unlatched. He swung it open.

Waters turned and spoke in Spanish to the men holding the horses. "Bring the horses up!"

A handful of men brought up ten horses with empty packs.

Waters spoke to Blackie's guards in Spanish. "Bring him in, but keep an eye on him."

Fred Tyson led the way inside, followed by several desperados and Blackie.

Waters asked Blackie, "Over a woman?"

"Yeah."

"I knew it! Never kill over a woman, boy. They're not worth it. For a twenty dollar gold piece you can buy a week with one of the prettiest women you ever wanta see."

Waters spoke to the banker: "Where's the gold? We want the gold ingots."

Fred Tyson answered sadly, "They're in the safe."

"Well, open it! And hurry! We ain't got all day."

Fred Tyson knelt before the safe and spun the dials while everyone watched in silent anticipation. The banker dialed five numbers, and then turned the door handle. He pulled the door open to reveal stacks of fifty pound gold ingots. The desperados inside the bank let out several high pitched cries called the *guaco*, a ki-yi that told of their joy.

El Lobo turned to his men and spoke in Spanish. "You men start loading these on the horses."

Abner Waters said to El Lobo in Spanish, "I'll round up the men." To Blackie's guards, he said, "Come with me."

Waters said in English to Blackie, "Come along, boy."

As they walked along, Waters explained: "I just wanta hear some English. I been in Mexico ten years, and I like it; but sometimes I just wanta hear English talked. I talk it with Lobo now and then when we don't want these cabrones to know what we're sayin'; but he don't talk it good. The other day, here in town, was the first time I talked English with an American in three years."

They encountered two desperados in front of a store, stacking loot on the boardwalk.

Waters said to Blackie, "They can't take all that. We don't have the horses for it. We ride with a lotta extra horses; but that's so's we can switch to fresher horses when we need to. If you load up your spare horses, then they're just as tired. You get too greedy and you get your tail shot off."

Waters spoke to the desperados in Spanish. "Get on your horses, and be ready to ride. Forget that stuff. We've got gold!"

They walked on, passing homes and businesses along Main Street with doors and windows bashed in. They encountered three desperados drinking whiskey.

Waters told them in Spanish, "Get on your horses and be ready to ride."

To Blackie he boasted, "I'm second in command of this outfit."

They went on up the street a ways, and Waters asked Blackie, "You ever see a man hanged?"

"No."

"It ain't a nice way to die. Maybe you oughta think about ridin' outa here with us."

"Maybe I should."

"Ridin' with Lobo is a hard life, though. When we leave here, we'll be ridin' twenty hours a day until 'way past Dog Springs. Some of the horses'll go lame or break down, and we'll have to shoot 'em. Some of them girls won't be able to take it either. They're not used to it. If you let one fall off her horse and live, they'll all do it; so, you gotta kill them that falls off so's to keep the rest agoin'. You gotta be a hard man to ride in this outfit."

Waters told more desperados to get their horses.

He said to Blackie, "If somebody don't take charge and tell these hombres what to do, they'd hang around all day, and get themselves shot by some miners who come to town. I planned this whole raid. And I know there are a-plenty miners out in them hills, and a lot of 'em have horses and guns. I allowed us two hours to get what we want and then get the hell out. It looks like we're gonna get out sooner."

Waters spoke Spanish to four desperados they encountered. "Pass the word: Be ready to ride!"

They met two desperados who had made a prisoner of a cute thirteen year old girl. She was terrified.

Blackie said urgently to Waters, "Mister, that's one of the banker's daughters!"

"That right? I wouldn't've recognized her if you hadn't said somethin'."

Waters seemed disinclined to do anything about it.

Blackie said, "I was thinking of your promise to the banker."

"I wouldn't know I was breakin' my promise if you hadn't said so."

"That's why I spoke up, sir."

Waters was both irritated and amused. "You got a lotta nerve, boy."

Waters turned to the girl's captors and explained in Spanish the bargain he had made with her father. They did not like it, but he insisted. After some haggling, they gave her up.

Waters grabbed the girl roughly by the arm and pushed her to Blackie. "Here, she's yours."

Blackie put a protective arm around her and spoke to Waters. "You're a man of your word, sir."

"Naw, I'm just gettin' soft. You're bad for me, boy. You didn't really kill anybody, did you?"

"Yes."

"What'd he do to deserve it?"

"Shot at me first."

Waters nodded. "Will they hang you?"

"I don't think so—now that the Marshal's dead."

Waters nodded. They walked up to the Marshal's office.

Waters said to the guards, "Get them women outa there and get 'em on horses. We're gonna ride!"

He said to Blackie, "Somethin' about you bothers me.... so I'm gonna lock you and this girl up in the jail and take the key; that way none of our men'll get her out while I'm not lookin'. If you told me the truth about your shootin' in self-defense, you'll be all right. If not, that's your hard luck."

Benito Gonzales was just now walking Stella O'Connor up from down the street where he had raped her with her dead brother lying on the floor beside the bed. Stella's eyes were glazed and she did not quite know where she was. Her walk was unsteady and she was trembling badly.

Gonzales and Blackie looked each other full in the face. Gonzales looked at the girl under Blackie's arm; she cringed from him and pressed tightly against Blackie, trying actually to physically merge with Blackie and disappear. Gonzales looked back to Blackie with pure hatred.

Waters told Gonzales to get Stella onto a horse.

Across the street in the empty store building, two desperados sloshed coal oil over the building and on all of the guns they did not want and the ammunition and powder they could not carry. One touched a burning match to the oil and they exited.

Down the street, wherever there was a block of buildings close together, desperados fired one of the buildings. It was Waters' plan that the townspeople should become involved in the immediate job of saving their homes and businesses. That might keep them from organizing a chase for a few hours. And with no horses and guns, the townspeople might not come after them at all.

Sixteen

Forget the house!" Abner Waters ordered impatiently in Spanish.

But the two bandits ignored him and continued riding on over toward the Sheffield house anyway. The Sheffield dogs were barking loudly and fiercely.

It had been Waters' intention to bypass the house and come around behind the barn to the corral and get the horses. There was nothing, he felt, that the house could offer to compare with the gold they already had aboard the pack horses. To mess with the occupants of the house was merely a waste of valuable time. Time they should be using to put a distance between them and Gold Creek. All he was interested in here was the good horseflesh he had seen in the corral a few days ago. They could use good horses, and he did not want the horses to be available to any pursuers.

But discipline was not one of the strong points of El Lobo's current gang.

Waters led the rest of the gang, the captives, and the spare horses rapidly by on the Gold Creek Road about seventy yards from the house.

Inside the house, Sarah had been watching the desperados and their captives approach since they had left the outskirts of town. Sarah had no intention of initiating any shooting as long as the desperados passed her ranch by. There was no chance that she could win a shootout with so many men.

But, as the two men approached the house on horseback, Sarah put her rifle down and picked up a double barreled shotgun loaded with buckshot. One man sidled up near the side of the house, peering at the windows. The other man approached from the front, a little further out. Sarah stood well back from the side window, knowing that, from outside, she would be hard to see.

She drew a bead on the man approaching from the side and squeezed the trigger. There was the explosion, the recoil, the window blowing out, and the man pitching bloodily from his horse. The horse took off galloping by itself, its reins trailing the ground.

Suddenly aware of his helpless vulnerability, and terrified, the man in front of the house shouted in Spanish, "They have guns!"

He fired blindly into the house. While he reloaded, Sarah let go with her other barrel through a front window. The man and his horse both went down. The man was dead instantly; but the horse groaned and kicked for a few seconds before it died.

Meanwhile, the rest of the desperados had stopped in their circle of the house. They raised their guns and fired a fusillade blindly into the house.

One of the bullets hit Sarah in the left calf. The shock and pain caused her to drop her shotgun and fall to the floor. She gripped her calf where she lay amid the broken glass from the windows blown in by the desperados' bullets. Blood quickly soaked her bluejeans and her hands. With bloody hands, she grabbed the rifle that leaned against the table. On her knees, she moved over to a window on the south side of the house. She aimed the rifle and fired. The man between the house and El Lobo pitched toward El Lobo and fell dead to the ground.

El Lobo spurred his horse and shouted, "Forget the house! Get the horses!"

Sarah fumbled for another .45-70 cartridge. The pain in her leg slowed her thinking. Now she remembered that she had left the rifle cartridges on the table. She crawled over and snatched a box of them. She crawled back to a window just as the desperados, their captives, and their spare horses were galloping out of sight behind the barn. Dragging her rifle, Sarah crawled toward the kids' bedroom. The pain in her left leg was intense. She was sweating.

Behind the barn, El Lobo ordered two men to go on foot along the sides of the barn to cover the house. He ordered two other men to rope the horses in the corral and bring them out to the herd of spare horses they were already driving. One man walked into the barn to look around. He spotted two coal oil lanterns. Motivated by senseless malice, he poured the oil out onto the straw and wood around the barn. He lit a match to it and quickly walked out.

In the house, inside the kid's bedroom, Sarah realized that she was bleeding too much. She grabbed one of Blackie's shirts and tied a tourniquet around her leg just below the knee.

Within a few seconds, the dry wood of the barn had practically exploded into flames. Smoke began steaming from the barn through cracks and openings.

Meanwhile, the horses were being led from the corral.

In the back bedroom, Sarah stood on one leg and looked out of the back window. She could see the two desperados watching the house from each side of the barn. She raised her rifle, but her condition had weakened and, on one leg, she could not hold the rifle steadily enough to aim. She decided to rest her rifle on the window sill. With sweat covering her face, she hopped one-legged over beside the window, unlatched it and started swinging it slowly open.

One of the desperados saw the window swinging open, and fired at it.

The window blew in, and Sarah fell to the floor, unhurt. The two men fired blindly at the bedroom. Bullets continued to rip through the outer wall a few seconds apart. Sarah stayed down for a minute or two, and then started crawling from the bedroom, heading for the little hall and the back door of the house.

El Lobo spoke in Spanish to the men doing the shooting. "That's enough! Let's go!"

The roof of the barn was vigorously burning. Above the barn, the leaves of the big overhanging cottonwood trees first dried, then crinkled, and then burst into flame. Inside the barn, the smoke was very thick, and in the hayloft, the surface of the hay was burning in patches. Beneath the hay, Dusty was breathing smoke. Against her will, her body began to cough. It was obvious to her that the barn had not caught fire by itself, and that the ones—probably Apaches—who had started the fire were still nearby; she had heard them shooting. She stood the smoke as long as she could, until she knew that she was suffocating. She pushed the hay from her. The heat was scorching, so she instantly pulled her jacket over her head with just a peep hole held closed with her left hand. Coughing, clutching her shotgun, she rose and scrambled for the loft opening at the back of the barn. She leaped.

Dusty hit the ground rolling, somersault fashion. Her shotgun necessarily flew loose from her grip.

The desperado who had shot out the back window of the house was walking by at that moment. He was nonplused by the sudden appearance of someone tumbling along the ground. Dusty sprang to her feet, pulling her jacket back, coughing and gulping fresh air; and in an instant she perceived the desperados and their captives. She looked for her shotgun, spotted it and dashed for it. The near desperado saw what she was doing and he sprang to intercept her. They collided. He threw his arms around her, clumsily holding his rifle with one hand. The Sheffield dogs had been keeping a respectful distance from the desperados, but now they dashed forward barking and snarling fiercely at the desperado grappling with the girl. Dusty struggled, and out flashed her knife. She stabbed quickly and violently, twice. The man cried out and slipped to the ground.

El Lobo spurred his horse forward as Dusty, knife in hand, started again for her shotgun. El Lobo swung his rifle by the barrel, and when Dusty came up with her shotgun, there was a sickening crack as the rifle butt bounced off of her head. She sprawled in the dirt, unconscious. The two dogs stood over her, barking and growling viciously up at El Lobo.

El Lobo pulled his revolver from his belt, cocked it, aimed, and fired, killing one dog. The other dog leaped at El Lobo's foot in the stirrup and bit through the boot leather. The man hollered. He aimed, and as the dog cleared the horse for another jump, he shot it dead.

El Lobo dismounted. Limping on his bitten foot, and cursing, he led the dead man's horse over and heaved Dusty up onto the horse, belly down over the saddle. He cut a piece from the lariat on the saddle and, running the rope under the horse's belly, tied one end to her hands and the other to her feet. He then tied her body to the saddle so that the horse could gallop and she would not fall off.

Sarah inched open the rear door of the house. She could see the barn engulfed in flames. There was no sign of the desperados who had been at the side of the barn watching the house. She prayed that Dusty was not still in the barn. She had heard the dogs barking and the two shots followed by the dogs' silence, and she had guessed what had happened to them. Sliding her rifle with her, she crawled down the back steps and out and around the barn. The effort increased her bleeding. When she got around the barn, the desperados were gone. She saw the dead man. And she saw Dusty's blue handled knife and her shotgun lying a few feet away. The dead dogs were there too. She knew, then, that Dusty was not in the barn. She called out the girl's name several times. She was aware that her voice was weak; but she knew that if Dusty had been nearby, and alive, she would have heard it. It was most likely that the girl had been taken prisoner.

Keeping a sharp eye, Sarah lay there and rested.

Finally, she thought about her circumstances. It might be some time before someone came to help. Probably, the people in town would be preoccupied with their own problems. She had no idea what Blackie's fate had been.

Consequently, her chickens and ducks, locked in the hot sheds all day, could die from thirst or heat.

In severe pain, Sarah crawled to the three chicken coops and the duck shed to release the animals. Then, drenched with sweat, stopping to rest several times, she crawled back to the house to tend to her wound.

She had already lost too much blood.

Seventeen

Jasper Odin lay on the ground breathing in gasps, his chest and stomach heaving. His face was smudged with soot and dirt, and sweat had run down it and left muddy ridges. Beneath the smudges, his face was unnaturally red.

The desperados had set fire to five buildings, one of which had been the hardware store. It was three buildings down from The Gold Creek Saloon, and as it had burned, it had caught fire to its neighbor. Almost every able bodied man, woman, and child who had not been tending to wounded and injured had been pressed into service to get the fires out. Men had stood as close as possible to the burning buildings and shoveled dirt into the flames. Other people had joined the bucket brigades and buckets of water had been passed from hand to hand up from the creek to be thrown onto the fires. Seven bucket brigades had been in operation around the town.

As the minutes stretched on, a lot of children, unused to such frantic exertion, had begun to wear out and stagger with the buckets and slop out part of the water, and the buckets had begun to arrive with less water. Soon, there had been those who could not keep up the pace. And, as the minutes had turned into hours, most just could not continue. Many women also gave way under the exertion. More and more men had begun to take breaks, their shoulders, arms, and hands aching from the strain, and the fire fighting had slowed. But, Jasper Odin, overweight, and "out of training," had kept going beyond exhaustion.

The hardware store had burned to the ground despite their efforts. They had retarded the burning of the second building, but they had just held their own for a long time. A bucket of water would put out the flames on a beam, and then a couple of minutes later it would break out burning again. Altogether, it had taken them three hours to get the fire completely out. They had had to throw water on the third building also, to keep it from igniting. It was scorched, but saved. The Gold Creek Saloon, fortunately, was untouched.

Odin had been gasping for a long time, and his throat had been raw, paining him to breath. He had kept going by shear determination. When it had been agreed that the fire here was out, Odin had turned away, gasping, feeling dizzy, and had collapsed and rolled over onto his back.

Very tired people had been lying all over the place, so no one had paid Odin much attention for a bit. Finally, a man came over and looked at him.

Exhausted as the man was, he grabbed a pail and ran down to the creek, filled the pail with water and ran, wheezing, back up and threw the water on Odin. He threw the pail to another man.

"Get some more water!" the man wheezed. "Quick! This man could die!"

The other man ran to the creek and filled the bucket and ran back. At the first man's directions he threw the water over Odin's head and trunk.

With the second bucket of cold stream water, Odin emerged from serious danger. He had been over-heated and the first man had guessed it. The two men now helped him up the back steps of his saloon where he lay down on the floor in the kitchen. Odin had stopped gasping, but it still hurt him to breath through his wind-burnt throat.

Mrs. Odin gave him water which he swallowed gingerly. Finally, Mrs. Odin and Cathy Haggarty put a quilt on the floor and helped him onto it. In his exhaustion, he began to doze and dream.

A big chested man who was a friend of bartender Ed Ringsley came in the back door of the saloon and saw Odin dozing on the floor. He went on through into the bar where Ed Ringsley lay on the floor with a blanket over him. To the big chested man's surprise, Ed was still alive.

"How you doin'?" the man asked.

Ed slowly shook his head. In a weak voice, he asked, "I'm done for it, ain't I?"

The big chested man nodded.

The bullet had gone through Ed's belly. Ed had heard the desperados breaking into the saloon and he had come downstairs, and they had shot him on the stairs and he had fallen down the rest of the way and broken his wrist too.

"This is a lonely way to die."

"I'm sorry. We been fightin' that fire. We got it out now."

"You reckon Doc could do anything?"

"I don't think so—but I'll try to fetch him if you want."

Ed nodded.

Doc came back with the man ten minutes later. There was a lot of competition for Doc's services, so the big chested man had told him it would take him only a minute of his time. He came in and looked at Ed's wound and shook his head.

Ed said weakly to the big chested man, "You know, I'd like to see Blackie before....I.... Do you think....?"

Doc raised his eyebrows. "Blackie's with the outlaws. They say he was a-struttin' around town this morning just like he owned the place. Nobody's seen him the last couple days and we figure he musta led them outlaws here."

The big chested man said impatiently, "What in hell are you talkin' about?"

Doc, who always wilted in the face of force, said, "I'm just tellin' you what people say. They say he was walkin' around town with the outlaws."

"Was he armed?"

"I suppose so."

"You suppose so?"

Ed spoke feebly. "He was out at Carpenter Springs with his sister the last couple days. I went out there and fetched 'em back. We got back last night. So, he couldn't a-brought no outlaws."

Doc excused himself and rushed out.

The big chested man told Ed, "I'll see if I can't find Blackie."

He went out and southward down the street. A group of about thirty people were standing in the street, trying to buy the horse and the rifle of a miner who, having seen the smoke from the fires, had ridden into town.

The big chested man asked, "Anybody seen Blackie Sheffield?"

A man said quickly, "He went with the bandits."

"What in hell was he doin' with the bandits?"

Another man said, "Word is that he led them here."

"Word is? What do you mean, 'Word is?!' He was in the mountains with his sister for two or three days, and Ed Ringsley went out there to get 'em. They got home last night. That's what your 'Word is' is worth. Did anybody here see him with the outlaws?"

Several people said they had.

"Was he armed?"

Some people said he was, some said not.

The big chested man said, "Well, it seems most likely to me that he must've been taken prisoner. Has anybody seen his mother or sister?"

"There's no one alive out there," said one man. "When the bandits left here, they went out there and shot the place up and burnt the barn down and stole their horses. I watched it from the edge of town. You can see the empty corral and the burnt down barn."

"Well, that pretty well tells you that Blackie was took prisoner. Do you think if he was armed he'd allowed the bandits to kill his kin?" The big chested man added impatiently, "I never saw the like of some folks!"

He turned on his heel and walked back to the Gold Creek Saloon where he stayed with Ed Ringsley until Ed died.

* * *

From a distance, people had seen the empty store building burn to the ground across from the Marshal's office. No one had gone up there to fight it. They knew that it contained powder and ammunition and was dangerous; besides, there were no buildings nearby to be endangered except for the

Marshal's office. Moreover, the owner of the building did not live in town and there was no one to be very concerned about it.

*   *   *

Altogether, six miners rode into town as a result of seeing the smoke. But, none of them was willing to sell his horse or rifle. Apaches were one worry. Outlaws were another. Claim jumpers were yet another. Mining claim laws were such that it was difficult to prove your claim if you had left it and someone else moved in and started working it. All he had to do was to burn your claim markers and replace them with his own. He could kill you, saying that you had tried to jump his claim. Consequently, at least one partner of a claim had to stay on the claim ready to shoot any trespassers who failed to move off when ordered to do so. If a fellow had no gun to defend his claim, that was too bad for him. He could be shot or bludgeoned and his body thrown off the claim.

Finally, a collection was taken and two men were sent into the mountains on foot to see if they could buy, rent, or borrow two horses and two rifles so that they could ride to Silver City to get horses and guns sent up.

The two men got back late that afternoon with a horse and rifle apiece. They left immediately for Silver City.

Eighteen

Quite weak from loss of blood, and in pain, Sarah lay on her bed until late afternoon. A rifle and a shotgun lay beside her. She knew that if Blackie had been able, he would have come home long ago, so he was either still in the jail or he was seriously hurt—or dead.

She had been thirsty a lot today; and right now she was thirsty again. She leaned over the edge of the bed and lifted the dipper from the water bucket she had dragged from the front room this morning. She swallowed some water, replaced the dipper, and then lay back, feeling dizzy and tired from the effort.

She knew that she could die if she did not get help. After some mental debate, she decided to crawl out to the porch and shoot the rifle as a signal. It was bound to be heard. What the hearers made of the sound might be another matter, however.

Getting onto her hands and knees on the floor proved to be painful and difficult. Crawling, dragging the rifle, she had to rest twice before she finally made the front porch. The floor seemed surprisingly cold to her.

On the porch, after another rest, Sarah pointed the rifle generally toward the burnt-out hillside to the west of town. She pulled the trigger, and the .45-70 banged loudly. She waited a few minutes, but saw no one appear at the south edge of town. She noticed that her vision was somewhat dimmed.

Chilled, and now trembling, Sarah was aware that she should not feel so cold in the heat of the afternoon. She fired her rifle again. Shivering, she waited only a couple of minutes and then crawled back into the house. Near the kitchen stove, she opened the cabinet where leftovers were kept. Nearly all of last night's supper was there. She took two chicken legs and two biscuits, wrapped them in a towel and, after a rest, dragged them and the rifle back to the bedroom. She rested again before crawling onto the bed and under the covers.

Cold, exhausted, in pain, and now suddenly depressed, Sarah felt alone, her life in ruin. The life she had built from the age of seventeen now seemed laid waste. The husband whom she had loved so much had now been dead three years. Her son might be dead in town. Her daughter, if she was still alive, was in the hands of some terrible men, and the probability was very high that, even if the girl lived, Sarah would never see her again.

She turned her head now and looked at the family portrait in its silver frame on her dresser. It had been taken at a photographer's studio in Silver City five years ago. Blackie stood there in his first suit, looking so self reliant at the age of twelve. The blonde streaks in his brown hair were all that was left of the blonde hair he had been born with. Sarah had thought that he would grow up a blonde like his father, but most of his hair had gradually turned brown. Beside him, Dusty's guileless beauty was already evident at the age of eleven. She resembled her father in more ways than one. Butch, in the role that he loved the most, that of father and husband, stood there with his hand on Sarah's shoulder. Sarah had been quite proud of this husband of hers, a man whom women generally could not keep their eyes from, and she had been pleased one day when he had told her that she was so good looking it made him proud to be seen with her.

*   *   *

She had been born Sarah Carter Bowen on a farm near Cincinnati, Ohio on December second, 1842. The family had pulled up stakes in 1846, when Sarah was three, and had moved by covered wagon to St. Louis where her parents then had opened a general store. It proved to be a fortunate move; for in 1846 the United States had gone to war with Mexico, and, after two years of it, Mexico had—with the treaty of Guadalupe de Hildago—given up California and New Mexico (which included Arizona in those days). There had followed that year—1848—and later, several spectacular gold, silver, and copper strikes in California, Arizona, Nevada, New Mexico, South Dakota, and Wyoming. Consequently, St. Louis, which was the main jumping off point for immigrants and adventurers heading for all points west, became a hotbed of commercial activity. Many of these immigrants and adventurers had provisioned themselves from Bowen's General Store. So the Bowen family had done well in St. Louis, and had lived comfortably on five acres in town.

When Sarah was eight, her parents let her start raising her own chickens and ducks and selling them and their eggs to neighbors and other townspeople. It was profitable, and her mother helped her open a savings account at a nearby bank. Piano lessons were among the things Sarah bought with her own money.

At fifteen years of age, when her mother allowed her to start dating, Sarah was in immediate demand. She had both beauty and intelligence. Furthermore, she was well read, and had a large working vocabulary. School work was fascinating. Learning came so easily for her, it was as if she had known all these things before, a long time ago, and was merely being reminded of them.

On top of her other attributes and accomplishments, she played piano with skill.

So she never lacked invitations to parties, picnics, and outings of all sorts.

Marriage, though, was not in her plans for a while—she wanted to be a school teacher. She loved and respected knowledge and learning; and she hoped, upon graduation, to get a job teaching in the private school she attended.

But, then, one evening when she was seventeen, Sarah met Butch Sheffield at a social event for some politically prominent families. Sarah had been invited by a girl friend from school and asked if she would mind playing the piano. Of course she did not mind. So she played with her usual expertise that night, and afterward received her due praise. Moreover, the Governor of Missouri introduced himself to her and her escort and said how pleased he was that she had come.

Sarah's escort beamed with pride.

Minutes later, a schoolgirl chum came by with her own date in tow. Showing him off, she introduced Sarah to Butch Sheffield. Sarah had never seen such a handsome man in her life. A rugged blonde, twenty-two years of age, he exuded good natured charm. Sarah was immediately taken with him. And he very quickly made a play for her. She thought that, under the circumstances, it was bad manners on his part; but she was flattered nonetheless. The girl friend whisked him off then.

Four or five weeks later, Sarah ran into Butch at a cold weather cookout on the bank of the Mississippi River. He was with a different girl this time, another one of her school mates. Butch and Sarah had a chance to talk for a while, and she was quite impressed with his easy manner and quiet self-confidence. He told her that he was employed as a secretary to a politician, but that he did not have enough work to keep him busy; and that it bothered him a little. The politician just seemed to like having him around.

But, what he really knew, Butch told Sarah, was hunting. He had hunted after school and on weekends all of his life. He had even worked a couple of years ago for a railroad as a professional hunter, supplying construction crews with wild game. Hence his nickname, "Butch," which, as everyone knew, was short for butcher. He speculated that he could earn a very decent living supplying game to mining camps Out West.

Over the next few weeks, Sarah kept running into Butch, and he kept asking her out. And she kept turning him down because on each occasion he had been dating one of her school mates more or less steadily.

Butch went through two girl friends in three months that Sarah knew about. There were rumors at school that his current girl friend had admitted to making love with him. It was juicy gossip. Supposedly, when they made love, Butch withdrew at the last second to avoid getting the girl with child.

Butch finally dropped that girl friend too, and he started coming by Sarah's home and charming her family. Her people took to Butch right off. Even her brother liked him. Sarah dated him several times then, and thought that she was falling in love with him. Butch casually mentioned marriage, but Sarah skittered off the subject. She had a strong resolve to finish her education. Besides, she was unsure how serious he was about marriage.

Unfortunately for Sarah, Butch's last girl friend was bitter about his dropping her; and, when the opportunity presented itself, she warned Sarah about his fickleness. In defense, Sarah told the girl that Butch had mentioned marriage.

"Oh, he talked marriage to me, too," the girl lied, "but, all he wanted was to get into me. You watch, he'll get into you and then throw you over too."

Butch was a charmingly persuasive man with everyone Sarah saw him deal with; and, to a girl in love with him, he was practically irresistible; so in the end he succeeded in seducing Sarah. And, she, confident that he would take measures to avoid getting her with child, made love to him eagerly and with intense passion. It was beautiful. But afterward she was frightened because he had not withdrawn at the last instant. She did not let him make love to her again until after she had her monthly—until she had proven to herself what she had heard some girls claim: that making love did not automatically make babies.

So she found it easy to give in to Butch again.

But she missed her next monthly. And remembering what her school mate had said about Butch tossing her over, she was frightened. To give birth to a child out of wedlock would make her a social outcast. She could never expect to get a teaching job then. Worse, the child, a "bastard," would be a social outcast too. She would have to move far away and pretend to be a widow. Frightened as she was, she did not lose her head. She gave herself two additional weeks to make sure that it was not just something out of rhythm in her body.

After two weeks, she was sure; so she made plans to discuss it with Butch—and she made contingency plans. She knew that one of the local churches maintained a home for unwed mothers in Memphis, Tennessee. If Butch walked away from her now, she would go to that church for help.

That night, her breath coming in thimblefuls, she told Butch that she was with child.

Butch was simply thrilled. But he could see that she was frightened.

He smiled happily, took her hands in his, and said easily, "Good. Now you have to marry me."

The fear peeled off of her in laughter.

When she had had her last giggle, he took her in his arms and said, "Now I know why you've been acting so oddly the last couple of weeks."

"I was scared."

He patted her back. "And all unnecessarily." He gave her a gentle commandment: "Please don't keep secrets from me ever again. They could ruin our marriage."

So, then, she revealed to him what his ex-girl friend had told her about his throwing Sarah over after "getting into" her.

Butch shook his head. "Well, now that she's made our affair public.... She was the one who hinted at marriage; I steered clear of the subject. In fact, I did what I could to avoid making a baby. With you, it was different; I'm in love with you."

She kissed him fiercely.

He added gently, "Next time somebody tells you anything bad about me, do me the courtesy of telling me right away. It could save us a lot of trouble."

"All right, darling."

Their marriage was immediate.

Butch, who had enjoyed life before he had met Sarah, made it clear to her that he had never been so happy as now.

It thrilled him to come home after work and find her there, to have her next to him when they walked down the street, to awaken in the night and find her sleeping beside him. Just touching his hand to her in the night gave him the sensation of something warm and pleasurable rushing up his arm to his shoulder where it then flooded his whole body.

According to him, she was the best thing that had ever happened to him.

For Sarah, life before marriage had been fun, but marriage to Butch was glorious. The only exception was for a couple of months during that first pregnancy. So as to not have to wait until next summer, they started out westward by wagon right in the middle of her gestation. And, of course, no one rode much in the wagons. It was hard enough on four mules to draw the big, laden wagons all day long, into and out of gullies and sandy washes and creek beds and across rivers and up and down hills and mountains without having to lug passengers too. To spare the mules, everyone but the smallest children walked much of the time. And along the way, beside the trail, they kept seeing fine furniture and good tools and rotted food that had been cast from overloaded wagons that had preceded them on the trail. Sometimes, they saw graves too.

However, when Sarah thought that she might miscarry, Butch made her ride. But the grinding and jolting was hard on her too. And on the baby.

She was cross and temperamental. Butch was his old even tempered self, never taking offense. He apologized for his stupidity at starting out while she was pregnant. And he did everything he could to make it easier on her. They both knew, however, that they could not stop now that they were on their way. To drop out of the wagon train would be to risk death from several causes out there.

At any rate, she did not miscarry; and Blackie was born James Steven on November eight, 1861 in New Mexico Territory, at Pinos Altos, a gold mining camp originally settled by Spaniards in 1804. The town had been re-founded by Americans in 1859, the Spaniards having been driven out by Apaches early in the century.

With the experience of her first pregnancy behind them, Butch made sure that everything was just so for Sarah during her pregnancy with Dusty. And it was an easy pregnancy; and Dusty was a quiet, happy baby too.

In her extensive reading, Sarah had somewhere read that bad things which happen during pregnancy can sometimes affect the child in later life. And over the years she had wondered if that rough pregnancy, with her uncharacteristic temperamentalness, had not been where Blackie's temperamentalness had come from. Well, she had no way of knowing for sure. At any rate, Blackie had surely not inherited it from Butch.

For all of Butch's strong points, he had one important shortcoming: he spent too much money. So Sarah had realized right away in St. Louis that she would have to manage their money. Butch had agreed easily, saying he was lucky to have a wife so capable as she.

At Pinos Altos, that rough and tumble camp where most people were striving to get rich quickly, Sarah immediately started raising chickens and ducks again. Butch took up market hunting again too. Sarah and Butch were satisfied to get rich slowly.

When the gold rush at Gold Creek started, Butch rode up there and took a look. Then he took Sarah up for a look, and together, they decided to move to Gold Creek.

It was eight years after Dusty's birth before Sarah was pregnant again. The whole family looked forward to this new addition. The children were quite excited about the expected birth. Butch, who loved and was loved by children—even Blackie's and Dusty's friends loved him—was making sure that everything was right for Sarah and the newcomer.

Despite everything, she miscarried twins; and the whole family was terribly upset. The children cried, and Butch turned actually pale for a couple of days. Nine year old Blackie tried to be brave in Sarah's presence and not cry, and he stayed home from school for the three days that she was in bed, and he did his chores and then sat the rest of each day close at hand in case he could do anything for her. Sarah did not insist that he go to school; she recognized that he was terribly upset over the loss of his siblings.

Nineteen

See, there he is," the small boy half whispered to another boy his age.

It was twilight, the day of the raid on Gold Creek, and the boys were peeking through the door into the darkened Marshal's office where the Marshal's dead body lay in the bed. They were convinced that they were not supposed to be there, and it was frightening to be looking at a dead man there in the semi-darkness with no grown-ups nearby.

"Is he dead?" the second boy, uncertain, half whispered.

"Sure, he's dead, you dummy."

Suddenly, they heard the sound of muffled footsteps.

Then Blackie's voice said, "Hey, you boys."

The boys screamed, turned, and ran.

Through the bars on the jail cell door, Blackie shouted, "Hey! Come back! Heyyyyyyy!"

The boys ran for all they were worth, putting as much distance as they could between them and the Marshal's "ghost."

Blackie grabbed the bars in the door and jerked at them in frustration. He and the banker's daughter—Amy Tyson was her name—had taken turns shouting throughout the day. But, no one had come to let them out. The heat from the fire across the road had heated the Marshal's Office, and then the summer sun had beat down on the un-ventilated jail cell all day long; it was stifling in there. They had sweated the day through; but there had been no drinking water to replace what their bodies lost.

They had known each other only by sight before; and so, to pass the time, they had talked on and off throughout the day, getting to know each other; but, finally, with the heat and the thirst and the hunger, they had grown silent.

Blackie was sure that something had happened to his mother and sister. Had they been able to, they would have come for him by now. He felt physically sick about it.

Twenty

At sundown of the following day, Blackie and Amy Tyson were still in the jail, and by now their tongues were swollen from lack of water, and their speech was slurred by that swelling and by the dryness of their mouths and throats. There was hardly any talk, however, because they were dozing and dreaming a lot. Their dreams were semi-hallucinatory in nature, as commonly occurs to people dying of thirst.

It was after dark when a burly man walked up to the Marshal's office carrying a lantern and a rifle. He peered in through the open door, and then walked inside and looked around. He looked at the jail door.

"Anybody here?"

No one answered him.

Blackie had heard him, but he had been dreaming and the man's footsteps and voice had weaved right into his dream.

The burly man turned and looked at the dead Marshal. They had forgotten about him today when they had buried the rest of the dead. Well, they could do it tomorrow. The burly man was exhausted tonight. He walked from the office and headed toward home.

Blackie had heard the man walk out of the office, and it suddenly occurred to him that it was not part of his dream. It occurred to him then that the question might not have been part of his dream either.

Blackie answered, "Y...." His voice cracked.

Mustering all his remaining strength, he sprang to his feet and to the jail door. Through the bars, he made a noise.

"Yaath!"

The burly man heard the noise, but he did not know what it was. He turned his head as he walked.

It came again, a faint, "Yaath."

The man stopped and turned. He listened.

There was a weak noise that might have been, "Hey!" It did not quite sound like human speech, but what else could it be?

The man retraced his steps.

In front of the Marshal's office, he called out, "Anybody here?"

The voice came from inside: "Yaath!"

Excited, the man went back in with his lantern and saw Blackie's strained face at the barred window.

"I'll be switched! Your ma insisted you'd be here. But I didn't think so, 'cause people said you rode out with them bandits. Look here, where did the Marshal keep the key? I'll get you outa there."

The man barely understood Blackie when he said there was no key, to get an ax, but to give "uthh" water first. Blackie lisped his s's badly.

"Us? You got somebody else in there?"

"Amy Tythnnn."

"Amy Tyson?! Her people think the bandits took her! Wait'll they hear...."

"Barney! Water!"

"Oh! Sure!"

In his condition, Blackie was a little panicky about the water.

Barney brought the water bucket over and handed Blackie a full dipper through the bars. Blackie drank it very slowly and then handed it back empty. Barney refilled it and handed it through the bars. Blackie took it and turned away.

"Amy! Water."

Barney said, "I'll go fetch an ax."

When he returned, he told the youngsters to stand clear of the door. He began work on splitting the door in the center. It was built strongly, and it took him several minutes to cave it in. He wrenched the two pieces out of the way, and Blackie and Amy slowly walked out. Blackie had his arm around Amy, supporting her. They were both weak.

The youngsters drank more water and then the three of them walked down the steps into the street. Amy leaned on Blackie. Blackie's other hand gripped Barney's near shoulder for support. Barney carried the lantern.

The cool, fresh air smelled sweet to the youngsters and helped to revive them.

Blackie could talk just a little better now; and he found that if he talked very slowly and took care, he could avoid the heavy lisp.

"I think....I'm too weak....to walk home. Can I borrow....your horth?"

"My horse is dead. The bandits shot every horse they didn't take with 'em. We figure they did it to keep us from followin' 'em."

They moved slowly down Main Street toward the center of town.

Right now, thoughts and words came with an effort to Blackie. He had to formulate what he wanted to ask Barney.

"If my mother and....sister," he said very slowly, "had been all right....they would've come for me yethterday.... I've had two dayth....to get ready for it.... You can tell me....the....worst."

Barney looked at him and nodded. "I went out there. My younguns needed milk and eggs. And your ma hadn't delivered in a couple days, so I went out there late today. Found a couple dead bandits in the yard—that's where I got this rifle—and I found your ma inside, shot in the leg. She was runnin' a fever and was a little out of her head and was weak as a kitten. She can't get around at all; and the bandits got your horses. She insisted you were in jail; but I was so sure from what people'd said that the bandits took you with 'em, I went ahead and fed the chickens and ducks, and gathered the eggs. And I milked the cows. They was mooin' up a storm! Must've been in dreadful pain. Hadn't been milked in two days. Their tits was drippin' milk, and it was clabbered."

"And Dusty?"

Barney hesitated. "Looks like they took Dusty."

Amy reacted. "Oh, Blackie!"

Barney went on. "A shotgun and a knife—your ma says they're Dusty's—they was on the ground back of the what's left of the barn—they burnt it down, the bandits did. The knife was bloody; but, the blood probably belongs to a bandit who's layin' there dead from stabbin'.

"Blackie, you might think somebody ought'n to've gone out there sooner; but, God, there's been enough to keep everybody busy here in town. We had to get them fires out before they spread any more. It took us hours. And the dead and wounded had to be cared for. We had to dig graves and bury more'n fifty people today. And the horse carcasses are still all over the place. They say some mule skinners'll be down from the sawmill tomorrow to drag the carcasses out of town.... And then the Army was here this morning."

"The Army?"

"Yep. About twenty soldiers, and two Apache scouts. Seems they been lookin' for the bandits for days. They took up the chase from here. Two townspeople went with 'em: Jed Simmons, the squawman, and Randy Hicks whose wife got took by the bandits.

"Anyway, my missus is out there with your ma now; so don't worry about her. She's awful weak, I guess she bled a lot, but I think she's gonna be all right."

They walked on down the street, and the youngsters had to stop and rest twice. They walked over to Carver Street and up to the Tyson's big house that had a big, oval, etched glass window in the front door. They walked up the steps, and Amy opened the door. They walked inside, and down the hall, their footsteps clearly audible.

At the sound of the footsteps, Mrs. Tyson walked from the living room into the hall. Her eyes jumped wide and she clapped her hand over her mouth and nearly fainted. Seeing her react so, her husband and four other children rushed into the hall.

It was gleeful Pandemonium for several minutes.

The Tysons tried to feed Blackie, but he had been three days without food, and his stomach had shrunk; so he vomited the little bit of leftovers they got him to swallow. Consequently, Mrs. Tyson sent two of her children canvassing neighbors for soup. Blackie was able to hold down a few spoonfuls of what they brought back. A pile of neighbors, informed by the Tyson kids, came to see Amy, and to offer congratulations to the Tysons, and to hear the story.

Amy still could not speak well, so everyone got very quiet while she told how Blackie had saved her from the desperados. Mrs. Tyson cried and came over to Blackie where he sat and hugged his head to her breast.

*   *   *

Later, when Blackie and Barney walked up the steps and into the Sheffield house, they could smell chicken broth cooking on the stove. A lantern was burning in Sarah's bedroom. Barney's short, stocky wife Gert came to the bedroom doorway in a faded blue dress.

"God, Almighty," said Gert. "Were you in the jail?"

"Yeah."

"We were so sure you'd gone with the bandits. But, your ma insisted you weren't with 'em when they came here."

Barney said to his wife, "And that ain't all—the Tyson girl was in there with him."

"Praise God."

"Her people are a mighty happy bunch right now."

Blackie went on into the bedroom. He was shocked by what he saw.

All of his life his mother had been beautiful. He had often found pleasure in just looking at her, of comparing her with other women in town and in Slilver City. But, tonight, her face was drawn and bloodless, and there were dark circles around her sunken eyes.

He approached the bed, bent down, and they hugged. She held onto him feebly for a long time.

Finally, Barney said, "We'll be goin' on home now. We'll come back in the mornin' and I'll help you milk them cows—I don't imagine you'll be feelin' strong enough to do all of 'em by yourself yet. And Gert will be wantin' to see to you, Mrs. Sheffield."

Sarah said faintly, "Good night. And thank you for everything."

Blackie walked out of the bedroom. "Did you get your eggs?"

"Oh," said Barney, "eggs. I would've forgot 'em. We'll need a couple dozen." Barney fumbled in his pocket for money.

Blackie said, "Forget about money. Just take whatever you need from the crock in the hallway."

"Well, that's mighty gen'rous of you."

"For the next year, your milk and eggs are free."

Gert said, "Oh, now, we can't take that. That's too much."

"No, it's not."

She smiled, "We'll see you tomorrow mornin' about sun up, and we can argue it then."

Watching Barney and Gert from the front doorway as they walked down the front steps with their lantern and started across the yard, Blackie was suddenly aware of his exhaustion. He turned and went back into his mother's bedroom. He knelt beside the bed and took her hand. She squeezed his weakly. She started to cry.

"Oh, Blackie, they've got Dusty."

"I know."

She continued to cry, and he leaned over and put his arms around her.

He had never seen her vulnerable before. She had always been the one who was on top of things, the one who could think things out, and who never stopped until things were handled. Even when his father had turned up missing, it was she who had organized the search for him, and it was she who had finally called it off when it became apparent to her that he must be dead and that it was a waste to continue searching. She had cried then too, but it had been different. She had shed her tears while she still ran the household and kept life going on.

Twenty-One

Mr. and Mrs. Tyson walked across the Sheffield front yard the following day about noon. The dead horse was still there, bloated in death, drawing flies, and stinking. The dead men had been buried now by men Blackie had hired. He had been too weak to do it himself.

Fred Tyson carried a large wicker basket with a cloth over the top. They climbed the steps of the porch and Mrs. Tyson rapped lightly on the front door, opened it, and peeked in.

"Yoo-hoo! It's the Tysons."

Dressed except for boots, Blackie walked from his bedroom where he had been lying down. He smiled.

"Come on in."

The Tysons came in. Seeing Blackie smile, Fred Tyson was reminded of what his wife and daughters had said: Blackie had a smile that would warm even the Devil's heart.

Fred asked, "How are you feeling?"

"Still a bit weak. I went down the creek about four miles a while ago, tracking the horse that belonged to one of the desperados my mother shot. He was spooky and I had to do a lot of running to catch him. The effort wore me out. I was just resting up."

Mrs. Tyson said to her husband, "Fred, you visit with Blackie. I'm going to see to his mother." She said to Blackie, "We brought a basket of food that just takes warming up."

"Much obliged."

Blackie sat on the couch.

Fred Tyson set the basket on the dining table. He looked around the big room. Most of the windows had been shot out. There was a rack of several rifles and shotguns on the wall. Fred Tyson took a chair. He was tired and worried. He tried to not think of what worried him. He managed a smile.

"Well, Blackie, I may as well tell you that Amy thinks you're the world's biggest hero."

171

Blackie smiled.

Fred went on, "This has been the biggest adventure of her life. And, don't say I told you so, but she's developed quite a crush on you."

"God, I don't see how. That hot, stinky jail cell seems hardly a place to win a girl's heart."

Fred smiled merrily. "That just goes to show that you must be quite a man."

Blackie laughed. Fred watched him laugh and then joined in.

After they had had their laugh, Fred's worry crept back up on him. He sighed.

"You know, Blackie, just an hour ago, I finished an audit of the bank. They got away with close to a hundred thousand dollars in gold ingots that belonged to the Yellow Lode. Besides that, they got some five thousand dollars in gold and silver coin. They could have gotten more, but they seemed in a hurry. They missed all the greenbacks. Probably the paper money wouldn't be any good down in Mexico anyway. That American fellow somehow knew about the ingots, and that was what he was after. Anyway, because of what you did for Amy, I've made sure that your mother's account is safe. You know, she's saved a lot of money from her chickens and cows, and from your and your father's hunting. Her money's over there in the bottom of that basket we just brought. All of it."

"That's awfully nice of you."

Fred nodded. "As for myself, I hope those soldiers catch up with the desperados, because if they don't I'm bankrupt."

Blackie restrained his tongue for a moment, but finally said, "I hate to be a wet blanket, but the soldiers won't catch them. The desperados had a day and a half head start, and they'll have been riding night and day. They were going south past Silver, picking up the Old Janos Trail that goes down through Playas Valley and Dog Springs into Chihuahua. Now, that's a hundred and fifty miles. But, you can bet your money that they're already in Mexico."

"Do you think that's possible? After all, they had all those girls with them, and pack horses. That would surely slow them down."

Blackie's voice turned hard. "They'll drive the horses until they die. They'll have already killed any of the women who couldn't keep up."

Fred Tyson shuddered. Finally, he asked, "How are you so sure?"

"The American told me how it was going to be."

Fred said glumly, "A lot of people are pinning hopes on the Army. You paint a discouraging picture."

"I'm sorry."

"Your outlook doesn't lay down much hope for anyone, including your sister, does it?"

"Dusty's a good horsewoman. She's used to long rides. Besides that, she was dressed warmly when they took her; that'll help save her strength."

"What I meant was hope of her ever coming home."

After a moment's hesitation, Blackie said, "I've made plans.... I sent a rider for Morgan on that horse I found. Morgan could be here tomorrow night with horses, and I should be strong enough to leave the next morning." He added slowly and emphatically, *"If my sister's alive, I intend to bring her back."*

Twenty-Two

Blackie read aloud, "Jim and Mathilda embraced and kissed and told each other of their love. The End." It was the day after the Tysons' visit, and he was sitting in a straight backed chair beside his mother's bed. The story was in a magazine from New York that had come in on the stage.

"Thank you, dear," his mother said.

"Did you like it?"

"Not very much. How about you?"

"Well, Jim seemed....uh....I don't know...."

"Uncommunicative?"

"Exactly. And I didn't like him much. And Mathilda was silly and weak. I couldn't have fallen in love with anybody like her. I like strong women like you."

Sarah gave a little smile. "I don't feel very strong right now."

"This is the first time I've ever seen you out of action. Now, this Mathilda gal, she would've let those desperados ride right up and do with her what they wanted while she screamed for a man to come help her."

Sarah reached and patted Blackie's knee.

Blackie asked, "You want to hear another story?"

"Oh, don't let me use up your entire day. I'm sure you've got some important things to do."

"I've got everything handled. I'm just waiting for Morgan now. I'm hoping he'll be here tonight."

"Is the posse all set?"

"Yes."

"How big?"

"Only three people besides me and Morgan," he admitted. "The Army being here ruined things as far as a posse is concerned. Everybody is hoping the Army will catch up with the desperados. And a lot of people have it fixed in their minds that the Army will catch them. It reminds me of something

174

you once told me: When the truth is unpleasant, some people will substitute an illusion."

"I don't remember telling you that, but it's true."

He did not tell his mother about the people who had infuriated him by telling him that if the soldiers could not handle the desperados, it was foolish for him to think that he could.

Sarah asked Blackie, "Who's in the posse?"

"Otis Shales, for one; they took his wife Becky. And then there's David Brown; they got his wife too. They have a baby girl, and he's got somebody to take care of her while we're gone. And Charles Cistrom. You know, he's been like a puppy around Dusty since she was thirteen. He probably thinks that if he rides up and helps save her, she'll fall in love with him. I don't think he has a chance of that. You know how Dusty is. She's not likely to confuse gratefulness with love."

Unspoken between Sarah and Blackie, of course, was the thought that Dusty might already be dead.

Blackie continued, "Now, two men went with the soldiers when they came through here. If those two didn't go on by themselves when the soldiers turned back, we'll meet them on their way home. They may want to go with us."

"That's not a very big posse." Sarah was concerned.

"I know. But I went all over town, and only three said they would go with me.... Well, not quite. Jet Stevens wanted to go; but, you know, with his back trouble we couldn't take him. He'd get ten-twenty miles on horseback and we'd have to bring him back by wagon."

"I hate to even think of Jettie being in the hands of those men. She's such a nice girl."

Blackie nodded agreement.

Sarah went on, "I don't mean any of the other girls weren't nice. None of them deserved this."

"I know what you meant. Jettie is a nice girl. Really nice."

"It's odd how evil people like to take what is beautiful or nice and ruin it."

Blackie thought about her last comment. Then he nodded. "That's one of those things you say to me that I'll be thinking about for the next month."

He thought some more about it and then said, "Well, anyway, about the posse: horses are a problem. We don't have horses yet. Three and a half days ago, a couple riders went to Silver to bring back some horses. They're not back yet, and I won't wait. I'll go tomorrow even if I have to go alone. I'll get a couple of horses one way or another."

"Don't you think Morgan will get here tonight?"

"I don't see why not. But if he doesn't for some reason, I'm leaving in the morning anyway. I'll leave a map of the route I think they're taking. And I'll leave markers along the way."

"Do you think that's wise? to go by yourself?"

"Yes. It's been four days already. Every day I wait, the more chance of my not overtaking them. Or of them splitting up and of me following the wrong ones and never finding Dusty. And the more chance of somebody turning up dead." He did not say anything for a moment, and then, in a choked voice, said harshly, "I'm not waiting!"

Sarah saw tears in his eyes. He got up and walked from the room.

Lying there, with the pain in her leg a distraction, Sarah had mixed feelings about Blackie going after his sister. On the one hand, she wanted him to do everything possible to save Dusty if she was still alive. But, on the other hand, if Blackie died trying to save Dusty, Sarah would have lost them both.

Sarah remembered now a family picnic which she and Butch and the kids had gone on twelve years ago. The four of them had ridden down Gold Creek Road in the buckboard; Butch, so achingly handsome, had been driving; and the kids, aged five and four, had been happily riding in the back. And Sarah had suddenly realized what a truly wonderful thing she and Butch were doing, giving these two people, Blackie (James in those days) and Dusty, a chance to live life. By some magic that could be performed only by a man and a woman together, they had conceived these people, and Sarah had borne them, and together she and Butch were taking them through the period of several years when the youngsters could not survive by themselves. It was, she had realized, a priceless gift that she and Butch were giving.

And now, lying wounded, Sarah felt it was important that at least one of her offspring should survive and give that same gift to others.

But, while it was unthinkable for Sarah to abandon Dusty to her fate, the alternative was the very real possibility of Blackie's death. It was one of those choices with which no mother wants to be faced. However, as a matter of fact, she was not faced with it; she knew that she had no choice in the matter.

Ever since that day in the buckboard years ago, she had never lost sight of the fact that Dusty and Blackie, her children, were people who had minds of their own. They had ideas, preferences, and desires that were their own and that did not necessarily reflect hers. Consequently, Sarah had, piecemeal, relinquished control over their lives as quickly as they had shown her that they were willing and able to control themselves. Finally, they had done pretty much as they pleased so long as they performed all the duties that being part of the family required of them. There were, of course, a few things which Sarah had insisted upon having her way about; one thing was their education. The kids had never given her much trouble over those things. Furthermore, they never had seriously questioned that, in the final analysis, around this house, she was the boss.

However, for several years now, Sarah had been quite aware that any control she had over the kids depended upon their agreement that she was the boss. And she knew there would be limits to that agreement, limits beyond which she could not go. Blackie simply would never stay home when there was any hope that Dusty was alive. However mixed were Sarah's feelings about Blackie's going, there would be no talking him out of it. So, lying there, she decided that there was no reason to give it any further thought. He was going, and that was that. There was nothing to be gained by worrying about it.

Blackie was out in the front room for about five minutes getting himself under control.

When he came back, he said, "Don't worry. Morgan will be here tonight."

He sat down, leafed through the magazine, found a story, and began reading aloud.

* * *

The packs and saddles and bridles had burnt in the barn, so Blackie had sent word for Morgan to bring all the necessary tack with him.

Blackie had three piles of supplies and equipment in the front room. He had made one pile for each of two pack horses. The third and much smaller pile was what Blackie would carry on his saddle horse. It included his .45-70 Sharps. On his pack horse, he would carry a small-bore shotgun—a twenty-eight gauge—for rabbits and birds, and his .45-110 Sharps express rifle, both in oil cloth sheaths. He was taking plenty of ammunition. They had always had plenty around the house.

Blackie was restless, and he went over the piles again, writing down what was in each. He took the lists to his mother and had her go over them, mainly just to involve her and keep her company.

When she had gone over them she said, "It looks like you've thought of everything."

The new dog, tied by a rope to the porch to keep it from running off, announced the arrival of the Tyson family with his barking. Blackie was suddenly giddy. Their arrival signaled an end to an afternoon of waiting for things to start happening.

Mrs. Tyson rapped, opened the door, and peeked in.

Blackie said heartily, "Come on in."

They came in, milling around. The five youngsters, three boys and two girls, were excited, especially Amy. She had a cloth bag of clothes and some personal things.

Blackie said to Amy, "Take your things right into that bedroom and put them on Dusty's bed. Hers is the smaller one. Tomorrow, after I leave you can use my bed; it's bigger. Poor Dusty—when we get back, I've got to make her a bigger bed. She's had that same one since she was eleven."

Mrs. Tyson tried to smile. "Couldn't Amy sleep out here on the floor tonight?"

The Tysons had a bigger house, and the boys slept in one bedroom and the girls in another.

Blackie gave a surprised laugh. "Mrs. Tyson, Amy and I spent two days and a night in an eight by eight jail cell. There wasn't much chance for privacy there. So, if you're concerned about modesty, it's too late. As for anything else, Amy and I are good friends, but we're not lovers." He winked at Amy. "Yet."

Disconcerted, Mrs. Tyson blushed. She pulled Blackie aside and spoke in a low, stressed voice.

"The child is infatuated with you!"

Blackie could not help being amused by Mrs. Tyson.

"There is really nothing to worry about, but if you feel this way, I'll sleep out here on the floor tonight. And Amy can sleep in my bed."

Fred Tyson cut in, "Oh, nonsense. If we don't know that Blackie is an honorable man, we don't know anything. And Amy is a responsible young lady or I wouldn't let her stay out here at all." He ordered with finality, "Amy, you sleep in Dusty's bed tonight; and Blackie, you sleep in your own bed."

Mrs. Tyson was embarrassed by the flap she had started. She said, "I'll go in and see to Sarah."

Amy took her things into the bedroom.

Blackie called to her, "The shotgun under your bed is loaded. It's Dusty's. It's yours while you're here. Have you ever shot one?"

"No," she called from the bedroom.

"I'll take you over against the hillside in a little bit and show you how to work it."

Mrs. Tyson could not help herself. Concerned, she stepped from Sarah's bedroom.

"Do you think there's any need?"

"Probably not. But who would have thought that those desperados would come by here? Mrs. Tyson, if my mother hadn't had guns and known how to shoot them the other morning, she would be dead or in Mexico today."

Mrs. Tyson looked at Blackie for a moment and then she realized whom she was talking to. It was Blackie Sheffield, in September of 1878. He was the young man who, with his presence of mind, had saved Amy the other morning. Mrs. Tyson's brow cleared

"All right, Blackie. I'll leave it to your judgment. I'm sorry to have been such a fussbudget."

Later, when the family was walking home without Amy, Mrs. Tyson would say to Fred, "I suppose if something did happen, we couldn't hope for a better son-in-law. He's such a nice boy. And they're certainly not poor. I didn't know how well off they were until I saw all that money in the basket yesterday. Speaking of money reminds me: will we have to give up our house?"

"We'll have to give up everything. We might be able to get three thousand for the house, which will cover only part of the bank deposits. I guess it won't hurt us to live in a shanty up on the hillside until I get started again at something. At least we have Amy."

"Yes." She thought for a bit about their situation. Then, "Anyway, as I was saying about Blackie: I hear that he's a hard worker. And, if nothing else, he certainly is a handsome devil."

Her husband put a reassuring arm around her. "Well, nothing is going to happen. We're just giving Amy a chance to repay Blackie. I never saw anyone so relieved as Blackie this morning when I suggested that Amy stay out there to

look after his mother. And you and other ladies will be looking in on them throughout the day. It'll be a good experience
for her; and we've got to stop thinking of her as a child. She'll
be married and gone before we know it."

Meanwhile, Blackie and Amy were collecting the afternoon eggs from the nests in the chicken coops. He showed
her where the feed was kept in its shed, and showed her how
much to give the ducks and chickens.

Amy finally said, "I'm sorry about the fuss my mother
made."

"Oh, she's gotten used to things in that big house of yours.
Out here, we're just like most other people: I take a bath
every Saturday night in a wash tub beside the stove with my
mother and sister right there doing dishes or whatever. And
whoever is handy washes my back. The only thing I don't like
about it is that I have to take my bath after they do. Do you
think it's fair that men have to use the bath water last?"

Amy was uncertain how to answer him. She wanted to be
agreeable. But finally she caught on that he wasn't serious in
his complaint. She grinned impishly. "Well, sure its fair."

"I might have known. You're a woman, after all."

His calling her a woman—and not a girl—filled her with
pleasure.

It was almost sundown when Morgan arrived with six
horses. Two horses with saddles and bridles, two spare saddle
horses, and two pack horses with empty packs. Blackie heard
them crossing the creek, and then the dog barking, and he
went out and waited on the porch. Neither spoke as the big
man rode across the yard and up to the hitching rail. Morgan
dismounted and tied the horses. He walked up the stairs to
the porch where his friend stood with an expression that said
thanks and a lot of other things. They gripped each other's
hand. Blackie threw his arm around Morgan's shoulders and
gave a hug. The big man returned the gesture.

"How's your mother?"

"She'll be wanting to see you right away."

Morgan reached into his pocket, withdrew some gold pieces and handed them to Blackie.

"Your change. Collier sold me some mighty good horses reasonably. They said to tell you they are praying for Dusty. Billy Cape didn't get there till the middle of the night, so he's laying over and will start at first light tomorrow. He says if you're gone when he gets here, he'll leave your horse at Buzby's Livery unless you leave word otherwise."

"That's good. Our hay burnt up in the barn."

"Coming up the creek road, I overtook a horse trader from Silver with about a score of horses and a small wagon carrying guns. Two Gold Creekers were with him. They all should be along in an hour or so."

"Good. Now we'll have a posse of five instead of two."

"Is that all you could raise?"

"Yeah."

A half hour later, they took their horses into town to Buzby's Livery where they could be stabled and fed for the night. Walking back, they met two armed men riding into town from the south. In the twilight, Blackie could not say that he had seen either before. But Morgan turned when they rode by and mumbled, "Mac," half under his breath.

"Blackie, I've got some people to see. It may take me a while. Don't wait up for me."

Twenty-Three

The following morning, Blackie was up well before daylight, lighting a fire in the wood-burning range, slipping outside with his boots in his hand, and walking to town and bringing the six horses back and tying them to the hitching rail in front of the house.

He pulled his boots off again and went inside to start breakfast. Despite efforts to be quiet, he clanked the stove top lightly as he removed the round iron cover from the fire. Morgan still snored very quietly in his bedroll on the floor across the room. But Amy in her flannel night dress quickly appeared beside Blackie, illuminated by the flames in the stove.

She whispered, "What should I cook?"

He whispered, "Coffee and oatmeal and biscuits and bacon and eggs. Here, I'll light a lantern and show you where everything is."

He lit a lantern, and when he had shown her where things were, he patted her on the back and left her to her work. He was grateful to her for offering to handle breakfast.

He opened the front door and began moving the equipment and supplies out onto the porch. Morgan awoke then and dressed and took the horses down to the creek to water them. As Blackie worked he could hear the familiar noise of biscuit batter being beaten and he could smell the coffee and oatmeal cooking. The pre-dawn light told him that sun-up was not far off.

The new dog was barking now. Two men crossed the creek on foot and waved to Blackie as they walked by the house on their way to the corral where the milk cows were kept at night now. Blackie had made arrangements with the two men to milk and look after the cows while he was gone. The steers would be allowed to range. If he did not get back soon they might all be lost to rustlers.

Morgan brought the horses back and he and Blackie loaded their packs and saddle bags from the piles on the porch. Then they went in and sat down to coffee and oatmeal. Very shortly, they had bacon, eggs and biscuits before them. Amy sat down with them and ate some oatmeal.

Amy kept glancing up at Blackie. The situation—being with him and away from her family, the darkness of the early morning, his handsome face softly illuminated by the lantern, him eating breakfast which she had cooked for him—gave her a special feeling like nothing she had ever felt before. Blackie looked up and smiled at her. She finished her oatmeal and went into the bedroom to dress.

Sarah had lit a lantern in her room, and Blackie now took a cup of chicken broth in to her. Her condition had improved some, and she was sitting up, propped with pillows against the headboard. Blackie put her broth on the night stand, and then sat on the bedside, facing her.

"We'll be leaving as soon as the rest of them get here."

"All right."

"You're looking better every day."

"I must have looked a fright the other evening. You seemed shocked."

"I never saw you look like that before."

"I guess I wasn't far from death." She smiled slightly. "Hand me a mirror, will you?"

He gave her a hand mirror from the dresser. She looked at herself.

"I do look awful. I wonder what Morgan must have thought last night."

Blackie leaned close and whispered, "He's in love with you. He's not likely to let your being wounded bother him."

Sarah was too pale to blush. It came only as a smile.

"Here, give me the hair brush."

She laid the mirror down and slowly brushed her hair. The effort tired her. She examined her work in the mirror.

"Well, that will have to do."

Blackie leaned over and kissed her forehead. Her skin felt better to the touch; warmer and more alive.

When Blackie sat back, Sarah looked past him and smiled. "Come in."

Turning and seeing Morgan walk in. Blackie got up.

"Would you keep Mom company while I do some things? I'll call you when the others get here."

Walking in, Morgan glanced at the family portrait in its silver frame on the dresser. His heart fell. Last night, when he had come into the bedroom, he had been so frightened by Sarah's appearance that he had had no attention for anything else. Now, seeing a photograph of Butch for the first time, he was suddenly less self-confident. He had heard that Butch had been handsome, but he simply had not been prepared for the reality of it. The man had been remarkably handsome. Morgan doubted that he could compete with Butch's memory.

Blackie walked outside and down the porch steps where he stood beside his new horse for a few seconds. The morning air was pleasantly cool. The horse, a powerful bay, stood calmly waiting. Blackie caressingly ran his hand over the animal's muscular shoulder. He immediately felt an increased friendship for the horse. He reached and ran his hand over the whip coiled around his saddle horn. Out on the trail, should one of his trailing horses, tied by rope to his saddle, get a notion to slow down, Blackie need merely lift the whip and show it to the slacker. He would not have to use it; the horse would instinctively know what it meant and would step lively.

He began to talk to his horses each in its turn, getting to know them and letting them get to know him. He touched them as he talked. The horses responded to his words and caresses by twitching their ears, nodding their heads, nibbling at him, shifting their weights, and blowing from their noses. After a bit, Blackie looked up and saw two men walking briskly toward him from town. One was Fred Tyson.

Inside the house, Morgan was sitting on the edge of Sarah's bed. At first they had made small talk about how she was feeling. Now the conversation was about rebuilding the barn when he and Blackie got back.

Eventually, Sarah said, "I know we're asking a great deal of you to go after Dusty like this."

Morgan smiled gently. "I want to go."

He did not say that mingled with his shock and horror over Dusty's abduction was his feeling of honor that Sarah and Blackie had turned to him in their time of need.

Sarah lay her hand on top of his on the bed. "I mean there are over forty bandits, and your posse is quite small. You would be hard pressed to find something more dangerous to do."

Morgan smiled gently. "Yes, I suppose you're right.... We'll try not to take any unnecessary chances."

What else could he say? He knew well the dangers of a manhunt. The desperados would be on the lookout for a posse. These bandits in particular were quite dangerous because they were led by some very clever men. Sarah need not remind him of the odds against him and the other posse members. That he might die a few days from now was a real possibility. He had thought it all out since about three o'clock yesterday morning when Billy Cape had arrived with Blackie's letter, waking the whole Collier Ranch with the news of the raid.

Sitting there, propped up against the headboard, Sarah knew that she might never see Morgan again. She wanted him to be aware that she knew how brave he was.

She said, "Your courage gives me strength."

Her blue eyes seemed to reach inside him.

Morgan experienced a thrill. Sarah's admiration was the most valuable commodity he could possibly want. Was it worth dying for? He reckoned it was. Was he a big fool? Maybe so; but he knew that he would go to his death now before he would allow her to think him even a little cowardly.

Morgan had had time to do a lot of thinking during his ride in from Collier's Ranch yesterday. He had been as honest with himself as he had ever been in his life. For example, he had admitted to himself that he was truly in love for the first time. Additionally, he had mulled over the strange fact that he had left Gold Creek and gone to Collier's Ranch when he could have stayed and gotten a job at a local mine; when he could have stayed and been close to the woman he loved and the family he cared for. Instead, he had "drifted," had left town. It had seemed perfectly reasonable to him until Dusty, by her questions on the morning of his departure, had pointed out the contradictions. She had, by her questions, made him take a peek at the fact that he was leaving because he was in love with Sarah. Confused, he had declined to examine his motives and behavior any more that day. But, thinking about it on the ride back in from Collier's yesterday, he had conceded that his behavior had been irrational. He had thought about it, and in the end, with sudden insight, he had realized that he had always drifted. He had always left town when things had come to a certain point with a woman. Although he had never been in love like this before, he had cared for other women. Some of them would have made good wives too. But he had drifted when things got to the point where he should have spoken about marriage.

And so, riding in from Collier's, he had determined that if Sarah was not too sick from her wound, he would let her know his feelings. But, now, after having seen Butch's photograph, he found himself unable to bring the subject up.

Outside, Blackie watched Fred Tyson and his companion come across the creek, across the yard, and up to him. The other man carried an oil cloth pouch in his left hand.

Fred Tyson smiled at Blackie. "Blackie Sheffield, this is John McHenry."

Blackie said, "Oh, I remember seeing you before. You're the owner of the Yellow Lode Mine."

McHenry and Blackie gripped each other's hand.

"That's right. Blackie, I'm pleased to make your acquaintance. I've heard nothing but good things about you since I arrived last night."

"Thank you. I'm pleased to meet you too."

Blackie realized that this was the "Mac" whom Morgan had recognized yesterday at about dusk.

"Is Morgan here?" McHenry asked.

Blackie smiled. "He's inside sparking with my mom."

McHenry smiled too. "Well, we won't interrupt him, then. Anyway, we talked to him last night. He said we'd have to talk to you.

"Blackie, if after a few days on the trail of these outlaws, you find out that your sister is....ah—God forbid—no longer alive, what will you do then?"

"Come home. That is, unless Otis' wife Becky and David's wife Suzanna are alive. If they are, we go on. If we believe the three are dead, we come home. That's the agreement."

"You wouldn't go on for the sake of vengeance?"

"If I'm hot on their trail, maybe. But to traipse all over Mexico just to kill somebody when it won't bring my sister back—no. I'm needed here."

"All right, that's reasonable. But, we'd like to make you a proposition. I and several other people in town, including Fred, here, want you to press on even if your sister is not alive. The families of those girls want them back alive. They're willing to pay a reward. There are people who lost money and valuables. They'll pay half of the value if you return it to them. That includes me. I'll give you and whoever goes with you half of the value of any gold ingot you return to me. It cost me eighty thousand dollars to extract that gold from the ground; so, even if you got the whole hundred thousand back, after taking your half, I'd still be a loser—but less of a loser. Howsomever, I don't expect you to get all of it. They'll have squandered at least some of it before you catch them."

Fred Tyson added, "And that's not all. We had a Town Meeting last night, and got pledges of reward money for those outlaws. A thousand dollars for the leader, seven hundred and fifty dollars for the American, and one hundred each for the rest of them. And when our letter reaches the Governor in Santa Fe, there'll probably be even more reward money."

Blackie did not respond immediately. He was looking at the ground.

McHenry said, "Blackie, most people don't make a thousand dollars in a whole year."

"I know...." Blackie was troubled. "What did Morgan say?"

"He's all for it, but he says he needs your eyes, and your marksmanship."

Blackie frowned for a long moment. Then he explained himself. "If they didn't have Dusty, I wouldn't go at all. It's not that I don't want to help those other girls. But my mom needs me here. She's going to be in bed for weeks, and maybe have trouble walking for months. We've got all this stock to care for."

McHenry said, "The Town Meeting agreed to extend the arrangements you've made for the care of your mother and her stock."

Blackie looked at McHenry evenly. "It's a possibility that I won't come back at all."

McHenry nodded. "In that case, I will personally see that your mother is taken care of until she's fully recovered."

Blackie thought for a long time. The guarantee of his mother's welfare tipped the scales. But he knew that his mission might end in failure, and it troubled him that someone might count too much on him just as many townspeople were counting on the soldiers.

"All right.... But don't get your hopes up too high. I'll do what I can."

"That's fair enough."

The three gravely shook hands. McHenry handed Blackie the oilcloth pouch.

"This is for Morgan. It contains affidavits before the Justice of The Peace swearing to the raid, the losses, who owns what, and so on. You might need it with the Mexican authorities."

Fred Tyson went up on the porch and stuck his head in the door and asked his daughter how she was doing. From her response and appearance he could tell that she was having the time of her life and that the saddle of all this responsibility suited her just fine.

Although Amy could not have put it into words, she felt for the first time in her life that she was doing something truly important, that she was making a difference in events beyond the narrow confines of a child's world that she had, until now, been restricted to by adults. She was making it possible for Blackie to go on a mission to save his sister and those other girls they had seen file from the jail that terrible morning. She was helping to save lives—if the posse succeeded.

Fred Tyson and John McHenry had returned to town by the time David Brown and Charles Cistrom rode up. Blackie now wondered where the hell Otis Shales was. Another delay!

David Brown, a broad shouldered young man with a big head, spoke: "Blackie, we couldn't get extra horses. With horses so hard to come by all of a sudden, they're going for five times what they sold for last week. I couldn't afford another horse. Otis couldn't even pay for one horse, so he's not coming."

Blackie was amazed that Otis Shales was not coming. He did not know Otis' wife Becky all that well; she was a well built young woman of twenty with clean good looks and dark, curly hair and a large bust accentuated by her slimness. But Otis had no children or other family to look after, so Blackie found it hard to accept that he would not use this opportunity to try to rescue Becky, that he would so easily abandon her to her fate. Had Blackie been in Otis' shoes, he would have gone to everyone in town asking for a loan, and not quit until he had the money. Blackie knew that it was not a matter of the money; it was a matter of Otis' lack of will and courage.

He looked at the horses the young men had bought. They were not good horses. The Silver City trader had probably taken advantage of Gold Creek's desperate need to rid himself of some inferior horseflesh while charging inflated prices.

"We'll manage," Blackie said. "We'll probably pass some ranches on the way where we can get some horses cheap."

Charles Cistrom said, "These rifles cost us an arm and a leg too."

Blackie nodded. "I'll get Morgan."

In his mother's bedroom, Blackie handed Morgan the oil-cloth pouch, and he explained to his mother the agreement he had just made with McHenry and Tyson. He leaned over the bed to her. They kissed and hugged.

"Good luck," she said.

She was like that. She would not tell him to be careful or anything like that. They both knew that the mission he was about to undertake was brimming over with risk.

Blackie walked out, leaving Morgan to say good-by. He walked up to Amy and gave her a hug.

"See if you can't figure out some way to wash my mother's hair without her having to stand, will you? And would you keep it brushed for her? She likes to be neat, and it's hard for her right now."

"Okay."

He hugged her again. They went out onto the porch, and Blackie walked down the steps.

In her bedroom, Sarah gave Morgan a couple of important tips on how to get along with Blackie. Morgan promised to heed her advice.

Morgan stood. He said, "Well, this is good-by for now."

"Good luck."

"Thanks." He knew they would need it.

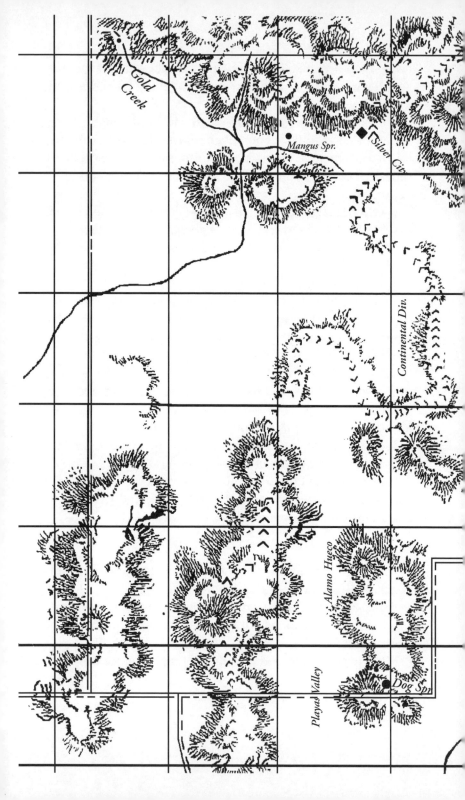

He turned and walked from the bedroom and through the living room and outside onto the porch. He addressed the young men.

"Boys, because of the danger of a manhunt, there's a rule I'd like to lay down. It's about guns. From this moment until we return whatever prisoners and loot we recover, I don't want you boys to be more than half an arm's length from your guns at any time. Having to take a step to reach your gun could be the split second that gets you or one of the rest of us killed." He paused. "Does that seem like a sensible rule to everyone?"

The three young men agreed.

Morgan stepped down beside his horse where he put the oilcloth pouch into his saddle bag. He pulled a map from his vest, and spread it against his saddle. The young men gathered around. As Morgan spoke, he traced the map with his finger.

"Here we are. Now, if the American bandit told Blackie the truth about going through Dog Springs, it means they were going into the State of Chihuahua. They'll pick up the Old Janos Trail south of Silver and follow it south into Chihuahua, crossing the border at Dog Springs. Once across the border, Janos is about the only place to go if you want to buy grub.

"Where they'll go from Janos, I don't know. Maybe east to Juarez. Maybe south to Casas Grandes.

"There is, of course, the possibility that they won't go to Janos; they could cut west through San Luis Pass into the State of Sonora.

"Anyway, we'll be tracking them the whole way. With over a hundred horses, they won't be hard to follow unless we have rain. At this time of year, rain is always a possibility."

Morgan re-folded his map and put it away.

The men mounted and turned their horses toward the creek, walking them at first to warm them up.

Amy called from the porch, "Godspeed!"

Twenty-Four

They rode south on the Gold Creek wagon road, intermittently loping and jogging for seven hours before they encountered the first grave. Vultures rose into the air as they approached. The grave was a few feet off the wagon trail, and was the work of soldiers in a hurry; it was so shallow that the earth had been mounded to cover the body, and coyotes had dug away the covering easily and vultures had done the rest. The remnants of a white cotton night dress were scattered around.

For some reason, the scene effected Charles Cistrom profoundly. It was not as if he had seen no dead people in the last few days, but the sight of this girl—or what was left of her—out here alone and abandoned, ripped and torn and consumed by carrion eaters, for some unaccountable reason caused involuntary stirrings in his mind. He watched Blackie quickly dismount and with his boot remove the dirt from the forehead and hairline. The hair was filled with dirt, but it was obviously brown. The face from the eyes down had been ravaged by carrion eaters, but the forehead was intact except for a dark hole in the left lobe. Charles felt a chill spread up the back of his neck, through the scalp, to the top of his head.

David Brown dismounted and looked the hair and the hairline over. He looked at Blackie and shook his head.

Blackie said, "I think it's Stella O'Connor; her hair is light brown, and she's about this size. She looked pretty bad when I saw her last. Like she wouldn't be able to ride very far."

David Brown's relief that it was not his wife was countered by the fearful reality that his wife might already have met a similar fate further down the trail.

Quickly, Morgan and Blackie switched to their spare saddle horses, and then they all rode on. Eventually, the posse came to the Gila River, forded it, and picked up the road to Mangus Springs. They rode on, driving the horses hard.

David's and Charles' horses showed severe fatigue, and began to slow the posse down. Just before sundown, riding up the shallow Mangus Valley, the posse approached Mangus Springs.

Near the newly settled springs, the desperados' trail looped south-west. The posse followed the tracks to what looked to be a place where the desperados had stopped. Blackie, studying the signs, sorted out what had happened. The desperados had made temporary camp and unloaded the girls and the gold to hide them from the settlers; and then they had taken the horses to the springs for water.

The posse rode into Mangus Springs and up to the log cabin on one of the two farms. The barking dogs alerted the inhabitants, and the farmer and two of his larger sons came outside.

"Howdy," Morgan said.

"How do," answered the farmer.

"We'd like to water our horses."

"You're welcome to help yourselves."

"Thanks.... Did you have a big party of visitors four days ago?"

"Yep."

"They give you trouble?"

"No; and I thank God for that. They just came in and used the springs without askin' our leave and we wasn't about to give 'em no trouble 'cause they was all armed and lookin' pretty mean."

"Some soldiers come by the next day?"

"Yep. The soldiers camped here overnight."

"I suppose they told you what those other men did at Gold Creek."

"Yep. But two men came by here the morning before the soldiers. They was the first to tell us. They was on their way to Silver to get horses and guns. I'll tell you what I told them: we didn't see no women. The men from Gold Creek said the Mexicans took a bunch of women and gold. The soldiers said the same thing, and one of the boys with the soldiers said they had his wife. But we didn't see no women."

Blackie said, "They unloaded the women a half mile due west of here and hid them while they brought the horses over."

"I reckoned as much."

Blackie asked, "Do you have any good horses you want to sell?"

"I might if the price is right."

Blackie turned to his companions. "Could you boys water the horses while I go look at this man's stock?"

Blackie was carrying twenty-eight hundred dollars for various reasons which included—if it came to that—ransoming Dusty.

When the posse saw Blackie again, he was leading two strong horses that he had bought with cash plus the trade of David's and Charles' tired horses.

It was almost dark when they rode on, following the desperados' trail as it continued up Mangus Valley, heading for the Continental Divide. The posse rode in the dark by bright moonlight, following an ancient trail, and after a few hours came to some Indian wells in the otherwise dry creek bed. They watered their sweaty horses, and Blackie and Morgan switched horses again. The posse rode on, climbing steadily, eventually crossing some low mountains which were covered with grass and mesquite and small cedar and were only about six thousand feet in altitude where they crossed. The posse members did not know and did not care that they had crossed the Continental Divide. Toward morning, they came to the desperados' first camp. There was grass for the horses but no water. And there was a grave. Bigger and deeper than the last.

"They just keep on killin', don't they?" David Brown stated through clenched teeth.

They made no attempt to dig up the corpses. The riders needed rest, and they expected to meet the soldiers coming back from the border at any time. The soldiers would furnish a description of the dead.

* * *

"We've got company," Blackie said. "About a mile east, in line with the north drop of that mountain."

The mountain, a gigantic peak that jutted up suddenly and starkly from the valley floor a couple of miles east of them, was Big Hatchet Peak, which, according to Morgan's map, was maybe thirty miles north of the Mexican border.

The fatigued posse had been on the trail for two and one-half days, and they were now in a semi-arid valley that seemed to go on forever and was just east of the Continental Divide. They had seen several herds of antelope in the valley, and plenty of deer, and even a herd of eighteen buffalo.

They stopped and Morgan looked through his telescope at what Blackie had seen.

"It's an Apache."

There could be no doubt about the distinctive Apache dress. The man was on horseback, and had stopped, and was looking their way.

Morgan added, "He could be a scout for the soldiers or for an Apache plunder party."

They rode on, and after a quarter of an hour, they spotted a bunch of riders a long way off to the south on the trail, headed their way.

They stopped for Morgan to scope the riders. "It's soldiers. That's about all I can tell from here."

They stopped again some minutes later. Looking through his telescope, Morgan said, "It's soldiers.... And two civilians from Gold Creek, Jed Simmons and young Randy Hicks. No women."

* * *

"We followed them a half day's ride past Dog Springs," Lieutenant Hodges said. "Against regulations, of course; but we hoped they'd get careless and take a rest. They didn't."

197

The posse and the Army company had come abreast, and Hodges was giving the posse members a rundown of the pursuit.

Morgan said to him, "On the way, we saw three graves that you dug. How many bodies did you find?"

"Six. That may not be all, but it's all that was along the trail. We gave them all proper burials."

Charles Cistrom thought, *Except the first one.*

David Brown pushed his horse forward. "Can you describe them?"

"Yes, we have complete, written descriptions."

Lieutenant Hodges reached into his saddle bag and withdrew a notebook.

Randy Hicks, with rough good looks and ginger hair, one of the two civilians with the soldiers, spoke up. "No need for that, David, your wife was one of those we buried two days out from Gold Creek."

Two days ride for the soldiers meant they had found her body at the desperado's first camp.

David had been halfway expecting it, but it stunned him nonetheless. For a few seconds he held it back, but then he broke down. He wheeled his horse and rode about forty yards from the group. He sat there with his back to them. His back quaked.

Hodges handed the notebook to Morgan. Morgan read the descriptions; he handed the notebook to Blackie and quickly looked away. Blackie, prepared for the worst, opened the notebook. He was able to start down the list more or less calmly. With his mother's close scrape with death, with Dusty's abduction, and with over fifty dead in town, he was somewhat hardened against horror by now. The first entry was Stella O'Connor. Shot through the forehead on Gold Creek Road. The second entry and the third and fourth were at the desperados' first camp. The second entry was without a name, but from the description, Blackie knew it was fourteen year old Prudie Babcock. She had been shot through the mouth. The third entry was a blonde, beaten almost beyond recognition, but tentatively identified by Randy Hicks as sixteen year old Etta Johnson. Shot in the face, she had been clad in a flannel night dress; so it was very unlikely to have been Dusty. The fourth entry was Suzanna Brown, beaten and shot through the temple. The fifth and sixth entries were at the desperados' second camp. Fifth was Mary Jean Hicks: multiple bruises, and shot through the back. Reading the sixth and final name, Blackie felt slightly nauseous. Jettie Stevens had been dragged by rope behind a horse for some distance, had been badly battered by rocks and brush, and much of her skin had been worn off. Her throat had been slit after being dragged; the soldiers had known that because the dried blood from her throat had been on the ground where she lay.

Blackie handed the notebook to Charles, and then looked at Randy.

Randy nodded. "Yep. My wife was one of those we buried too. I already did my bawlin'." There was fleeting grief on his face when he spoke of it.

"I'm sorry, Randy." After a moment, Blackie added, "I'm after my sister."

"They got her too? I didn't know. Well, you're lucky so far....I guess. What I mean is that at least we didn't find her remains.... That is, unless that blonde girl...."

"I don't think so. Dusty was dressed in boots and denims and a flannel shirt with a jacket."

Randy Hicks nodded, glad for Blackie.

Blackie said, "We're going on into Mexico to chase those men down to the end. Will you come with us?"

Randy Hicks did not answer immediately. Finally he said, "Blackie, there are four of you. I'd make five. There are over forty of them. I don't like your chances.... If my wife was still alive, maybe I'd be a fool and go. But not now."

Blackie looked at Jed Simmons. "Mr. Simmons? How about you? There are thousands of dollars in reward."

"I have all the sympathy in the world for you, but I'm with Randy; I don't like your chances. Besides, I've got a wife and kids waiting in Gold Creek."

Charles Cistrom was having doubts. He turned to Lieutenant Hodges.

"What do you think of our chances, sir?"

"Eleven to one? You ever been in a gunfight, son?"

Charles' voice got small. "No."

"Eleven to one is bad odds in a shootout."

Morgan spoke: "Lieutenant, could you draw us a map of the trail from here to where you turned around? If you include landmarks, we could travel tonight by moonlight. If we rely just on our own tracking, we'll have to stop when it gets dark."

"I'm sure you'll be okay if you stay on the trail to Janos. There isn't any place else for them to go as far as I can see. But I'll draw you a map anyway."

He tore a blank page from his journal and began to draw a map.

Meanwhile, David Brown had gotten himself under control and had ridden back over to his companions.

"Listen, boys," he said. "There's no sense in my goin' on now. I'm gonna go back to Gold Creek with the soldiers, here."

No one knew what to say for a moment. Finally, Morgan said, "I know you've had a bitter loss, David. But I urge you to keep on with us for the sake of the other prisoners. And think of the reward. Most men don't make a thousand dollars in a year."

"What's the use? My wife's dead. Nothin' else means anything to me. I just feel powerful tired."

"All right, David." There was no criticism in Morgan's voice.

"Jesus!" Charles exclaimed. "That makes just three us. What kind of odds is that?"

Morgan looked at him, realizing that the young man was quite fearful. "Are you thinking of going home too?"

"I'm thinking about it."

Morgan thought that a scared man would probably be unreliable, and perhaps troublesome.

"Well," said Morgan in a kindly voice, "you had better do it then. No one can fault you for it."

When Hodges finished the map, Morgan and Blackie quickly said their good-byes and trotted their horses southward.

Hodges looked after them. To him they were a couple of reckless fools.

Charles Cistrom could not help himself. He hated Blackie and Morgan bitterly for having the courage to go on by themselves.

David Brown looked after them, knowing that he had gone back on his agreement to continue as long as either Suzanna or Dusty was believed to be alive. It bothered him some to go back on his word to Blackie, but not enough to make him go on with the posse. He had been head over heels in love with his wife, and now she was gone and life seemed cruel and miserable to him. Too bad about Dusty. All that meant anything to him now was his baby daughter back in Gold Creek. He decided right there that he would get the hell out of Gold Creek with her and take her someplace where it was safe to live. That he would be bothered for the rest of his life by breaking his word to Blackie on such a deadly mission did not even occur to him.

* * *

Not too long after leaving the soldiers, Morgan and Blackie came to Las Cienagas Springs, a marsh right there in the middle of the valley. A herd of antelope ran off a short ways and watched to see how long they might stay. With his shotgun, Blackie killed a big jack rabbit, and that spooked the antelope to fly off to a greater distance. While Blackie cooked the rabbit, Morgan watered and grazed the horses. When the rabbit was done, Blackie packed half of it away for later, and divided the remainder between Morgan and himself. They would eat while they rode. They mounted up, and made eighteen miles south to Alamo Hueco Springs on the eastern side of Playas Valley. The springs was visible from miles away: a big green clump of aspen trees up in a low saddle on the side of the brown Alamo Hueco Mountains. From there, the trail led south along the mountain seven miles to a low east-west pass. South of the pass were the Dog Mountains. Riding by moonlight now, the pursuers turned eastward, climbing the pass, and then rode down the other side, following the shallow Horse Canyon three miles, and then turned south again for a couple of miles. Finally, twelve miles from Alamo Hueco Springs, now in the Dog Mountains, the posse of two came upon Dog Springs.

They approached the ancient cottonwood and willow trees of the Springs with caution. At this time of year, on this trail, travelers just might encounter an Apache plunder party going to or coming from Mexico. However, tonight, there were only wild hogs at the springs when they rode up. The hogs grunted and raced off through thick mesquite into the night. The hogs' presence told them there were no humans but themselves in the area.

The pursuers watered their horses and rested them for a couple of hours while coyotes howled a serenade from the hills above the pass. When the men mounted up, they took the trail that led southward, and soon they crossed the border into Mexico.

Twenty-Five

Morgan and Blackie had been three and a half days on the trail, and they were now in the Mexican State of Chihuahua, at close to six thousand feet in altitude on the eastern side of a semi-arid valley that was perhaps twenty-five miles wide east to west, but in length, stretched on and on southward until it ran into some far high mountains that jutted eastward.

The clouds had first started coming piecemeal over Sierra Madre, the mountains of the Continental Divide, fifteen or so miles to the west. The big clouds scudded over, going east, casting giant moving shadows across the huge dry lake and the grass land of the valley. Then a heavy gray and white bank of clouds bunched up over the mountains, extending north and south as far as could be seen, and then the mountains disappeared behind a gray wall that was the rain, and the storm front moved relentlessly eastward toward Blackie and Morgan, the edge of it raising dust clouds as the huge rain drops, falling several thousand feet, pounded the dry earth. The dust would rise up several hundred feet only to be washed back to earth when the rain overtook it. But the wall of rain kept advancing and throwing up new dust on its edge as it advanced.

The lightning was spectacular. All along the rain front, it darted and forked and webbed—sometimes it stood or danced for several seconds—to be followed by roaring, deafening claps of thunder. Blackie, who had always loved thunderstorms, was furious with this one.

They halted while Blackie pulled oil cloth rifle sheaths from his pack. He handed one to Morgan, and they sheathed the rifles in their saddle scabbards. Blackie put on a waterproof coat.

In another five minutes the rain was upon them, coming down on them as if they were riding under a waterfall. The brims of their hats collapsed down around their heads and faces. Within seconds, notwithstanding Blackie's so-called waterproof coat, they were both drenched to the skin. Their bedrolls were sopping. The water went right on through the canvas covered packs on the pack horses. The two men took their hats off to get the brims out of their eyes. The rain washed into their eyes, blurring their vision. They rode with their hands against their foreheads, like men shading their eyes from the sun, but instead now trying to keep the rain from them.

The horses that they were leading, having no man aboard to make them feel safe and protected, got very spooky from the pounding rain and from the closeness of the lightning and thunder; so the men had to keep those horses on short rope and alongside them.

Visibility was down to a few yards. Everything was gray except when lightning struck nearby.

No hoof marks would survive this downpour, so it was the end of tracking the desperados for a few days. Perhaps forever.

They stayed on the trail that headed southeastward, hoping that the desperados had gone to Janos. There was nothing else to be done now. The desperados had preceded them by four days, and so the tracks that they would make when the rain stopped would not be seen by the pursuers for perhaps four days—perhaps never—because the pursuers did not know where to look for them.

The two men finally halted at a muddy torrent that was obviously well over their heads in depth. It roared violently down a gully, apparently heading for the huge dry lake bed on the southwestern side of the valley. There was no chance of swimming the torrent. They dismounted and waited.

The rain kept coming down like that for perhaps three quarters of an hour. Then it turned less heavy for another half hour. Finally, rather suddenly, it stopped and the clouds cleared somewhat, and patches of hot sunlight appeared around the valley. There were still some clouds, and some of them were dumping rain elsewhere in the valley; but for the most part the rain had passed on to the east.

Nevertheless, the flow of water down the gully had increased and the level had risen perhaps five feet higher than when they had first stopped. The two men ate some wet crackers and jerky while they waited. There was no dry wood to burn, and their matches were soaked; consequently, they were unable to make coffee or to cook anything.

The rain had flattened the grass all around; so, while they waited for the torrent to subside, they went around pulling grass up by the roots and feeding it to the horses.

It was at least another three hours before the torrent had subsided enough for them to cross it. During that time, the clouds had cleared away, and the hot sun had turned the air humid.

When they started again, they kept the horses at a walk. Every square inch of the valley was slippery, sticky mud, and they dared not gallop or trot lest the horses slip or fall and perhaps injure themselves or the riders.

"If it's any consolation," Morgan said, "the desperados probably were stopped by this rain too—wherever they are."

Blackie nodded; his anger had long since dissipated. "Don't mind me. I don't know why I get mad over things I can't do anything about."

The horses plodded along, slipping now and then in the mud. The mud balled up on the bottoms of their hooves and made it difficult for them to walk.

Blackie said, "That's one thing about my mom: she doesn't often bother her mind over things she can't do anything about."

Morgan nodded and gave some thought to what the young man had said. "Your mother is an unusual woman."

"Do you think she's unusual?"

"Yes. Don't you?"

"Yeah, I admit that I do. I think she's awful smart, for one thing. Now, I suppose somebody would say, 'Well, it's his mother; so of course he thinks so.'"

"Oh, I wouldn't say so. A lot of men your age think their mothers are pretty dull. They don't want anyone else to say anything bad about their mothers, but they themselves have lots of complaints. It seems to be all part of being about your age. Do you know anyone your age who talks about his mother the way you do?"

Blackie thought for a moment. "Dusty."

Morgan chuckled. "Anyone else?"

"The fact is, I can't think of anybody right now. So maybe you're right. I guess you could say I brag on my mom."

"Oh, I wouldn't put it that way. There's certainly nothing wrong with being proud of your mother. And, in my opinion, you've got a lot to be proud of."

Blackie beamed. "Did you know that my mom read all of Shakspere by the time she was fifteen?"

"Well, that's unusual all right. I've only read three or four of his plays and I'm forty."

"She says she's always loved to read. You know, my grandma taught her to read when she was four, and later enrolled her in a lending library there in Saint Louis. Through it, she met some people who had their own libraries. So, she's read all kinds of books: Thomas Jefferson, Benjamin Franklin, Voltaire, and people I never heard of. I asked her a while back how many more books she's read than I have, and she said maybe twenty times as many. Twenty times!"

Blackie's enthusiasm for his mother charmed the older man. Besides, Morgan was very interested in anything about Sarah, so he listened to the boy with pleasure.

Blackie went on, "Another thing: Mom has always been a saver. She says that when she was little, she saved bits of money they gave her, and, when she was eight, she bought two hens and a rooster and started breeding chickens and selling fryers and eggs. They had five acres there in Saint Louis; and she says that pretty soon she had chickens and ducks all over the place. She had her own savings account at the bank, and she had money to pay for piano lessons and for yardage so that she could make her own clothes according to the latest fashions. My dad told me it was Mom's money that bought the wagon and team and paid for the trip out here right after they got married."

"How old was she when she married?"

"Seventeen."

"Well, I'd say she was a pretty rare young lady."

Blackie and Morgan rode most of the night by moonlight, heading south by east, going from one valley to another, generally losing altitude, stopping only for about three hours along a river bank to graze the horses on the rich grass. Their bedrolls were still soaked, so the men sat huddled together in the wet grass with their knees drawn up, trying to doze. Their clothes had not dried before nightfall because of the humidity, and a breeze came up in the night; as a result, they were chilled to the bone. And Morgan was genuinely concerned that one or both of them might come down with a cold or worse.

Later in the night, riding the Janos Trail, they came across a dead horse. A few miles further, they encountered another one. Right after dawn they found a third one. Consequently, they were fairly sure that they were on the trail the desperados had taken.

They reached Janos, a former Spanish garrison, at about noon. It turned out to be a town of small size, made up of adobe buildings.

They rode in cautiously, with their rifles at the ready. They stopped at the general store which was made of adobe with wooden bars over the windows; there was no glass in the windows, and the wooden shutters inside were closed. Morgan dismounted and tried the door. It was barred from inside. He looked up at the sun.

"It's siesta."

They watered their horses and then rode around the town, looking for any signs of the desperados. They found no such signs.

"I suppose," Morgan said, "we ought to dry our gear out."

They made a camp of sorts outside town and unloaded the horses. They spread the canvas pack covers out on the ground and spread everything else out on the canvasses. They draped their blankets over brush to get them both sunshine and air. The ground was still wet from yesterday's rain, and so they lay down on the edge of the canvasses and slept in the hot sun. They were very, very tired. The horses slept where they stood.

* * *

"Buenos dias, Señor," said the proprietor of the general store when Morgan entered.

Siesta was over.

The proprietor stood up from where he had been sitting behind the counter. His wife remained seated. Three small children, two boys and a girl, who had been playing on the dirt floor, got quickly silent and stared at the big man with pale skin.

"Buenos dias," Morgan answered.

In Spanish, Morgan ordered two boxes of matches, some of the hard flat bread, and some beef jerky. They chatted in Spanish about yesterday's storm, and about where Morgan could buy grain for the horses.

Finally, Morgan asked, "Recently, have some men been in town buying provisions for a large party?"

"Yes, four days ago. And two of them are still here. They have been drunk since they came."

"Where can I find them?"

"At Doña Maria's Boarding House. It is on the next street over," the proprietor pointed northeast, "and, ah, about eight buildings down. It has a high wall around it."

Morgan thanked him and paid for the supplies.

The proprietor asked, "Are they your friends?"

"No."

"They are bandits, are they not?"

"Yes."

"Everybody knows it. They have too much money. And they spend it wildly."

Morgan smiled and nodded and went outside to where Blackie waited with the horses. The proprietor, his wife, and his children came to the door to watch them. Morgan relayed in English what the proprietor had just told him.

Blackie nodded and smiled his appreciation at the proprietor.

The proprietor asked in Spanish, "Did they take something of yours?"

Morgan answered, "Yes. These men are part of a gang that took fifteen girls from a town in New Mexico. They've killed some, but some are still alive. At least we hope they are."

The proprietor momentarily stared at Morgan; then he involuntarily glanced at his own little daughter. He looked back to the pursuers. "May God be with you and may He protect the girls."

The pursuers rode over to the next street and down the street toward a seven foot high adobe wall that surrounded about two acres of land. They approached cautiously, one on each side of the street, their rifles at the ready. In front of the boarding house, they tied their horses securely. To hide his express rifle on the pack horse, Blackie threw his bedroll over it. Morgan opened the wooden door in the arched gateway and slipped in. A moment later, Blackie slipped in.

Blackie latched the gate behind him because inside the wall there were chickens and goats everywhere. The place was a virtual barnyard. The animals were obviously accustomed to humans walking about in their midst because other than a couple of bleats from goats, they made no fuss. With extreme care, Blackie and Morgan moved among the four buildings, looking in through the windows. The windows had no glass; they were rectangular openings in the adobe with wooden bars on the outside and shutters swung open inside. It was dangerous work because the men outside were lit by the sunshine, while anyone who might be inside would be in the gloom. In between looking through the windows, Blackie kept his eyelids slitted so that his irises stayed dilated. In the first building, there was only one elderly man. In the next two buildings, they found no one; the residents were probably at work. The remaining building was at the back of the compound. From inside it, a very fat woman with white hair saw them and came out and asked in Spanish what they wanted.

Morgan talked with her for a couple of minutes, and then turned to Blackie.

"This is Doña Maria. The two men left this morning. They didn't tell her where they were going. However, she says that the second day they were here, five men came after them about noon, but the two were too drunk to ride." Morgan's voice took an encouraging tone. "That must mean the whole gang lay by overnight and at least part of the next day. So, we're gaining on them."

They went out then and got their horses and went to a sort of stable where they bought corn. Blackie fed and rubbed and combed the horses while Morgan walked around the town looking for leads. Morgan was back in a half hour, excited.

"Found a kid playing in a mud puddle who says he saw the strangers ride out of town this morning, heading south. He showed me where they started out, and sure enough there are tracks of two horses going south. That probably means they're heading for Casas Grandes. We have to hope the rest of the desperados headed that way too. If we take these two alive, we should be able to find out."

"They could have been abandoned, and don't know where the others are."

"Yes, that's possible, but it's more likely that they knew where the others were going. They're our best hope right now."

Twenty-Six

The pursuers rode south until after sundown, following the tracks of the two desperados easily in the damp earth. There were no other tracks on the trail now since the rain.

That night, they made camp on the Janos River. They slept in their clothes except for their boots, and in the morning they were up at the first hint of light in the east. They pulled on their boots and ran out to catch their horses, which, although hobbled, had wandered two and three hundred yards in the night. They ate hard bread and jerky with cold water while they saddled the horses. They forded the Janos River and struck out at a trot for the Casas Grandes River. When the sun rose, their horses were warmed up and they took them up to a gallop. A light wind was blowing.

They found the two desperados' camp about three hours later. The ashes were still warm where the fire had been. Blackie first caught sight of their quarry a couple of hours after that when the outlaws topped a rise about three miles ahead of them.

"There they are! About three miles out! We better change horses now."

They reined in, dismounted, and moved their saddles to the fresher horses. In less than three minutes, they had completed the switch and were galloping hard again.

About twenty minutes later, one of the desperados, despite the wind, thought that he heard something. He turned in his saddle and was startled to see two men and six horses about three hundred yards away, galloping toward them.

"Huh!" he blurted.

The other man looked at him and then behind them. He too was startled.

"What is it?"

"I don't know."

"Bandits?"

"Must be. Their rifles are out."

Even bandits must be on guard against other bandits. They reined in their horses, withdrew their rifles from their scabbards, and turned the horses around. The first one raised his rifle threateningly.

Blackie saw the move and reined in his horses. Turning his mount sideways, he quickly aimed and fired. The first desperado fell backwards from his saddle to the ground. The second desperado, a so-so shot, fired, missing Morgan. He wheeled his horse and kicked it to a gallop, trying to reload on the run.

Morgan was now galloping the trail fifty yards ahead of where Blackie sat. Blackie had reloaded and now took aim at the fleeing desperado's horse. He fired. The horse collapsed, sending the rider hurtling through brush and plowing to a halt in the soft dirt. Morgan galloped hard toward the man. The man staggered to his feet, half stunned, looking for his weapons. He was mortally afraid. Searching frantically where he had hit the ground, he found his revolver half buried in the dirt, came up with it, shook the dirt from it, and aimed at Morgan who was now only about thirty yards out. Morgan moved his feet so that only his toes engaged his stirrups and he leaned low over his saddle horn and hid behind his horse's neck. At about twenty yards, the man fired, hitting the horse in the neck. The horse stumbled and fell, throwing Morgan head over heels through the brush. Morgan's spare and pack horses were tied by thin ropes to leather thongs on his saddle. When they came to the end of their ropes, they both whipped around, the thongs snapping. But they fell anyway. Quickly, they struggled to their feet, obscuring the desperado's sight of Morgan.

Blackie had been galloping, but when Morgan went down, Blackie reined his horses up again, and took aim at the outlaw's midsection. The man moved to get a shot at Morgan where he lay in the brush. Blackie fired. The desperado dropped his revolver and fell backwards to the ground, clutching his belly.

Morgan got up dirty, scraped, and bruised. He rushed to the wounded man and demanded in Spanish, "Where is El Lobo?"

The man did not answer, but merely groaned in pain. His hand probed his stomach.

Finally, the man said fearfully, "I am going to die."

"We'll give you a Christian burial if you help us. I'll pray for your forgiveness. I swear by all that is holy I will."

The man looked hopefully up at Morgan. Morgan began asking his questions, and had to kneel and lean close to hear the answers. In the meantime, Blackie rode up and dismounted. The man died before Morgan got many questions answered. Morgan got to his feet. Blackie looked expectantly at him.

Morgan said, "El Lobo is on the way to the City of Chihuahua to sell the gold. But they planned to rest up for two days on the river south of Casas Grandes. Eight girls were still alive at Janos. That means one more is dead that the soldiers didn't account for. When I asked him about a blonde, he got confused. You remember, there were three blondes in the original fifteen women."

Blackie radiated frustration. "God damn it! I gut shot him because I hoped he'd live longer!"

Morgan nodded. "You saved my life."

Blackie mounted up and went out and caught Morgan's two horses and also the first desperado's horse. Meanwhile, Morgan went through the dead men's pockets for money and valuables, and he cut the right ear off of each man. When Blackie brought Morgan's horses up, Morgan was searching the pack spillage where the pack horse had fallen. He retrieved two leather pouches from the spillage and put the loot in one and poured salt into the other one and put the ears into the salted one.

Blackie watched him with curiosity.

Morgan said, "Proof. These ears are worth one hundred dollars each."

The salt, of course, would help preserve the ears until they got them home—if they ever got home.

Each of the two dead horses lay on part of its saddle. Blackie un-cinched those saddles and, with a lariat tied to his saddle horn, pulled the saddles free. Meanwhile, Morgan had taken a shovel and was engaged in digging a grave. Sweating, he glanced up and saw Blackie looking at him.

He explained, "Just this one. I promised him a Christian burial if he talked."

Morgan dug on while Blackie put the dead men's weapons and saddles on the pack horses. Then Morgan dragged the one dead man into the shallow grave, and Blackie took the shovel and covered the man, mounding the dirt over him. Morgan made a cross of sorts from brush, planted it at the head of the grave, and then said a short prayer, asking forgiveness for the man.

Finished, he said to Blackie, "Your mother's comments about keeping one's word weren't lost on me."

"What comments?"

"The morning after I got fired, when I left for Colliers' Ranch, she said something to you about no one respecting a man who doesn't keep his word, least of all the man himself."

"Oh, yeah. She says so many things."

"I'll tell you, if I'd had your mother's counsel when I was your age, I could have saved myself a lot of trouble in life."

Morgan knew right then that he was through hesitating. When—and if—he got home, he would ask Sarah to marry him. If she said no, well then at least the uncertainty would be over.

He plunged: "I guess I might as well admit to you right now that I'm in love with your mother."

Blackie smiled gently. "As far as I'm concerned, she's the best choice you could make."

Morgan chuckled. "I don't know what I expected you to say, but I was afraid that you might object."

"Not me."

"Look, this is a hell of a place to be talking about something like this—two dead men lying about and a bag of ears in my hand."

*   *   *

They rode south toward Casas Grandes, pushing their horses hard. The desperado's horse began to limp, and upon inspection they discovered that he had thrown a shoe from his right hind hoof. Blackie had packed shoes, nails, pliers, a file, and a hammer for just such an eventuality, so they re-shoed the horse right there on the trail.

They reached the outskirts of Casas Grandes after night-fall where they camped along the river, hobbling the horses and turning them loose. In the morning, they went carefully into town and rode around. It was a small town on the river, serving farmers and ranchers. Morgan, looking unkempt with six days growth of beard, asked around until he found someone who would feed them hot food. It was simple fare, beef and beans and tortillas, but it tasted delicious after several days on the trail.

Afterward they went to the cantina—saloon—and Morgan went inside while Blackie stayed with the horses. Blackie leaned against a tree in the shade with his hat pulled low over his eyes. It would not do for any of El Lobo's men to recognize him here; they must not suspect that they had pursuers. He watched people moving down the dirt street that had holes which could break the axle of a fast moving wagon.

Morgan walked out, jubilant. He came close.

"Two days ago, three men bought enough liquor there to last them a year. Loaded it up on two pack horses. The proprietor didn't recognize them as being from around here."

Blackie was elated. The three men had most likely been from El Lobo's gang, and they had probably believed that they were safe from pursuers. Otherwise, it seemed unlikely that they would have bought so much liquor.

The pursuers rode south along the Casas Grandes River, Morgan on the east bank, Blackie on the west. Sixteen miles south of town, Morgan shouted. Blackie forded the river and saw the remnants of a large camp. There were ashes from several fires, many empty liquor bottles, a scorched blanket, the remains of a steer carcass, and plenty of horse manure.

Blackie dismounted and walked around, looking at the ground carefully. There had been so much foot and horse traffic that nothing was very distinct. However, there were bare footprints of girls.

He wandered into a stand of cottonwoods and was out of Morgan's sight for perhaps a minute.

When he emerged, he said, "There's a dead bandit I recognize here in the trees. He must have bled to death—he was castrated."

"Castrated?!"

"Yep."

"What the hell?"

While Morgan went to look for himself, Blackie mounted up and started a circle of the camp.

A couple of minutes later Blackie called out, "Here's where they headed out, going east. There's a dew crust on the tracks, so they left yesterday or the day before."

Morgan rode over. "Look here. Our horses are about played out. We'd better find a place where we can buy fresh ones."

"We'll lose almost a day if we go back to Casas Grandes."

"We're not going to get anywhere on dead horses. We better rest them a couple of hours here where the grass is good and green."

Blackie protested, "I can smell rain coming."

Morgan pulled the telescope from his saddle bag and glassed the rain clouds on Sierra Madre.

Blackie continued, "I want to be sure of their general heading before the rain washes out the tracks."

"Okay. But, we've got to give these horses a rest. Their horses are rested at least a day, and maybe two. And they haven't been driving them as hard the last four days."

They galloped eastward while the storm clouds closed in on them. Later, they were caught in a downpour amid thunder and lightning.

* * *

Two tired men with six tired horses climbed to the summit of a low east-west mountain pass at about noon the next day. The men looked eastward down the other side of the summit into a river valley populated by rolling hills.

"That should be the Santa Maria River," Morgan said, looking through his telescope. "Let's camp there and rest the horses."

The men both looked forward to the rest. Last night, they had stopped for the sake of the horses, but the men's bedrolls had been so wet that neither man had done more than doze, sitting with their backs against each other for warmth.

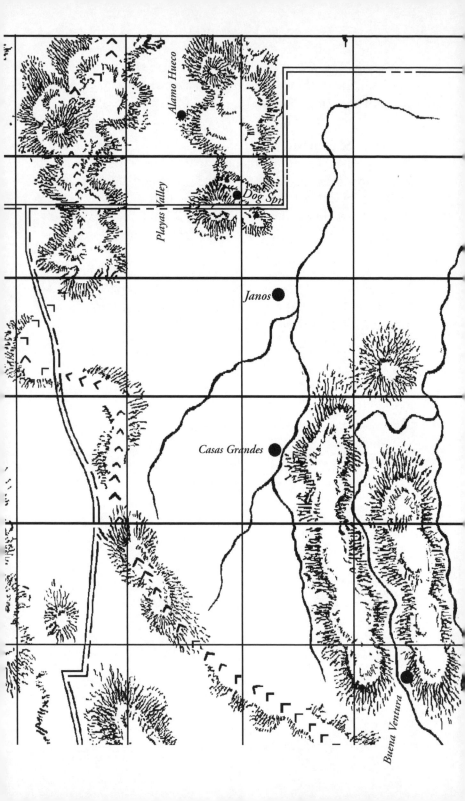

Twenty-seven

That afternoon, they made camp on the bank of the Santa Maria River where they hobbled one horse and turned the others loose. They dared not shoot any game because they had no way of knowing where the desperados were. For all they knew, the bandits might be camped within sound of gunshot. So the pursuers cooked and ate a stew made of bread and jerky.

Afterward, they huddled over Morgan's map. With a carpenter's pencil, Morgan marked where they were at the moment, then he pointed to the town of Buena Ventura.

"Buena Ventura. It looks to be about two days ride south, and it's on the way to Chihuahua. Maybe we can pick up their trail there."

Each took his turn standing guard while the other bathed and washed his clothes in the shallow river. Then they took turns shaving with the aid of a mirror hung on a tree trunk. Morgan was surprised at how haggard he appeared in the mirror. He glanced at Blackie; the boy looked tired as hell.

They laid their bedrolls about thirty feet apart and, as usual, spread dead twigs and leaves all around them to prevent anyone from approaching close without awakening them. They then lay down and slept on and off throughout the afternoon. Just as the sun was setting, Blackie lay awake thinking. He looked over at Morgan where he lay and saw that he too was awake now.

"You know," Blackie said restfully, "I've been lying here thinking about something Mom said to me the other day. She said that it's odd how evil people seem to want to ruin people and things that are beautiful or good.... Now, wouldn't you say that that's the difference between good people and evil people? Evil people destroy what is good and beautiful. I mean if they didn't do that, you wouldn't say they were evil, would you? If a man killed a rattlesnake in your house, you wouldn't say he was evil. But, if he walked in and deliberately killed your dog, you'd say he was a bad man."

Morgan rolled onto his side and looked at Blackie. This was one of the things that, when he had first gotten to know this young man, he had right away liked about him—you could discuss ideas with him.

"That's a good point," Morgan said.

Suddenly, Morgan's long dormant college habits surfaced. "But I suppose it would be wise to make clear what you mean by 'good' and 'beautiful.'"

Blackie looked at Morgan in surprise. "Well, I....I never really thought it out. Beautiful has to be something you like to look at, I guess.... No. It's more than that.... When I see a pretty girl, it makes me smile.... And I feel good inside. And when I see a pretty flower, I may not smile outwardly, but I feel kind of the same inside. It's like I'm smiling inside. I feel good inside. The same thing with a beautiful horse."

"What about beautiful sounds?"

"Oh! I forgot. Yeah. Sometimes we go to the Stevens' or the Conte's and Mom will play the piano. She says she's away out of practice and not very good anymore, but to me it's beautiful and I just sit there and smile all the way through. Her piano playing sure makes me feel good inside. And at dances when the fiddlers and the banjo players are good, I love it."

"So, beautiful things make you feel good inside?"

"That's right. Don't they do that to you?"

"They sure do...." Morgan sat up, enjoying this. "But what about the fellow who feels good inside about someone else's misfortune?"

"Well...." said Blackie, momentarily stumped. "Well, I'd guess he's got something turned around backwards inside of him. Something's wrong with him. What do you think?"

Morgan nodded, pleased with the young man's quickness. "I suspect you're right. And I wonder if buried deep down inside of him he's cringing at his own corruption."

"Maybe so. I don't know."

"Well, now," said Morgan, not even aware that he was sounding just like one of his long ago college professors, old Dr. Harkness. "What about 'good?' What is goodness?"

Blackie sat up and considered for a bit. "I kind of know; but I can't put it into words; so maybe I really don't know. It came up when we were discussing Jettie Stevens. We both thought she was a really nice girl. Mom didn't use the word 'good,' but I think she meant pretty much the same. Anyway, I've always thought that everybody knows what good is, but here I am having trouble putting it into other words."

Morgan's excitement suddenly showed, and he abandoned the image of old Dr. Harkness. "You know, I've never totally sorted this stuff out either. Now, what about a horse? When is a horse a good horse?"

Blackie was infected by Morgan's excitement. "When he behaves. When he does what he's supposed to."

"What about the horse that throws you every time you get on him?"

"No. He's got to be a bad horse."

"So, a good horse adds to your life; he contributes to your well being; makes your life better. A bad horse takes away from your survival. He breaks arms or tramples you, causes pain.... It's the same with people, isn't it?"

"Well, sure."

"What was it about Jettie that made her good?"

"She was pleasant to be around...."

"Did she ever hurt you, or try to?"

"No.... Well, wait a minute. Once when I was eleven, I pulled her pigtail too hard and she slapped me. But I brought that on myself. After we got over being mad at each other, we got along ever since."

"What was so good about her?"

"Well....she had good manners, for one thing. And she was gentle....she didn't try to hurt people. And she always treated me mighty nicely. You know, sometimes people can be pretty mean. You can be trying to just get along and before you know it you're defending yourself—they're finding fault with you for things that aren't wrong with you, or complaining to others about you. Well, Jettie wasn't like that. She...."

Morgan could not contain himself. "It seems to me that good people add to your survival and bad people subtract from it. It's a simple definition, but it's also true."

Blackie nodded. "So you're saying a good person is helpful."

"Right."

"And an evil person is unhelpful."

"Yes.... Wait." Morgan gave that some thought. "No, not necessarily. An evil person's got to somehow detract from your life—take something away. Don't you think? I mean, if a person just leaves you alone, he might be unhelpful but not harmful."

"Yes, I see what you mean."

"You know, I'm glad you said that about helpfulness; because....there's something else here. Some people just like to be left alone. It seems to me that one of the greatest virtues is being able to let people live their lives without interference, to let them make their own decisions, to let them be responsible for themselves."

"Yes, of course. I hadn't thought of that."

"Doc's a good example of that," Morgan said. "He's always meddling in other people's affairs. He wanted to be President of the Town Meeting so badly he could hardly stand it. And when he was elected, he used his position to do what he'd been doing in a smaller way all along, meddle in other people's lives. And look what happened."

"Do you think he's evil?"

"Sure. Look what happened. Don't pay any attention to what he says. He'll fill your ears full of excuses and reasons-why. Just look at his actions. That tells the real story. I should have had this conversation with you a long time ago. Maybe back then I could have recognized Doc for what he was. You know, he talked behind people's backs constantly, hurting their reputations. So he was destructive all along. He was just that much more destructive when he got power."

"I see."

They fell silent and Morgan finally lay back down, pleased with his new insight.

After a bit, Blackie said, "I'll go change the night horse."

He got up and went out and caught the hobbled horse, rode down river and drove the other horses back up toward camp. He hobbled one of the other horses and turned loose the one he had been riding.

* * *

During the next two days, the horses showed definite signs of the strain, and the men did not push them as hard. It would have been a major setback if the horses had given out before the pursuers got to where they could replace them.

At twilight on their ninth day out from Gold Creek, they rode into the little town of Buena Ventura, hoping they would find some sign of the desperados there. They were quite worried; they had found not a trace of the outlaws since the last rain storm. They walked the horses down the main street of Buena Ventura, looking around them. Children stood about, self-consciously watching the Norte Americanos—North Americans—ride by. They rode up to an adobe stable which had a wooden sign saying, "Caballerizas Buena Venturas," Buena Ventura Horse Stables. Morgan bargained in Spanish with the owner while Blackie kept his eyes peeled for any of El Lobo's men.

In the stable, while the horses ate, Blackie combed them and rubbed them down and kept an eye on their packs and saddles. Morgan walked around town talking to people. When he came back, he appeared hopeful.

"Turned up a possibility. Two strangers came to town the day before yesterday and bought a large amount of salt and corn meal. It could have been someone from one of the haciendas out there, but they usually grow their own corn, and the store owner says he'd never seen these two men before. He said they were very, very dirty, and their clothes stank like men who haven't changed for weeks."

Blackie nodded, thinking about it. "Could be. I suppose they could have been prospectors, though."

"Yes."

"By the way, are we going to buy horses here?"

"I think we ought to. I haven't seen any good ones. But maybe what we can buy will do until we pass a hacienda close on our trail."

Their present horses were, of course, jaded, and needed four or five days of rest before they would be any good again. Needless to say, the pursuers did not have those days to spare.

The following morning, at a rancho just south of town, they bought six fresh horses, paying for them with the desperados' guns and saddles, and leaving their fatigued horses as part of the bargain.

They had not ridden more than four hours when Blackie's new mount came up lame. Examining the horse's right fore-leg, Blackie realized it was an old injury that they had failed to detect when they had bought the animal.

"May as well turn him loose," Blackie said. "He'll just slow us down."

He transferred his bridle and saddle to his spare horse and they started again.

That night, they camped along the river. The next morning, riding southward, they began to see small groups of cattle here and there. Morgan stayed on the river with his horses and Blackie's pack horse, proceeding at a walk while Blackie kept riding back and forth across the broad, rolling valley, working his horse hard, looking for some indication of the desperados. Blackie had been riding like this for several hours when he came up to Morgan to swap horses.

"I found something. Tracks of two horses and a heifer. The tracks follow the same horse tracks coming the other way, as if a couple of men rode out and got this heifer and took her back where they came from. It could be nothing, but it seems odd that some cowboys would ride out and get just one heifer. Anyway, from a hilltop, I saw up-river a couple miles to where there's a big lot of trees. I'm guessing that's where those tracks are heading. I'll follow them for a ways."

Blackie went back out to follow the tracks, and Morgan continued following the river, eventually coming to where he saw that Blackie had crossed it. It was Blackie all right; he had scratched a big "V" in the firm, damp sand beside the water. The "V" pointed across the river. Sure enough, there were tracks of two other horses and a heifer there too. Morgan crossed the river and followed the tracks south. Finally, he could see by the tracks that Blackie was galloping his horse. Morgan moved his horses up to a gallop.

Morgan heard Blackie shout up ahead of him. "Yahoo! Here's where they camped! We've got their trail now!"

By the time Morgan galloped up, vultures were flapping and sailing in the sky above the camp, having been scared off by Blackie's arrival. The boy was off his horse, walking around, looking at tracks and debris. There were the partial remains of a cow carcass, empty liquor bottles, tracks, and more tracks. Blackie went to the edge of the shallow river where a big sand bar extended out to where the stream eddied. The eddy made a water hole that looked to be about waist deep. The sand bar was low and damp and firm, and was made up more of mud than sand near the bank. To get to the water here, one had to walk across that sand bar, leaving clear, almost perfect tracks in the wet mud and sand. Blackie was so intent on some tracks there that Morgan watched him with curiosity. The young man squatted and studied the tracks a long time. Finally, he stood and looked at Morgan. All his elation was gone.

"It looks like the girls bathed here." He pointed at the deep place in the current. Then, pointing to the wet sandbar, he continued, "Seven different pairs of feet. I never paid that much attention to Dusty's bare foot tracks—just kind of without thinking about it. But hers aren't here."

"Maybe she didn't take a bath that day."

"Maybe." A pause. "And maybe another girl is dead now. If we can believe that bandit we buried, there should be eight pairs of feet."

Morgan nodded. The soldiers had found six dead girls. But, according to the bandit who they had buried north of Casas Grandes, there were seven girls dead by the time the desperados got to Janos. Dusty could have died any time in the last fourteen days, and her body could have gone undetected, especially when he and Blackie had ridden by night.

From the abandoned camp now, they followed the desperados' trail southward, pressing their own horses hard, and in the late afternoon, they discovered another camp. They knew something was dead because the vultures flapped into the air, scared off by the pursuers' approach. It might be the remains of an animal, but Blackie's heart pounded in fear that he would find Dusty there.

It was not Dusty. The hair was dark brown. The body was mostly bones now. It was hard to tell whom it had been. Already known to be dead were Prudence Babcock, Suzanna Brown, Mary Jean Hicks, Etta Johnson, Stella O'Connor, and Jettie Stevens. Blackie knew that these remains were not of Connie Watkins, the redhead, nor of Jinny Rowe, whose hair was auburn, nor of Trudy Belvedere, whose hair was light brown, nor of Ella York, whose hair was a very fine light brown. Nor of Rebecca Shales, whose hair was black. So it had to be one of three girls: Clarissa Blackford, Dianna Ramsey, or Minnie Stapleton. Blackie did not know any of them well enough to identify her from these remains.

In fact it was Dianna Ramsey. If they had known the truth about her last few days, they would have wondered how she had lasted this far down the trail. Her rib had been broken when she had first fought her abductors; and in the first night on the trail, partly because of pain from her rib and partly from obstinacy, she had resisted her first rapist. He had then proceeded to beat her without mercy, loosening two of her teeth and worsening the break in her rib in the process. From then on, she had tolerated the agonizing rib pain while being used by the men because she had known that if she did not, they would kill her. And, from then on, she had been unable to lift a saddle or to pull a cinch to saddle her own horse; so one of the other girls had done it for her every morning to save Dianna's life.

But, what had destroyed Dianna's survival potential more than anything had been an occurrence on the third morning out from Gold Creek. She, along with the other girls, had been forced to witness the sadistic murder of Jettie Stevens. The desperados and their captives had camped in rocky terrain, and in the confusion of breaking camp that morning, Jettie had, on the pretext of relieving herself, gone into the brush and then had run off. When her absence had finally been noted, a furious El Lobo had ordered a hunt.

Seeking through terror to put an end to escapes, El Lobo had given explicit instructions as to what to do when the searchers caught her. The men, of course, had been on horseback, and, Jettie, running on bare feet, had been able to cover only a half mile. She had hidden in some rocks; but her white night dress had been spotted, and her captor, following El Lobo's orders, had roped her and dragged her behind his horse through the rocks and brush to camp where she lay battered, gouged, and bleeding, with a lot of her skin missing—a horrifying sight to the other girls. Then one of the bandits, grabbing her by her hair, had pulled Jettie to her knees and another man had slit her throat.

The rest of the girls had seen the blood spurting from the wound with the beats of the dying girl's heart.

Dianna Ramsey, weak from the constant pain of her rib, and unable to draw enough breath to scream, had burst into tears. Noticing her crying, the American desperado, Abner Waters, like a cat torturing a helpless mouse, and seeking to totally subjugate Dianna, had quietly given instructions to Jettie's executioners in Spanish. Those men had then forced Dianna to kneel, facing Jettie who now lay on her back with dead eyes, the gash in her throat still glistening, and blood all down the front of her. Then Jettie's executioner had placed the bloody knife to Dianna's throat. In terror, she had urinated. It had been then that Abner Waters had appeared to intercede. He had told her that if she promised to do whatever she was told, he would not let the men kill her. She had promised. And she had thereafter felt utterly degraded, as if she herself did not exist. Furthermore, Dianna had felt indebted to Abner Waters; felt she owed him her life. She had even been grateful to him, and had sought his company, believing he would protect her.

However, her condition had continued to worsen, and on her last morning, feeling faint, she had tried to mount her horse, but had gotten only half-way up and had fallen to the ground onto her back. The impact on the broken rib had knocked her unconscious for a few seconds, and, when she had come to, she had been unable to get up. A man had kicked her, but she had not gotten up. After a minute of entreaties from the other girls, and commands from the bandits, someone had walked over with a pistol. Dianna had looked pleadingly to Abner Waters, but he had gazed at her indifferently. Tears had flooded her eyes then, and, because she had no breath, she had said softly, "Ohhhhh, No...."

While Blackie dug the grave, Morgan sketched the girl as best he could and measured her, and wrote down the description of her remains, including her teeth, in hopes that something he described would identify her back home. They buried her, and Morgan said a short prayer.

They rode on southward and Morgan for the first time felt like a man through whose fingers sand was slipping. Important sand. And there seemed nothing he could do to stop it. Would the next abandoned camp contain another body? Would they lose the trail altogether?

That evening they camped beside the river, and in the morning they found that one of their horses was down and couldn't get up. The beast was trembling, and its eyes were glazed.

To avoid the sound of a gunshot, Blackie pulled out his sticker and from behind the animal's head, in one deft stroke, slit its throat.

They rode on now without spare saddle horses, and, because of that, they did not trot the horses much that day. They left the Santa Maria River and followed the desperados' trail along the foothills of Sierra Madre. Blackie kept his eyes peeled for any sign of a hacienda or even a rancho. He saw none that day.

At twilight, however, they came across something Blackie had been dreading since before they had left Gold Creek. Blackie dismounted and walked about, carefully studying the horse tracks. Morgan generally knew what had happened, but Blackie gave him the situation in detail.

"About twenty-five horses forked to the left. The rest forked to the right, heading off along the foothills. My black and Dusty's sorrel are among those that went to the right." He paused. "There's nothing to say that she's riding her own horse, though."

Morgan nodded. And they could not help but hold each other's eyes.

Blackie conceded, "Or that she's even alive."

Morgan looked the tracks over. Finally, he asked, "What do you think?"

"I don't know why they split up at this point, or who went where. What do you think?"

"I reckon El Lobo will stay with the gold. He's the boss. And besides, he may not trust too many of the others. I know I wouldn't."

"That doesn't exactly tell us which way to go."

Morgan sighed. "I don't know which way to go. But I lean toward the larger group."

"So do I. So let's go to the right."

"All right. But there's one possibility we didn't consider: they may know they're being followed now, and the split may be a rear guard maneuver. I think we should ride with the assumption that we may be the targets of an ambush."

About mid-morning the next day, Blackie spotted some regular shapes about three miles west of them, up a long arroyo that came gradually down out of the mountains. Morgan got out his telescope.

"It's a Rancho, all right. Corrals out back. Even got a windmill to pump the well. I hope they've got good horses."

They rode three miles up the arroyo to the house. Two dogs were barking as they rode into the yard. A handsome, slender Spaniard with light brown skin walked around the side of the house. He was about fifty, and had hair that was turning silver.

Morgan said, "Buenos dias, Señor."

The man answered in accented English. "Good day, Señores."

Blackie and Morgan were surprised, and the man was pleased with the effect. He explained:

"I lived in Texas ten years. My name is Benedicto Alvorado."

"Mine is Morgan Blaylock, and this is Blackie Sheffield. Our business is to buy horses."

Alvorado shook his head. "Oh, Señores, I am sorry to say that I have no horses for sale."

"We will pay well."

"I have only enough horses to run my little rancho. But, seven leagues—ah, twenty-one miles—east of here, is a large hacienda owned by my cousin, Don Ignacio Medina. He has many, many horses. If you are rich enough, he might even sell you race horses."

"Is there an hacienda south of here?"

"No, nothing for many, many leagues. Why not go to my cousin's, buy your horses, and then go south?"

"We can't. We're following the trail of some bandits."

"Bandits?"

"A gang led by a man known as El Lobo."

"*El Lobo?* In these parts?!" Alvorado gave a troubled frown. "This is bad."

"They went by here yesterday about three miles—a league—east of here."

"Why are you following them? And where are you from?"

"We're from New Mexico. They raided a town there, and took much loot and fifteen girls. Seven or eight of the girls are still with them. They've killed the rest."

Alvorado was revolted by the news.

Now that fresh horses were out of the question, Blackie felt that a high energy horse feed was their next best option. He asked, "Do you have any oats we can buy?"

"I have no oats," Alvorado said. "But I offer you some very good forage up behind the corrals. It will cost you nothing."

The horses badly needed rest and good forage. Blackie looked at Morgan.

Morgan nodded. "We'd better lay by for two or three hours."

Morgan addressed Alvorado. "We'd be much obliged to you."

From inside the house, a girl had been gazing out through a glass-less window at Blackie. She was sixteen and darker than her father and quite lovely. Blackie had spotted her right away, and now that the horse and feed question had been settled, he turned and looked steadily at her. They both smiled.

Señor Alvorado's eyes followed Blackie's gaze. The girl moved out of sight. "Ah," he said to Blackie, "you have seen my daughter, Catarina."

"She's very pretty."

"Thank you. I have a son your age, too. He went up the arroyo for a load of firewood."

* * *

In such outlying regions, strangers were always an event, and Norte Americanos (North Americans) were a rarity. So, the Alvorados were pleased to host their unexpected guests. Señora Alvorado, a Mexican, dark and a good deal younger than her husband, was quite shy toward them. She busied herself in the kitchen preparing a meal. The kitchen was in an alcove off the main living area. Two bedrooms and a large pantry were the only other rooms.

Alvorado placed hot water and a sharp razor at the disposal of the two strangers.

Morgan shaved while Blackie watered the horses, unsaddled them, and then took them five hundred yards to the upper pasture. While up there he noticed a cow lying in the shade of a tree peacefully chewing her cud, and he noticed a few goats here and there around the arroyo. Blackie came back down to the house and shaved himself. When he was through, Señora Alvorado set the table with a pot of beans and goat meat along with corn bread. The guests fell upon the hot meal with undisguised gusto.

When the Americans had finished eating, they thanked their hosts profusely. The men now sat in chairs away from the table, and Señora Alvorado and Catarina cleaned up. To the Alvorados, Morgan began describing in Spanish the raid on Gold Creek and his and Blackie's chase up to now. Catarina kept stealing glances at Blackie. Occasionally, Blackie would look up, catching her, and smile at her, and the girl would smile and look down. Señora Alvorado noticed this byplay.

She said in Spanish, "Catarina, go bring in the cow."

The girl was startled. "Now?! At midday?"

"Do as I say."

On her way to the open rear door, Catarina walked past Blackie's chair and subtly brushed her hand against his shoulder and arm. Blackie, who had no idea where she was going or why, looked up and watched her walk to the door. She had thick, glossy black hair that hung to the small of her back. She was barefoot, and her slender ankles and the swell of her calves were visible and pretty below the hem of her skirt. At the door, she glanced back and saw him looking at her hips. She smiled shyly and went out. Blackie got up and followed. Seeing this, Señora Alvorado did not know what to do about it without creating a fuss. She gave up; but she stood by the window where she could watch them.

Señora Alvorado had been surprised by her daughter's behavior. Usually once a week in decent weather, vaqueros (cowboys) came from the Medina hacienda to court Catarina. Señora Alvorado did not encourage them, but she did not try to stop them either. It was Catarina's cousins, the Medinas, whom she encouraged. They were not penniless cowboys; and they would be well off when they married. But the thing was that while Catarina was gracious and seemed to find their company diverting, she had shown no particular romantic interest in any of them; and she had even mentioned casually that she might enter a convent (this had upset her father who wanted lots of grandchildren). But, now, here was this stranger from the United States whom Catarina would probably never see again, and she was suddenly a flirt. Señora Alvorado found Blackie much too handsome and she distrusted him on that account. She speculated that he had had his way with many girls and was the type who used them and tossed them aside. After all, her own husband—too handsome for his own good—had admitted to her that he had been a womanizer until he had met her at Hacienda Medina where her parents were employees. She had been fourteen when they had had to get married.

Anyway, not only did visitors regularly show up from Hacienda Medina, but, four times each year, the Alvorados sent first their son, Emilio, and then Catarina to Hacienda Medina for visits of from one to two weeks. At the hacienda, the youngsters mingled with other youngsters of their ages and experienced community life.

So, now, while Blackie and Catarina walked toward the upper meadow, flirting with their eyes, Blackie caught sight of a young man coming down the arroyo toward them riding a burro and leading two more burros piled high with dead mesquite branches. Blackie figured that this must be Catarina's brother, and of no danger; nevertheless, he was suddenly aware that he had left his rifle in the house. He thought that this was a good lesson for him; he would not make this mistake again. They walked up the trail at a very casual pace, taking their time. Catarina stopped and picked flowers that had grown up as result of the recent rains. She smelled them and gently put them in front of Blackie's nose for him to smell. They dawdled along up the trail like this until her brother came abreast of them and halted. He was a very good looking youth of eighteen. He looked Blackie over while he spoke rapidly back and forth with Catarina. Blackie watched as the boy grew excited at the things she was telling him. Catarina pointed at Blackie and said his name. She turned to Blackie and pointed at her brother and said, "Emilio." Blackie offered his hand and smiled a big friendly smile. They shook hands.

Catarina watched Blackie smile. Her own smile grew big and joyful, and she spoke excitedly to her brother. Emilio laughed. He reached and gave Blackie a good natured slap on the shoulder and then started his burros for the house. Blackie, pleased, took it that he now had Emilio's permission to flirt with his sister.

Blackie and Catarina walked on up to the upper meadow where Catarina broke a switch from a bush, and with it, proceeded to drive the cow toward the house. The cow stubbornly took its time. The two youngsters flirted on the way back. Catarina spoke to him in Spanish. He smiled and shrugged. She spoke to him again, her voice expressive, her face mobile, and her eyes shining. He marveled at how pretty she was. He wished that he could speak Spanish. He told her in English how pretty she was.

Inside the house, Morgan and Alvorado sat talking. Emilio was there now and had already been introduced, and, at the moment, he stood in the kitchen, snacking at leftovers and listening to the older men talk.

Abruptly the two dogs started barking out in front of the house. Morgan reached to his revolver in its holster and unhooked the leather thong from the hammer. He was suddenly aware of Blackie's rifle leaning against the wall.

Alvorado got up and went to the open front door and looked out. Morgan went to a window.

Up in the meadow, the two youngsters had heard the dogs barking down by the house. Blackie, suddenly alert, had scanned the hillsides and had seen nothing, but the house had obscured the trail from the valley below.

He said quickly, "I left my rifle in the house."

He took out running for the house, leaving a surprised Catarina to drive the cow alone.

Alvorado came out onto his front step. A man approached on horseback. Two more riders waited fifty yards out. All three were without rifles. They wore long, dirty panchos, and appeared to be unarmed except for the machetes attached to their saddles. The one rider came on up and halted in front of Alvorado. He had a long scar on the left side of his face. He was the desperado who had killed Bill O'Connor and his son, Hank, and who had raped and abducted Stella. He was Benito Gonzales.

Benito Gonzales said, "Buenos dias, Señor."

"Buenos dias," Alvorado answered.

Gonzales said in Spanish, "I and my companions seek work."

"Forgive me, but I have no jobs for you. Try Hacienda Medina. It is seven leagues east on that trail."

"Thank you." Gonzales appeared to hesitate. "It is too late to reach there today. May we do some work in exchange for a hot meal?"

"You and your companions may eat as my guests."

"It is a kindness."

Gonzales turned and waved his companions in.

At the house, the three desperados dismounted and tied their horses and followed Alvorado inside. The bandits smelled unwashed. Nevertheless, Alvorado, a pleasant host, introduced himself, his wife, and his son. Benito Gonzales gave his name, and the other two gave theirs. Alvorado turned their attention to Morgan who stood against the far wall of the room.

"This gentleman is also my guest. He is from the United States. He is here to find and kill El Lobo and his gang."

The desperados were visibly amazed.

"I have heard of this El Lobo," Gonzales said. "You must be a very brave man to hunt for him and his men by yourself."

That Gonzales believed he was talking to a fool was obvious. Morgan smiled courteously.

Alvorado chuckled. "He is not as brave as it appears. He did not come alone. He brought a boy with him."

The desperados laughed. It was good natured teasing on Alvorado's part.

Smiling, Gonzales said to Morgan, "Oh, Señor! And where is this boy?"

Morgan hesitated. For all he knew these men might be part of El Lobo's gang. Besides, there was something repulsive about this man who called himself Benito Gonzales. Morgan felt that these men should be lied to, but what could he say? Blackie saved Morgan the trouble by running up to the back door, breathing hard. Everyone looked up to see him at the door. Gonzales and Blackie each recognized the other immediately, and Gonzales' hand darted inside his serape.

Blackie jumped clear of the doorway.

Gonzales' hand reappeared with a revolver in it.

But Morgan, where he stood, had already gotten his revolver out and cocked the hammer, and he fired and hit Gonzales who fell against the wall and then to the floor. The other two desperados had now also drawn their revolvers. Morgan fired at the second one, who stumbled away, crashing into some chairs, and fell to the floor. The third desperado fired excitedly in Morgan's direction, but missed. Morgan fired and did not miss. The man doubled over and backed against the wall. Morgan was ready to let him live; but the bandit raised his revolver. Morgan fired again and the bandit fell to the floor. The second desperado, where he lay wounded, fumbled for his dropped revolver, got a grip on it and picked it up. Morgan fired again, killing the man. The room was hazy blue from black powder smoke. Morgan went over and kicked Gonzales to make sure he was not alive. He started reloading his revolver.

Alvorado stood rooted in the midst of the scene, just plain shocked. His wife was in wide eyed terror. Eighteen year old Emilio Alvorado was electrified where he stood. While the shooting had been going on, he had been afraid; but now that it was over, he was no longer afraid even though his body trembled in the aftermath of being afraid. He had the notion that he had witnessed a rare and never to be repeated scene.

Morgan shouted toward the back door, "Blackie! It's all right! You can come in!"

Blackie had run in an arc away from the doorway, circling back and diving over the corral's brushwork fence, landing on his right shoulder and rolling in the powdery dust and scrambling on all fours to the place on the fence where he had earlier draped his horse's pack. He had then pulled the pack down into the corral and extracted his express rifle and, crouching, with just his head visible from outside, had made it to the corral gate and unlatched it. By then, Morgan had called. Blackie stood erect now and went through the gate.

Morgan came to the back door and said to him, "Look around in case there are others out there."

Blackie started walking a circle of the house, looking outward.

Morgan went back inside and grabbed Gonzales' body by its feet and dragged it out of the back door and off to one side.

Emilio Alvorado's heart was beating rapidly; he went over and seized a foot belonging to one of the dead men. He had never touched a dead man before. The lifeless foot seemed strange to him. He experienced shock-like feelings along his own arms and back and head. He grabbed the other foot and began dragging the dead man for the door.

Morgan came back inside and saw streaks of blood on the floor where he had dragged Gonzales. He could hear Señora Alvorado hysterically whispering—hissing—to her husband.

Morgan listened to the whispering. He interrupted impatiently in Spanish:

"These men came to steal, rape, and murder. I saved your lives!" He paused for that to sink in, and then added more gently, "Now go out and let your daughter know you are all right."

Alvorado went out and called to his daughter to hurry to the house. Blackie had circled the house and had seen nothing. He snatched a bridle and his whip from the corral fence and took out running for their horses in the upper meadow. He passed Catarina on the way. Frightened, she stepped off the trail as he ran by.

Blackie caught the horses, de-hobbled them, mounted one bareback, and drove them down to the corral where, with Alvorado's help, he and Morgan saddled them. Emilio had wrestled the dead bodies onto a wagon and, to hide them, was now covering them with the firewood he had brought home a few minutes before. He and his father would bury them later.

Morgan apologized to Blackie. "They all had their six shooters out. It wasn't possible to take prisoners. I'm sorry."

Morgan turned to Alvorado. "I figure they are camped less than half a day's ride from here. So, don't let anyone in unless you know him. How many rifles do you have?"

"I have only a musket, amigo."

"These men probably left their rifles nearby under some bush, trying to look like vaqueros in need of work. If we find them close, I'll run them back to you."

The pursuers mounted and, leading their pack horses, galloped from the yard.

Blackie initially galloped the horses hard, tracking on the run; but, after it became apparent that the desperados were most likely camped in an arroyo or canyon in the nearby mountains, he slowed it down, trying to predict where the tracks would turn west. He did not want to be seen by a lookout from the camp.

*　　*　　*

The desperados' camp was in a meadow in a beautiful box canyon a dozen miles south of Rancho Alvorado. A stream ran beside the camp, flowing toward the valley to the east. Trees grew along the creek, and grew here and there on the edges of the meadow. The grass in the meadow was lush, but was trampled flat where the people were. At sundown that day there were three camp fires burning, and wood smoke rose and wafted above the camp. The men were lazing about. Some were drinking liquor, some were gambling. Two of them sat casual guard a couple hundred yards downstream, at the east end of the camp. The horses, unsaddled, grazed behind ropes knotted together across the canyon just west of camp. Five of the girls were cooking at the fires. The sixth, Otis Shales' twenty year old wife, Rebecca, walked by a man who grabbed her and pulled her down on top of him.

Trudy Belvedere was squatting by one of the fires, cooking steer meat on some wooden spits. She had lost weight. Serene and pretty a little over two weeks ago in Gold Creek, she was now haggard, sullen, and miserable. Her dirty face was pale from fatigue, and her hair was tangled and dirty. Her face and arms were bruised. The torn and soiled silk night gown, knotted together in the front, hid other bruises.

Beside Trudy squatted redheaded Connie Watkins, seventeen. These two girls had been sticking together without realizing why. The fact was that they had something in common: Connie's father, like Trudy's father and mother, had been killed when she had been seized. Connie had also lost weight, and she had a bruise just below her left eye, and others on her arms. Her flannel night dress was filthy.

A few feet away, at another fire, squatted Ella York, sixteen. Back in Gold Creek, she had been willowy with gorgeous blue eyes and shiny, very light brown hair; but now she was too thin and appeared ill, and she had a glazed look to her eyes.

Beside her was fifteen year old Jinny Rowe. Because of her unusual appearance, she had received extra use by the desperados, and now she had a beaten, bewildered expression. Her auburn hair was tangled and dirty and she did not care.

Cooking alone at another fire, waiting for Rebecca Shales to join her, was fifteen year old Minnie Stapleton. She had arrived in Gold Creek only a week before the raid, and although she had not known any of the girls before being abducted with them, she had formed a bond with them tighter than any she would ever likely form with anyone else under any other circumstances. It, the bond, would last for a lifetime—which seemed likely to them all to not be very long. The girls had seen too much death already for them to harbor any illusions about their own survival.

Now, sixteen days after the raid on Gold Creek, while the girls cooked the last of the camp's meat supply, Morgan and Blackie lay prone upon the north ridge above the canyon, looking down into the camp. Blackie, who had been using Morgan's telescope, handed it back to Morgan.

"Well, I guess that settles it."

Morgan offered, "Maybe she's in that clump of trees by the creek."

Blackie answered bitterly, "Yeah. Well, while I'm grasping at straws, here's another one for me: Lobo and the American and the pack horses with the gold aren't there. Maybe they took Dusty with them."

Morgan was surprised. "Not there? Damn! That must've been their tracks that branched east." He paused. "Yes, they might have taken her."

Blackie bellied backwards until out of sight of the camp. He stood, turning his back on Morgan. He was slightly nauseous. His breathing was effected by his emotions and, when he spoke, he had to catch his breath twice to complete his sentence.

"I suppose the most likely....answer is....that she's dead."

Morgan said quietly and gently, "There's another possibility that we can't totally ignore. She might have escaped."

"Another straw.... To hell with it! I'll have to stop thinking about her. I'm up and down like a jack in the box every day.

Whatever the truth is, whether she's dead or alive, worrying about it won't do one ounce of good." He paused and then added, "In the meantime, there are six girls down there who need help."

"Right. Do you want to plan this now?"

Blackie bellied forward and looked down on the camp. Morgan looked through his telescope as he spoke.

"There's no outlet to the west; just cliffs and a waterfall."

"Uh, huh."

Morgan looked up at the opposite ridge on the south side of the canyon. "I can't believe they don't have guards up here on the ridges. They must be awfully confident. They can't have any idea they've been followed."

Blackie said, "If Lobo or the American were there, I'll bet they'd have guards up here. I'm reminded of something the American told me about these hombres: if somebody doesn't tell them what to do, they'll get themselves shot."

"I hope he's right." Morgan studied the camp. "Look here, it seems to me that we might be able to kill most of them if we do it suddenly and don't let them get organized. If we drag it out, they'll kill us. There's no way we could win in a straight shootout. We should pick our positions carefully and get into them under cover of darkness, and start shooting when the light's good enough. We'll have to shoot fast and we can't afford to miss hardly a shot."

"What about us taking prisoners?"

"It's dangerous. I think we should kill everyone we can. If we try to take prisoners, we could jeopardize the girls and maybe get ourselves killed."

"I suppose the girls will know what happened to Dusty, but they may not know where the other desperados went."

"They must have gone to Chihuahua."

"All right," said Blackie. "But if the last couple of men throw down their guns and throw up their hands, I want to know where in Chihuahua Lobo went."

Twenty-Eight

L ying there on the north ridge above the desperados'
camp, they agreed that Blackie would take up position
behind a fallen cedar log down on this side of the canyon, about two hundred and fifty yards from the edge of the
desperados' camp. He could shoot effectively from that distance while at the same time be somewhat out of range for
the less skillful shooters among the bandits.

Morgan selected for himself a pile of rocks on the far side
of the canyon. It was only twenty yards from the nearest bandit's bedroll, but there was not much else to be done considering Morgan's eyesight limitations.

Before it got dark, Morgan rode his horse eastward about
a mile down the ridge toward the valley floor. He stopped
and waited for darkness to set in. After dark, he crossed over
to the south ridge. Then he rode westward up the ridge. He
had a hard time of it in the dark on account of his short eyesight; he kept thinking he was at the right place to go down to
the camp, but in the darkness he could not find the landmark
he had selected before dark by telescope from the north
ridge. He had to go much further before he found it, and he
had lost time in the confusion. He took his horse over on the
side of the ridge away from the desperados' camp and tied it
by his lariat to a bush in a grassy ravine. Now came the really
dangerous part. He had to literally inch down the north face
of the ridge on foot, being careful to not dislodge rocks. Even
a broken twig might be heard. In this lower latitude, stars and
moon could make a moving body possibly detectable; so
Morgan moved slowly, stopping often. He took an hour and a
half to get down there; and the night was half over by the
time he got into position.

This was by far the most reckless thing Morgan had ever
done in his life. They had counted exactly thirty desperados
in the camp. And now here Morgan was in a position from

which he could not escape so long as any desperado remained able and willing to shoot. Morgan was not under any illusions about his chances; shortly after first light today, his life might end.

He could have been sleeping soundly and comfortably at Collier's Ranch right now; and he would have been so sleeping if it were not for this family he had willingly gotten himself involved with.

There was Sarah: stunning even at thirty-five, and, in Morgan's estimation, extremely bright. Her son knew that she was "awful smart," but, at seventeen, perhaps he was not sophisticated enough yet to realize just how insightful and keen his mother's mind really was.

Then there was Dusty—or had been, if she was dead now. The girl's beauty probably blinded some people to other attributes which Morgan thought were even more important. She had power. You could not be around her without being affected by her. Most of the time, for instance, she seemed to shed joy around her as a dog shed hairs.

And finally there was Blackie. Morgan could say without hesitation that he would not be here now if it were not for the boy. He would not have ridden down here alone with anyone else. It was unthinkable and reckless; but, because the boy had counted on him, he had come. Billy Cape had carried a letter from Blackie out to Morgan at Collier's Ranch. The message had told briefly of the raid, of Dusty's abduction, and of Blackie's intention to bring her home. He had requested that Morgan buy six horses for them and requested that Morgan accompany him. Morgan had not even hesitated.

Remembering the letter now, Morgan could see in the wording that the boy had not doubted that Morgan would come with him. And when Morgan had climbed the steps at the Sheffield house thirteen days ago, having just arrived from Collier's Ranch, he had looked into the eyes of someone who radiated power, who knew what he wanted and was determined to have it. Blackie had made up his mind to bring his sister home and, even if she was now dead, it had been his intention that had gotten them here where they had now found a needle in a haystack. Morgan's experience and reason and his ability to speak Spanish had indeed been important; but without the young man's purpose, Morgan's talents would not have been put to use. That Blackie's sister was perhaps dead was no reflection on the boy's effectiveness; after all, here they were with a chance to save six of the girls.

Morgan thought that Sarah must know Blackie possessed unusual qualities. In Morgan's last couple of minutes with her, while the little posse waited for him outside, she had instructed him on how to handle Blackie. She had pointed out to Morgan that when Blackie got difficult you could always reason with him. Don't ever order him about, she had cautioned Morgan. *Ask* him to do things. You could get him to move mountains for you then.

Move mountains? A figure of speech. But, that the boy could be remarkably effective, and was capable of singleness of purpose, Morgan could plainly see now. He had not seen it before.

*　　*　　*

After dark, Blackie had inched down the mountainside in a crouch. He had carried his two Sharps rifles, both the .45-70 and the .45-110, and a bag of ammunition for each. When the barrel of his .45-110 got hot tomorrow, he would switch to his .45-70. And back again if necessary. He also carried a cleaning rod and flannel patches to clean the black powder from the barrels. A dirty barrel could ruin his accuracy.

He was in position long before Morgan was, and he settled down for a long night of waiting.

Unlike Morgan, Blackie did not consider his own death likely; he felt sure that he would survive somehow. Uppermost in his mind were two aims: to save the six girls, and to find out what had happened to Dusty. His death did not allow him to do those things, so he did not give it but fleeting consideration.

He was, however, concerned about Morgan's risk. The position from which Morgan had chosen to shoot was risky in the extreme. But there was not much else to be done if they were to utilize him. There was little that Blackie could do for Morgan other than kill all the men he could as fast as he could. The girls' safety required the same of him. So, he intended to do it.

The thing that caused Blackie strain in the night, however, was his worry about Dusty. He tried not to think of her, but thoughts of her drew his attention now and then regardless. It was almost a certainty that she was dead. The hope that, for some reason, Lobo and the American had taken her, and only her, with them wherever they had gone with the gold was stretching things. The seven pairs of footprints in the sandbar seemed to indicate that she had not been with them at the camp along the river a few days ago.

Blackie jerked his attention from thoughts of Dusty. He remembered his mother's attitude about worry. She said it did nothing for the person you worried about; and it distracted you and upset you. He remembered that in his younger years, whenever she had noticed him worrying, she had gently directed his attention to things in the environment. Now, sitting here behind the fallen log, Blackie looked at the silhouettes of the mountains, and then he looked at the stars, picking out ones that he had never seen in New Mexico. He soon felt better.

But, eventually, thoughts of Dusty crept back in. Memories of pleasant times with her drifted in and out of his thoughts. He remembered the time last year when they had painted the exterior of the barn together. It had never been painted before, so it had required lots of paint and lots of effort. They had painted and sweated and gotten the dark red paint on themselves and in their hair and they had laughed and talked and kidded around, and it had not seemed like work; and they had done a good job too. He was sure that if he had painted the barn with anyone else it would have been work.

Not that he minded work, but Dusty had some magic that turned work into play.

And, sitting there behind the fallen log in the night, he remembered one time when he had been angry with her. He had seen the smile on her face and the look in her eyes, and had known that she intended to get him over it. But he had not wanted her to, because he was feeling righteous about whatever it was—he could not even remember now what he had been mad about—and she had come over and put her hand behind his head and had pulled his forehead down on hers and looked up into his eyes and he had burst out laughing; and whatever it was that he had been angry about seemed so unimportant that he could not believe he had been mad about it.

There had been other times like that. She had never said or done the same thing twice; so there was no trick to it. It was just her.

Twenty-Nine

The sun was not yet up, but there was light enough for Blackie to see everything clearly. The two guards at the east end of the meadow were sitting on the ground with their knees drawn up, each wrapped in a blanket against the coolness of the night. Blackie could tell by the way one guard's head hung against his chest that he was asleep. Blackie adjusted the peep sights on both rifles for the distance and for the downhill shooting. He now put the sights of his .45-110 on the guard who was awake. He set the hair trigger. He touched the hair trigger—there was a roar followed by echoes and the guard fell over and did not move. While Blackie quickly opened the rifle's breech and extracted the spent cartridge, he heard the bark of Morgan's .44-40 Winchester followed by echoes. By the time Blackie had reloaded, the sleeping guard had awakened and had lurched to his knees. Blackie fired and the man sprawled and lay still. He heard Morgan's Winchester again. He reloaded and swung his rifle into the center of camp. Six men were standing. Other men were sitting up. Morgan's Winchester barked again, and one of the standing men fell. Blackie fired and another man went down. He reloaded and saw a man on his knees with a rifle in his hands. Blackie shot the man before the man could find a target.

Blackie shot rapidly and at a regular rate like a well oiled machine, choosing as his priority targets anyone who had picked up a gun. He did not miss a shot. He fired, opened the breech, reloaded, fired again, opened the breech, reloaded, fired, over and over. All with a cool hatred for the men he and Morgan were killing.

In the camp, confusion reigned. Four men near Morgan lay dead in their bedrolls. There were men who had gotten up only to be shot down. Some were moving about but did not even have their rifles.

The six girls wisely stayed flat on the ground. Two bellied toward the creek.

Sixteen desperados lay dead or dying before two men started shooting at Morgan. Morgan had to lay low behind the rocks. Blackie picked off those two men. But the smoke from his big rifle had now finally given his position away. Fire began to be directed his way. Most of the bullets impacted the dirt above and behind him. Guns shot up hill shoot high, and none of these men had experience shooting at such a steep angle. It would take them a few shots to learn how much to compensate, and most of them did not live long enough. Morgan began firing again. Blackie switched rifles and resumed shooting and killing.

A desperado ran for the horses, mounted one bareback and streaked down through camp and got away. Another, seeing him get away, ran for the horses, mounted bareback and got only a few yards before Blackie blew him off the horse.

Only seven desperados had not been shot when Morgan stopped for the second time to reload his Winchester's magazine. This was the break two desperados had been waiting for. They charged Morgan's position firing their revolvers, making him duck down behind the rocks. Blackie sighted on the back of one of the men and fired. The man fell forward on his face and lay still. Morgan popped up with his sixshooter, and was surprised that there was only one man charging him now. The man foolishly fired at Morgan on the run, his gun bouncing and jiggling as he ran, and so he missed. Morgan calmly aimed and fired at the onrushing desperado. The man stumbled backwards down the incline and fell and slowly bled to death. In the meantime Morgan finished reloading the Winchester's magazine while Blackie shot the one remaining man in the meadow.

The easy pickings were over. Blackie was drawing too much fire, and he had to clean his gun bores while out of sight behind the log. Two men had gotten in with the horses and out of Morgan's range of vision. Worse, three men had taken cover in the clump of trees along the creek. These three had been with El Lobo a long time and were experienced killers. And they concentrated their fire on Blackie's position. Blackie knew that there were some men in the trees, but he could not see them through the foliage. He sat up, trying to get a clear shot at one of the men among the horses. From the clump of trees a bullet struck the top of the cedar log and sprayed dust and splinters into Blackie's right eye. The pain was instantaneous and excruciating, and his hand darted to his eye, but he restrained it. He did not rub the eye; instead, he ducked down behind the log and blinked and blinked uncontrollably. He tried to let the tears wash his eye. The pain had him almost entirely distracted.

Morgan could not see the men in the trees nor the two among the horses. He could not even see the trees distinctly. He could hear them shooting from the trees, and, alarmingly, he could not hear the boom of Blackie's big rifle returning the fire. He wondered if Blackie had been killed. With his telescope, he glassed Blackie's position; there was no sign of his friend. He pointed the scope down to the creek and glassed the trees carefully. He could see nothing through the leaves and underbrush.

Morgan heard galloping of horses. He saw two (or was it four?) gray shadows running eastward down through camp. He was unable to fix his telescope on any one of the shadows to determine whether it was a loose horse, a bandit, or a Gold Creek girl.

Blackie had popped up and seen the two desperados escape on the unsaddled horses. He had popped immediately back down and three shots had sounded from the trees. His right eye was cleaning itself, although it pained him and its vision was still blurred.

It was several minutes before Blackie regained good vision in his right eye. The eye nevertheless still pained him. He finally looked over the log and searched the trees. He saw dirt spray in front of his log and he heard the rifle shot from the trees. He ducked down and he heard two more rifle shots.

Blackie could not think of anything to do at this point. He was pinned down, and Morgan was pretty much out of action now so long as the men stayed in the trees. He wondered if the desperados who had escaped by horse might come up on the ridge behind him and shoot down on him. If they did, he would be in serious danger.

From the trees, a bullet ricocheted off the rock in front of Morgan. He ducked down. He crawled to the other end of the rock pile and found a space between the rocks where he could, by craning his neck, glass the trees and the meadow. Several minutes had thus gone past when he saw, through his telescope, a young woman belly up from the creek to a dead desperado and take the man's Winchester. She levered the breech partly open and checked to see that it was loaded, and then she bellied back down to the creek and toward the trees from which the desperados had been shooting. Morgan knew her by sight, but he had never known her name.

He figured that she would need help. He crawled to where he could shoot, and then fired his Winchester blindly into the trees to distract the bandits' attention. He levered and fired again. Two shots were returned and one ricocheted off the rock over which he leaned, and fragments of rock or lead stung his face. Morgan fired again, and then ducked down behind the rock.

The young woman, Rebecca Shales, bellied forward in her soiled flannel night dress, using her bare elbows and knees and feet to pull and push herself forward. The skin was being scraped from her knees and elbows, but she gave it no attention. Her face and body were already bruised and sore from three beatings she had sustained in the last few days. She inched through some underbrush and, from her prone position, could see the three desperados through the remaining underbrush.

Rebecca Shales took very careful aim at the side of the head of the nearest desperado. He was looking down his rifle barrel at where Morgan had been shooting from. Rebecca held her breath and squeezed the trigger. The rifle went off with a loud bang, kicking her right shoulder and puffing blu-ish smoke. She instantly rolled onto her left side and with her right hand levered a new cartridge into the chamber; she rolled back to aim at the second man. The second man, who had also been looking Morgan's way, realized that the gun-shot which felled his partner must have come from the side. He was looking Rebecca's way but he did not look low enough before she shot again, hitting him in the side. He slumped away from her, his feet and his right hand twitching three or four times; and then he lay still. The third desperado had been watching Blackie's position, but now he knew that something was amiss. He turned and looked at his two dead companions. Frantically, he looked for the shooter and, when he did see her, he found himself looking down her bar-rel. She fired, hitting him in the chest. He went down and was dead in three seconds.

Rebecca levered another round into the rifle's chamber. She looked carefully around the trees and brush. She saw no other men. She got up to a crouch and walked warily up onto the meadow.

Morgan had her in his telescope. He called out, "Are they all dead?!"

English! A man's voice speaking English! A thrill of relief ran through her.

She called back, "I think so!"

With his telescope, Morgan looked up to Blackie's posi-tion. Blackie was showing his eyes, looking out over the log onto the scene below.

Morgan stood and looked around with his naked eyes. Within the range of his sight, he saw no movement among the desperados; they all seemed dead. Two other girls got to their knees, hesitated momentarily, and then stood. Morgan walked down into the meadow. Other girls stood. All but newcomer Minnie Stapleton recognized Morgan. He walked across the meadow and up to Rebecca Shales.

"Young lady, you're handy with a rifle."

"My god, I've never been so glad to see anyone in my life! Who else is out there?"

"Blackie Sheffield."

"Blackie?.... Is that all?!"

"Yep."

"The two of you did all this?" She waved her hand at the carnage.

"Like shooting fish in a barrel. This has got to be one of the most stupid campsites an outlaw ever made. Not even a lookout on a ridge."

Rebecca nodded. "They started getting careless two days ago when Lobo left."

"We can all be grateful for that."

Morgan looked up to where Blackie was walking down to the creek. He decided to wait and let Blackie ask the questions that the young man wanted answered.

The other five girls, numb with shock and exhaustion, gathered around Morgan. He was the first safe man they had seen in seventeen days. All eyes watched Blackie come across the creek and up to them. He kept blinking his right eye which was badly bloodshot.

Blackie looked at Rebecca's Winchester. "How many did you shoot, Becky?"

"Three."

"You did a good thing."

He knew that those men could have had him tied up on the ridge until nightfall; and they then might have slipped out in the dark and taken some of the girls with them, or killed the girls. They might even have come up there in the dark and killed him.

Rebecca said, "Blackie, you have no idea what it's like seeing you again."

Blackie patted her on the back. He felt her flesh involuntarily flinch and quiver under his hand. He could see from her face and arms that she had been beaten.

Dreading the answer, his voice uncharacteristically weak, he asked, "Becky, what happened to Dusty?"

"She's with Lobo—the leader. They separated from us day before yesterday. Six of them and Dusty, and the pack horses with the gold. The American told Trudy they were going to a town called Chihuahua to sell the gold." Rebecca turned to Trudy.

"That's right," Trudy said, clutching her nightgown together so that it would cover as much as possible. "They're supposed to meet us here in a few days."

Blackie's relief was obvious to all of them. "Why did they take only Dusty with them?"

Rebecca answered, "Lobo's taken her for his own. He won't let anyone else touch her. He had...." Rebecca got a hard look on her face. "Look, we've seen some pretty rotten things. I'm not going to try to sound ladylike. A few days ago, all the men got drunk, and one tried to rape Dusty. Lobo had the man castrated."

Blackie nodded. "We found that man."

From his shirt pocket, Morgan pulled a list that contained the names of all the abducted girls. He had drawn lines through the names of girls he knew to be dead. He now asked the girls in the meadow to identify themselves to him. He put a check mark beside each girl's name as she gave it. Two girls remained unaccounted for.

Morgan addressed Rebecca. "We found a camp a couple of days ago. There were remains there, but we couldn't recognize them. Dark brown hair."

"Dianna." Rebecca felt her throat tighten. She paused. "I don't know her last name."

"Ramsey," said Trudy Belvedere.

With his carpenter's pencil, Morgan crossed out Dianna Ramsey's name.

He said, "That leaves only one girl unaccounted for—Clarisa Blackford."

No one wanted to speak for a moment. Finally, Jinny Rowe said, "Days ago—way back.... A horse fell on her.... So they killed her."

They had been riding at night south of Dog Springs, and Clarisa Blackford's horse had shied at something in the dark—they never knew at what—and the horse had fallen with her and broken her leg. Clarisa, crying and groaning and gasping in pain, had known without a doubt that she would be killed then, and to the other girls she had cried out, half crazy with pain, that she wanted her family to know that she loved them. One of the bandits had executed her by cutting her throat. Her body had been dragged several yards to the east of the trail to clear it for the rest of the party, and, consequently, Morgan and Blackie had passed it undetected in the night four days later when the rain had washed away much of the odor and the prevailing breeze had been from the west.

Now, while Morgan organized the girls, Blackie spent several minutes washing his eye in the creek. Minnie Stapleton built a fire and made coffee and cornmeal mush. There was nothing else to eat. The last of the meat had been eaten last evening. The three desperados who had died at Rancho Alvorado had probably been sent out to rustle cattle. The rancho had no doubt been seen when they passed it on their way to the canyon.

Rebecca was assigned lookout duty up on the hillside. The other girls went through the desperados' pockets and saddle bags, taking anything of value and throwing it onto a blanket in the meadow. Morgan preceded the girls, cutting off the right ear of each dead man. It was a good way to determine if a man was really dead. After what the women had been through in the last few days, this did not bother them in the slightest. Morgan found two men badly wounded but still alive; one was incoherent, the other did not know where in Chihuahua El Lobo had gone. Morgan executed both men with his sixshooter. He had no problem with it; these men were all guilty of rape and murder at the very least.

Blackie climbed up and over the north ridge to get the three horses he had left up there. When he led them down the steep incline into the canyon, one of the pack horses fell, spilling its pack. He finally got them down to the meadow where he put them in with the desperados' horses.

By now, the loot had been collected, and Morgan had made blanket packs for the desperados' firearms, and assigned the girls to collect the guns and ammunition. The girls were not awfully efficient right now; they were exhausted, confused, and easily distracted.

They finished while Blackie was up on the south ridge retrieving Morgan's saddle horse.

Morgan said, "All right, ladies, grab something to eat, and then saddle up. Saddle two horses for yourselves. Take a rifle and plenty of cartridges. I don't care if you've never shot one before. Pick up whatever else you think you need—like maybe a blanket.

"The nearest hacienda is thirty miles east of here. We're going to ride steadily. If the people at the hacienda are good people, we'll leave you there and fetch you on our way back from Chihuahua."

*　　*　　*

They had been on the trail for about two hours when Blackie, riding point, halted and let some of them pass him. The girls had their night dresses hiked up to their hips by sitting in the saddle. Their legs were peeling from bad sunburns. He fell in beside Rebecca. She tried to pull her dirty flannel night dress down over the thigh near him. There was a big bruise on that thigh where she had been kicked by a desperado. Blackie looked at the bruise and then looked her in the eyes. Her hair was a mess, and besides the facial bruises, her face was blotched from stress and exhaustion; moreover, her eyes had dark circles under them. That she needed a few days rest was quite obvious. He had other plans for her, though.

Blackie said, "I've been watching you. You handle a horse pretty well."

"I've always handled horses well."

"And rifles?"

"I've shot rifles. But I didn't know I could do what I did back there until I did it. Sometimes, when you have to do something, you just do it."

Blackie's tired face broke into a smile. He liked her attitude more and more.

He said, "You look pretty tired." He vainly hoped she would answer that she was all right or something of the kind.

Instead, she flashed anger at him. "Well, what did you expect?! The little time we weren't riding or cooking, we were being used by one man after another!" It had come ripping out of her mouth and she had been unable to stop it.

Blackie did not take offense. He merely nodded.

After a moment, Rebecca said in a conciliatory tone, "You look pretty tired yourself. Have you been on the trail all this time too?"

"No. I was in that jail without food and water for two days besides not having eaten the day before that, and when I got out, I was too weak to ride, and there weren't any horses anyway. We started four days late."

Rebecca nodded, thinking.

Finally, Blackie spoke what was on his mind. "Look, Becky, do you think you could make the ride to Chihuahua with me and Morgan? It's eighty or ninety miles."

She merely looked at him.

"You know these men by sight more surely than I do. I know I would recognize the American and Lobo, but I might miss some of the others. Besides, another pair of eyes, and another rifle might come in handy."

Rebecca was pleased despite her exhaustion. "If you need me, I'll go."

"We need you." He paused. "You know, Morgan can't see well at long distances. If something happens to me, I want him to go on after Dusty. He's nearsighted and he'll need somebody to see for him, and somebody who can shoot."

Rebecca nodded. She thought for a bit as they rode. Then, "Dusty said you would come for her."

"Did she?"

"Yes. But after a big rainstorm a week ago, she said you might not be able to find us. At first I think we all had some hope of being saved. But it didn't last long." Emotions began to distort Rebecca's face. "They kept killing girls and you were scared to death. You did what they told you to because those who didn't got killed. They shot Stella 'cause she couldn't control her horse. Then that night, at the first camp, they gave us all a beating—everyone had a beating. They just did it for no reason that I could see. And then the raping started. One girl started screaming and wouldn't stop. They beat her and beat her but she wouldn't stop; so they beat her unconscious and when she came to she started screaming again. Lobo shouted something and then someone walked over and shot her. I guess to shut her up. And there was a girl that night, Prudie Babcock, who bled so badly she was too weak to stand, so they shot her. Susanna Brown's legs were so raw from rubbing on saddle leather that she begged them to not make her get on a horse, so they shot her."

Rebecca's face turned red and distorted. "Oh, Blackie, it was so awful!" She cried, tears running down her dirty face leaving clean tracks on her cheeks. She sobbed for a couple of minutes.

Blackie rode alongside her, showing her no sympathy, just looking at her gently.

She finally wiped her eyes and glanced at him.

Blackie said forcefully, "In the end, you beat them, Becky."

She started laughing then. It was an uncontrolled laugh, no real humor to it, almost hysterical. It was the sixteen days of terror streaming from her. She finally settled down and gave him a thankful little smile.

"I guess I did at that."

He smiled gently back at her.

Rebecca studied his face. She marveled at how safe she felt riding beside him. After what she had been through, she might have expected someone to wring his hands and say how sorry he was for her. Instead, Blackie had a little smile for her.

It reminded her of Dusty.

She said, "You know, your sister is a rare one."

Blackie lit up. "How so?"

"I don't really know. It just made me feel better when she was near. I remember we were camped beside a river and I was feeling...." The emotions began to twist her face again. "I don't know how to describe how bad I felt. Everything was so awful.... Blackie, I can't tell you how it was. At first the groveling fear—we were so terrified we stank from it. I remember the sweat running down my sides even after dark. And we were treated....like....like animals. They spoke to us in Spanish and when we didn't understand them, they hit us or kicked us. And I knew that they might just kill me for any reason at all. I could reckon the miles we were covering, and after several days, I knew no one would come and save us, and I didn't feel scared anymore....just hopeless. I was just waiting to die. That hopelessness was the worst thing I've felt in my life. I knew I was going to die, and nothing was any use anymore. I didn't care what they did to me."

Rebecca was silent for a long time. Then, "Well, anyway, we camped on the bank of this river four or five days ago, and they rustled a heifer and slaughtered her and made us cook her. Dusty and I ended up cooking over the same fire, and she told me she was learning Spanish from Lobo and the American so she could use it to escape. She said I should learn it too. I told her it was nonsense, that we were all dead. But, she kept talking with me and pretty soon I wanted to believe her, that we would get away. And I started crying. I got afraid they would come over and kill me if I didn't stop my bawling. Then we started talking low about how we might escape. She said she was pretty sure Lobo didn't want to kill her and probably wouldn't unless she tried to escape. In between hitting her and threatening her, she said, he seemed to be trying to get her to like him.

"And finally, in the midst of all this, there on the river bank, surrounded by all these killers, your sister said something funny, don't you see." Rebecca paused and glanced at

Blackie. "At first, I thought I hadn't heard her right, but I looked up and saw this little smile on her face and I realized she was joking.... And then I thought she'd gone crazy—from what was happening to us, don't you see. I thought she was crazy and didn't understand what was going on. I think it took me a few seconds before I thought her joke was funny. You can't appreciate what a little joke is worth in a situation like that.... I wish you could feel what I'm trying to tell you, because I can't find the words for it." Rebecca was silent for three or four seconds. "Oh, I know I'm not making myself clear."

"No, you are," Blackie said.

After a pause, Rebecca continued, "Well, just knowing that someone hadn't been so smashed down by what was happening to us that she couldn't joke.... It gave me.... It made me realise...."

Rebecca was silent for a bit, ruminating. Blacky just rode alongside her, looking at her, waiting for her to complete her thoughts.

Finally she spoke: "It pulled me out of the hell I was in just enough for me to know that I might not be done for." Rebecca was silent again for a few seconds.

"What did she say? What was the joke?"

Rebecca started to speak and then shook her head. "Oh, it was women's talk. It wouldn't be funny now. Only then and there."

Blackie nodded.

She was silent for a bit, thinking. Then, "Well, anyway, after that, I tried to stick as close as I could to her. Anyone who could make a joke in a situation like that has got to be something rare. And it was clear that she hadn't given up. And I thought....I felt...." Rebecca squinted, trying to get clear in her mind what she had felt. "I felt that if she could be brave and have hope, then I could too.

"But, when they took her away, I....I just knew I wouldn't live to see her again. And I felt that awful hopelessness again—until this morning when the shooting started and I saw those men dying. I saw them dying and I felt this strange feeling of something coursing through my body. And later, when I decided to kill the men there in the trees, I felt like something blew off the top of my head, and I knew I was going to kill them and I was not going to die."

Rebecca looked at Blackie. She could see in his eyes that nothing else mattered to him right now but what she was saying. She felt a great weight lift from her. She was suddenly aware that she no longer felt shame over what had happened to her.

She said, "God, I've been talking your leg off."

"I'm glad you talked to me."

"Well, you're easy to talk to. I wouldn't have thought I could've told anyone these things, least of all a man."

"Then I'm honored."

They rode in silence.

Blackie liked her. He admired her guts and her candor and he was glad that she had liked his sister.

Finally, Rebecca forced herself to ask, "You know my husband Otis, don't you?"

"Yes, I know Otis."

"Is he all right?"

"Yes, he's all right."

There was silence while Rebecca's tired mind worked.

She said, "I don't understand why you and Morgan came alone."

"It wasn't by choice. David Brown turned around north of the border when he found out his wife was dead. Charles Cistrom turned back then too because he was scared."

"Only four people?"

"The fathers of two of the girls were killed when they took the girls. And the rest had other family to take care of in Gold Creek. And they're afraid of an Apache attack now too. Besides, they were counting on some soldiers who followed you."

"Soldiers?"

"Yeah. They followed you for four days. They didn't keep the same pace you did, though. And they stopped just south of the border."

Rebecca finally got it out. "Why didn't Otis come?"

"He couldn't afford a horse and gun."

"Oh...." She experienced confusion. "Were they pretty expensive?"

"I don't know exactly. Around two hundred for a horse, I think."

She felt humiliation. That two or three hundred dollars had stood in the way of her husband coming after her was, to her mind, a reflection upon her worth as a wife. She tried to conceal her humiliation. "That's a lot. And we didn't have any money saved."

Blackie nodded.

She continued, "I guess I'm pretty lucky that you could get horses."

"If I couldn't have," said Blackie, unable to keep the resentment for Otis from his voice, "I would have come on foot."

She gave him a doubtful look.

He asserted, "You'd be surprised what a hard man can do on foot. I would've had Mrs. Simmons—the Apache lady—make me moccasins in case my feet blistered in my boots. And I would've taken one rifle and plenty of cartridges and a big pack of jerky and pemmican, and a canteen of water.

"A horse can beat a hard man for three or four days, Becky, but after that he breaks down because he has to graze for four hours; so he can't get rested. Or if he rests, he can't eat; so he gets weak. But a hard man can go eighteen hours, eating on the move, and sleep six hours and go for another eighteen hours, day after day. Now, I'm not in training; but in three or four days, I would've been, and then I could've run much of the day."

Rebecca looked at him with wonder.

Blackie saw that look and said, "I gave it serious thought until I caught a stray horse and sent a rider out to Collier's Ranch for Morgan."

"Is there no end to you?"

Blackie looked at her a long moment before he answered. "Maybe if a person wants something bad enough, there isn't any end to him, Becky."

Thirty

Dona Medina, Don Ignacio Medina's stout wife, entered the big front room from the kitchen carrying a tray on which was a crock of beans and meat along with goat cheese and corn tortillas. A tallow candle stood on the tray to help light her way. Her face registered immediate disapproval. It was some of the hacienda's vaqueros—cowboys—who were the targets of her disapproval. Seven of them were standing about in the candle-lit front room, and others were peering in through the front doorway at the six American girls. The girls all wore blankets now over their torn and soiled night clothes. Rebecca and Ella York had fallen asleep. In the faces and postures of the other four, exhaustion was apparent.

Doña Medina spoke in Spanish to the vaqueros, "Get out of here, you coyotes! Leave these poor girls alone. You can see them when they are properly dressed. Out! Out! Out!"

The men, some of them grinning good naturedly at Doña Medina, hurried and got out. Doña Medina looked at her two youngest sons, Jesus, twelve, and Benito, fourteen, and said, "You too. Out."

Casa Medina had nine feet high adobe walls which were five feet thick at the ground and tapered to a thickness of two feet at their tops. The floors were of large, hewn pine planks that had been worn smooth by decades of boots and bare feet. Remarkably, the floor planks had a lot of holes in them where the knots, shrinking over the years, had fallen out. The ceiling beams were of thick poles cut from a stand of hardwood in the mountains of Sierra Madre more than two hundred years ago. Notwithstanding the holes in the floor planks, the house was large and impressive.

The house and its outbuildings and the houses of families who had been employees for generations stood on high ground in a lush wash that was dry except right after rains.

But there was plenty of water only a few feet underground, and there were several wells that were pumped by windmills and others pumped by hand.

At this moment, the two oldest of Doña Medina's four sons were vacating their bedroom, moving out to the bunkhouse with the single vaqueros, so that the poor American girls could be in the house under Doña Medina's care and protection. There were other houses on the hacienda, lived in by vaqueros with families, and the girls could have been sequestered individually with those families, but Doña Medina wanted them together so that they would not feel any more frightened and abandoned than they already must feel.

In the morning, the girls would have baths, and Doña Medina's maid would boil their nightclothes and blankets in a caldron. You could smell the poor young ladies clear across the room.

Blackie and Morgan sat with Don Ignacio Medina in his study. By candle light, Don Madina was now penning a letter. He and Morgan had been speaking seriously but agreeably in Spanish, and now, while Medina wrote, Morgan turned to Blackie and explained to him what had passed between them.

"Don Medina is lending us three race horses to ride to Hacienda Ortega. It's thirty-two miles from here on the way to Chihuahua. The letter is for us to carry to Ortega, asking him to lend us fresh race horses to ride into Chihuahua."

Don Medina finished his letter, folded it, and handed it to Morgan. His manner was grave and efficient.

Morgan pulled out his map and he and Medina began marking on the map, placing Rancho Alvorado, the box canyon where the dead desperados lay, Hacienda Medina, and Hacienda Ortega.

Morgan explained to Medina that the Alvorados might be in danger from the three bandits who had escaped from the canyon. He suggested to Medina that he dispatch riders to Rancho Alvorado with a couple of the rifles Morgan had

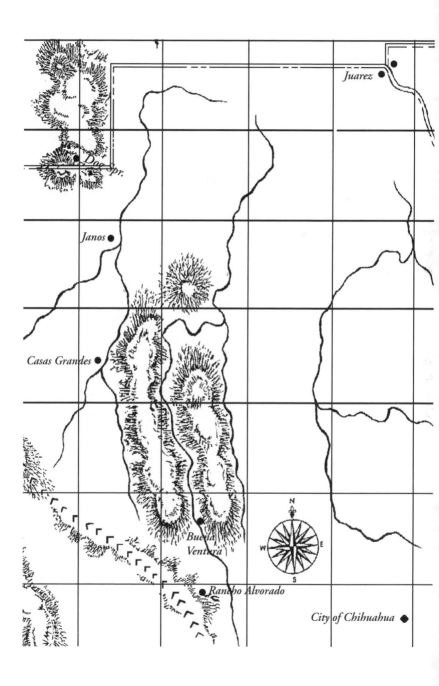

brought from the canyon. Medina said he would send his son, Pablo, and four other riders tonight.

They went out then, and the two Americans joined the four awake girls for supper at a big oak table. When Blackie had finished eating, he woke Rebecca and insisted that she eat. She closed her eyes and he had to put a spoonful of meat and beans against her lips. She opened her mouth, took it like a child, chewed dreamily, and swallowed. They repeated the action. Then she opened her eyes and smiled weakly.

"Do you think you can make it, Becky?"

"Yes."

"All right. Eat some more, and then get changed. The Medina boys lent you some clothes."

Rebecca ate, and then Blackie assigned two girls to help her dress. He worried that she might give out on the trail and hold them up. He vacillated now on telling her to stay here. But, when she emerged from the bedroom, she seemed all right. She was a slim woman but Benito Medina's pants were a little too tight for her, and so was the shirt—especially the shirt, where the buttons strained over her large bust. On top of that, the boots they got for her belonged to the seventeen year old Medina boy and were a bit too big for her.

Twenty year old Pablo Medina, a dashingly good looking young man, hurried through the front room on his way to the corral. He carried his kit and three rifles, two of which Morgan was sending with him for Alvorado and his son. Pablo Medina kissed his mother good-by and went on out.

A few minutes later, in front of the house, the rest of the Medinas held candles inside glass hurricane chimneys while Morgan, Blackie, and Rebecca mounted Don Medina's remarkably beautiful thoroughbreds. Because Rebecca weighed the least, Blackie had attached his extra rifle, the Sharps .45-110, to her saddle along with her Winchester. The horses were nervous and shifted about, blowing through their nostrils. The five American girls were apprehensively saying their good-byes to the trio. All were speaking at once. Doña Medina was speaking in Spanish to Rebecca.

Morgan translated, "She says may God ride with you and protect you."

Blackie reined his horse around and the others followed

They pressed the horses hard that night on the wagon road to Hacienda Ortega. The horses were in training and were fresh, and they took it well. At first light, the riders kicked them to a gallop.

It was still morning when the trio, amid a pack of barking dogs, galloped in among the corrals and tack rooms and up to Casa Ortega.

Morgan jumped off. "You two take care of the horses while I speak to Ortega."

Blackie and Rebecca dismounted and began walking the horses to cool them down. Some vaqueros came over and asked them where they were from. Blackie told them, "Yo no entiendo español," which meant, "I do not understand Spanish," and was some of the very little Spanish he knew. The vaqueros nodded at that and simply watched them. They knew there was something very different about them besides being Norte Americanos. The pair's obvious exhaustion and the girl's bruised face and their exceptional horses and their air of mission combined to intrigue the vaqueros.

Blackie and Rebecca were watering the horses when Morgan came out of the house with a man whose bearing spelled "Boss." The man, Ortega, issued orders in Spanish to three vaqueros to take over the care of the horses from the Americans.

Rebecca and Blackie walked over to Morgan who said, "Don Ortega invites us to eat and rest in his house."

Rebecca said, "I just want to lie down and sleep somewhere."

Morgan answered, "You better eat to keep your strength up. We've got a thirty mile ride ahead of us. We'll eat and take an hour's nap here."

*   *   *

It was mid-afternoon when finally in the city of Chihuahua the trio, haggard and grimy, trotted their horses up to a building with a sign beside its door that said, "Consuldado Estados Unidos de America," American Consulate. The horses were every inch wet with sweat that was muddied with dust. They had been galloped almost steadily since leaving Hacienda Ortega. The riders dismounted and Morgan pulled the oil cloth pouch from his saddle bag. Blackie began walking the horses to cool them down. Morgan and Rebecca went inside the consulate where Rebecca slumped into the first chair she found and closed her eyes. Morgan approached the Mexican lady behind the desk.

"Is the American Consul in?"

"Yes. Your business?"

Morgan opened the oilcloth pouch and removed documents from it.

*　　*　　*

They went to a hotel and were put in a room on the second floor. The main bed stood on legs and was like a rectangular box with short sides. The sides held the straw in place. Over the straw was a cowhide. Over the cowhide was a feather mattress with a dirty flannel sheet. Then a dirty blanket.

Morgan and Blackie lay down fully clothed on the main bed with their rifles at their sides. They were too tall for the bed and their feet hung over the end, but they went promptly to sleep. Rebecca used a child's bed that slid out from under the main bed and was a smaller copy of the main bed. She had to draw up her legs to fit into it. She did not mind. Her Winchester leaned against the wall next to her. A wash stand with a pitcher and wash pan were next to a window. Blackie's .45-110 leaned next to it.

It was dark out when Blackie awoke to the sound of footsteps in the hallway. He quietly picked up his .45-70 and placed his thumb on the hammer. There came a knock on the door. He and Morgan were on their feet immediately. Rebecca blinked awake. Candle light shone under the door.

Morgan asked in Spanish, "Who is it?"

From behind the door, a man's voice said in English, "Roderer, the American Consul."

Revolver in hand, Morgan opened up while Blackie covered him. Roderer came in carrying a candle in a holder; he was elated.

"They've got them! The soldiers arrested them!"

The trio was both relieved and excited. Blackie's eyes shone; he wanted to shout and he could barely restrain himself from interrupting Roderer to ask after Dusty.

Roderer was saying, "The Army had alerted the banks. And the bandits went through a broker who tried to peddle the gold at Banco de Minera. The bank then sent a runner for the soldiers. They came and arrested the broker and he led them to the bandits. There were so many soldiers that the bandits gave up without a fight."

Roderer suddenly got serious. "There's just one thing." He hesitated. "There was no girl with them."

Blackie was so stricken that he could not speak. The others looked at him. Everyone was silent. He turned away and looked out of the window.

* * *

Four sullen desperados, including the American, were illuminated in their cell by an oil lantern held by a guard outside the barred door. They looked toward the light.

Rebecca turned away from the cell. "All of these men are members of Lobo's gang."

Roderer translated her words to the Mexican Army Colonel who escorted them. The Colonel's satisfied look increased.

Rebecca asked, "Where are the rest of them?"

Roderer translated to the Colonel who replied in Spanish.

Roderer said to Rebecca, "He says that's all of them."

Rebecca said, "Six men started out for here. One of them was Lobo."

Roderer was startled. "Isn't El Lobo one of these men?"

"No."

He frowned. "Are you sure?"

Rebecca flashed angrily, "Am I sure?! After riding with that beast for two weeks?!"

She turned to Blackie.

Blackie said to Roderer. "He's not in there."

Roderer told this to the Colonel. The Colonel was dumb-struck for a moment. Then he barked at an aid to assemble a company of armed men.

Blackie pulled Roderer away from the guardhouse. "Ask the Colonel to get the American out of there and into a room with just me. I might be able to find out what's going on."

They put Blackie, unarmed, into a small adobe room where he sat on one of two small crude chairs at a small crude table. A lantern burned, hanging on a wall. The door opened and the American bandit, Abner Waters, was pushed in by two guards. He stood there looking at Blackie. The door closed behind him. He was sullen and he stayed so.

Blackie said, "Well, they didn't hang me."

"So I see."

"Sit down?"

"Why not?"

Abner Waters sat down. They looked at one another for a moment. Waters looked away. Blackie gazed at Waters steadily and expectantly.

Finally, Waters asked, "What're you doin' here, boy?"

"Hunting El Lobo."

"Yeah?"

"He's got something I want."

"Mmmmm. Well, you won't kech 'im."

"Why not?"

Waters fell silent. After a bit, Blackie spoke:

"You know, your gang is almost all dead."

Waters did not speak. He did not believe Blackie.

Blackie continued, "I killed two south of Janos. You'd left them in Janos, drunk. Then at a rancho about a hundred miles from here, my friend killed three more. One of them called himself Benito Gonzales. Had a scar on his face." Blackie paused. "You saw that girl out there. She and the other five were at a camp in a box canyon. Twenty-seven of your men were killed there yesterday morning in a few minutes. Three got away, but they won't get far. They were bare-back and had only their rifles." Blackie paused. "So, with you four here, that leaves only Lobo and one other man at large."

This information shook the bandit. He cared nothing about the men; but news of their deaths reinforced the feeling of his own impending doom.

Blackie asked, "Where can I find Lobo?"

No answer.

Blackie said, "If you help me, I'll speak for you to the Colonel."

"Lotta good that'll do."

After a long silence, Blackie said, "To hell with Lobo. What I'm really after is the blonde girl called Dusty."

"That girl! I wished I'd never laid eyes on that bitch! She's bad luck! That goddam Lobo went plumb loco over her! Didn't even want her to take baths with the rest of the girls 'cause the men'd stand around and watch. He didn't want 'em to see his woman! That stupid old fool.

"I'll tell you about that girl: She ain't to be fooled with. I mean she ain't safe—you can see it in her eyes. The funny thing is, I think that's one of the things Lobo likes about her, that she's dangerous. He talked proud-like about the way she stabbed one of his own men to death.

"Now, I'll tell you a secret about captives. You take 'em by force, and you kill them that don't do as you say. The rest are so terrified that when you don't kill 'em, they feel grateful to you. Like you done 'em a favor. They must get to where they feel like they owe you somethin'.

"And, then, after a while, if you be nice to 'em, why, they get downright chummy. They'll wanta please you. Even though they know you'll kill 'em if they try to get away.

"But, that ain't so about that bitch of Lobo's. You can see it in her eyes.

"I'll tell you this much: now that he ain't got no gang of men around, he'll have to watch her every minute. You can see it in her eyes like you can in the eyes of a bad horse—one of them horses that's waitin' for the chance, waitin' for you to get careless and the next thing you know your head's stove in."

Just as suddenly as he had erupted, Waters fell silent.

"I see," said Blackie.

Blackie waited, gazing expectantly at Waters.

Suddenly, Waters spoke again. "Lobo ain't in town. Somebody might recognize 'im. Besides, he can't bring that girl in town. She start hollerin' and we'd be in trouble for sure. So, he stayed outa town."

"Where"

"Won't do you no good to know. We had another man with us. He stayed with Lobo. He'll have come to town to find out what happened to us. They've hightailed it by now."

"To where?"

Waters did not answer.

Blackie waited expectantly. Finally, he asked again, "To where?"

"Oh, to friends' places...."

Waters found it hard to stay quiet with this boy. He wanted him to know that he, Waters, was not just a stupid bandit. He wanted the boy to know that he was a smart bandit.

Before Blackie knew it, he was being lectured, instructed: "You know, you can ride only so long as a gang. When the gangs chasin' you get bigger'n yours, you gotta split up and hide out until they kinda lose interest. The only way you can hide out and stay hid out is with friends. They hide you at their homes. They go to market and buy the grub and stuff. You just stay indoors if its in town, or you stay in the country if its a hacienda or at a mine."

Waters fell silent for a moment. Then said, "Lobo's got friends."

"Where?"

"Sonora."

"Where in Sonora?"

Waters shook his head.

A few yards from the room, Morgan and Rebecca sat asleep on the ground with their backs against an adobe wall. Roderer sat impatiently on an overturned bucket. Several times over the next three hours, he would want to go over and find out what was going on in the room. However, he restrained himself.

Blackie and Waters had been in there more than three hours when Blackie finally came to the door and called out, "Somebody bring us a piece of paper and something to draw with!"

*   *   *

"They're gone all right," Blackie said.

They had come directly from the Army compound to this camp about five miles outside Chihuahua. While Blackie had reconnoitered on foot, Morgan and Rebecca had waited in the dark, sitting on their horses, with Blackie's horse beside them. Now he was back.

"I figure he'll go to the canyon where he thinks his men are.... But I'm not absolutely sure. He might just run out on them. I think we better camp here until first light so we can pick up his trail and be sure of where he's going."

"I agree," Morgan said.

At first light the next morning, the three riders picked up the trail of six horses galloping west. They pushed their own horses hard and, in the afternoon, they finally trotted up to Casa Ortega, ate a hurried meal, thanked Ortega graciously, mounted Medina's horses and trotted north a mile, warming up the horses. There they picked up El Lobo's trail and galloped west again.

At sunset, they halted for a conference.

Morgan said, "We've got the same problem we had last night."

"I'd like to gamble." Blackie said. "But, if they turn off and don't go to the canyon, we'll have to come back here day after tomorrow and pick up their trail again."

"Right. A loss of over twenty-four hours instead of seven. And it might rain or blow in between. Then we would be in real trouble."

Blackie said, "Let's find a place to camp."

Thirty-One

T
he American," said Blackie with his mouth partly full, "whose name is Ab Waters, incidentally...."

"Yeah, he told us," said Connie Watkins, the redhead. "He likes to talk."

The five American girls, somewhat rested, and washed and combed, and dressed in borrowed clothes, were looking better—even with their bruises.

It was mid-morning, and the pursuers and the five American girls and Don and Doña Medina, and three of their four sons were in the coolness of Casa Medina with its massive walls, sitting on cowhide covered oak chairs at the big oak table which had come from Spain more than two centuries before. The pursuers had followed the trail of El Lobo and Dusty where it had gone across Hacienda Ortega on the wagon road, and across Hacienda Medina on the same road until about three miles from the main house. There, the outlaws and their captive had looped south, avoiding the populated area of the Hacienda. El Lobo was obviously too canny to take Dusty near any civilized people. The haciendas had too many armed men for the bandits to chance a confrontation.

Blackie nodded and smiled at Connie Watkins. "Anyway, Waters said that they'd intended to lie low in the U. S. until things cooled off down here. But they just couldn't resist it when they found out Gold Creek was unarmed. They figured it would be an easy two or three thousand dollars apiece, and...." Blackie looked at the girls. "And some women."

Morgan was translating to the Medinas while Blackie talked.

"He said they sure as hell...." Blackie looked at his audience which included the girls and Doña Medina. "Excuse me.... He said they didn't expect to lose seven men at Gold Creek. He said that, usually, it's the getaways that are the

275

dangerous part—when people get organized and come after you. So they did everything they could to keep people from being able to do that. They killed and took all the horses, and they started fires."

Blackie swallowed some food.

Ella York, looking too thin and perhaps ill, but with the glaze gone from her blue eyes, asked, "How far did you say Lobo and Dusty are ahead of you?"

"Right now, I figure about eight or ten hours. We've had to stop at night because we couldn't track in the dark. But, they haven't stopped. There's not been one campsite. The only time they stopped was to water the horses. They didn't even let the horses eat but a little. The men are pretty scared. We could tell by the gait of their horses that they ran them in a panic for the first ten-eleven miles; part of that time was after dark. Then they settled down to a steady grind. But they haven't stopped.

"That's why I didn't want to stay here long enough to eat. We figure they went to the canyon and changed horses. I'm really sorry now about leaving all those horses up in the canyon."

Jinny Rowe jerked a look at Blackie and then turned to Connie Watkins.

"Oh!" said Connie Watkins. "The vaqueros brought those horses in last night."

"What?"

"Yeah. They brought in a bunch of horses last night. Jinny and I recognized them; they were from the canyon, all right."

Morgan spoke to Medina in Spanish. Medina answered him, and then Morgan turned to Blackie.

"He says they brought all the horses from there."

Blackie was elated. Now he did not object so much to the time spent eating here.

He and Morgan and Rebecca had broken off their pursuit about two miles due south of Casa Medina and had ridden in to return Medina's horses and to retrieve their own horses.

Their arrival had been heralded by shouts. Children had run to see them, others had run to tell all around of their arrival. The pursuers had dismounted hurriedly and unsaddled the horses. Grooms had taken over the horses and walked them to cool them down.

The crowd that had gathered around them had been like one you would expect on a day of celebration. Morgan began answering questions in Spanish to the Mexicans. The American girls ran from the house and began peppering Rebecca and Blackie with questions about what had happened in Chihuahua. A lot of vaqueros came and stood around, enjoying getting a good look at the girls without Doña Medina shooing them off.

Standing there with her two trail companions, Rebecca became acutely aware of the contrast between her and the other girls.

Distressed, she turned to Blackie and asked, "Don't I have time for a bath? I'm the only one who's still dirty."

Startled, Blackie looked at her. Her face and neck and hands were grimy, and her hair was a mess and shot through with trail dust.

"Oh.... Becky, not now!.... Tonight, maybe."

He felt that every daylight minute was critical and should be spent closing the gap between them and Dusty.

"Oh, Blackie," she pleaded, "I've never smelt like this."

She had had no chance to wash away the odor of fear that she had felt until two days ago. Nor the odor of the men.

"Becky, I stink too," Blackie said, trying to convince her it was natural to get dirty and sweaty on the trail. Which it was.

Rebecca said crossly, "Well, it's different with you! You're an old billy goat!"

Blackie laughed. Rebecca looked at him half crossly for a moment and then she laughed too.

Blackie then went over to where Morgan was talking with Medina. "Would you ask Don Medina for our horses?"

"I've already asked. He insists that we eat something. He says it'll take a few minutes for the vaqueros to get our horses, and in that time we should eat. So, I compromised. We'll eat leftovers—no time spent cooking."

*   *   *

Now, having finished eating, they came outside once again. Three vaqueros stood waiting with three thoroughbreds. Blackie turned and looked at Medina questioningly. Medina smiled and spoke to him in Spanish.

Morgan translated, "He's lending us fresh race horses for as long as it takes to catch Lobo."

In heartfelt thanks, Blackie grabbed Medina's hand with both of his.

*   *   *

They trotted south to pick up their quarry's trail again. It looped all the way around Casa Medina and re-joined the wagon road going west toward Sierra Madre. The road was covered to its edges and beyond by horse tracks coming east. The tracks must have been those of the horses brought in from the box canyon. Over the top of those tracks could be seen the tracks of thirteen horses going west. Only six of those west-going horse tracks interested the pursuers, of course. With their own horses now warmed up, the pursuers followed that road while alternating between a lope and a jog until they came to a shallow river where they stopped to water their sweaty horses. They let the horses crop grass for a quarter hour, and Rebecca washed her face and arms and hair in the stream. Then they crossed the river and kicked their horses to a lope again.

A few miles west of the river, they went up a hill, the crest of which was covered with hard, brown sandstone, some of which was broken and some of which was in solid, long slabs that went on for hundreds of yards in either direction of the road where it cut through a narrow gap. It was a fair ambush spot, so the pursuers rode up the hill carefully, spread out and with their eyes peeled, scanning the rocks on either side of the road. But, no one was waiting in ambush and the pursuers followed the road over the hill and down the other side seventy or eighty yards.

Suddenly, Blackie reined in his horse. He turned sharply, looking a little scared. "They've cut off!"

Rebecca looked at the jumble of tracks on the road. Sure enough, there were fewer tracks going west. But, how did he know which were which? They all looked pretty much the same to her.

He galloped back past her, going up the hill. Rebecca and Morgan turned their horses and started after Blackie.

At the top of the hill, Blackie waited for them, no longer scared. He pointed to the ground on the south side of the rutted wagon road.

"Six horses went up here. We better go up together and spread out. They might be camped somewhere in these rocks."

They went up on the rock slab and spread out. About a quarter mile south, the rocks split for a few yards, separated by dirt, and Rebecca found the tracks of six horses heading across the break where they disappeared onto the rocks on the other side. Another quarter mile south, the rocks ended and they saw the tracks of the six horses plainly in the sand of the hill. The desperados, taking a cross-country shortcut to the box canyon, had tried to elude possible trackers by leaving the road on the hard sandstone.

The pursuers and their sweaty mounts followed that shortcut, trotting where they could, and arrived at the canyon's mouth by late afternoon. There, they slowed, scanning the hillsides, and cautiously started up the canyon. They rode spread wide apart with Blackie in the middle following the tracks of the six horses. Blackie stopped and beckoned them over. He pointed to tracks coming out of the canyon.

"Here's where they came back out." He then looked up the canyon and said in a suddenly fatigued voice, "I guess we better go up and have a look in case they killed Dusty up there."

Morgan asked, "Why would they do that now?"

Fatigue. "I don't know. Maybe revenge."

They rode slowly up the canyon, approaching the trees which bordered the east end of the meadow. The light breeze coming down the canyon carried the stench of the dead bodies. The pursuers broke through the trees and the sight was something to be remembered. Vultures took flight in huge numbers. The corpses had been well picked apart. And flies were present in force. The pursuers rode around and found no sign of Dusty. Blackie's extra fatigue lifted.

They watered their horses and let them eat some and then left the canyon, following their quarry's trail northward.

At twilight, Morgan called a halt.

He asked Blackie, "Well, what do you think?"

"The horses have to have water," Blackie answered. "And the only place we know of hereabouts is the Alvorado place. Besides, they've got good forage."

Blackie said to Rebecca, "This is a place we stopped at the day before the ambush in the canyon. It's maybe a couple of hours ride from here. They've got a well, and good forage."

Morgan said, "We might not be welcome. Señora Alvorado was terrified the other day."

Blackie turned back to Rebecca. "You know Benito Gonzales? He was one of the bandits. He had a long scar on his left cheek."

Rebecca gave an involuntary shudder. "God, I know who you mean. He is one of the most....most....slimy....I don't know what." She shuddered again, remembering his hands on her.

Blackie nodded. "Well, Morgan shot and killed him and two other men right in these people's house the day before the ambush."

"That explains what happened to them. They went away and I never saw them again."

Morgan said, "So, we might not be too welcome. I don't think they'll deny us water and forage, though. And we can sleep up there on the pasture with the horses."

Morgan and Rebecca relied on Blackie to get them there in the dark. By the time they arrived, the Alvorados had gone to bed. The dogs were barking when the trio stopped a couple hundred yards out.

Morgan called out, "Hola, Alvorado!"

The dogs barked louder. After a minute, Morgan called again.

Finally, Alvorado's voice called back in Spanish, "Who is it?"

Morgan shouted in English, "Morgan Blaylock and Blackie Sheffield! ....And a woman!"

"Welcome, amigos!"

The trio rode up to the house. The door now stood open, and a couple of candles burned inside. Alvorado, in a night shirt, stood outside holding in one hand a candle that burned in a glass chimney. In his other hand, he held a rifle, one of two that Morgan had sent. Behind him were Señora Alvorado and Catarina in night dresses. Catarina peered earnestly, trying to see Blackie in the dark beyond her father. The Alvorado boy, Emilio, was at one of the windows with a rifle. One of the Medina boys, twenty year old Pablo, whom the pursuers had met at Hacienda Madina, was at the other window also with a rifle. The young men now came to the door where they stood in pants but no shirts or shoes.

The saddle-weary Americans dismounted. Morgan introduced Rebecca to the Alvorados. Alvorado asked if they remembered Pablo and they said they did.

Alvorado said, "I thank you for sending these rifles, and for thinking of our safety. Pablo and four vaqueros came two mornings after you left. The vaqueros went home but Pablo stayed because you said three bandits escaped. We watched for them, and this morning two men and a yellow haired girl rode by, going up the arroyo. We guessed they were bandits because of the girl."

The sighting of Dusty had an exhilarating effect on Blackie. "The girl was my sister!"

Morgan added, "One of the men was El Lobo."

Alvorado raised his eyebrows. He said, "I fired a warning shot. They turned away and rode by at a distance, going up the arroyo. Maybe they wanted horses. Their horses looked very bad—they walked with their heads hanging low."

Blackie said, "They've ridden those same horses from Chihuahua without a rest."

Alvorado shook his head. Then he said, "I am worried they will come back in the night for our horses. But, with you people here, I feel safer. You will stay the night, won't you?"

"Very kind of you," Morgan said.

Alvorado asked if they had eaten. They said they had not, and he very politely asked his wife to prepare something for their guests.

Señora Alvorado was still a little frightened by the men, and now here was this young woman who, according to the stories Pablo had told, had killed three men. Señora Alvorado had never before associated with people who had killed humans—let alone anyone who had done it in her house.

Catarina had lost the momentary fear she had felt the other day. From the stories Pablo had carried from the hacienda, and from what her own perceptions told her, she was convinced that Blackie was an unusual young man. She looked at him boldly. She thought that she might never see him again, so now was not the time to be coy.

The pursuers came into the house now. Blackie looked at Catarina in her night dress. Her dark brown eyes shone at him. Her skin had a clean, velvety sheen, and her black hair was glossy in the candle light. The nipples of her upturned breasts were clearly outlined beneath the delicate white cotton material. Blackie felt a shortness of breath.

Rebecca watched the byplay between the two; and she was pleased when Blackie turned to her and stated quietly, "You want your bath, don't you."

She smiled gratefully and nodded.

Rebecca had a cold water bath in a wooden wash tub out beside the well while the horses drank greedily nearby and Blackie stood guard in the dark. The cold water momentarily revived her; she had been so weary her head had buzzed faintly. Afterwards, she emptied the tub and rinsed it thoroughly and then stood guard while Blackie took a bath.

Inside, while giving an account of their adventures since they were last here, Morgan washed his upper body at the wash stand, and then shaved. His arms felt heavy with fatigue.

When Rebecca and Blackie came in, Señora Alvorado and Catarina set the table with three bowls of hastily prepared jerky stew along with goat cheese and some re-heated tortillas.

Everyone sat around the table. There were not enough chairs, so Catarina got the milking stool from outside and sat close beside Blackie. Señora Alvorado did not like it, but she said nothing. Pablo Medina sat stony faced for a while.

Finally, Pablo turned to Rebecca, smiled, and spoke to her.

Morgan translated, "He says you are very pretty."

Rebecca fingered her damp hair, straight now after her bath. Her gold wedding ring had been taken by a bandit, and the sun had tanned away the whiteness of her finger where the ring had been. She knew that men usually liked to look at her, but she knew that under the circumstances—more than two weeks of terror, and three weeks of constant exhaustion and poor diet—she could hardly look her best. She also guessed that Pablo was merely trying to create an effect on Catarina. But she smiled at him and told Morgan to thank him.

Rebecca thought of her husband Otis, presumably safe back in Gold Creek. She no longer felt any loyalty to him. She felt sure now that if she got home alive—and there was no certainty of that—she would leave Otis. She had no idea right now where she would go and what she would do; she would cross that bridge when she came to it. It wasn't just that he had not come down here to save her. It was that over the last few days of close association with Morgan and Blackie, she had changed her mind about what her man should be like. Otis simply did not measure up.

More importantly, Rebecca herself was no longer the same person who had lived with Otis along the creek in the Mogollon Mountains until three weeks ago. The biggest change was not the result of the terror or of the beatings or of witnessing the murders. No, the biggest change in her had occurred when she had taken that rifle and killed those three outlaws. The world no longer seemed so large and out of control to her as it had until those last few moments of the gunfight in the box canyon. She conceived herself bigger now when compared with the world; and it, the world, seemed more manageable.

She turned to Blackie. "Do you think Otis could have borrowed the money for a horse?"

Surprised at her bringing it up now, he answered, "Becky, I would have lent him the money. But he didn't ask. He sent word by others that he wasn't coming."

Rebecca nodded. Her gaze drifted. Money was just one of the things wrong with her marriage. If she were to go back to Otis, she would have to go back to living from payday to payday. Otis made good money in the mine, but he liked to whoop it up with the boys after work.

Rebecca looked up and studied Morgan's face while he talked to the Alvorados in Spanish. There was this eye-pleasing ruggedness about him, a ruggedness that made him look indestructible. But despite his obvious toughness, there was a gentleness and a kindliness that came through from him and touched you.

Morgan dealt with Blackie in a way that surprised her. She had never before seen two men so far separated in age treat each other with such obvious respect.

Four days ago, when the shooting had finally come to an end there in the canyon and Rebecca had first seen Morgan stand up behind the rocks, and had recognized him, she had felt it only natural that he, the former Marshal of Gold Creek, should be there, saving her and the rest of the girls. But, a couple of minutes later, she had reconsidered. Considering that he was no longer the Marshal, and especially considering that there was only one other person with him, it had no longer seemed natural. It had seemed extraordinary and courageous—incredibly courageous. She had wondered but had not asked why he was there. In Gold Creek, there had been some gossip that he was sweet on Mrs. Sheffield. And Rebecca, now sitting in the Alvorado house, guessed that Morgan's involvement with the family was the reason he was here. Rebecca's eyes misted over at the idea of Dusty being without a father but having someone like Morgan willing to fill in and perhaps die trying to save her. Dusty, if not already dead, might yet die never knowing of this fact. All Dusty had expressed certainty about was that her brother was somewhere looking for her. How had she known that? A few days ago, Rebecca had believed that Dusty had fixed upon the idea out of wild hopefulness and desperation. Now, sitting beside Blackie, Rebecca guessed that Dusty must know her brother awfully well.

Rebecca glanced at Blackie. He was looking at Catarina on his other side. In her life Rebecca had not exchanged more than three dozen words with him until four days ago. Yes, she had known him, but certainly not well. All that she had known about him in Gold Creek was his name and that he was a market hunter and was said to be an extraordinary shot. Oh, and his wonderful smile—you would never miss that.

But, here in Mexico in the last four days, she had learned a great deal about him that she would never have been able to learn back in Gold Creek. He was a hard driving man. He was willing to risk not only his own life to save Dusty, but Morgan's and Rebecca's as well. He put everything on the line to accomplish his end. Moreover, he made no bones about it. He moved and acted with such a natural certainty that it filled Rebecca with confidence and made her want to follow him.

And Rebecca thought that despite the never-ending, back-killing, leg-killing, exhausting, rump-pounding-on-the-saddle riding, despite the weariness and the craving for a decent meal and for a decent bed, despite the recurring dread that they would at any time find Dusty's corpse along the trail, despite all she had been through, despite everything, she knew that she did not want to be anywhere else right now than with these two men, sharing their mission. It was the first time in her life that she felt as though her presence and actions made a difference in something important. She knew, for example, that, there in the canyon, the gunfight could have gone all wrong. Those three men in the trees could have turned their rifles on her and the other girls. It was conceivable that they might have killed Morgan and Blackie. At the very least, the bandits might have escaped in the night. What she had done, her actions, had made everything turn out right.

Alvorado was saying in English, "Miss Shales can sleep with Catarina. The two boys are using Emilio's bed. Do you two," he asked Morgan and Blackie, "mind sleeping in here on the floor?"

Blackie said to Alvorado, "I'm going to sleep up in the meadow with the horses."

"Do you think that is wise?"

"It's wisest. I don't want to lose the horses, and I don't want the bandits to have them."

Alvorado nodded. He turned and explained the sleeping arrangements to his family. Catarina protested to Blackie in Spanish.

Alvorado smiled at Blackie. "My daughter is afraid for you."

Blackie, who found pleasure in her closeness, smiled at her while he spoke to her father. "Tell her not to worry. A spider's footstep will wake me up."

*　　*　　*

At first light Blackie brought the horses down from the meadow to the water trough. The dogs barking at him woke the others. Blackie was unwilling to spend time eating. He wanted to leave immediately.

As soon as the horses were saddled, they said their good-byes. Catarina stood watching Blackie from the back door, a blanket wrapped around her shoulders over her night dress. He smiled at her for a long moment. She broke into a smile and came out into the yard. She said something which did not get translated because Morgan was listening to Alvorado wish them God's favor.

The pursuers mounted up, and, chewing jerky, trotted up the arroyo, following a cattle and game trail.

They went like that for two hours before they saw the first dead horse. Meat had been cut from the horse's hind leg. But no camp fire had been made.

"They must be out of food," Morgan said. "But they must have been too scared to stop. They were scared when they left Chihuahua; but I'll bet when they saw all those dead men in that canyon, they probably imagined the country was crawling with soldiers or militia. They're unlikely to suspect there are only three of us."

The pursuers hurried on. About noon, they came across a second dead horse. The desperados had stopped this time and built a fire. Meat had been cut from this horse too.

Later, Blackie pointed to the tracks they were following. "You see how their horses have been dragging their hooves? I'll bet we're moving three or four times as fast as they are. We should catch them today or early tomorrow."

In the late afternoon, the pursuers were still in chaparral, trotting steadily up the grade. Up ahead on the mountain, maybe nine hundred yards away, the timber started.

Suddenly, Blackie spoke in a low, calm voice. "There they are."

"Where?!" Rebecca exclaimed.

"Shh. About seven hundred yards out. Slightly to the left, just below the timber."

Rebecca shielded her eyes from the sun. "I see them. What're they doing?"

"Horse down. Lobo's saddling a spare one."

Rebecca could see a difference in Blackie now that action was impending. He was as cool as ice. You would have thought that he did this every day.

*   *   *

El Lobo, standing beside the horse, had not seen the pursuers seven hundred yards down the slope from him. He was having some difficulty with the cinches on the saddle. He was exhausted to the point of semi-consciousness and his face sagged and the whites of his eyes were inflamed from lack of sleep and his hands would not work just right.

The horse stood asleep while El Lobo tried to fix the saddle.

Dusty stood nearby. She had lost some weight. She had circles under her eyes and the whites of those eyes were inflamed.

Dusty had never before experienced such fatigue. Even so, she was not as tired as the two men and she still had her wits about her. The three of them had ridden single file the whole way. Lobo had made her ride in the middle where he could keep an eye on her. The man in the lead had had to keep the three of them on the trail, keep a lookout, and set the pace. Lobo had had to watch their rear as well. So, the men had had to stay awake the entire time. Dusty, however, had been able to doze some in the saddle. Even so, she had not been careless about it; no, she knew that if she did not keep up, if she slowed them down, Lobo would kill her.

She knew that Lobo had wanted to keep her. And she knew now, that he had wanted to get her with child. Five days ago, when she had started her monthly, he had crazily slapped her around and generally raised hell with her. However, she was under no illusions that Lobo, now running for his life, would let her live if not with him.

So Dusty had dozed some in the saddle, feeling the horse's rhythm under her. Whenever its rhythm had changed, she had awakened suddenly and looked to see whether the men had changed pace or whether her own horse had slacked.

When her horse had slacked, she had kicked it and whipped it with the reins to make it keep up.

She could only speculate about what had happened in Chihuahua; but it had been obvious to her that the men believed their lives were in danger. And she had been sure since Chihuahua that if they felt that she was in any way dangerous to them, they would kill her.

So, the entire way, she had tried to appear helpless and submissive. But when Lobo and his henchman had seen the dead men in the canyon, they had seemed to go crazy with fear. For a moment there, she had been frightened that Lobo would kill her. It had been in his eyes—the sudden hatred. To save her life, she had pushed her own fear from her mind and had looked him steadily in the eyes, and finally he had calmed down and looked away. But, she had gotten the impression that, at least for a while, he had crazily held her responsible for what was happening.

She had seen, as the two men had, that there were no dead girls. But it was unclear to her just what had happened to them. Hastily, she had counted maybe twenty-five dead men. It meant, she thought, that some men must have survived the shootout. Maybe the girls were with the men. Maybe not. Maybe the other eight or ten men had given up and had been taken prisoner.

In any event, since leaving the canyon, Dusty had certainly not taken her own survival for granted.

Now, up here on the mountain, while El Lobo was bogged down at the simple task of cinching a saddle, the other man, El Lobo's henchman, was slumped in his saddle with his head hanging and his eyes closed. His exhaustion was such that the only thing keeping him going now was the certainty that if he stopped, El Lobo would kill him. There had been moments when he had wished that they would get overtaken and arrested; anything had seemed better than this unrelieved exhaustion. He had tried to talk El Lobo into taking a couple hours rest; but El Lobo had coldly told him that the reason he, Lobo, was alive today was that he did not take stupid chances. When the man had argued with him, El Lobo had told him in no uncertain terms that the only rest the man would get was the final one, the one brought on by a bullet. The man had gone on because he knew that the exhaustion was better than immediate death. But he had not understood what was keeping El Lobo going; El Lobo had to be as exhausted as he, but the old bandit kept going hour after hour, day after day.

Yesterday, as happens in severe exhaustion, the man had begun to hallucinate. And he had begun to imagine that El Lobo was actually the Devil. That explained for him how the old bandit could keep going when everything and everyone else would have stopped. With the Devil at his back, El Lobo's henchman had kept going.

Now, up on the mountainside, the man opened his eyes, raised his head, and looked down the slope. In his exhaustion, it took him a few seconds to realize what it was that he saw.

He pointed and called out, "Jinetes!" Riders!

El Lobo and Dusty turned and looked. The sight shook El Lobo from his semi-consciousness. He turned and tightened the cinch. He stepped back and pulled his revolver from his belt and waved it at Dusty. Dusty mounted the horse he had just saddled. El Lobo mounted his own horse. He pulled his lariat loose from his saddle and gave Dusty's horse a whack on its rump. The horse took off at a slow trot. El Lobo spurred his own horse to a unwilling gallop and whipped Dusty's horse to a gallop. The other man was ahead of them galloping for the timber, his horse stumbling as it ran.

Down the mountainside, Blackie reined his horse over against Rebecca's and jerked his .45-110 from its scabbard on her horse.

"Whoa!" Blackie reined in his horse and jumped to the ground.

Morgan reined in and asked, "What're you doing?!"

"They've seen us, and they're running for the timber. They can bushwhack us in timber country, so I'm going to get Lobo now."

"Seven hundred yards? That's too far."

"It's been done," Blackie grimly asserted.

Blackie checked his rifle's breech to make sure it was loaded, and then sat down on the ground. "Becky, grab my horse's reins. He'll spook when I shoot and nobody's on him."

Blackie folded out his vernier peep sight and assumed a shooting position with his elbows just forward of his knees, the muscles of the back side of his arms resting on his knees. He looked at the fleeing riders and judged the distance. He took his time adjusting the sight; he adjusted for the distance and for shooting uphill. If he misjudged, he probably would not get another shot today.

Morgan fumbled in his saddle bag. Out came his telescope, but it was never firmly in his grasp, and it dropped to the ground. He cursed and dismounted.

Rebecca fidgeted while she watched the fleeing riders get closer and closer to the timber, increasing the yardage for Blackie to shoot. Her palms sweated.

Blackie's ams were again on his knees. His rifle barrel was supported by his left finger tips. The powerful fingers moved the barrel ever so slightly and smoothly with the gait of El Lobo's horse. Then he adjusted his sights for the lead that he judged to be correct—the distance the barrel must point in front of El Lobo so that by the time the bullet got there, El Lobo would have ridden to the same spot. It would be a spot in space where Blackie predicted the bullet and El Lobo would arrive at the same time. If he misjudged, he would miss and El Lobo would be gone. And so would Dusty.

Blackie squeezed the rear trigger which thereby set the forward trigger, making it a "hair" trigger. Now he moved his trigger finger to the hair trigger.

The riders were now only fifty yards from the timber.

Blackie's sights swung past El Lobo, past him again, swung past again, and again, and then, as they crossed him again, Blackie applied a tiny pressure to the hair trigger.

The explosion of the big gun going off seemed surprisingly loud to Rebecca. She saw the recoil and the cloud of bluish smoke.

Blackie looked up over the rifle's sights, up the mountainside. He quickly extracted the spent cartridge and inserted another.

Morgan had picked up his telescope and had blown and wiped dust from the lenses. Now he put it to his eye and focused it and glassed until he saw El Lobo where he lay on his back. El Lobo moved and then rolled onto his right side. The big bullet, having spent much of its energy plowing through eight hundred yards of air, had un-horsed him, but had not killed him. Morgan glassed until he saw the other desperado gallop into the timber. Then he found Dusty. She was up ahead of where El Lobo lay, and she was just now turning her horse around. She trotted the stumbling animal down to El Lobo where he lay on his right side, beckoning with his left hand, apparently asking for help.

Dusty dismounted and knelt down beside him. He rolled onto his back and put his right arm around her shoulders. She helped him sit up. With his right arm around her shoulders, the butcher knife on his right hip was now exposed.

In a blur, Dusty jerked the knife from its sheath and plunged it into El Lobo's heart. He fell back to the ground.

Dusty got to her feet, looking at him, and then turned and walked to his horse. She slid the rifle from its scabbard and checked to see that it was loaded. She led the horse down to her horse and then led them both down the slope.

Farther down the mountainside, Blackie was hastily untying his bedroll from his saddle. He turned and handed it to Rebecca.

"Find a level spot in the shade and put this down for her. I want her to go right to sleep."

He mounted his horse. "Morgan, would you watch for the other man in case he comes back out of the timber? Give a shot in the air if you see him."

"All right."

Morgan kept his telescope to his eye.

Blackie trotted his horse up the slope about five hundred yards to where he met Dusty. They both stopped and looked at each other. She appeared near exhaustion; nevertheless, she still had spark.

She said, "I knew you would come."

He dismounted then and they hugged, not letting go.

Her head against his chest, she asked, "What about Mom?"

"Shot in the leg; but she'll be all right."

Dusty nodded her head against him.

They hugged a long time. He kept looking over her head to the timber, watching for the other man. The man did not show.

Finally, Blackie took Lobo's rifle from her and put it in its scabbard. He grabbed all three horses' reins, and then he picked Dusty up and started back down the mountainside carrying her.

Letting him know that it wasn't necessary to carry her, she said, "I can walk."

"I know," he said gently, "but I want to carry you."

Dusty went promptly to sleep while her brother carried her down the slope.

END